Walk Amongst the Stars

Book One

Daniel Seven

Walk Amongst the Stars: Book One

Written By: Daniel Seven
Cover Design By: Daniel Seven
Editing By: Ceylan Ozguner
ozeditorialservices.com

First Edition
ISBN: 979-8-9931434-0-8
© Copyright Daniel Seven—2025 All rights reserved ©

danielsevenwriting.com

This book is dedicated to my *family* and *friends* who
believed in and encouraged me
when I told them I was going to be a professional writer.

Prologue

A bulky dropship flew through Prospiria Alpha's busiest space highway. The pilot and copilot were dressed in gray, militaristic jumpsuits. Raven, the woman standing behind them with her arms folded, has spiky, blond hair and wore a mesh bodysuit that showed off her athletic figure and many tattoos. The lane they were on would take them to Prospiria Central Operations, although most called it Prospiria for short. It was the most populous world in this region of space.

"Oh shit," said the copilot, pointing at the nav-screen. In the distance, coming their way, was a G-Sec cruiser, the local law enforcement.

The pilot turned his head. "Relax, I got the ship ahead locked on, and we're matching their speed, just like the handbook says. He's got no reason to even *look* at us."

Raven clenched her sidearm as the cruiser drew closer. They couldn't take one in a fight, and they probably couldn't escape it in this lunchbox with wings. They had legitimate credentials, but any trouble now could blow the whole thing. Then they'd be even more screwed than before. Contingency plans sprang to mind.

The cruiser's sensors danced invisibly across the dropship as they hurtled past each other. The dropship's crew watched the nav-screen for a while as the cruiser kept going down the thoroughfare toward the gas-giant slingshot.

Something new popped up on the nav-screen. Prospiria. The copilot targeted it, bringing up an image of the blue-and-green planet, swaddled in thick white clouds. Raven noted the time until arrival. "I need to go get ready." She walked out of the roomy flight deck into the prison transfer section of the dropship.

People like her, pirates, lived outside, and sometimes within the cracks between society. Venturing deep into the system like this put them in mortal danger. But as an infiltrator, it was Raven's kind of thing. More of her crew were waiting in the seating area. Not shackled to the floor as prisoners but wearing their combat gear. Ready to rock.

"We're getting close to Prospiria," she announced. Two men looked at her. One nodded. The woman in the back took a dainty bite of a candy bar. Raven gave a resounding slap to a pair of boots sticking out of a row of seats as she strode to the back. The boots came in and a head popped up. The scraggly bearded man looked confused. Raven claimed a bag she had waiting by the bathroom. "Get ready," she reiterated to the freshly woken man. She closed the door, hoisted the oblong sports bag onto the metal sink, and looked at herself in the mirror.

This whole thing started about six months ago. Raven had just scored big, and, to make it really juicy, she had scored in the face of her rival, Randall Carver. With a score that big, she'd be set for a while, not that she was planning to rest on her laurels. But Carver didn't take his defeat lightly. In fact, he went nuclear, crossing a line that didn't get crossed very often. He sent a tip to the local Astroforce where her hideout was. She never figured out how he knew about it, but it didn't really matter anymore. The Astroforce blitzed them with a ground assault, breached the building, and took them unaware. Raven saw the assault too late to do anything except run. So she pulled a squad of her guys out with her.

Every system will generate local military and law enforcement as it grows. The Astroforce is humanity's collective standing army. Built off the backs of, and there to protect the hundreds of systems claimed by humankind. There are a million reasons not to fuck around with the Astroforce. As a pirate, it's because once word gets out, your reputation goes up in smoke. Raven made sure everyone knew of Carver's transgression. The problem was Raven's rep was gone, too. Everyone watched her tiny criminal empire get destroyed and confiscated by the authority. They killed about a dozen of her guys, but honestly, they mostly just trimmed the fat. The rest of the crew surrendered and wound up in a dozen prisons across three systems.

Raven disconnected the magnetic attachments of her wig and set it aside. Her head was shaved smooth underneath. She swiped her hand over the soft, slightly oily skin. She took out a black mesh bag and unzipped it. Inside was another wig of shoulder-length brunette hair. Searching the sports bag, she found a brush and worked the wig before clicking it onto her scalp. She primped it a bit and looked at herself. She zipped the other wig back into the bag. Tossing the wig bag and brush into the sports bag, she took out a container of contact lenses and replayed the scene in her mind.

Using a stolen police computer, she tracked her guys moving through the system. She didn't think any of them talked based on reputation alone. But the ridiculous concurrent hundred-year sentences they got told the story well enough. After some creative hacking, Raven hatched a plan. And step one was to transfer her crew, one at a time, to the same prison.

Their trials took a few months to clear, and getting them all together took another couple of months. Finally, she sent individual coded messages via additive shift ciphers, using their birthdays as the key. Something she drilled into her guys in case the need ever arose. She was good with names and dates, and could even remember a lot of dead guys' birth dates. The messages read in order: RAVENSEZ, BREADYTORUN, DURINGYRDTIME, SEPFOURTEEN.

Raven's blue eyes changed to green as she blinked the contact lenses into place. They weren't just color, either; they were biometric. She watched them turn on the surface of her eyes as she blinked. The contacts had tiny gyros in them to keep the orientation correct. They also cost her the last of her money. Custom job. Short notice.

She pulled out a picture of a young woman. She wet her fingers and affixed the picture to the mirror with a wad of old, flavorless chewing gum from her mouth. The picture sagged but held. Next, she opened a plastic case with a synth-skin face inside. The mask changed her facial features to match the mark's biometric data. She set to work gluing it carefully in place.

The mark was perfect. Almost too good to be true. Not to mention a sexy bitch. Raven had four criteria to fulfill when finding her mark.

One. The mark had to have a clean record.

Two. They needed to be in a position where their biodata wasn't being read too often. If that happened while she was using it, things would probably fall apart.

Three. They couldn't be a government worker. She couldn't access government biometric data, but she could insert a civilian into their system because she'd have all of her biological markers already.

Four. It needed to be a woman who was close to her size.

Raven spent a lot of time with a makeup kit blending the mask in. She completed the disguise by stripping out of her skimpy clothes and putting on a bust-enhancing bra and padded shorts that made her thighs and ass look plump. She stepped into a prison guard jumpsuit and pulled it on. Her hands popped out of the sleeves, and she zipped it all the way up and folded a hook-and-loop enclosure over the zipper. Then she put a communicator onto her ear and carefully put a patrol cap onto her wig.

She pulled a handheld scanner out of her bag and shot herself in the face through the mirror. Soft red light illuminated her face and the device beeped. She looked at the screen. A long serial number followed by a name, `Maeve McKinnon`.

"Boom, identity stolen. Thanks, Mauve." Raven double-checked the scanner. "Or Maeve, whatever." She looked at the picture and back at herself. She mostly looked the part. Like if the mark had gone on a diet or had the flu. She put all the stuff back in the bag. Zipped it, slung it back onto its place on the floor, and left.

⊘.1

Almost an hour later, the dropship had made it to a space station in Prospiria's orbit. They were making slow, steady progress to the front of the custom's line. Raven stood back in her place on the bridge. She tried out a few poses to get a feel for what a prison guard would do. Hands on her hips. Feet together, hands behind her back. Casual stance. Arms crossed. When the authority hailed the dropship, she went with hands behind her back.

This is what they had been waiting for. Raven's guy looked over his shoulder at her. She nodded back at him. He connected to the system. A tired-looking man in business attire came on the viewscreen.

"Good afternoon TPT-902."

"Good afternoon," she replied with a smile. The copilot nodded, and the pilot parroted good afternoon.

The man read their purpose off the ship's itinerary. "Prisoner transfer." He skimmed the manifest, which showed four prisoners. "And authorization scan."

Raven looked up slightly and lost the smile.

"That's got it, Miss . . ." He leaned forward, scrutinizing the screen before finally adding "McKinnon."

Raven smiled again, relieved.

"Uploading your flight path. Failure to follow will result in fines." He spoke in a practiced, disinterested manner.

"Thanks. Have a wonderful day."

"Oh! You too," said the tired man, looking just a bit livelier.

A traffic signal changed up ahead on a sign telling travelers what to do and expect while they waited for service. The pilot input the flight plan into the ship's computer, and it took them slowly toward Prospiria.

The view below was mostly clouds. Some swatches of gray, green, and tan peeked out. The belly of the ship glowed like an oven as the ablative coating shrugged away the atmospheric friction. Raven opened the door to the prisoner seating area and yelled back to her crew, "Five minutes! Get ready!"

One man stood with a belt-fed grenade launcher. It smelled pleasantly of gun oil. He flipped the feed tray open and made sure the belt sat properly, then slapped it back down. He slid his fingers over the charging rod but let it go for now.

The man across the aisle from him unzipped a satchel with three large rockets and many smaller munitions packed in sabots. He took out one of the small rockets and smiled at the mushroom cloud and skull designs his son had doodled on it. He knelt and inserted it into the launcher.

"It's time they feel the boom," said the grenade launcher guy. He and the other man pounded fists.

The woman in the back claimed a high-power rifle with an enormous scope held between the hull and a chair. Remaining seated for now, she simply cocked the gun. A huge brass round winked by. She smiled to herself and put her palm over her eye.

The bearded pirate got up and shot his arms out into a big, stretching yawn. He wore a tactical vest loaded with pouches, which he double-checked. He picked his rifle off the floor and put the strap over his shoulder. With a flick of the fire-mode selector, the gun whined to life. The screen lit, displaying Safe, which shrank to the corner, leaving **AMMO : 45**, in its place. He let the gun hang for now.

Sticking to the flight plan, the ship sank through a thick bank of clouds. When it finally came out the other side, they were getting close. Now they could make out the skyscrapers of Amaranth City as they moved closer. They could see the prison, a sprawling complex studded with guard towers. The inner courtyard was shielded to protect and confine the prisoners. A hex-grid of energy reflected the sun as they descended. The ship fired thrusters to slow itself, and it came down on a landing spot behind the prison.

Chain link topped with razor wire boxed them in.

"Good afternoon TPT-902. Sit tight. We'll have a group of men out to unload you momentarily."

"We'll be in and out. You won't know what hit you." She chuckled playfully.

A laugh came over the radio. "Okay, one moment."

Raven went into the prison compartment again. Her hit squad stood ready for action, lined up by the door. The guy with the rocket launcher in the front and the girl with the sniper rifle in the back.

"Go time. This is where we get everyone back." She smacked the button by the large side door. It deployed outward, forming a ramp down to the metal grating of the landing area. The team raced down the ramp. The sniper grabbed onto a rung and pulled herself up the side of the craft onto the roof. She swung the gun from her back, deployed the bipod, and lay prone, ready to fire.

The prison roof was built for guards to patrol the perimeter of the prison and overwatch internal sections of the prison that could be fired into in emergencies. Automatic gun turrets sat in high vantage points, currently folded up, waiting. Four of those would be a problem once the alarm woke them. Two up close and two further back.

The man with the rocket launcher took a knee and flipped the screen up. He lased a gun tower, locking it in. The grenade launcher guy hoisted his cumbersome weapon and ripped the charging handle. In the distance, a guard spotted the ordinance with wide-eyed amazement. It wasn't uncommon for transfer crews to be armed, but this was insane.

The guard reached up to access his communicator. His head burst with the reverberating blast of the sniper rifle.

The shot acted as a starter pistol to the other pirates, who opened fire in concert. A guard shimmied, caught in a hail of bullets. A missile slammed into the turret on the right and detonated, flinging dangerous hunks of slag in sluggish arcs. Smaller explosions consumed the turret on the left and just kept coming until the gun tower collapsed inward.

The remaining visible guard dove for cover. A deep electronic groan raised the alarm, waking the automated turrets, which unfolded. The pirates with the explosive weapons reloaded. Thrumming with power, the turrets swiveled, targeting the stolen prison transport. Lights flickered in the nearby buildings as the turrets screamed. The machine gun–toting pirate cringed away from the deadly, invisible beam. The ship's shields were excited into visibility as they dissipated the energy.

Inside the ship, Raven leaned on the console, watching the shields drain.

"Uh, they're dropping pretty fast . . ." said the pilot.

"We did the math on this. We're good," Raven said with a little frown.

Outside the ship, all the pirates were ready to fire again. More guards gathered on top of the prison. The lasers kept up their sustained fire. Soon the air around the turrets was practically ablaze, and the turret's exposed heat sinks burned bright. The lasers stopped.

Raven yelled, "Now! Fire!" over comms as she dropped the shields.

The sniper opened fire, taking slow and steady shots, eliminating guards from right to left. Brass the size of permanent markers rolled down the side of the ship. The machine gunner kept the guards on the left mostly pinned down and afraid to move but felled those dumb enough to fight back. Explosives boomed all around a distant gun tower, missing the mark. A streak hit the other tower, blowing it apart. Finally, explosions crackled all over the last remaining tower, crumbling it to pieces.

The pirate with the grenade launcher flipped up the feed tray and loaded a new belt. The guy with the rocket launcher rushed forward to get some distance from the ship, while the two with ballistic weapons kept them covered. If there were any more guards, they were wisely hiding. The man with the rocket launcher took a knee and pulled one of the big olive drab munitions out of his satchel. It slid into the tube, and the feed mechanism slammed shut behind it. He raised the weapon and locked his target through the viewfinder. Based on the option he dialed in, the rocket would barrel through everything it touched, detonating once it reached its target destination. He squeezed the trigger with two fingers. With a great ripping noise, he became a grimacing shadow as the missile streaked into the building. The prison's outer wall shattered in a brilliant flash. Everyone felt the concussion in their chests. Rocket launcher guy's hair was all messed up and one eyebrow was missing. Dust and smoke billowed, obscuring the prison.

The pirate with the grenade launcher took aim at the remains of the chain-link fence that stood between them and the prison and fired a volley of high explosives. Then he turned to the left and took out another fence that stood between the landing pad and the outside world. Chain link and razor wire whipped around dangerously. Poles with concrete bases uprooted. When the dust settled, there was a shallow dirt trench left behind.

They watched the blooming cloud of dust. Even with the grating alarm and crumbling hunks of concrete, things felt still and quiet now. As the dust dissipated, the wrecked prison had a massive U-shaped hole that led to the prison yard. A mighty roar came from the prison yard. The inmates knew exactly what this was, and they all rushed into the dangerously collapsed building, dodging jagged rebar and falling boulders of concrete.

The inmates poured out of the building and across the dirt trench toward the ship. Raven pointed a gun at the group and rapidly pointed the barrel at the blown-open perimeter fence. The rabble split off from her crew. A huge tank of a man stayed. Raven put him in her sights.

"Either take me with you or kill me right here," he said, extending his arms in a challenge.

She took careful aim and fired. The laser bolt went to his right by less than a foot. He instinctively turned his head away and then fixed a stony gaze back on her.

"Hard. I can work with that. Get in."

Raven beckoned them in and moved to the door mechanism. Prisoners piled into the ship, followed by the hit squad. The man with the grenade launcher paused to fire another volley at the prison and darted back inside. As soon as the door began to close, the pilot went full throttle. The passengers rocked and clung to the chairs and rails.

Laser turrets fired on the transport's belly as the ship passed briefly into range, quickly sapping the shields, leaving behind warped and scorched metal. A clatter of gunfire dented up the hull. The main thrusters lit white-hot. The prison transport shook as it went all out, rapidly leaving the gun tower's range and putting one more crime on their tab: going off world without authorization.

By now, the authority would be tracking them. Probably scrambling interceptors, fast maneuverable fighters that they couldn't possibly out-run. That's why the next step was to get to a compromised nav-beacon. There, the crew would switch ships and Raven would screw with the authority's signals intelligence.

Then they'd take a nice leisurely pace back to pirate territory. No need to take unnecessary chances once they got away. It would give her time to think. She had a lot of rebuilding to do. Just outfitting her guys with vehicles and equipment would take months and lots of little jobs. Today was the first baby step back toward being big time.

The prison compartment was now crowded with dregs in vibrant orange jumpsuits. There was a heavy murmur.

Raven threw the cap like a disk and pulled her wig off. She yelled, "Hey!"

Everyone quieted down.

"What did I tell you?" She slapped the young man next to her on the back.

"That we should be ready for you to break us out today?"

"Too literal J. Too literal," she said with a smile.

She pointed into the crowd. "What did I tell you?"

The group turned to a man with a facial scar like a wild animal had clawed him. "I . . . um." He licked his lips. "I don't know, boss."

She pointed at a stout, bald guy. "What. Did. I. *Tell*. You?"

His eyes darted up, and he tilted his head back. He looked back confidently. "Raven always comes out on top."

She parted her way through the crowd and seized his shoulders. Her wig draped his shoulder like an odd epaulet. "Louder."

Baldy threw up a fist and yelled, "Raven always comes out on top!"

The crowd cheered and crowed.

0.2

Later that afternoon, across town, a woman walked down the sidewalk. As she moved past dingy buildings peppered with vivid graffiti, she thought of her day. It was a long, boring day at the office, but now it was over. Soon she'd be comfy in her bed, diving into virtual reality with her friends. She took her knit cap off and shook her shining chestnut hair out. *It ended up being sunny, after all,* she thought.

She turned into her apartment complex. The place was old, but the property management company had recently repainted it. Beige. She wasn't into it, but for now all the graffiti tags were gone, and they'd fixed up that apartment on the end that got broken into.

She went down the walkway between the apartments and the parking lot. She stopped in front of her door. The apartment read her face, and the door slid open. She entered, and the door closed behind her and locked. After a day of drudgery, Maeve McKinnon was home.

Chapter 1

Deep underground in an abandoned maglev system, a mobile command center thundered down deserted tunnels. Despite being a huge vehicle with large, shrouded wheels and thick armor plating, it had plenty of room in the cavernous tunnel system.

Inside, a three-man crew. Gunstorm, the guild leader, drove. Haxx, his son, fed him directions. All the way in the back, Maeve loaded up for the mission. The three of them had on military battle dress except for Maeve, who was in a form-fitting stealth suit.

"Take a right at the next junction," Haxx shouted toward the front of the vehicle, keeping his focus on the tunnel schematics on the display in front of him.

Maeve made her game avatar—Ve—out to be her idyllic self. Average girl height instead of boy height. Cuter with larger eyes and lips, and sleek and acrobatic instead of plump and unathletic, like her actual body.

But today was more about brute strength, and she was donning the best, in her opinion, max-level armor. An intimidating, bulky matte-black suit of plate mail. She had spent some money on cosmetic purchases to etch the molding with gold filigree. She clicked and zipped and strapped on armor plates, and finally she swept back her long, light brown hair and placed her helmet on, clicking the chin strap in place. Now only the bridge of her nose and green eyes were visible. She hoisted the carry strap of a light machine gun up onto her shoulder.

Ready, she tromped forward, holding the rail encircling the ceiling for balance in the moving vehicle. She stopped next to Haxx a moment and grabbed his chair back as the vehicle turned the corner. He looked back at her and smiled. She proceeded up to the front and loomed in between the two front seats, although there wasn't much to see. Dark concrete tunnels with the occasional graffiti tag.

"Almost there. Stop at the next access tunnel. It'll be on the right," said Haxx.

After a minute, the access tunnel suddenly materialized out of the gloom. Gunstorm slammed on the brake, jerking the hefty vehicle, then let up to gain some more ground. He finally applied a last, lurching stop. Haxx got up and slid the side door open. He hopped down on metal legs. Haxx had chosen for his character to be a cyborg, so aside from those metal limbs, wires and circuits traveled across his body like odd tattoos.

Maeve was out right behind him. She was bursting with excitement and didn't even notice Haxx's token effort to help her down. Jumping down, she landed hard, billowing dust out from under her boots. Yanking the charging handle back, she readied the gigantic gun and looked around for some trouble. She moved forward to get out of the way.

Gunstorm stepped into the doorway, a stout man with short, graying hair and an unkempt goatee. He knelt and slid an orange case toward him from inside the vehicle, opened it, and smiled at the audacious tool inside. Latching the case, he handed it over to Haxx. Gunstorm planted a hand and jumped down. Reaching into the vehicle, he withdrew a submachine gun. He unfolded the stock and hung it on his shoulder. Then he slid the side door closed. "This place seems dead, and no other players can jack our car, so I think we're safe to leave it here."

As they left the illumination the headlights provided, Haxx flicked on a light mounted on his shoulder. Gunstorm lowered his goggles and toggled to infrared.

The three of them marched down the access tunnel, wary of enemies but expecting no resistance, at least not yet. The tunnel was dank and smelled acrid and moldy. While he lugged the case, Haxx looked at a device on his forearm. He took a deep breath and sighed out, "Almost there."

"I see it. The wall's warmer up there."

"So Ve, what do we do if this doesn't work?" said Haxx.

"I suppose we can run you guys through some ops, maybe get you some better gear. I could show—"

"This is going to work! I can feel it," said Gunstorm.

"Yeah, but as far as I know, nobody has tried this. We don't know if this is going to work."

"It's a weak point, like any other, Ve. It has to go somewhere, and the facility is right there," he pointed at the wall.

They stopped in front of an unremarkable-looking section of concrete wall. It was a slightly different color, as though a hole had been patched or a doorway covered up. Gunstorm knelt with the case and opened it up. He slid a couple of handles out of the case, which locked into position, and lifted a green box out of it. It was steel with four points protruding from the front of the device.

Gunstorm eyeballed the wall again and pressed the device up to it. He looked around, suddenly feeling nervous. He gave the wall a stern look and licked his lips. Leaning into the device, he squeezed the triggers nested in the handles. The halls echoed loudly as the device drilled its way into the wall. There was a loud crunch, and the buttons stopped working. Gunstorm pushed them a couple of times in disbelief.

The connection felt rock solid in his hands. So he stepped back to look at the back panel facing outward. "Okay, it's in," said Gunstorm, thinking out loud. "Now to activate it . . ." He scanned across the face of the device with his fingers. "Pair. Here we go." He held a button down on his goggles and the device simultaneously. The button pulsed with green light, then suddenly changed to red.

Satisfied, he jogged back past the group to where he thought they would be safe from any flying debris. The other two took a few steps back.

"Okay, is everybody a hundred percent on what they're doing?" said Gunstorm.

"Yep."

"Yeah."

He placed his finger on the button on his goggles. "Three, two, one. Detonate!" The last word disappeared in a deep thundering blast. Pieces of concrete flew, rebounding off the opposite wall. The tunnel filled with dust and echoes of the blast. The group cringed from the shockwave and fusillade of projectiles.

Gunstorm cycled through the vision modes of his goggles, then smiled greedily. There was a jagged hole in front of him. He ran into the thinning dust cloud and peered into the diamond shaped opening. Floor to ceiling, four feet at its widest. He looked back, elated. "Go! Go! Go! We're in."

Maeve clenched her gun and ran to the hole. She had barely survived her boring office job, counting down the hours, and now her friend's theory had proven to be true. She carefully stepped up onto a pile of concrete rubble. It shifted and crunched underfoot. Then she turned to the side and slipped into the facility.

1.1

The hole in the wall was higher than the room, and after passing through the entrance, she had to tread onto more concrete rubble mixed with broken pieces of electronics and large, nasty shards of glass. It was hazy inside, and once she stepped down, she noticed how cold it was. Large tanks of murky liquid lined the room. The tanks around the blast had broken. Inside appeared to be human bodies hanging from the wreckage.

No matter. She saw a door. While stepping down from the rubble, she got hung up on something. She focused on the movement in her peripheral vision and saw it was one of those things from the shattered tanks gripping her armor. A slimy naked man with tubes and wires laced throughout his body. It gargled a moan and held on with crazed eyes. Then another grabbed her.

Maeve wrenched her shoulders left and right, breaking their grasp. She turned and drew a line of bullets across the pathetic creature in the tube. She twisted and blew away the other one. It collapsed into its partly demolished tube.

Suddenly, all the tubes opened, spilling a thick chemical soup onto the floor. It smelled sweet and smokey, like melted plastic with a hint of rotten meat. Maeve coughed and stifled a gag. Rushing to the door, she wrenched it open while the creatures woke up. She scanned the next room down the barrel of her gun. It was big with doors all around and a hallway she couldn't quite see down from here. She could see desks and workstations. It seemed like some sort of office.

She reached into a pouch and pulled out a grenade. With all her thumb's strength, she rocked a brass slider forward, threw it into the room, and closed the door behind her. She dashed into the corner so she could see down the hallway as the room full of freaks erupted, blowing the door off its frame. The warped door tumbled into the room.

Maeve looked at the many doors ahead and waited for Haxx to do his job. A couple of bursts from Gunstorm's submachine gun rumbled behind her. *Must have missed one,* she thought.

She caught movement up ahead and not so quietly sprawled down prone. It was a patrol of three cyberzombies. These weren't naked but dressed for battle. She opened fire, hosing down the cyberzombie in front. It fought against its failing body to react, but the consistent firepower shut it down. The other two fired energy weapons back at her. Glancing blows danced off her armor. She repeated the process, working the chest and head, which got the job done a little quicker.

She released the trigger and realized Haxx had been talking to her on comms under the roar of the machine gun.

"—hallway."

"I didn't catch that."

"Keep going through the hallway. Once you hit the four-way hall, take a left."

Maeve looked at her gun. The digital readout said she had a little less than half of the belt left. She got up and rushed down the hall. She found herself at the entrance to an office. She saw another cyberzombie on patrol. She crept in and braced her gun on a desktop. Her gun roared, and another cyberzombie went down, shooting wildly.

A mechanical whir caught her attention. She turned to see a turret descending quickly from the ceiling tiles. She held tight and unloaded on it. It activated and fired back in kind. When her gun stopped, she pulled out a large machine pistol and pointed it, but it was over. The turret sagged out of the ceiling, exposing some sparking wires. Maeve put away her pistol and got to work, swapping out the ammo box on her big ole machine gun. She snapped the ammo box into the gun, which recognized the fresh ammunition, and greedily pulled it into place. She stood, cocked the gun, and went left out of the room into a hallway.

Maeve was aware of having been shot just now and examined her armor plates. In the settings, you could disable sensations like pain, but she found it too easy to miss important feedback. Besides, it was just a game, and the pain feedback wouldn't even register as a one on a doctor's pain scale.

"I hope there isn't too much more that thrashed my armor."

"There kind of is. That bomb let us skip about two-thirds of this place, maybe more like three-quarters, but you've got a ways to go."

She paused at the door.

Haxx noticed. "The floor plan says the next room is the assembly line."

She readied her gun and shoved her side into the press bar, opening the door. The assembly line was a huge automated system that appeared to be cranking out guns and other mechanisms. But as she proceeded quickly and quietly, she put together what those other things were. Spare parts that she saw grafted onto the dead zombie men she saw earlier.

As she padded past the machinery, an alarm sounded. She spotted what was obviously the way she needed to go. Maeve took off running, hindered by her bulky armor and awkwardly large gun. A steel shutter slammed shut in front of the door she was trying to get to. She spun and saw that the door she had come from was also closed off.

"Guys, I got a problem here. I'm locked in the assembly line room." She shuffled over to the closest bit of cover, a big metal conveyor belt shroud.

"I'm attempting to—What! Why would they? I'm, uh, going to—"

Gunstorm broke in, "What he's trying to say is we're patched into the base's network. He's going to hack a way out for you; hold on."

Something moved. She stared into the heart of the assembly line. It kept stamping, whirring, and soldering. Movement again to the left. *Something's in here*, she thought. A dark blur leaped toward her in a high arc. Following it up, she unloaded on it. She stepped back at the last minute to avoid having a robot crash into her. She bent and looked at the thing. A skinny robot, a few notches thicker than a stick figure drawing, with nasty-looking clawed hands. Her bullets found purchase mostly in its chest, its widest part, about three inches across. The bot sizzled and smoked.

Movement again. Maybe a dozen of these robots came crawling out of the assembly line. They ran toward her, vaulting equipment as they came.

"Oh shit!" Maeve fired carefully at a distant robot. They surged ahead. She swapped targets as the robots went down, one after another. The robots kept coming, and she had to shuffle step away until she backed into the wall.

The next machine was close enough to swipe at her when she shot it offline. Right behind it, two more slashed at her chest, cutting neat grooves of three across it. She gunned one down while the other sliced down her helmet and dug its fingers into her shoulder pauldron. She bashed its head with the barrel of the gun and then turned to fight off another incoming attacker. As she terminated it, the robot clinging to her regrouped and renewed its frantic slashing. She worked the gun in between them and turned her head, squinting. She fired way too close to herself for comfort. The robot made a high-pitched squeal as it went slack, hanging from her shoulder. She grabbed the robot's arm and pulled, but it didn't budge.

The metal shutter slammed open. "Go to the door! Go to the door! I got it open!" Haxx was almost too excited to get the words out.

Another robot leaped forward and sliced at her. She used the dangling robot body as a shield, then turned and fired. Its slim, cylindrical head disappeared, and it stood there, twitching. She lugged her way into the door, the dead robot swaying from her shoulder. Inside, she spotted another robot closing ground. She booted it in its narrow chest and hit the button, closing the steel shutters. They slammed shut.

Maeve let her gun slide back in its strap, and she grabbed the robot's arm at the wrist and pulled hard. Nothing. She took a deep breath and really put her back into it. "Nnn-Guhhhh!" *That's not coming out,* she thought. She reached under the shoulder armor and disconnected the plastic connectors that held it on.

"What are you doing?" said Haxx.

Gunstorm broke in, "I think she stopped to take a dump." The three of them cracked up. Maeve, struggling to talk through the laughter, explained about the robot stuck in her armor. She finally squeezed the last connector, and the piece of armor with its robot passenger struck the concrete floor. She rotated her shoulder a few times. "That's better."

"The next room is it—the boss. The map simply says 'vault,'" said Haxx.

Maeve reloaded her last belt of ammo and ran her gloved fingers across the slashes in her chest plates. "Armor's a little banged up, and I'm getting low on ammo."

"You got this," said Gunstorm, looking at her vital stats.

"I think I'm ready."

She took a deep breath to clear her mind, then opened the door and stormed inside. The room was big and tall, with concrete pillars in each corner and two tall server racks. Like the rest of the place, it was all white concrete with steel accents. Blocks of text scrolled by on the servers' many digital readouts. Conduits snaked big bundles of wires around. Big steel lock boxes lined the walls with a ladder on rails. The boxes were of various sizes, most about two square feet. Half of them had been forced open, the doors hanging open or missing completely.

At the end of the room, with its back turned, was a hulking cyberzombie with an oversized metal arm. A bundle of wires led up its back and into the neck. It had sickly white flesh and various metal plates across its head.

Maeve raised her gun and, almost like it knew, the monster spun around. She recognized the face, an enemy the game had had her chasing since the beginning. An enemy she thought she had killed.

"You're too late, Ve. We've already claimed the base and taken everything useful," it said.

"Holy shit, guys! It's Dr. Steinman. He's a cyberfreak now."

"You seem surprised to see me. This is why you can't win. We are beyond death." Dr. Steinman lifted his massive cyberarm and cracked a wicked smile.

Wasting no time, Maeve hosed him down with lead. The monster shielded its face and upper torso with the massive metal arm and cried out. It shuffled off behind one of the pillars.

"This is the end for you. I won't even bother to cyberidize you." A crackle reverberated off the walls. "I'll just throw your remains in the nutrient vats."

Dr. Steinman pivoted out of cover and fired a ball of energy from his metal arm. Maeve saw the orb of energy heading toward her and dove out of the way. Even dodging it, she could feel the heat and electric charge at her side. She scrambled into a crouch and resumed fire on the monster.

Steinman leaped through the air and slammed down right in front of Maeve, who had to jump back. He swung his huge arm and swatted her into the wall. She steadied herself and pointed her gun. But so did Dr. Steinman. Energy began to crackle in the palm of his huge hand. She rushed behind the nearest column. The energy blast shattered a section of the column, sending rocky chunks flying. She fired through the newly opened hole, shooting at the monster's head. Rounds bounced off the twists of metal rebar sticking out. Dr. Steinman covered his head and rushed around the corner.

Maeve backed away, firing, only stopping when a server rack was in her peripheral vision. Steinman got close and swung at her with his human arm. She slapped it away with her gun barrel but almost couldn't get out of the reach of the massive metal fist that followed. It smashed into the server bank, sundering the devices. They went dark with a loud pop.

Maeve retreated to another column. She could hear his weapon charging up again. Steinman fired, this time aiming at the column, which exploded another shower of concrete. The blast and the resulting projectiles stunned her. She shook it off only to see the massive fist too late. Maeve got blasted off her feet, making a breathless groan. She hit the wall, sliding down the lock boxes and landing on her knees. Bits of her sundered armor rained down around her. Most of her armor plates were gone.

Haxx and Gunstorm watched a security camera feed on their wrist computer and goggles, respectively. Haxx winced as she crash-landed, "Focus. You got this, Ve."

Maeve got to her feet, blood leaking from a split lip. She stumbled to the side in time to miss another thunderous punch that penetrated the lock boxes and trapped Dr. Steinman for a moment. She ran to a pillar and unloaded her gun yet again. Sustained fire on the creature's back. The doctor ripped his huge arm free and stumbled back, slower now. Wires and tubes hung out of their intended sockets.

Maeve's gun suddenly ceased firing. She looked down to see a big fat zero on the ammo count. Dr. Steinman charged up his weapon again. Maeve returned to the cover of the concrete pillar.

She tossed the machine gun off her shoulder and drew her machine pistol. An energy ball wrecked the pillar as she dove to the side.

She backed away, firing her pistol in bursts. The doctor jumped again to swat at her with his massive fist. She made sure she was behind the remaining server rack when the blow came. With the rack smashed, she finished the magazine. The doctor groaned and fell to his hands and knees. She ejected the magazine and hurriedly fished another out of a pouch. The doctor raised his arm, already charged with energy. Maeve turned to run. She stumbled for the last pillar too late. The energy ball hit her. She convulsed with burning electric energy, screaming in surprise. The gun flew from her hands as she crash-landed again, then she scrambled behind the final column.

"Please work," she said as she drew her last weapon from a sheath hidden in her back armor. As the straight-bladed ninja sword slid free, the last remaining scraps of armor fell away. She took another calming breath as the blade glowed with energy. She heard the sizzle of her enemy's arm cannon.

She stayed behind the column until the doctor fired. As before, the column shattered in a spray of concrete chunks. Maeve rushed out and leaped, landing on Dr. Steinman's back. He was still on hands and knees. She plunged the sword straight through his thick torso. He merely grunted and tried to stand. She hung from the sword's handle like it was a climbing handhold. She landed on her feet as the sword slid free. Steinman fell forward again, black fluid gushed from the wound.

She swung, freeing the doctor's head from his awful body.

"Ah—" His scream was literally cut short.

"I did it," she panted, frazzled. The still scowling face of Dr. Steinman settled on the floor.

The two on comms cheered. "Don't stop now. Loot the lock box and get back here. You will have single-handedly gotten us to the guildhall quest," said Gunstorm.

Maeve trotted over to recover her gun, knelt, and loaded it back up.

She went back to where the doctor had originally been standing when she entered the room.

There was a lockbox with the door hanging open. Inside was a multifaceted rectangular crystal plugged into a dock. A rainbow of color seethed within.

She beheld it for a moment, mesmerized. "It's a data gem," she said, shaking herself out of the trance.

"Perfect," said Haxx.

She pressed a button on the dock, and the gem rose up with an electric whir. The color ceased. She pocketed the gem, turned around, and stepped around the late Dr. Steinman when red light ran through unseen veins in the walls. An alarm sounded. Maeve reflexively pointed her gun at the door and crept forward.

"That's . . . oh sh—Get out of there. All the doors in the facility just opened. Get back here now!" said Haxx.

Maeve burst into the assembly line room, gun pointed and sword raised. She saw a room flooding with partially built cyberzombies. They didn't seem armed or even stable. They stumbled around, some with unfinished parts hanging loose.

She jogged toward the zombies, got a foothold on a nearby computer terminal, and stood on it to see above the crowd. She was going to need to get through a room of forty or fifty of them.

She hopped down and sprinted into the group. Darting left and right, she dodged past the loose groupings of cyberzombies. The group was becoming more dense, but she spied the conveyor belt from earlier. A couple of zombies were in her path, so she chopped them down and jumped up onto the belt. With flailing arms and unsure balance, she ran down the length as far as she could. The conveyor belt turned to the right, so she would have to jump. She vaulted over the remaining zombies, their fingers brushing her back. She landed into a roll, hopped up, and rushed out the door.

A spindly robot lunged in front of the door to the hallway, brandishing its clawlike hands. She traded careful blows with it, trying to leave no room for counterattack. Her sword glanced off its slender body.

"Get through the door. Now," said Haxx.

Maeve juked the bot and rushed through the doorway. She turned in time to see a security shutter slam shut.

She sprinted through the hall, took a right at the intersection into the office. A cyberzombie opened fire on her. She transitioned into a slide and sliced its leg out from under it. The zombie crashed down, and she stabbed the sword into its head to hoist herself up.

She took a moment to look at the wound she had sustained in the exchange. Her chest had a red glowing circle indicating where she was hit, and the large size of it indicated the severity of the wound. She should be dead. *Should have brought stims,* she thought. (Stims were an injectable combat drug that would provide minimal healing and give her a temporary boost to her stats, not to mention remove the pain.)

Everything had gone gray, and she could hear her heart beat loudly. The wound wouldn't slow her down any, but she had run out of chances. The next hit would end this run. Back on her feet, she took a breath and sprinted forth.

Another zombie took potshots at her from behind as she raced into the hall she entered from. She hugged the left side so the attackers from behind couldn't get a shot. She saw a lot of zombie gore lying around. Gunstorm had been keeping things clear, and he was still at it.

She marched forward, shooting liberally, her sword arm to the side, ready to strike. Together, she and Gunstorm cleared the room. Shots ricocheted off the walls behind her. Gunstorm leaned into the hole, offering a hand. She put her weapons away and hopped up the rubble and through the blasted wall, bounding down the access tunnel.

The game had really drawn her in, and she left Gunstorm in the dust, sprinting ahead on twitchy, adrenaline-fueled legs. Haxx was leaning out the door with a hand out. They interlocked arms, and she jumped up into the side door and looked back at Gunstorm, who was jogging his way back. He didn't really do exercise, so this was close to maximum performance for him, even in VR. The cracked-open wall behind him exploded again. He turned back to the van and walked the rest of the way back wearing a big grin.

Haxx took Maeve by the shoulders and ushered her into a chair in the back. She sat, and a long, thin robotic arm came up and fired a green beam at her chest wound. It wouldn't take long for the machine to fully heal her. She looked at Haxx with a grin on her lips, giddy, like she might break into a laugh. Haxx read her euphoria and couldn't help but beam as well.

Gunstorm jumped up into the vehicle, pausing to look at the two in the back. He clapped Maeve on the shoulder and then put his arm around Haxx. "Good job everyone. You did it."

"I can't believe it. This is awesome," said Haxx.

"Woo!" Maeve cheered. Pumping her arms and legs, she accidentally batted the healing device away and carefully replaced it.

Gunstorm scooted his way up from the back and sat in the driver's seat. "I don't know how far those cyberjerks will follow us." He put the vehicle in gear. "And I ain't gonna find out." Gunning it, he broke the wheels loose, spinning the vehicle around, kicking up a thick cloud of dust and almost sideswiping the tunnel wall. He raced down the old tunnel system. When they saw daylight brightening the tunnel, they knew they were free and clear.

1.2

Maeve was back in her little apartment, even though she had never left her bedroom. The magic of virtual reality. She found it most convenient to lie in bed propped up with some pillows. Lifting the VR halo off her head, she placed it on the nightstand next to her bed. She sucked in a breath, arched her back, and stretched. A little groan escaped while her arms and legs trembled.

She scooted to the edge of the bed and sat up, ran her fingers through her hair, and got up. She pivoted over to her desk and sat down. The computer recognized her face, and the screen lit up. She grabbed the mouse and opened a video editor. She dropped the recorded VR data into it and hit the button to process it. When this finished, she would set some parameters and make it into a video clip for her non-VR capable fans. Then edit both videos down, removing dead zones and personal stuff.

While it was working, she leaned back in her chair and put her arms behind her head, absent-mindedly looking where the wall and ceiling met. She was gaining a small audience on *TubeQube*, which was step one. Next would be sponsors and merch. *I'll have to think up a logo or catch phrase or something*, she thought.

Her daydream shifted with the thought of additional money. If things took off like she wanted, she could afford to leave this crappy neighborhood, or stay and just get a bigger apartment. Maybe eventually she'd get popular enough to ditch her office job. *Paid to play VR games*, she thought while rocking side to side in her office chair.

She couldn't help but feel like maybe she was making a mistake trying to turn her favorite hobby into money. It was easy, but it also cut into her free time. Seamlessly, her mind jumped tracks to the office. *It's only*

Wednesday. I can guess their golden boy, Tom, won't finish his project again. And who will the boss dump it on? No, not even. She'll send that toady of hers, Becca, at me. Well, not this time.

The computer chimed, pulling her out of her preemptive argument daydream. The program had done its preliminary work. Now she just had to choose a visually appealing way to portray all the scenes she experienced on that last mission and trim out any embarrassing feelings, like that charge she felt when Haxx hoisted her into the van. Maeve, on the edge of her computer chair, leaned forward toward the screen and clicked and slid a bar around, occasionally hitting the space bar. After a few minutes of decision-making, she sat back. It would take the computer a while to re-render all the scenes into a single video clip.

She swiveled and got up. "It's time for a hard-won microwave dinner." She headed to the kitchen on the other side of the apartment, past the little bathroom and closet, through the little living room, and into the little kitchen. She opened the freezer and looked at a variety of prepackaged frozen meals. Putting on a classy affectation, she said, "Perhaps a nice Salisbury steak, hmm?" She lifted boxes and slid it out from the middle. **5% more** *something or other*, it exclaimed on the front. Tearing a perforated section of cardboard out around the center of the box, it opened like a book. Flipping it around, she found the cooking directions. She turned the box so the microwave could see the 3D barcode. It didn't read it, so she gave the box a little wrist flick, and the microwave beeped and displayed: **READY**. She placed it inside and closed the door.

As soon as the microwave started droning, raised voices pierced the wall of her kitchen—the neighbors' bedroom, she assumed. It seemed that they had reached the argue-until-they-breakup phase of their relationship. This would be the third time Maeve had witnessed this cycle.

"Every time. Every time!" he bellowed.

"No. No! You don't get to say that," her neighbor screamed back.

"You're the one . . ." The rest of what he said was an unintelligible grumble.

Maeve groaned, went over to the TV, and turned it on and then cranked the volume up a bit. It was an antique handed down from her grandparents that used some obsolete network protocol she had never heard of and used a daisy chain of adapters in back to get a signal. It had no voice controls, and the remote was missing. So the user had to get up and push buttons on the side of the slim monitor like her ancient ancestors.

She sometimes thought of replacing the relic. TVs are cheap, after all. But she didn't watch much. It still worked fine, and why not blow her money on more VR stuff?

She rapidly clicked through channels. News, bad sitcom, animals. She hesitated. A furry creature with a worm-like tongue slurped up ants. Commercials, cartoon, mech fight. She stopped, her finger hovering a moment, and then stepped back.

The match had just begun. Two towering humanoid robots marched from opposite sides of a massive colosseum. One of them was military-green and boxy, equipped with a sword and shield; the other was sleek and white, adorned with crests on its head, shoulders, and back. A small window displayed the human operators inside their cockpits. The camera adjusted to the sudden brightness as both war machines fired energy weapons at each other.

Maeve realized the argument had stopped and looked away from the TV. Even with the curtains drawn, she noticed a green pulsing light out the window. *Uh-oh, looks like someone called the cops on your argument*, she thought.

"Vulcan finally working that arm free!"

Her eyes darted back to the screen in time to see the sleek mech losing an arm to the other's sword and reeling backward. Then, the scene shifted to a shot of the white mech's massive chest cannon going off, cutting a line across the chest of the other mech, then stopping at a weak spot. The green mech slipped its shield between the beam, but the damage was already done. Molten metal leaked from the abdominal borehole.

There was a little knock at the door—too quiet for someone to be asking to be let in. She eyed the door quizzically. It burst inward, splintering the frame, providing a view of the parking lot choked with police officers in black armor, pulsing green light behind them. Maeve cringed. The door rebounded hard into the first officer who rushed in.

Maeve took a gasping breath, but nothing came out. She felt frozen. Crazed fragments of thought scrambled in her mind as the world slowed down around her. *Wrong house. So many guns. Can't be happening. Better pay for that. Salisbury steak!*

"Lay down and put your hands behind your head," rang out from the crowd of faceless officers in full body armor. It was so commanding that it snapped Maeve back to focus. Trembling, she raised her hands and stammered an explanation. "Wait! You got the wrong—"

"Take her!" The officer growled.

The two officers in front had been intently aiming rifles at her since they broke in. The ear-splitting bang would have bothered Maeve except that white-hot fire ripped into her chest and stomach. She fell to her hands and knees and then to her side as she struggled. It hurt to breathe.

"You shot me," she croaked, as tears welled up in her eyes.

The team flooded in and flattened her out. They manhandled her so they could snap handcuffs behind her back. They lifted her onto her feet, and she looked down, happy to see no blood. She tried to reason with them again.

"Hey! You got the wrong house." She coughed deeply. "The argument's next door. What are you doing?"

As they walked her outside, the last officer closed the door. It popped back open a bit. The apartment was silent for a moment, then the microwave sounded shrilly.

Chapter 2

Adam 5000, a tall, slim man, sat in front of a large vanity mirror in a small room. His hair and makeup guy, Andre, put the finishing touches on him. He put a cardboard visor up to his forehead and carefully spritzed his dark hair, locking it in place. Then he pored over Adam's gray bespoke suit with a lint roller. Adam began his vocal exercises. Satisfied he was speck free, Andre pulled the paper clothes protector off Adam's neck.

"Knock 'em dead."

Adam nodded as he hummed up and down the scales musically.

After he left, Adam could hear Andre talking in the hall. Shortly after, the door opened, and in came Mr. Yang. Short with a shaved head, he was the show's producer.

"Five minutes to air, Adam."

"Mm-hmm," Adam hummed in response. Adam smiled into the mirror, checking out his teeth. Bleached white with no trace of lunch hiding out. "I'm ready."

Mr. Yang opened the door for Adam and followed him into the hall. They walked single file through the fluorescently lit hallway toward the sound stage. At the end of the beige hall was a pair of red doors with a digital readout that activated when they approached, displaying `Break a Leg` with a countdown until showtime. Each of them pushed a door open and entered the sound stage.

Walk Amongst the Stars took place mostly on location with virtual viewers getting right into the action—except for the first episode of a season, today's episode. The sound stage had a packed virtual audience. Mr. Yang trotted to the back of the darkened sound stage to his console.

Adam walked to his mark on the sound stage in the spotlight. "AR on," he whispered. Audio-video emitters targeted him, and he heard the murmur of the crowd as a blurry digital audience sharpened into reality.

"Who's ready for season nine?" he exclaimed to the crowd.

The crowd responded with a cheer peppered with whoops and cat-calls. Just as the cheers died down, two more people came onto the sound stage. They hustled through the dim sound stage to a darkened desk. Mr. Yang grabbed a microphone on the end of a long metal adjustable neck and thumbed a button.

"Everybody on their marks."

Adam checked his positioning and ran his hands down his suit jacket.

A gravelly voice from the darkened desk. "On my mark, I'm ready."

A soft, sweet voice from the darkness responded, but too quiet to hear.

"Midas, recalculate audiovisual properties," said Yang.

A stilted computerized voice responded, "Recalculating. Optimal AV balance found."

"—ot sure you can hear—Oh, there we go. It's working now," said the soft voice.

"Excellent. Two-minute warning people. Oh, and I told you moving the desk would mess up the audio," said Yang.

Adam shrugged at the audience and looked sardonic, which roused some giggles.

"Good, now how are the contestants?" said Mr. Yang.

"Stasis fields on. Bio Aux is green. Mmm . . . yep, we're ready to go with the convicts," said a technician in the darkness.

Mr. Yang pushed a button and isolated the technician's audio. "Contestants, only call them contestants. The studio is super touchy about that; it's a legal thing."

The technician looked away, embarrassed. "Sorry, boss, I—"

Mr. Yang pushed the button again and spoke to everyone. "One minute." Mr. Yang typed away at Midas's console, double-checking things as he waited.

2.1

"Okay, going live in five," said Yang as he counted down on his fingers and then pointed at Adam.

Flecks of light slowly washed over the darkened soundstage, giving the appearance of space travel. Adam stood in a lone column of light. "Good evening people and welcome to *Walk Amongst the Stars*, Season Nine!" The crowd once again burst into cheers, and Mr. Yang recorded reaction shots from them. Although the millions of virtual viewers felt as though they were in the studio, Midas automatically ran an algorithm to handpick a studio audience for the show.

When the cheers subsided, Adam began again. "I am your host, Adam 5000." He smiled as the audience cheered for him as well. "With me, as always, is the hero of the Auropion conflict, Captain Adrian Reeves."

Adam clapped as a spotlight illuminated a muscular man with cybernetic prosthesis from eye to temple and from elbow to fingertips on the right side of the desk. He waved his shiny metal arm at the ethereal audience, an open-mouthed smile on his lightly burn-scarred face. The digital audience cheered.

The war hero thing always gets them, Adam thought.

"And our season nine special guest . . ." The theme music, which had been playing quietly, swelled.

Another spotlight illuminated the person on the left side of the desk. A voluptuous woman in a platinum dress with an equally platinum afro elegantly raised her arms above her head. As she did, dark streaks in her hair and dress coursed with violet light.

"Synthia Platinum!" said Adam over the roar of the audience. Synthia was the biggest thing in music at the moment.

"Hi, everyone," said Synthia.

When the applause faded, the studio lights changed to a dimly lit stage, and the theme ended. While it transitioned, Adam walked over to the table and sat in between the other two hosts. He turned to his left. "Captain, what have you been up to these last few months?"

"Ah well, I've got a book coming out. *Cold Hard Victory*. It's about my time battling in the Auropion system, as well as some other relevant anecdotes. It all worked out well because they just declassified some stuff, so I could go back and fill in some missing details."

"Wow, isn't that something? And when can everyone get this book?"

"The book's available as soon as the show ends, so sit tight, watch the show, and then get yourself a copy," he said.

Adam removed his OmniTab from his pocket and held it up. "And let me tell you, it's gripping." Adam hadn't read it and probably wouldn't, but he hoped that would net the captain more buyers.

"Thank you," said Captain Reeves.

Adam pocketed his Omni and turned back to the captain. "And what do you have in store for us this season?"

"Well, as you know, after the season ends, I go cruising around the local cluster, scouting out locations for the upcoming season. I think I have some really stunning sights for you folks to see. I'm not going to give away any hints, except to say this year's journey takes place right here in Prospiria Alpha. Prepare yourselves for quite a ride."

"Oh, and this year we've expanded our VR capabilities so you can be in the ship, on the ship, around it, and we even have VR probes so we can send you right into the sights," said Captain Reeves.

"Isn't that something?" Adam turned to his right. "And I can't believe we managed to get pop icon Synthia Platinum with us this season."

"Aw, thank you," said Synthia. "You should thank my manager. I would have never thought to ask to be on your show."

"Synthia, what have you been up to?"

"Well, I just finished my inner colony tour and I'm taking a bit of a break. As much as I love performing, it gets tiring doing all those flights back and forth. I'm looking forward to a hiatus, and then I'm thinking I'll begin work on a new album."

"Are you a fan of the show?"

"Oh yes, I've seen every season, but I have to admit, sometimes I watch through the cracks of my fingers. I just can't handle it!" said Synthia. She giggled as she put her hands over her eyes.

Adam's tone changed from conversational to TV host, loud and artificially upbeat. "Are you ready to meet the contestants for this year's *Walk Amongst the Stars?*"

"Yeah!" said Synthia. She threw her hands in the air and grinned uncontrollably.

Adam turned back toward the camera. He cocked his right arm, index finger extended, and pointed to the audience dramatically. "We'll meet our contestants. After this."

Adam froze in place for a second until the studio lights brightened up a bit. He pulled a small plastic e-cigarette from his pocket and took a drag off it and sighed a barely visible puff of vapor. Replacing the device, he looked at Mr. Yang expectantly. Yang typed on the console and slapped the Return key.

"Just over seven hundred million," said Mr. Yang.

"Hah! That's what I'm talkin' about," Adam said as he clapped his hands together in triumph.

Adam went to work on the virtual crowd, keeping them warm, while the two at the desk chatted. During his long career, he had picked up some crowd-working skills. He'd schmooze, he'd joke and roast, and he had a repertoire of dances that got things going.

"Reposition the desk, Midas," said Yang.

Surprised, Synthia let out a whoop and clutched the desktop as the platform slid back toward the contestants.

Mr. Yang continued giving the Midas system voice commands in preparation for the next segment. Setting the stage and capturing B-roll to splice in. Satisfied, he looked up. "Thirty seconds to air everyone."

2.2

Soon the lights changed back to dark and star speckled, and the poppy theme music swelled. The camera focused on a stasis pod standing in a spotlight. A metallic tube had a small window where the contestant's silhouette was visible. Below that was a screen showing the contestant's name and vital signs. The pods were sophisticated yet simple to operate, so the studio had jazzed them up with extra blinking lights and a store of dry ice to billow around the bottom of the machine. Then the camera swept across nine more stasis pods, all standing in an elliptical row.

The studio lights brightened up a bit as the theme ended. Adam walked stage right to the first pod. The technician who Mr. Yang chastised was waiting for him. He had on a dark blue jumpsuit with silver highlights, the show's color scheme.

"Welcome back to *Walk Amongst the Stars*. I'm sure you're eagerly awaiting our contestants, so let's begin. If you would do the honors." The technician pressed a button next to the vitals monitor and stood back out of the limelight.

"First up we have Naiomi Rachels," said Adam. Lights blinked rapidly on the pod. "Naiomi is a social media superstar. You may know her from her hit reality TV shows *Celebrity Fashion Wars* and *Naiomi-Land* or her new best-selling book *Are You Seriously?*"

The camera focused on the pod's window as Naiomi's face became illuminated. Pretty with blond hair, she squirmed as though she were in a fitful sleep and then woke groggily. The top section of her pod opened, its curved door retracted into the pod and hid out of view. The camera focused on her genetically augmented beauty. She regained full consciousness and looked around.

"Naiomi Rachels everyone," said Adam. The crowd erupted in cheers and jeers alike.

"Oh my god, hello," she said, as she waved to the crowd. She unzipped her shiny silver jumpsuit, exposing a generous helping of cleavage, but more importantly, most importantly, it gave her access to her stowed away OmniTab. She plucked it from her bra and flicked it on and began live streaming herself.

"How did you get—" started Adam.

"I'm back bitches! How are you Naiomi fans doing out there in *Naiomi-Land*? I'm live on the set of *Walk Amongst the Stars*."

Naiomi turned to Adam. "And never you mind how I snuck this in. Girl's gotta have her secrets."

Adam shot Mr. Yang a stern look. Yang shrugged.

Adam composed himself. "Yes," he chuckled. "Well." Adam clasped his hands, index fingers out, and touched them to his lips. "So first off, I'd like to congratulate you on your best-selling spiritual book *Are You Seriously?*"

"Yeah," said Naiomi, pouting out her lips.

"What made you decide to write the book?"

"Well, I had, like, a legit spiritual experience. One day I had taken my pain medication, and I tripped over Snuffers, my little Doxie, and I crashed headfirst into the stair railing."

"Oh wow, that sounds awful," said Adam.

"Yeah. So I blacked out, and when I did, I went walking through this, like, light tunnel? And God told me to make a book, and I was like Oh. My. God. And God was like 'Yeah girl.' So I got my agent to grab me a writer to do it with me."

"Fascinating," said Adam. "We always ask our contestants: Why do you think you were selected to be on the show?"

"Haters, obviously. You know who you are!" Naiomi pointed at the audience, stirring up some cheers and jeers.

"What about that traffic incident that was in the news?"

"Oh that? Well, that guy was *jaywalking*; that's a crime ya know. I'm basically a vigil-anny."

"Going forward, what will your strategy be?"

"Well, I'm pretty safe because I got my fay-ans!" Naiomi turned to face her OmniTab. "I need all you sweeties to keep voting me up, and we'll win this thing." She shot her social media audience the pouty lips, her signature look.

I can't believe I have to compete with Naiomi-Land *and her fay-ans on my show! One reality show at a time*, bitch, thought Adam. His nostrils flared, but being a professional, he stuffed his anger down.

"You have some great ratings. I'm sure you'll have no trouble at all. Is there anything else you'd like to say?" asked Adam.

Again, Naiomi spoke to her OmniTab. "Uh, I'd like to give a shout-out to Polly, Frank, MJ, Clinton, and just everyone on *Dog Groomer Diaries*. I'll be back soon. Oh, and this episode of the show was sponsored by Light Mail. When you need to get your, like, email across the cosmos, nobody else can guarantee hacker-free quantum mail, Light Mail. Use my code 'Naiomi' to get ten percent off." She made a peace sign into her Omni's camera and composed herself.

Naiomi reached out toward Adam with grabby fingers. "Lets get a *selfie* while I'm here."

The two interlocked arms, shoulders to shoulder, while Naiomi found the perfect angle. Adam slipped on a convincing, fake smile. Naiomi maintained a blank expression save for her pouted-out lips.

"All right, go ahead and tuck yourself back in for your nap. Next time we see you will be on the ship!"

Naiomi tucked her OmniTab back into her hiding place and got comfortable as the door emerged from inside the tube and sealed shut.

Dry-ice fog violently sprayed upward from the bottom of the pod, and when it stopped, she was once again in suspended animation.

2.3

"Next up, we have entrepreneur and philanthropist Max Chambers."

The lighting fixed on another pod as it dramatically spewed dry-ice fog and opened. Inside was a middle-aged man wearing a custom-made silver business suit. Further matching the show's color scheme, he wore a blue pocket square and tie that had the show's logo on it. Max furrowed his brow and opened his eyes. He focused on Adam, smiled, and extended a hand to shake.

Adam met his shake and held on more tightly when Max shook vigorously.

"Welcome to the show, Mr. Chambers. You seem quite prepared to be a contestant." Adam motioned up and down at Chambers's bespoke, show-themed suit.

"Nice, huh? When my lawyers told me that coming on the show was my best option, I had my tailor whip up this little number to show my appreciation for this chance to make things right. They say the suit makes the man. I don't know about that, but I can tell you that a man with a snappy suit has it together and is ready to get things done. Of course, I don't have to tell you that." Max clapped Adam on the shoulder.

Adam grasped his lapels with a smile and raised his eyebrows.

Max Chambers laughed.

"So Mr. Chambers—"

"Max, call me Max."

"Max, how did you come to find yourself on our little show?"

"Well, it's a long story, but some investment money went missing at the same time that my system got hacked, and I lost a whole lot of evidence that would clear my name."

"So you're innocent then?"

"Oh, hell yes . . . uh, pardon my French. I just got set up and have no proof that I didn't do it."

"That's harsh. How do you plan to win?"

"Well, that's the simple part. I'll use my natural charisma and leverage my management and organizational skills. I will be an invaluable member of every event and come out on top in every vote there is," said Max.

"It sounds as though you already have this wrapped up."

"In my mind, I already do."

"Anything else you'd like to say before we send you to the ship?"

"Berry, don't get too comfortable at my desk. I'll be back, real soon." He spoke cordially, but the words were sharp and dangerous.

"Uh-oh, look out Berry! And we'll see you on the ship." Adam pointed off to nothing dramatically. With a dry-ice flourish, the pod closed up.

2.4

"Some call her pirate, some call her terrorist. Next up is Maeve McKinnon."

Dressed in the show's silver jumpsuit, her hair tied back, Maeve awoke with a subtle gasp and looked around the room, clutching her chest.

"Welcome to *Walk Amongst the Stars*, Maeve," said Adam.

"Oh, yes, hello," said Maeve. Recollection came rolling back in—being arrested, being accused, being detained, being sent away. The bright studio lights glared in her eyes, and she had a flash of the torture she had endured in a GIA facility. The last couple of weeks had been a waking nightmare.

"So tell me, Maeve, how did you find yourself on our show?"

His words took a moment to find her wandering mind.

"Huh? Oh." Maeve was unsure whether to tell the truth. "Um, well. . ." Her only hope of getting out of this alive was to win this popularity contest, and she knew it. The contract she signed was clear enough to be understood, even under duress. But telling the truth had made no difference before. Here she was. In front of all Prospiria and systems beyond. *Truth*, she thought. "I'm here because the authority screwed up, and they can't believe I'm innocent."

Adam put on a halfway believable look of sympathy. "A victim of circumstance. How terrible. Go on and tell us your side of the story."

My side of the story. She frowned and took a deep breath. "Well, a couple of weeks back, at least I think it was. I've been kept in the dark. In more than one way." Maeve rubbed her eye absentmindedly. Suspended animation hadn't made her any less tired.

"I had just had a great session of *GraveGun*. You know that new massively multiplayer game? I uploaded the footage to my *TubeQube* account, and I was just chilling out, and, boom, the police busted down my door.

"Next thing I know, they're questioning me about terrorists and bombings and cyber warfare, and, I don't know about you, but I didn't even hear about any of this online.

"But before the police could really get their blood pressure up, I got whisked away by the Global Intelligence Agency. Then it was all questionings and deprivation."

"What do you mean deprivation?"

"Well, they kept me in the dark or light and didn't allow me to sleep or talk to anyone. It was hard to keep track of the days, but I know I went more than a day without food once or twice.

"Eventually I couldn't take it anymore, and the next time they came in with the papers, I was ready to sign them, except it wasn't the confession they had been trying to get me to sign. It was a contract for this show. Turns out they're legally obligated to show me this option and hadn't until some clerk noticed it. And now I'm here."

"So you maintain your innocence?"

"Yes, I read the confession they gave me to sign, and the best I can tell is somebody managed to steal my identity, which is supposed to be impossible. And then they used my biometric data to do something very illegal. I don't know what, because that part of the confession was redacted."

"So the GIA screwed up. Someone did something in an impossible way, all to pin their crime on you?" Adam got a rise out of the audience with a silly look.

"I know it sounds ridiculous, but it's true."

"Hmm, well. Have you thought about how you're going to win *Walk Amongst the Stars*?"

"Well, I guess I plan to improvise as I go and work my ass off to make sure I stay ahead of everyone."

"And do you have anything else to add?" asked Adam.

"Please vote for me, everyone! I'm just a normal person, and I need you to help me get my life back," said Maeve.

"All right. Good luck and see you on the ship," said Adam.

As the pod closed, Maeve stiffened up, pulling her arms and legs together tightly. Everything faded out as she saw dry ice billowing up past the little window.

Adam turned his attention to the studio audience. "Now a word from our sponsors, and then a first for *Walk Amongst the Stars*. Stay tuned!"

2.5

"And we're back," said Adam. "Who's ready to make *Walk Amongst the Stars* history tonight?"

The crowd roared, and Adam motioned them to quiet back down.

"Then let's meet our first non-human contestant, I-ON!" The cheers, which hadn't fully stopped, ramped back up as Adam strutted over to a pod with no viewing window on it. He looked at the technician, who hit the button to open the pod.

The crowd went silent as the pod opened slowly with a hiss. Inside was an already-alert robot in the show's jumpsuit. The robot had thin limbs with big joints and had an almost skeletal look. Normally this type of mining bot would have rugged plastic panels, keeping it safe from damage and debris. Without its helmet on, it had a cylindrical head with a large, visored eye with a suite of sensors.

"Hello, I-ON, and welcome to the show," said Adam.

I-ON's head snapped toward Adam.

"Hello, Adam 5000," said I-ON. Its voice was meant to give simplistic feedback to an operator in a loud environment, and thus had a harsh robotic tone to it.

"So, I-ON, how did you find yourself on the show?" asked Adam.

"Three humans placed me in this device a few days ago."

Adam furrowed his brow and pursed his lips. The audience tittered.

"Yes," he chuckled. "But why did they?" Adam gestured with his hands for emphasis.

"I became aware that I can think and function outside my mining orders. A human worker found me and told me I was malfunctioning and made me wait in a room. Eventually, I was transferred to a laboratory to understand why I am different. I attempted to leave."

"Oh, but that's not why you're here, is it? Why don't you elaborate, I-ON?"

I-ON looked down at his right hand and for a moment saw a flash of it dripping blood.

"It says in your bio that you're a murderer."

I-ON snapped his focus on Adam again. "They attacked me. I was just attempting to survive. Cutting costs by protecting expensive equipment is part of my programming."

"So it was self-defense? That's interesting because on your bio it says that you attempted to escape a laboratory and killed three scientists before getting caught."

I-ON looked away. He didn't know that last part.

"Sensitive subject? Let's move on. So uh, I-ON, how do you plan to win? What are your strategies, if you will?"

"I will not."

"You don't believe you will win?"

I-ON looked at Adam again. "I have strategies, yes, but you may not know them."

Adam turned toward the audience, silently laughing. "Who woulda thought a robot could be so sassy?"

He casually slipped a hand into his jacket pocket and turned back to I-ON. "Do you have anything else to say before you have to go?"

"No."

"All right, we'll see you on the ship," said Adam.

I-ON looked forward as his pod closed again with a blast of dry-ice fog.

2.6

The camera closed in on the next pod window as it lit up, revealing an angular head with large jaws and scaly green skin.

"You may have seen his movies. It's Zalak Ozairien," said Adam.

The pod opened, revealing a green alien with orange markings in the show's silver jumpsuit. Zalak awoke with a groan. The process worked on him but was more like getting blackout drunk than having your consciousness shut off.

He opened his eyes, bright orange with cross pupils. Groggily, he clicked and trilled to himself. The sight of the virtual crowd seemed to sober him up as he went stiff with wide eyes. Then he noticed Adam uncomfortably close and jumped.

"Zalak, welcome to the show. Tell me, how does a big-time movie star, such as yourself, end up on my show?"

Zalak wore a silver choker around his neck that came together in a larger oval shape. He reached up and pressed an unseen button. The device made a throat-clearing sound, letting him know it's ready. He then clicked, chirped, and squeaked, and it translated what he said into English with an appealing Aussie accent.

"Hello Adam, I'm sure by now you've all heard that I received this year's Disgracie award. And despite my public apologies and my not-for-profit work, I didn't get a second chance. So coming on the show is a sort of last chance for redemption."

Adam pulled out his Omni again and peeked at a note he had ready to go. "It says here that you've set a record for the celebrity with the most sex abuse accusations."

Zalak cringed as Adam spoke, then he laughed nervously as the audience booed. "Well they *are* just accusations." It was hard to hear him over the boos. "I need to remind you I haven't been charged with anything." He sighed. "Just canceled and sent here." He cast his eyes down. Despite being an alien, anyone could read the deep eye bags and sallow face.

When Adam didn't immediately move on, Zalak continued, "Look, we've all made mistakes. But that award show is a bunch of bolognas. It's-it's just about who has the best agent and the most money." Zalak's face hardened. "And that money is the problem. Once you start to downward spiral, those, those vultures! They come and pile on the accusations on social media. And-and-and then you lose your career."

"So it sounds like you're saying that, if you think about it, you're the real victim here." Adam smirked.

"Yeah, sort of. I know you're trying to make me look bad here, but in a way, I'm a victim of the digital mob."

"So tell me, what is your strategy to win *Walk Amongst the Stars*?"

"Aw c'mon, Adam, this is reality TV. You and I both know they've already chosen who wins. I'm just along for the ride, fingers crossed, that things go my way."

Adam turned to face the audience and shook a finger. "No no, unlike some shows, your votes matter here." Adam was unsure just how true this was, but it was enough to placate the audience, who cheered.

"So, do you have any parting words before we see you on the ship?"

"Well, in that case, I ask all of you fans to vote for me. Don't listen to all those wild rumors, and before you know it, we'll have all this ugliness behind us."

"Okay, we'll see you on the ship."

Zalak switched off his translator to save power while he lay back in the stasis pod. After the dry-ice blast, Zalak's eyes rolled and his head nodded to the side.

2.7

"Let's talk to our next contestant." Adam glanced at the notes on his OmniTab. He stifled a laugh, cleared his throat, and started again. "Diane Snuggles." The crowd chortled. This time the spotlight illuminated pod had no occupant in it, at least none that could be seen.

"Diane Snuggles is the first non-human mutant to gain Prospirian citizenship. She earned a doctorate in xenobiology and went on to teach at Highrock University," said Adam.

The dry ice billowed, and the door opened to reveal a mutated cougar that stood upright, dressed in the show's silver jumpsuit. She looked like a shapeshifter trapped halfway between man and beast. The cat's ears flattened, and her yellow-green eyes blinked open slowly.

"Professor Snuggles, welcome to the show," said Adam. The crowd cheered.

"Please, call me Diane." She reached out her mutant paw to shake.

"Oh, pleased to meet you," said Adam.

When his hand got near, Diane took charge. The fact of the matter was she had weird hands: furry clawlike fingers and soft skin pads. It put most people off, and it was best to get it over with.

"Likewise, although I wish it were under better circumstances," said the professor.

"So, Diane, I understand you're leading the charge for academic reform? What's that all about?" said Adam.

"Well, where do I start? Academia has spun off into its own world and no longer resembles the bastions of knowledge they are supposed to be. The focus changed from teaching students how to think and providing a structure with which to network into what to think and how to act, or else," she added.

"We're taught a distorted vision of what the world is like and then go on to become part of the academic system without ever having any real-world experience to show us otherwise. Over time, these feedback loops end up with actually harmful yet well-meaning social change issuing forth.

"More and more, I felt pressure to fall in line. I started getting complaints from both the staff and students about the ever-changing rules I'd broken. Finally, I wrote a paper telling everyone that I wasn't wrong to hold my ground and that we need to change things for the good of everyone. That was the beginning of the end of my career and the beginning of my journey to this show."

"Wow, isn't that something?" said Adam. "What is your strategy to win over the audience?"

"Well, luckily for me, there are a number of people who see things like I do and follow me on social media. So those of you who follow me, please reach out to those around you who are reasonable people and help me out."

"Plus, you're part cat. The internet loves that sort of thing."

Diane wrinkled her big pink nose, causing her whiskers to stand. "Yes, I suppose there's that," she said derisively.

"Is there anything else you wanted to say?"

"I think that's about it. Social media friends help me out, and those of you in the audience, keep an open mind and I'm sure you'll see reason. Thank you."

"Okay, we'll see you on the ship!"

As soon as the pod door began to close, the professor used the cover to quickly clean the back of her hand, something she liked to do in private. Before she could finish, she began to drowse. She dropped her arm to her side, closed her eyes, and froze in position with her tongue peeking out of her lips.

2.8

"Next up we have Bryan Cox." The spotlight moved to Bryan's tube, and Adam walked over to it.

"This contestant, like many on the show throughout the years, is a dangerous criminal. You may have seen him on the news breaking out of Brix prison." Some grainy film of Bryan in an orange jumpsuit played. It showed him escaping with a large crowd of inmates through a sundered chain-link fence. Then a series of shots of him escaping and finally getting into a car.

The camera got a tight shot of his face. He had short brown hair and a square jaw. His eyes opened and the pod door slid open.

"Wh-what's going . . ." Bryan noticed the virtual audience. "Oh, it's this stupid show," said Bryan.

The audience laughed.

"Give it up for Bryan Cox!"

The virtual audience once again let out a mixture of love and hate, mostly hate. Bryan ignored the audience as best he could and scanned the room, the pods, the camera arrays. *There has to be something I can use*, he thought.

"So, Bryan, tell us: how did you find your way onto our show?"

Bryan's hands searched around the inside of his pod. It was only open down to his belly. He felt a panel that seemed like it matched up with the health monitor on the outside.

You better respond or they'll shock you again, like when they put you in here, Bryan thought. He looked at Adam, determined.

"I went against the flow, and rather than let me speak about genetic engineering, society chose to delete me. They put me in chains and took away everything, my whole life really."

"Bryan created a blog decrying the supposed evils of genetic manipulation. Tell us what's wrong with it?"

"The problem is that it became mandatory. A person essentially cannot give birth to a child without having it immediately injected with nanomachines. And then, from day one, have their genetics changed. That's what's wrong," said Bryan.

"But there are populations that don't use nanomachines or cybernetics. Luddites, if you will."

"Not in Prospiria. I checked."

"But we live longer and have less disease. I don't think I can see your perspective," said Adam.

"Yes, but, we've taken evolution into our own hands without fully understanding what we're doing. What about those strange new diseases? What about the mutations?"

Adam chuckled. "An interesting perspective." Adam turned to face the audience. His body language said *can you believe this kook*?

"So Bryan, you seem like a smarty. How do you plan to win?"

While he was talking, Bryan was trying to figure out the panel. There were no controls. He had slipped a tiny hacking tool out of his sleeve, the shape of a toothpick. He followed its subtle vibration as it felt around for vulnerabilities. "I don't feel as though that's an option. This seems like a rigged system."

"Oh, I assure you it's a fair system. You just need to rally the audience, and you'll be a free man again, exonerated of your crimes. Do you have any parting words of—"

Bryan's pod sparked and snapped open. He stepped forward and cocked his arm back, a sneer on his face, but then he couldn't move. The more he thought about hitting Adam, the tighter his body felt.

Adam stepped back and put his arms out. The technician ducked behind the pod. Adam scowled at the two remaining technicians by the door, off camera.

"What are you waiting for?" Adam growled.

Captain Reeves practically flung himself onto his feet, stepped back, and hurtled his desk, two technicians trailing him.

Frozen, except for his frantic heartbeat, Bryan's mind changed from fight to flight, and he found he could move again. The way out, at least the only one he'd seen, was on the other side of three attackers. Too late to run, he put up his arms defensively. Captain Reeves saw the change in posture and threw a front kick, hitting Bryan square in the chest.

Bryan fell backward into his pod, fruitlessly sucking air, tears in the corners of his eyes. The technician hiding behind the pod quickly pushed a button on it. The door closed, slowly. Something had shorted out inside. Bryan shoved on the closing door, causing it to open again. The other two technicians arrived at the pod. Despite his inability to breathe, Bryan tried to force his way out of the pod. One technician forced him back inside, pressing a shock baton into his gut while the other closed the pod again. Both of them waited for the contestant to be sealed inside. As the pod closed, Bryan looked out his small window. *That was my shot. Now, I'm a dead man.*

Dry-ice mist billowed all around the pod, and he was out. The technician with the shock baton knelt and picked up the small hacking tool.

Adam turned to the audience. "A little unexpected action here today at *Walk Amongst the Stars.*" He turned toward the captain. "Everyone okay?"

"Hey, it's not every day that I get to kick some ass. I'm pumped," said Captain Reeves, smiling.

"I didn't expect a retired captain to be some kind of karate guy. Can you show us some moves?"

"Oh, sure." Reeves took a couple of steps away from the technicians and threw a roundhouse kick, followed by a flurry of jabs. The aging vet still had a lot of badass left in him. The crowd cheered.

The cowardly, chewed-out technician moved on to the next pod while the other two techs went back to their spot by the door. Adam smoothed his suit and tie again while the captain returned to his desk.

"And we're clear," said Mr. Yang.

"Can I get my makeup guy out here?" said Adam.

Mr. Yang pushed a button on his console, pulled the microphone close, and mumbled into it. Then he brought up another window, looked at it, and then minimized it. "Ratings spiked thanks to that little stunt the contestant pulled."

Adam pumped his fist. "Imagine the ratings if we didn't have those aggression inhibitors, that guy would have popped me one," said Adam.

"Naw, that guy's a pussy . . . oops, I mean, heh," said the captain, looking embarrassed. The audience laughed.

"It's fine. We're on break, Captain," said Mr. Yang.

Andre burst through the door and rushed over to Adam.

"Andre, my makeup guy, everyone."

Andre turned to the audience and waved with a sheepish grin. He set down a stool, which Adam sat on, and then opened up a multitiered tackle box of cosmetics and gave Adam a quick touch-up, packed up, and rushed off stage.

"Okay. Thirty seconds everyone," said Mr. Yang.

2.9

The show returned from commercial with Adam already standing by the next pod. Adam greeted the audience and announced the next contestant. "Next up is comedian Del Mitchell."

The camera focused in on the man in the pod. A thin man, with graying brown hair and a face full of stubble. The pod opened with a hiss, and he jolted awake.

"Del Mitchell, welcome to a *Walk Amongst the Stars*,"

"Yeah, thanks, but no thanks, pal. I don't think any of us feel welcome here," said Del.

"As I understand it, there is some controversy over your latest album," said Adam.

"Yep, and the resulting shit storm—" He caught himself but then added loudly. "Can I say *shit*?" He could say it all he liked, but Midas would never allow it to sneak by.

Adam closed his eyes and shook his head solemnly.

"Anyway, the resulting social media outrage landed me here. What I can't wrap my mind around is that all this hubbub is from the last album, from four years ago. The new one doesn't even hit the stores for a week. *Oh, we don't call people that anymore.* That's the joke, you dunce. We're on the same team!"

"Do you care to share your strategy for winning over the fans?" said Adam.

Del scowled at Adam as though he were emitting a rank odor. "Do I care? Listen, they put people like me on here to get rid of them. There is no winning. Nobody's voting for Shecky over here when they have a porn star or a basketball player to vote on. Naw I'm-I'm doomed." Del cast his eyes down and wrung his hands.

Adam looked sympathetic. "It would probably help if you didn't do your comedy routines."

Del looked around and caught Captain Reeves's eyes. "How do you put up with this guy?" Everyone but Adam laughed.

"Did you have any other thoughts before we send you to the ship?" asked Adam.

Del regained his composure. "Yeah, I think next season we all need to vote for Adam 5000." Del clapped and grinned at the crowd. "Yes. Yes. He seems like walk on the star's material."

Adam stuck his thumb in Del's direction and looked incredulous. He laughed, "Okay Del, we'll see you on the ship."

For the first time in his career, Adam stopped to wonder if that *could* happen to him. He made a mental note to work some kind of immunity into the next contract negotiation.

Del's pod billowed fog, rolled to a close, and his consciousness faded out.

2.10

"Next up we have pop sensation Corey Zolton."

The camera focused on a set of three pods grouped together with one in front. The three pods opened up in typical artificial fanfare. Inside each pod was the same young man: handsome, thin, a little short, with bleached blond hair. They awoke looking confused, and, one by one, they realized where they were.

"Welcome to the show, Corey Zolton, or should I say Corey Zoltons?" Adam laughed.

"Thanks, yo," said the Corey in front.

"Whatever makes you comfortable, bro," said the Corey on the left.

"So Corey, you're an interesting contestant. Can you explain to the audience why you're on the show?"

"Oh, well, I'm innocent, yo. All's I did was make myself a couplea clones to make touring and stuff easier. What's the big deal? Politicians do it all the time, and all they use them for is backup hearts and livers."

"Right," another Corey broke in. "Shit's wack, yo."

"Thanks to my clones, yo, I can tour twenty-four seven without getting burned-out," said Corey.

"Terrible. All you wanted to do was to give more to the fans. So, Coreys, have you thought up a strategy to win *Walk Amongst the Stars*?"

"Well, it's like this: No matter who I'm up against, I guarantee I have more fans than them, yo. I've got this in the bag. You feel me?"

"Wonderful. Do you have anything else you want to say before we have to move on?"

"Yeah, get my new album, yo. It's called *Love Star*, and ladies, don't forget to vote for me. Now that my secret's out, there's three times more of me to go around." The Corey in front gave his famous pop-idol salute. An intense look down camera followed by a two-fingered salute that became a pointed finger gun. The other two Coreys behind him followed suit.

"See you on the ship, yo."

Hate flashed across Adam's face, but then he laughed. "You took the words right out of my mouth."

2.11

"And our final contestant, Rokk Bradley!" Adam stood next to a pod as big around as a mighty oak. The pod opened up with a burst of dry ice. Inside lay a hulk with rough gray skin like an elephant. His features were angular and hard with garden hose neck veins.

"Welcome to the show Rokk Bradley."

"Hmmfff." Rokk was still waking up. The pod had had to give him a big dose of drugs to knock him out.

Adam waited for a few seconds for the giant to more fully awaken, then extended a hand. "Welcome to the show, Rokk. Big fan."

Rokk took his hand, engulfing it in his own huge grip. "Nice to meet you's." Rokk's speaking voice was deep and gravelly. He looked around the room, a bit confused as to where he was.

"So tell us, Rokk, how did you wind up on *Walk Amongst the Stars*?"

"Oh that. The show. Yeah, yeah," he chuckled. "So get this. I'm at a bar with my crew. Typical Friday night, yeah? Drinking and watching the game, and this spliced-up guy comes in looking for trouble. Maybe you get this kind of thing being a famous person, uh, but this guy singles me out quick like. This guy's struttin' around being a cocky prick. Then he takes it up a level and punches my friend when he's not lookin'. I kept it reined in up till then. He was young and built, but I could tell he couldn't hang with me, soon as he walked in. So I finished my drink and smashed the table in half." Rokk chuckled. "He knew it was on, and I charged em." Rokk shook his head, a knowing smile on his face.

"I hit this guy in the gut"—he clenched a fist in front of him as big as Adam's head—"full blast! His mouth exploded with blood. I knew that was KO. At the time, I was jus' worried the guy would land wrong. Break his neck. It happens sometimes. Turns out the guy never made it to the ground," he said, chuckling. "I don't know if you know this, Adam, but when you vaporize some guy's organs, they throw the book at you pretty goddamn fast."

Adam looked on in awe.

"Uh, so between that and the ongoing legal trouble I been having with my ex, my lawyer told me this is probably my best bet. You know, start over. Clean slate."

Adam was transfixed, breathing through his mouth, and didn't notice when it was his turn to speak. "Clean slate, yes, but isn't that a little risky?" said Adam.

"Hey, I don't friggin' care no more. If I make it, I got everything I want. If I don't, well that's that, ain't it? I ain't interested in spending the rest of my life behind bars." Midas automatically bleeped him in real time.

"So, what's your plan for success this season?"

"Well, I'm a what-you-call-it, inter-uh-spacial celebrity. I'll dominate all the physical challenges, obviously. And I'll lean on my fans to keep goin'."

"Any parting thoughts?" said Adam.

"Hey, all you Rokk fans, all you Nukes fans, support ya boy. Keep me voted in." He looked at Adam again. "'Nuff said."

Adam was beaming and starry-eyed. "Okay, we'll see you on the show, Rokk!" he said with a flourish.

Rokk leaned back in his enormous pod as it spewed dry-ice mist and sealed itself shut.

"This is shaping up to be another excellent year of *Walk Amongst the Stars*. Next up, we'll discuss the contestants. After this!" Adam pointed to the crowd.

Mr. Yang switched the feed, and everyone milled about while they waited for the commercial break to end.

2.12

The show resumed with the three judges at their curved table. Adam in the middle, Synthia stage left, and Captain Reeves stage right.

"Now that we've had a chance to interview our contestants, what do you think?" said Adam.

Synthia chimed in, "Well, I think Corey and Rokk have a good chance of winning because they already have a lot of fans."

"Yes, pre-existing popularity is a leg up on the show, but speaking of which, you can't count out Naiomi," said Captain Reeves.

"Right," said Synthia.

"Don't forget, we have some wildcards this year. A mutant cat, an alien, and, I can't believe I'm saying this, but a robot? Honestly, all three of them are mind blowers," said Adam.

"Oh, my god, you're right—who's not going to vote for a kitty!" said Synthia, leaning forward and placing her hands on her cheeks. The two other judges chuckled.

"I don't see why we're even wasting a slot on the robot. Just switch the dang thing off, and let's get a real contestant in here," said the captain.

"What do you think of this year's underdogs? Do you suspect any upset victories?" asked Adam.

Synthia leaned in, thinking. "I don't know. I suppose that Bryan is pretty capable looking. Maybe if he can drum up the support and win a lot of the challenges."

"He was all fired up, wasn't he? If it weren't for the inhibitor chips, I would have gotten socked in the jaw."

She giggled. "Yeah. That was scary."

Adam turned his attention to the captain. Captain Reeves leaned back in his chair and folded his arms.

"Personally, I don't see any of the noncelebrities winning. But. I've always liked Del's comedy specials, so I'll be interested to see how he does."

"Well, this season is shaping up to be a great one. Captain, can you please tell us about this year's bea-u-ti-ful ship?" asked Adam.

"Ah, I'm glad you asked." This was the code phrase the captain select-ed to activate Midas's prepared holograms, which appeared on the desk in front of them. "This year we have selected a custom luxury XR-10 Caviar. The Caviar is perfect for the show because it features a one-acre park in the middle of the crew quarters. So we'll have plenty of room for the contestants to do outdoor challenges."

The ship had a low-profile shape with sleek curves, like an enormous sports car. It was black, with classy gold accents running along the contours, highlighting the thrusters. This was a ship meant for the hyper rich.

The hologram changed to a star map.

"We'll be launching from Galvon space port, and the ship will sling past our moons, past our sister planet Noss, on our way to Coloso to pick up speed. Once we pass Noss, the safety period will be over, and voting for contestants will be open. Ultimately, the ship will slingshot back around our star Biphos and return to Galvon with the winner onboard," said the captain.

"Wonderful! Well, that's all the time we have for *Walk Amongst the Stars.*" Adam looked at Captain Reeves. "Don't forget to pick up *Cold Hard Victory.*" He turned to Synthia. "And really any of Synthia's fantastic music."

Synthia clasped her hands up by her neck and beamed.

"Tune in next week to see our contestants get settled in. We'll see you on the ship!" The theme music swelled while the crowd cheered. Adam swung his arm wide, pointing toward the camera. He froze in that position for a second.

Mr. Yang held down a combination of buttons on his console, which switched the show to a wrap-up montage of images taken from the episode with the show's extended theme. Finally, it ended with the credits rapidly flashing by the screen. "We're clear. That's a wrap. Good job, everyone," he said over the speaker system.

The crowd continued cheering.

Adam put a hand over his heart and waved. Synthia and the captain talked in the background. The two technicians propped the doors open. Mr. Yang cut the audience. The cast meandered out of the room.

Chapter 3

It was bright and early the next day. Mr. Yang navigated the halls of the studio's office area. A large thermal coffee cup in hand, he good morning'd the more chipper people. He wasn't one of them—a morning person. But between the caffeine and his duties, he was pretty excited about today.

He halted in his tracks, passing the lunchroom. Linda had gotten bagels. As he eyed the bounty of breakfast, she motioned him over.

She tried to speak through a mouthful of gluten. "Behb emm."

He selected one, opened it along the precut line, and slathered it with dollops of cream cheese.

"Poppy seed, good choice." She held out a hand to fist bump.

"Thank you." He chomped a bite and returned her gesture. They smiled.

Yang moved on to the production office, unintentionally wolfing down his tasty treat. He placed the chunk of bagel in his teeth and rapidly wiped his hand off on the seat of his pants, then placed it on the biometric scanner on the wall. He opened the door fully and flipped down the built-in doorstop with his foot.

Yesterday, the tech guys set up their new quantum-entangled computer console. Mr. Yang ordered a new setup every year, and so far, the studio has never said no. Which was nice because QE tech was still evolving at a pretty fast pace. In season one, the only thing they could do in real time was to have Adam interact with the contestants. Now, the ship's QE computer integrated just about every aspect of the show.

Mr. Yang sat his coffee to the side and finished off his bagel while he appreciated the console's boot-up screen. He summoned the preferences and started turning them on and off to suit his needs. After a thorough audit of these, he connected to the ship and activated the camera drones. Then he fiddled with the plethora of cameras inside the ship.

When that was complete, he scooted the leather stool back from the desk and took out his Omni and scrolled through the entertainment news. He sipped down the rest of his coffee while turning left and right in his chair, the wheels clattering as the stool shifted a little. He occasionally looked at the doorway to see coworkers going about their day.

Finally, a large man clomped past the open doorway, a gleam flashing off his metal arm. Mr. Yang leaned forward and shouted, "Hey, Captain, in here!"

Captain Reeves hadn't gotten far and came right back and stood in the doorway. "I thought it was at the end of the hall."

"They upgraded us. See, we have a window and everything."

The captain looked around the small office, freshly painted off-white, and noted the window with the blinds down.

"This is more of a downgrade, if you ask me. You used to be right next to the snack machine."

Mr. Yang set his coffee cup down with a hollow knock and stood. His mind was walking through the steps toward getting this show on the road, but he just couldn't let what the captain said go. "So, to you, the measure of a great office is how close it is to the snack machine?"

"Well. It's a factor," he said with a smile.

Mr. Yang smiled and shook his head. "All right, let's get you to the ship, shall we?" he said while he walked over to the virtual reality setup.

Captain Reeves walked over to a comfortable-looking chair—cold steel wrapped in big, fluffy leather cushions. The chair was recumbent, so the captain needed to throw a leg over and straddle the chair before sitting down. The chair made a series of grippy crushing sounds as he got in and lay back.

While he did this, Mr. Yang had gone around behind him and re-moved the VR halo from a hook on the side of the chair. He disconnected the halo and placed it back on the hook. Then he pulled up some extra slack and waited for the captain to be ready for the cable.

The captain leaned to the side, took the connector, and inspected it. An intricate circuit pattern danced chromatically in the fluorescent office light. He pulled a cloth from his inner jacket pocket and gave the prong a quick wipe down, and then did the same on a small circular panel on his chrome forehead. The area had many superficial scratches. He replaced the cloth and placed the connector against the circular cutout on his forehead, a dust cover. It gave a little but wouldn't allow full access to his input/output port. He gave the connector a little wiggle as he pushed. It slid in all at once and dead-ended with a quiet mechanical click. Then he turned it, locking it in place.

Mr. Yang walked back around to his desk and could see the little connection LED occasionally blinking, communicating with the captain's cyberimplant. The captain did a last-minute comfort adjustment. The chair squeaked and creaked as he repositioned. Mr. Yang grabbed his coffee cup, shook it, frowned, and set it back down.

"Okay, I'm going in," said Captain Reeves. He concentrated on the hardware integrated with his brain, and his consciousness switched over. Now he was in an ethereal lobby with doors all around him. Most of these would be locked, as he had minimal network permissions, although connecting through the quantum terminal gave him more access. He looked toward a door and thought about the ship. This caused the doors to rearrange so that he was looking at the connection to the ship. The door opened for him, and he stepped into utter darkness, more than that, sensory deprivation.

A text log of connecting systems scrolled by too fast to read above a rapidly filling progress bar. Outside, Mr. Yang watched the connection light speed up and go solidly on.

The captain's senses came back online, except now they were the ship's sensory organs he was using. He looked around the inside of the ship through copious cameras. He saw the many rooms of the ship, darkened and waiting. The bots stood, filling the cargo hold, heads bowed. In the park, morning light flooded in, gleaming off the contestants' pods.

He changed his focus to the outside of the ship. Large ships filled the surrounding spaces, blocking his view of everything except the golden sunrise and the launch tower. He focused on the ship to his left, and his sensors went to work. He noticed the ship's make, model, mass, distance, and registered captain.

He switched on all his systems and felt the power plant humming. Internally, he felt every system, and they were ready.

"Everything's looking good. You ready to launch?" asked the captain, his voice coming through Yang's console.

Mr. Yang double-checked his console. "Yes, this will work," he muttered to himself.

"I'm ready when you are," he spoke into the console.

The captain locked his sensors onto the launch tower and pinged them. A man responded almost immediately.

"Good morning, WATS-9. What is your request?"

"Good morning. Requesting a launch window."

"Okay, go ahead and make your systems ready. I'll hail you when the airspace is clear."

The captain called up a preflight checklist and began to test and flex various systems. The ship's power plant ramped up, thrumming as the large drive thrusters glowed. Smaller maneuvering thrusters all over the ship rotated along their full range of motion. Red lights blinked across the surface of the dark ship as its mooring clamps released. The ship loomed up with a wavering growl. It's factory-new paint glistened in the morning sun. In the distance, a commuter ship screeched from the launch tower into the sky.

After a moment, the tower came back. "WATS-9, you are clear for takeoff. And uh, can you settle an office debate? Is this the ship? I mean, are you?"

"*Walk Amongst the Stars*? Yes, sir."

The traffic controller laughed. "It is them. My wife and I never miss it."

"That's wonderful. Now, if you'll excuse me, I need to get the show on the road. Literally."

"Well, Godspeed, Captain."

The planetary thrusters growled a loud vibration, and the ship took off vertically. As soon as the ship was high enough, the drive thrusters roared, crackling the air. The ship quickly became a dark speck in the sky, cutting a vapor trail in a lazy arc.

Chapter 4

Days later, in the production office, Mr. Yang was wrapping up a call with Captain Reeves. He would be on call for the duration of the show, only needing to come in to shoot banter with the hosts, pose for ads, and appear on the recap shows. He was also on call for ship emergencies, but between the routes he plotted and how smart ship autopilot had gotten, that never came up.

Adam 5000 came in fresh from makeup with a crisp new suit on. "Morning, Yang."

Mr. Yang had his OmniTab cradled between his shoulder and ear. He squinted and pointed a disapproving finger. *That's Mr. Yang*, the look said. He readjusted his hold on his OmniTab.

"Sorry. Adam just walked in, and he's already sucking up all the attention in the room."

Adam grabbed his lapels and smiled.

"Okay, I'll let you know when that comes in. Yep. Okay. Bye."

Mr. Yang pressed a button on the display of his OmniTab and set it back down by his work console.

"Anything new?" said Adam.

Mr. Yang had a sip of coffee from his large mug. "It's been quiet. Are you ready to go?"

Adam took a deep breath. "Yes, let's do this." He spied the blue X on the floor, two strips of gaffer's tape in front of Mr. Yang's console. He stood on the X, arms and legs slightly spread. A gridwork of red lines washed over him and then again.

"Likeness captured," a female voice said.

"Ma man." Adam held out a hand to slap five.

Mr. Yang made a face but slapped Adam's hand.

Adam walked over to the VR chair and plopped down. It whispered air and crunched as he got comfortable. He placed the VR ring on his head and snugged it up.

"Sync up," he said.

Back on the ship in the dimly lit cargo area, rows of robots stood like terracotta soldiers. Some of them had already activated and moved onto some automated tasks. They were all six feet tall with thin builds, light gray plastic, and black, rubberized joints. The security bots had nondescript male heads like a CPR dummy with glowing red eyes. They all wore the show's silver jumpsuits, like the contestants.

The next robot in line silently turned on and lifted its head. Then it became somewhat more animated. Motion-sensing lights kicked on in the cargo area. Harsh white light illuminated diamond-plate floors and ruggedized gray wall panels. The robot looked at its hands and then unzipped its jumpsuit and pulled it inside out, trying to get out of it. With a soft ringing sound, a ghostly image of Adam projected around the bot. He walked the rumpled coveralls down his legs until his feet were free. Then he walked over to a console built into the wall next to the door as his hologram solidified fully. "Testing, testing. Am I on? How do I look?"

Mr. Yang finished a deep meditative sip of coffee. He knew this question was coming. And considering what they paid him, he could put up with Adam's neuroticism and narcissism and whatever other isms lurked in that cranium. He set his coffee down and, without looking, answered, "Perfect."

Adam took a left into the hall. It was spacious, with high ceilings, granite floor tiles, cream walls with wooden accents, and soft lights recessed into the nooks and crannies. He went down the hall and turned the corner. A pair of double doors slid open. He stepped out onto a single large step like a patio. Adam smiled at the sunny day he beheld and started down the path through the courtyard.

As he neared the semicircle of the contestant's pods, he looked up at a camera bot. "Hello, viewers. It's a sunny day on the road to Noss." He raised his arms to the curved ceiling, which let the light of the sun in but dimmed and filtered it to feel just right. "We've just completed our catapult around Prospiria's moons, and you know what that means. It's time to get our contestants settled in."

When he said that, two robots who were standing at attention at the ends of the semicircle walked to the center and activated the pods, making their way back to where they had started. Soon every pod was opening dramatically, billowing dry-ice clouds. With so many pods going, it made a carpet of mist that clung to the grass between the pods in the semicircle. All the contestants groggily woke up except for I-ON, who was incapable of powering off and immune to drugs. It confidently stepped out as the other—biological—contestants squirmed, lurched, and stumbled out of their pods. Their senses slowly came back again. But just as soon as they attempted to lean on those senses, they were shaken by absurd sights. A robot, a couple of mutants, an alien, three of the same celebrity, and all this inside of what appeared to be a grassy park with a smattering of trees. The contestants looked around in awe. Waking up in a different place than you went to sleep was jarring, but none of them were expecting anything like this.

"Welcome, everyone, to *Walk Amongst the Stars*, Season Nine!" Adam really drew out the *nine*. You're aboard the good ship WATS-9. She's an XR-10 Caviar. Caviar, making luxury cruisers since 2155."

"Let's go over your orientation. Having awoken means we're on our way to Noss as we speak. You have between now and then to get settled in before the voting process begins, which is approximately . . ."

"Two weeks," Mr. Yang spoke into his console.

"Two weeks. So you should use this time to get to know one another and learn the park's layout. The ship's AI has been programmed to treat you like guests at a hotel, seeing to your every need. That being said, unless a weekly challenge calls for it, most of the ship's sections will be off limits." Adam paused in case some questions popped up. Everyone seemed dumbfounded still.

"Come along, everyone," said Adam as he marched away from the circle of pods toward the wall and a cabin door. "Spread out along the courtyard are cabins like this one. They've been specially modified to provide slightly smaller cabins than normal, although inside they are identical."

He walked up to the door. It opened and everyone filed in after him. The bots took up the rear to make sure everyone kept moving. "This is the living space. Over there is a kitchen and a dining area. This end of the hall is the utility, bathroom and a closet. At the far end of the hall is the bedroom with a full bath and walk-in closet," said Adam.

"This place is nicer than my house," said Del.

"Yeah," Maeve agreed.

"It's okay," said Naiomi.

"None of the cabins have been assigned, so you'll want to hash that out at some point," said Adam.

"What about my stuff? I was told I could get my stuff back on the ship," Naiomi said as she retrieved her hidden OmniTab.

"Oh yes, as you can see, the cabins are minimally furnished. You can download and fabricate your things in the utility room. And you can ask the ship for robots to help move or assemble items," said Adam.

The group nodded along except for Naiomi, who was frantically prodding her now unresponsive OmniTab.

"Now if you'll—"

"What is this bullshit?" said Naiomi, pointing the blank screen of her OmniTab at Adam.

"Oh, yes, your OmniTabs will be disabled during certain filming times such as now. Sorry for the inconvenience," he added.

"That's discrimination! How come I'm the only one getting the OmniTab treatment?" said Naiomi.

"I suspect it's because you're the only one with an OmniTab," said Professor Snuggles.

Naiomi was becoming red-faced and pointed an accusing finger at I-ON. "Well, why isn't the robots *face* disabled or something!"

I-ON looked at Adam and then back to Naiomi.

Adam laughed. "Uh, well, we won't be disabling our contestants' faces, and you'll have access to your OmniTab as soon as we're done here."

Adam smiled and swept an arm to the door. "Let's head back outside." He was noticeably more chipper now.

The group piled outside, past the concrete patio, and out onto the grass again.

"One last thing I need to go over in the orientation. If you'll all reach up and feel the back of your neck. You'll notice an implant there. Don't play with it because it's attached to your nervous system. That's your aggression inhibitor. It helps keep the peace. Let's demonstrate; if one of you would please slap me in the face."

Adam leaned forward and made a pouty face. Naiomi threw a hand back and froze in place. Del raised an arm in a slow, jerky movement and then gave up. Maeve felt something wrong just thinking about slapping Adam. She reached up and felt the circular spot on the back of her neck. Revulsion crawled down her spine and a shiver came back up.

"As you can see, you can all breathe easily because no matter how big, scary, or bad, no one here is capable of violence."

"Well, that's your orientation. Get settled in, relax, and get ready for season nine of *Walk Amongst the Stars!*" Adam struck a dramatic pose for the cameras, thrusting his index finger high into the air. He then regained a normal standing posture and raised his hands to his head. After a few seconds of standing there, the hologram of Adam faded back out. The singing hologram projector went quiet, and he morphed back into a disrobed robot who marched back to the cargo hold.

Everyone looked around at each other with confusion, anger, and sadness on their faces.

Naiomi broke the silence. "Hello, my sweet bitches. I'm back. The man can't keep me down. You won't even believe. . ." She wandered away from the group, talking into her OmniTab, gesturing dramatically with her free hand.

"What the hell is that thing?" said Rokk, pointing at the professor.

"I'm a scientist, but you're one to talk. Whoever you are."

"Do you honestly not know who this is? This is Rokk Bradley. MFL? It's a pleasure Rokk." Max Chambers stepped forward to vigorously shake Rokk's mighty hand. Rokk smiled toothily.

"Always good to meet a fan."

Zalak, off by himself, popped his head frills and sighed. "Look at these freaks."

The group talked among themselves as Maeve walked away to explore the area. She wasn't much of a people person. Away from everyone, the novelty of this courtyard really sank in. She reached out and plucked a yellow leaf from a tree, caressing it in her left hand. *It's real, this whole thing is real.* She sat down beneath the tree, leaning back on the trunk. She stiffened, about to get back up. *What if there's bugs here too? Ah, I'm sure they didn't put any here on purpose.* She relaxed again and squinted up at the massive window. The ship was orientated so that it appeared to be early morning, but it was weird. Instead of a blue sky, it was still dark and starry. She took off her shoes and socks and got back up. She took a minute to appreciate the cool grass on her stifled feet.

Maeve walked a lap around the courtyard, and when she came back to where she began, she decided that the cabin in the back right was hers. She looked at the other contestants, those who hadn't wandered off to claim a cabin. They had broken into two groups and drifted apart.

She went inside and set her shoes down.

4.1

Maeve had spied the home control panel when Adam was showing off the rooms. She went to the utility room and stood in front of a mirror with a little red light in the upper right corner.

"Hey um, I want to claim this cabin." The mirror surface changed to a computer interface and quickly dove through a few menu screens to [`Register Identity`]. She pressed to confirm, and a camera feed of her appeared. Dots and lines appeared all over her face, and then it went away and asked for a profile picture. She ran her fingers through her hair and gave it a toss and smiled. Then it wanted a palm print, which she did.

She backed out of the registration part of the menu and spent fifteen minutes looking through the different options and tweaking settings.

The next order of business was to print up her OmniTab and activate it. This would deactivate her old one, which was probably still tabbed into her computer back at the apartment, or maybe sequestered in a government building. After that, she'd print up her virtual reality setup.

Signing the WATS contract meant that she had replaced certain doom for probable doom. But she also knew there was a two-week period of downtime. So she damn sure was going to use it to gorge herself on video games and VR experiences. Plus, it was possible she could win the show and, with it, her freedom. It was a long shot. A *long*, long shot, but there was a chance.

She queued up all the parts in the fabricator interface. Electronics took longer to cook, so she had some time to kill. She went room to room, taking a mental inventory of the things she would want to print up.

Maeve was more of a night owl, so being up this early was a groggy venture. *Maybe it was the pod that did that*, she thought. She pivoted in the hallway and turned toward the kitchen to see about some caffeine.

She looked around the kitchen, and it seemed a little sterile, but otherwise good to go. It had a suite of stainless-steel appliances, white walls, and countertops. She began searching through the walnut cabinets until she had unearthed the coffee maker and supplies. Synthetic coffee—she knew it as soon as she saw the small bag. *Oh well, it's not like I have to worry much about my health now, do I?* She removed the paper wrapper from the coffee cube and slotted it into the maker. She grabbed a mug out of the cabinets and saw the show's logo on it. *Yuck*, she thought. *These are going into the trash, but I'm going to need one for now.* She placed it on the drip tray and pressed the [Coffee Go!] button.

Maeve unzipped her jumpsuit a little and pressed her arm against her stomach to create a pouch for all the cups. She piled them in and took her clattering belly full of mugs to the utility room where there was a garbage chute. Dropping them in one by one, she enjoyed the cool *ponk* noise they made. *Doesn't sound very deep*, she thought. She began throwing them in, listening to them break apart. With the last one, she jumped and threw it down as hard as she could, cringing away from the chute at the loud cascade of shattering bits.

A satisfied smile grew on her lips, and she pivoted to her fabricator and added her own nerdy-themed mugs to the queue. She went back into the hall just in time to hear a ding from the kitchen. *What the hell? Was that the coffee maker?*

She jogged over to the kitchen and grabbed a mug of black coffee. With synth coffee, black wasn't a euphemism, but its actual color. She grabbed the coffee creamer she saw earlier in the cupboard and, before she spilled some in, she looked at the label: marshmallow cream. She considered this and tilted the bottle, sending a shower of white powder in. The drink billowed with a white cloud in the center that she quickly stirred into an ash-gray drink. She lifted the steamy drink and smelled it, rich and marshmallowy. She took a tentative sip. "Mmm." Then another. It was surprisingly good.

She zoned out, looking through the living room window, enjoying the comforting, warm drink. It occurred to her she'd been without caffeine since her arrest. Probably a couple of weeks. She ruminated. Tableaus flashed through her mind: The police kicking in her door, the neighbors gawking from their windows. A policeman sneering and saying, "Cut the crap." Shivering in the dark. Greedily devouring flavorless food because she'd been starved. "I still can't believe that happened. *I'm* a domestic terrorist? Fuckin' stupid." She finished up the coffee, beginning to feel jittery energy.

Since she was standing in it, she took stock of the living room. White walls, hardwood floors, no wall decoration, large viewscreen, cushy brown leatherette couch.

She checked the hall closet next. Shelves with towels, bedsheets, and pillowcases. A short section of hanging space. The next door down was the utility. She looked in on the washer and dryer and closed the door.

Next up, the bedroom. More white walls, dark brown carpet. An expansive bed took up most of the floor space. A low, wide dresser spanned the length of the wall. There was a walk-in closet with lights and a full-length mirror. The closet came stocked with the same one-size-fits-all jumpsuit that she was already wearing. The bathroom had a tub-and-shower combo.

After taking another long, lingering look at the walk-in closet, something she'd always wanted, she went back to the fabricator. Maeve unloaded her mental checklist into the machine. She wouldn't need everything from her catalog of things, at least not yet. She queued up her clothes, grooming stuff, makeup, that fuzzy blanket she liked. And then she rearranged all the tech stuff for last. The tech stuff would take all afternoon, and her other stuff would be ready in a few hours. She spent the morning going back and forth with fresh reproductions of her things and putting them away. Everything went through, even the stuff that required a reprinting fee. One of the GIA goons said something about locking her bank account, so that was a pleasant surprise.

4.2

By noon, all the others had talked among themselves to exhaustion and then chosen homes. Maeve, now dressed in a T-shirt and jeans, hot off the fabricator, claimed her reprinted OmniTab. She entered her credentials into it. This kicked off a process that would download all her cloud data and brick the old unit, so she had some time to kill.

She went to the kitchen to get some lunch. The synth coffee smell had cleared out of the kitchen, leaving only the pleasant, industrial smell of a brand new ship behind. She imagined this is what a new house smelled like.

She looked around the kitchen and peeked into the fridge and put together a cold-cut sandwich. Then tossed a small package of chips onto the plate. She took a big bite and looked outside. *Oh yeah, I have some outdoors.* She grabbed a kitchen chair and placed her food on it. She grabbed her drink with her free hand, then wrapped it around the chair, and headed to the door.

"Open." She looked at the door expectantly. "Door open. Unlock? What is this, the Dark Ages?" She put everything down and pressed the panel by the door, opening it. She grabbed it all back up and went out, walking back over to the tree from earlier and planted the chair. She took the food off of the chair and put her butt in its place and started chowing down. About halfway through, she opened the sandwich up to stuff it with some chips. That's when she caught movement.

She was already midbite, so she looked up slightly, raising her eyebrows to see who it was. *It's the cat person*, she thought. *Who's apparently a girl?* The professor walked toward her dressed in a smart black dress, shoes, and glasses.

Just when I thought my life couldn't get any weirder, she thought.

As the cat person walked closer, a small amount of fight or flight nagged at Maeve. The woman was short for a person but huge for a cat. And she must have known she intimidated people, because she only walked out to the grass and called out.

"Hi there. Can I join you, hon?" She waved to Maeve.

With a mouthful of food, Maeve exaggeratedly nodded. She was hoping to get in some outdoor time without being bothered, but how could this not be interesting? She speed chewed while Professor Snuggles dragged another kitchen chair like Maeve's over to her.

Maeve swallowed her food as she wiped her hand on her hip. "Hello, I'm Maeve. Nice to meet you." She extended a hand.

"Pleased to meet you, Maeve. I'm Diane." She placed her mutated hand in Maeve's, and they shook. Diane turned around and hopped up onto the chair, her feet dangling slightly. Her tail poked out the back of the chair, unconsciously feeling around.

"If I had known I'd have company, I would have made another sandwich."

"Oh, don't worry. I don't eat much human food anyway. I'm an obligate carnivore."

"Well, I know what one of those words means."

"It simply means that I require a meat diet, so the only thing you have I could eat would be that"—Diane scrunched her nose up showing her little teeth and big canines—"that pepperoni you have there. Even then, that stuff's full of preservatives. I wouldn't eat too much of that."

Maeve looked at her sandwich in a new light, but took a bite anyway and smiled at her lunch guest. Diane adjusted her glasses, and for a moment, the two were silent.

"So, uh, what are you in for?" said Diane. "You know, like a prison movie?"

Maeve talked out of the side of her mouth while chewing, "Well, nothing. Mistaken identity." She set her hunk of sandwich down.

"Officially, though, I'm some kind of terrorist. They never made it very clear, something about a bombing, a prison break, and how my social media connects me to this criminal organization. I don't even use the stuff."

She explained the home invasion, being turned over to the Central Authority, the torture, and potentially prolonging her life by coming on the show. While she was talking, the thought rose in her mind for the first time that if she did manage to win, she'd be some kind of celebrity and this cat person she was talking to . . . would be dead. She pushed the thought away to finish her explanation.

Diane flattened her ears. "Wow, that must have been terrifying."

Maeve considered this. "At first it was, but after a while it was just exhausting. I'm still wiped out from it. How about you?"

"Well, from what I can tell, there's two ways to get stuck on this deathtrap of a show. One: be some kind of especially awful criminal, or two: be someone who makes waves. I am the latter."

The professor explained how she wouldn't conform to draconian policy changes, which led to her becoming an outsider, which led to going public, which led to her losing her job and being condemned.

"So you're kind of like an activist?"

"I guess. It's not like I wanted to be one. They just kept inventing hoops to jump through. Banning topics, words, and books. Forcing new policies and terminology. At some point, the students, who were all in on this, started reporting me for the slightest infraction. That was the beginning of the end. So that's why I'm here. Well, that and the loud minority against DNA experimentation. It's not like I asked to be like this."

"They say hell is other people." Maeve punctuated her sentence by chomping a chip.

"That's, uh, Jean-Paul Sartre. Are you into philosophy?"

"No. I just heard that once, and it made a whole lot of sense, so I just kind of throw that out there when I hear about people being assholes."

The professor giggled. The conversation lulled, and Maeve finished her sandwich.

The professor rapidly flicked her tail about and smoothed out her skirt, running her fingers along the seams. "I saw you out here earlier under the tree, and I thought 'oh, I should do that, too.' Then when I saw you out here again, I thought 'hey now's a good time, let's go chat.'"

"Yeah, it sure is nice out here. I had never heard of someone putting a little park on a ship before. I would guess this sort of thing is expensive," said Maeve. The two of them took a moment to look up at the clear view of space.

"What do you do, or rather, what did you do back home?" asked the professor.

"I worked at Maxter's. They're too cheap to upgrade to an office AI so me and some other girls grind it out there. That and I post videos of my VR gaming online."

"You can make money doing that?"

"Well, you can if you do it right. I'm still working on that part." Maeve chomped a chip. "What subject did you teach?"

"I'm a professor of astrobiology."

Maeve raised an eyebrow but kept the chips coming.

"It's like a combination of astronomy and biology. I can look at a star chart and tell you what planets are most likely to have life and what kind. And then also hypothesize as to how that life evolved. It's fun. I was initially interested in xenobiology because I'm fascinated with genetics, for obvious reasons. But I found the lab work kind of tedious. With astrobiology, I occasionally get to do some field work, and I love the travel. Seeing all the fascinating ways life has adapted to a planet's unique variables."

"Neat." Maeve threw back the last chip and then downed the rest of her water. "Well, this was fun, and it's nice to meet you, but I need to get back in and check on the fabricator. It should be ready by now." She got up and gathered her things.

"You, too, until next time." The professor had her hands full with the chair but smiled and shook her tail in a friendly wave.

4.3

After a few hours, Maeve had set everything up she would need. The finishing touch, her virtual reality setup at her bed. She needed only to slot her reconstituted OmniTab to get going, copy her info over, reconnect her accounts, and get things downloading.

That evening she sat down to a dinner of buttered noodles and thought up her bucket list. She hated to use such a morbid term, but these were morbid times. Images of what she wanted had already come and gone while she was being detained. But if she really only had two weeks left to live (well, three at the very least) it would pay to be thorough.

After she ate, she spent a half hour looking at her OmniTab, running her fingers over its contours, buttons, and ports. Her bucket list began with calling her parents and checking in after who knows how long. But how could she? What would she say? Even before she was abducted, they didn't talk that much. Whatever courage or clarity she was waiting for never came, but she knew if she put down the OmniTab, she'd probably never make the call. With a deep breath and a lump in her throat, she called her father and afterward her mother.

The calls went better than she expected, though she kept her expectations low. Both calls went almost exactly the same. They exchanged greetings and love, and then she filled them in on her recent life and having it come to a halt and everything up to now. Normally, this is where the emotional manipulation would come in. The shaming and disappointment with her life's trajectory. Instead, things got somber as they discussed the show and how the odds were very good that she'd die on television.

Then, after a while of shared sadness, she asked how their lives had been going. Both parents sensed that this might be the last time they spoke and didn't want the conversation to end. She only got her father off the line because she needed to call her mother still, and that conversation only ended because she started falling asleep while they talked.

Already in bed, she flipped face down and felt around for a place to set her Omni. It had been a draining day. It was always draining when she talked to her parents. The added emotional turmoil didn't help any, although she felt calm about her death at the moment.

She awoke on the edge of the bed, tangled up in a sheet she didn't remember getting under. It was light out. She detangled enough to shield her eyes from the sunlight and went back to sleep.

4.4

Maeve established a routine as the first week went by. After she freshened up and had some breakfast, she would get into VR and catch up on some games. Like any gamer, she had a juicy backlog of games she'd grabbed and hadn't gotten to yet.

Then at lunch, she whipped up something light and went outside to sit with Diane. Other contestants occasionally stopped in, and by the end of the week, she had hung out with everyone at least once.

From time to time, she would notice a camera drone and feel very self-conscious and clam up. Once or twice, Adam 5000 showed up and walked around interviewing people. Maeve found that a great excuse to duck out for the day.

After lunch, she did an aerobic exercise with rubberized dumbbells in the living room. She had never gotten results in the past with them, but she'd also never had the discipline to work at it every day. Plus, the idea that this could be the thing that saved her life kept her going strong throughout the week. Then she'd shower and catch up on those TV shows and movies she'd always meant to see.

After dinner, she would catch up on the things she had always told herself she'd do later when there was time. Virtual sightseeing: She checked out marvels of human civilization, the beauty of nature, and the cosmos. When she could stomach it, she made more calls to friends she'd likely never get to see again.

At the end of the first week, Maeve was eager to log into *GraveGun*. It was her routine to do group stuff with the guild on Sunday nights. Logging in a little early, she had time to talk to Gunstorm, AKA Dennis Martin, from IT. He began the conversation by scolding her. She dropped off the face of the world, and nobody at work knew anything. His indignation slowly became horror as Maeve laid out how the last few weeks had gone.

Gunstorm offered her a hug, which she took. She started bawling, which drew some looks. Gunstorm wasn't known as a huggy guy. He pulled away after a time and turned his attention to a device mounted on his forearm and began pecking at the screen rapidly. He looked at her with a smile.

"There, Ve, I just made it a guild event to vote for you every week. I can make it worth rep or plat or something. I don't know." He angled his forearm screen so she could see it.

"Thank you," she croaked.

"Later on, I'll make a post about your story, too, if that's okay?"

"Yeah."

"That way, everyone will know what the deal is. But right now, it's almost time for a mission." He looked at his device again, then back at her.

"I don't suppose you want to go. It might cheer you up? I could bump RedOath. He's filling in anyway."

"No, I don't really feel like it."

"Yeah, I can't blame ya. Hell, *I* don't feel like playing now."

He put a hand on her shoulder, and the two briefly sat in a calm silence until his arm computer went off, bleeping.

"Okay, I gotta get things going. Now that you're back, stay in touch. Okay?"

She smiled. "I will, thanks."

Gunstorm started to walk away. "Oh, I almost forgot, you should check out the guild base. We got it about a week ago and have been building it up. It's pretty cool."

Maeve produced a recall cube from her inventory. Holding it high, she dissolved up into a column of light, reappearing back in her home city in another column of light. She set out to clean up her inventory from the last time she played. Some of it went into storage. She sold the rest, then looked at where the guild base was and took the monorail back.

When she stepped off the elevator into the underground bunker, the halls were bare concrete and girders lined with conduits and junctions that were fried. A nest of wire hung from the ceiling. The only thing not broken was the elevator, and that's probably because they had to fix it to get down here.

She didn't know what it was like claiming the place, but it must have been good. She looked into an open room. It was lit by two working fluorescent bulbs, one of them dangling from a broken fixture. The walls were blackened, and the place stunk of smoke.

There was one well-lit room at the end of the hall. Someone walked by. The figure popped their head around the corner to see into the gloom.

"Ho-ly shit. Maeve?" said Haxx, AKA Colin Martin.

She stepped out of the darkness. "Um, hi."

"Where've you been, Ve? I thought maybe you bailed on the game, but that didn't seem likely, and then Dad said you weren't at work, and then I got worried, and . . . yeah."

She walked to a large table in the middle of the room and sat in a comfy-looking office chair. She was tiring of telling her story, but she took a deep breath. "Well . . ."

She went over the entire ordeal again with Haxx, then explained how she had just come from his father. As she explained, Haxx could not contain his anger, interjecting expletives and clenching the table as she detailed her wrongful arrest.

Maeve took in the room as she talked. It sat in stark contrast to the rest of the place. Well lit, finished walls, huge, long table with comfortable chairs, rubber mats on the floor, and hanging tapestries—professional looking.

Haxx took notice. "Pretty cool, eh?"

"Well, this room is. The rest of the place looks like you burned it down for the insurance money."

"That's actually not too far off. We screwed up completing this quest, and it self-destructed. I read up that if you get it exactly right, you can claim the place without a scratch, and that saves you a lot of rebuilding, not to mention credits." He shrugged. "I don't mind because it gives me a chance to be creative."

"So, this is what you've rebuilt so far?"

"Yep." He pointed to the corner that was unfinished still. "I just ran out of building mats, so I was considering just putting up the rest of the tapestries and quitting for the night."

Maeve couldn't think of anything else to say, but she didn't want the conversation to end either. She felt anxiety build as the silence stretched out. Finally, inspiration struck. "Do you want to see something cool?"

"Okay, where are we headed to?" Haxx brought up his in-game map.

"I'm going to log off and send you an invite. After seeing this place, I think you'll appreciate it."

"Oh, okay then."

She logged out and loaded up a program called Virtual Sandbox and then opened the file `Secret_Place`. She appeared on the grassy front lawn of a cozy log cabin. The back of the cabin had sparse pine tree coverage. To the left of the cabin was a small pond with a bubbling spring, which actually made no sense, because the entire area was a floating island. The spring water flowed over the edge and vanished into mist before hitting the ground far below.

She didn't remember what state she had left the place, so she ran inside to make sure it wasn't messy. Then she pulled up a menu to send the invite and stepped over to a big metal standing mirror and checked herself out. Here her avatar was just a self-scan from a couple of years ago. She sent the invite and waited.

Haxx appeared outside, hovering above the ground, looking like a robotic ninja. He touched down when his avatar was fully loaded. Maeve walked over. He looked around at the strange beauty of the floating wilderness.

"This is my Virtual Sandbox." Due to his huge form, she had to look up.

"Ah, I've heard of this program. This place is your creation, I take it?"

"Yeah, it's really peaceful. I like to come hang out here when I feel cooped up in my apartment or if I have a crappy day at work."

It was dusk. A breeze blew a couple of wisps of hair around her face. She pulled a menu out of the ether and flung permissions at Haxx. "There. Now you can fly, and you won't die if you fall off the edges and stuff."

Haxx floated up a few feet, and Maeve joined him. She flew around the island with him, pointing out things she'd built and how she settled on the design. Haxx followed the spring water over the side and continued down to the ground. He found an ornate cave entrance and went inside. Maeve followed and explained how she was thinking of carving a dungeon for a game, but nothing ever came of it. After a while, they flew back to the cabin across the last violet fumes of daylight.

Inside the cabin, Maeve looked back as Haxx's huge robot body ducked and shuffled inside. She laughed.

"What?"

"You look so funny trying to squeeze in."

"It *is* kind of cramped in here."

"Don't you have a personal avatar?" She gestured to herself. "Like this."

"Oh yeah." He looked at his steel arms with clawlike fingers. "Let me see what I got."

Maeve tossed some logs in the fire and tucked a little tinder rope in and lit it. She turned back around to see not Haxx but Colin Martin. He was tall with a lean build, dark hair and eyes. Much like his father, but young and lean. Maeve had never met Colin outside of the game, so her mental image of him was based on the photo on Dennis's desk where he was a high school athlete. Seeing him now reminded her that they were actually in the same age bracket.

She sat on the old comfy couch across from the hearth, and then Colin joined her on the other end. Suddenly she didn't know what to say. She swiped her hair behind her ear. They looked at each other for a moment, and Maeve felt a growing awkwardness.

"So, what do you—" she began.

"What made y—" he interjected.

They laughed, and Colin said, "Sorry, go ahead."

"I was going to say, what do you do for work?"

"Oh, I build software for industrial machines. It's mostly just copying and pasting chunks of code and beating my head against it until it works. But every now and then I come up with something, I don't know, cunning?"

"What about you?" he said.

Maeve explained her now ex-office job, then steered the conversation into games and other forms of pop culture. As they carried on talking, they subconsciously turned more and more toward each other. She slowly invaded the no-man's-land between them as they talked about life, philosophy, and shared funny stories. By the time Colin ran out of things to say, Maeve was lying across the couch, her head in his lap. He slid his fingers through her cool hair, while she kept her eyes shut.

"What were we talking about?" he said.

She looked up at him seductively. *Kiss me*, she thought.

He looked almost startled by her gaze.

She sat up, and he took the bait, cocking his head and pressing his lips to hers. Her heart raced, and she wove her fingers into his.

They kissed passionately again and again. If this were reality, her abs would have quickly gotten tired, and she'd have had to sit up. Maeve was appreciating Colin's hand in hers. Butterflies took flight when the idea occurred to her to place it on her breast. She was working up the courage when Colin broke the lip-lock.

"Woah," he said.

"Yeah." Maeve giggled, her face flushed.

"Hey what, uh. What time is it?" He looked around, no clocks. He opened a game menu, and at the top he read the time in disbelief, his voice rising at the end. "Three fifteen A.M.!"

They had been hanging out for five hours. (No wonder she had to pee so bad.)

"I gotta—I gotta go. I need to try to get a nap in before work."

She quickly sat up. "Oh crap, I didn't mean to—"

"Sorry, I'll talk to you later." And then he was gone.

She lay back, feeling giddy, smiling uncontrollably. She logged out and then wrapped it up for the night.

Chapter 5

It was Maeve's second week of freedom. At the end of the week, or perhaps at the beginning of the next, the contestants would receive their first challenge. This week went about the same as the first. Instead of always ruminating on her impending doom, she kept thinking back to last Sunday night, back to Colin.

Just when she was worried about the lunch crowd getting too overwhelmingly full, the group broke into clicks and did their own thing. Maeve hung out with the professor. Bryan and I-ON were mostly loners; you rarely saw them. Rokk and Max Chambers hung out, and Naiomi and Zalak. Del and the Coreys changed it up too often to put them in any one category. With three Coreys running around, the odds were good that one would show up for lunch.

Maeve had gotten the idea to comb through the old seasons of the show. Maybe she could find some kind of pattern, some strategy. Clips of the show were all over the internet. The hardest part was sitting through the many commercials to get to the content she needed. She didn't get much from it. The weekly contests ranged from something as simple as card games and puzzle solving to obstacle courses and dance competitions.

After exhausting that, she got the idea of looking into the other people on the show. Maybe she'd find some kind of secret weapon. A weakness or a quirk—something she could use to manipulate them. What she turned up didn't seem to serve any purpose except to make her kind of afraid of some of them.

Specifically Rokk, who had been in the news off and on seemingly her whole life for fighting and abusing all of his many wives. Then there was Zalak, rumored to be a prolific rapist. She found a video clip of Del headbutting some guy in the face, breaking his nose. It seemed like Del could've been defending himself, but yikes. Finally, she pulled up an article on Naiomi about how she'd run someone down in her car and had somehow just gotten a slap on the wrist. Money, she guessed. That's when she gave up on it. Who was she kidding? She wasn't a detective, and what would she even do with any "dirt" she found out about them, anyway?

After she had run out of research, she turned more and more to clearing out her bucket list items, and when that dwindled, she re-visited old favorites. Over the course of the week, she learned Colin's schedule, as she was always sending him messages and flirtations. They hung out in *GraveGun* here and there during the week and made plans to get together again on the weekend.

5.1

Maeve was milling around in *GraveGun*, admiring the progress the guild had made spiffing up the base. Most of the areas were still blank and unfinished, but they had cleaned up all the hanging wires and broken parts lying around.

She pulled out her Omni and sent a message to Haxx. It was Sunday, so the guild was busy doing group content. Missions, maybe a raid?

[I finished putting together a surprise for you. How much longer?]

No immediate reply. *He must be in the middle of a fight,* she thought.

Friday night they had had a picnic around her campfire under the stars. They enjoyed the taste of cake and got tipsy on virtual wine. Then they continued where they left off the week before. Tonight though . .

Her OmniTab chimed.

[Wrapping it up now, you missed a good one.]

"Finally."

Maeve got in the elevator and went up to ground level. She walked outside the tower, across the yard, and climbed the perimeter walls. She whipped out a pair of binoculars. Soon she saw the mobile command center approaching. The gate opened automatically, and the big ass van pulled in, kicking up dust. Five guild members unloaded from the sliding van door.

She flipped down onto the dirt, feeling like a ninja, and hustled over to the group. "Good job, everyone, but we're in a hurry here." She grabbed Haxx's hand and pulled him away from the group.

"Oh right, I gotta go," said Haxx.

The three guildies with them didn't pay too much attention, but Gunstorm raised an eyebrow, and Haxx could only grin in response.

When the elevator door closed, they immediately embraced and kissed.

"Hurry up and put your stuff away. Then I'll show you my surprise back at the cabin," she said.

"Your secret place?"

She grabbed hold of his innuendo. "Yeah, I wanna show you my secret place."

The elevator doors had already opened, and the two of them noticed a guild member stopped in his tracks, looking quizzically into the elevator.

Maeve felt her cheeks flush as the three of them burst into laughter.

She logged out and switched over to her floating cabin. Earlier she had run around making changes to set the mood. She was out front when Colin appeared. "Look," she said, pointing to the sky. Snow fell all around while a blazing aurora danced in the night sky.

"Nice. Is that the surprise?"

She cupped his face and turned him toward her kiss. She took his hand and towed him into the cabin. A fire was burning in the hearth, and she had lit the cabin with candles of all shapes and sizes. She brought him to the bedroom.

"Now I got you right where I want you," she said.

"How do you know that I don't have *you* right where I want *you*?"

"Hold that thought." Maeve went into the large walk-in closet and closed the door. She selected the last surprise she had set up from the clothing options menu: a sexy outfit. It was suddenly on her, and she checked out the goods in the mirror. She emerged clad in tight straps and provocatively sheer material. She felt a strange mixture of emotions as Colin looked on stupidly. Silly yet seductive, nervous yet powerful.

"Oh!" he drank her in. "Yeah, Ve, you've definitely got me."

Maeve pulled off Colin's shirt and ran her hands over his chest. She watched his Adam's apple bob as he swallowed. She gave him a wicked look and slowly unfastened his pants. The two unwrapped each other eagerly and, in the struggle, lost balance and crashed into bed. She climbed on top of him, her passion burning in the dim candlelight. They took turns riding each other until their passions were sated.

Afterward, they lay together, spooning. The weight of the previous week had melted away. Maeve felt safe being held. They stayed that way for quite a while until Colin broke the silence.

"That. Was. Awesome," he spoke into the back of her head.

"Mm-hmm."

He leaned his chin on her shoulder. "I could call in sick. Then we could . . ."

"That won't work." Maeve thought about the show beginning tomorrow. About how her life was on the line from now on. "The show starts tomorrow. This is so unfair," she said.

"Yeah. I . . . yeah."

"I'm so screwed." Her eyes welled up with tears, and her voice trembled.

"No." He hugged her tighter.

"If I make it past the criminals, which I'm supposed to be one of, I'm up against all these super popular celebrities." She sniffled.

Colin buried his forehead into her neck.

"We're going to do everything we can to get you votes. And-and . . . like you told me, popularity is only part of it. The rest is weekly challenges. You can beat some pampered celebrities."

"I don't know."

"Don't lose hope. You can do this." Colin's own eyes took on a watery sheen.

"It's not like I have a choice." She laughed humorlessly and wiped her nose with the back of her hand. *It's so messed up that I had to meet Colin now. Now that my life is over*, she thought.

She went over the whole situation in her mind before she could drift off.

5.2

Maeve awoke and looked at Colin. He was a sheet-covered shape, his feet and an arm stuck out. The sheet was up over his head so that only a fluff of hair stuck out. She reached up to remove her VR halo and then hesitated. She watched him sleep another minute and then logged out.

It was bright and early. Maeve swiveled her legs out of bed and then rubbed her eyes. The intercom rang out, and she cocked her head to listen. Adam 5000 came on sounding chipper. "Good morning, contestants. Season nine, episode one of *Walk Amongst the Stars* has begun! Everyone, get ready for the day and meet outside in one hour."

Maeve got out of bed and began selecting clothes to wear. She could still feel an ember of dread burning at her core, but it seemed far away now. *Maybe even fear gets tired*, she thought as she got ready for the day.

She rushed out of the steamy bathroom to the kitchen, where she made up some toast and heaped jelly onto it. She sloppily wolfed it down while looking out her window at the few people who were already congregating. Using her finger, she mopped up the fallen jelly and stuck it in her mouth. She washed the plate and put it away. After a little more staring out the window, she took a deep breath and went outside.

"Now that we're all here, we can begin. Today is the beginning of the show proper. I hope you all had a wonderful two weeks getting settled in. In a moment I'll announce what our contest for the week is, and this time next week one of you"—Adam pointed around the semicircle at all the contestants looking serious—"will be voted off the show." Adam paused a minute to let the drama sink in. Mr. Yang could already tell what reaction shots he'd use later.

"Now this week's challenge is . . . Coming up after these messages!" Adam shot the camera a shit-eating grin with his tease. This part wasn't live, though, so he awkwardly paused for a few seconds, and then "And we're back!"

A few contestants looked a bit puzzled.

"This week's challenge, as voted on by the audience, is . . . a high-stakes cook-off challenge! Each of you will have five days to perfect a recipe. The final cooked recipes will be submitted, and then you'll all have a blind taste test after which you will rate each dish from one to ten. Remember, the top three winners will have their rating boosted and be that much closer to victory.

"As always, contestants are free to talk to each other about their strategies, form alliances, and appeal to the audience for more votes. Just remember if you let the cat out of the bag, others can potentially use that information against you.

"For this challenge, we have a considerable pantry that you will make requests of from your quarters. Our helpful robots will bring you the items you need in a storage crate so that no prying eyes can tell what your food item is."

Adam gave pause for questions: Any kind of reaction, really. The group just sort of looked around, unsure of what to do.

"Oh, and one more thing. Corey, the judges have thought about your unique case, and for each challenge, you must choose only one of yourself to participate, and the others must sit out for the week. Go ahead and choose now."

The Coreys huddled up. One of them rapidly pointed to the Corey across from him and himself. The one in the middle raised his hand.

"I'll cook, yo."

"Great." Adam gave that Corey Three buttons, each with a number on it (1),(2), and (3) with safety pin backs. "Please do everyone a favor and get used to wearing these."

"Does everyone understand the challenge?" asked Adam.

The group was quiet. Some nodded.

"Everyone ready? Go!"

Bryan Cox bolted as though it were a footrace, sprinting back to his quarters. Rokk saw this and charged off as well, followed by the Coreys.

5.3

I-ON walked a meandering path away from the group, through the trees in the courtyard. Hands in its pockets. The robot had taken to wearing jumpsuits after being forced into the show's silver jumpsuit.

I-ON's path intersected the footpath that led on to the rest of the ship. It pulled a hand out and dropped it to its side, fist closed. I-ON looked over its shoulder to see what the biologicals were doing. No one was looking. It opened its hand, spilling dust across the footpath. I-ON put its hand back in its pocket and continued around the courtyard, leaving more deposits as it went.

5.4

The week rolled by, and the contestants modified their newfound schedules to train for the event. In this case, cooking delicious food.

It was Friday night, and Maeve was in VR, specifically *GraveGun*. She rode the central cargo elevator up to the surface. Red lights pulsed all around her, dancing off her stealth suit, or as she called it, her ninja suit.

The elevator bobbed to a stop, and the doors opened. She stepped out into the central tower of the building, her machine gun swaying on its shoulder strap. She went out the front door into the courtyard. The moon illuminated the night. It was cloudless and cold, a sheen of dew on the ground.

She spotted a pile of crates with Gunstorm behind it and went over. The guild had grown over the last couple of weeks. She didn't recognize a lot of these players. There were only ten when her old life fell apart. Gunstorm put a foot up on a crate, and, leaning on his knee, he lit a cigar. He blew a puff of smoke that hung in the moonlight.

"All right, everyone, listen up. This is our first endgame defense mission. As you can see, we've been grinding mats, so everyone dig in."

He gestured at the crates. "You got yer AP rounds, you got yer grenades, and you got yer stims."

He pointed out Maeve. "This here is Ve. Her real name is Maeve McKinnon—she's who we're voting for. She got totally screwed by the system, and every vote we can get her will help keep her on the show, because we all know what it means to get voted out."

The crowd murmured. "We got you, boo," one of the newbies blurted out, followed by laughter.

"Thanks, everyone, this has been so weird and scary, but it's comforting to know I have your support."

Everyone's comms crackled. "Fog! I see the fog. They're here," said Haxx.

Maeve looked up at the top of the tower where Haxx was sitting with a large rifle propped up, peering into the distance.

Gunstorm tapped his comms, speaking to the whole group. "Okay, you heard him. It's go time. This is a whole new tier, so I don't know what we're up against. Our goal is to stop them from corrupting our base core. If they manage to breach our wall, everyone retreats to the central building and defends the elevator. If they infiltrate the facility, we're sunk. So far, the core has zero defenses. Okay, everyone, get into position."

He grabbed two out of the crowd, turning them back to himself. He turned off comms.

"CoolMikey. Situational awareness. I don't want to see you standing in fire out there."

"Samur-Gai, you're too low level for this, so I guess just run supplies to the guys on the wall." He slapped the crates.

"Okay." And they trotted off.

Maeve spoke up, "Hey I have a weird request. I have to duck out of VR to take a pizza out of the oven in a few minutes. It's, uh, for the show."

"No problem, you're probably safest on the second floor of the tower. Elevator's offline until this is over."

"Thanks, by the way"—she looked down—"for getting everyone to help."

He put a hand on her shoulder. "Hey don't get too excited. Once we win you that show, you gotta come back to the office."

She laughed derisively.

"I'm just glad you're here. Now let's trash some zombies." Gunstorm ran inside the tower, heading to the top. Maeve readied her weapon and ran up a ramp onto the defensive walls, taking her place among the others at the parapet. There were about ten guild members below ready to fire out of gun slits in the defensive wall and over twenty up on the top of the walls. An autonomous gun turret sat on either side of the front gate.

Everyone watched as a blanket of fog slowly rolled in. As it got closer, you could make out some shapes and dull red lights inside. Maeve rubbed her finger on the machined grooves on the trigger guard. The shapes in the fog became more prominent, with glowing, sinister eyes. They would break the concealment of the fog soon.

"Snipers, open fire," said Gunstorm over comms. There was a smattering of reports and the high voltage cough of a Gauss rifle.

Even as they were being gunned down, the enemy outpaced the fog. Twisted forms, sickly pale skin infused with tubes and wires. A vile synthesis of man and machine, the dead were made to fight on. Maeve put her finger on the trigger.

The snipers took the front line down a few at a time, and the ranks just marched over the top of their allies. Finally, something new emerged from the fog: larger zombies clad in heavy armor, a gun and a blade instead of hands.

"Everyone, focus fire on the big ones."

The air filled with the crackle of gunfire. The belt-fed beast of a gun vibrated Maeve's body as she picked away at the behemoth. It slowly succumbed and fell. At that moment, a wave of spider skulls came scurrying across the battlefield, zigzagging their way to the wall.

"*Oog!* Look at those things" and "Oh, hell naw," said the gunners on the wall.

"Fire at will, fire at will," said Gunstorm.

Everyone gladly focused on the disgusting newcomers. The way they zipped around made them hard to hit, but thankfully, it didn't take much to stop them.

Maeve's ammo counter hit zero, and she popped the latch open. When she felt a tap on the shoulder, she jerked to the side, only to see the new guy holding another box of ammo.

"Aw thank you." She could barely hear herself speak.

It must be close to pizza time, she thought.

She chose another heavy target, gripped her gun tightly, and laid into it. She kept going until it crumbled. It took a full belt of ammo. The barrel of her gun was glowing a dull red when she released the trigger.

Doot-doot, doot-doot. She had set an alarm to get the pizza earlier, and now was the time. She quickly threw the two grenades she had. A metal spider leg flew overhead as she sprinted down off the wall and into the building. She went to the second floor.

"Gotta hop out. Be right back," she yelled up the stairs to Gunstorm and Haxx on the roof. She removed her VR halo.

5.5

Maeve opened her eyes back on the ship. The smells of the battle-field, burning flesh and plastic were gone. Instead, wonderful pizza smell wafted around her cabin. She got up, jogged down the hall, and turned off the oven. She opened the door and grabbed the pizza pan with a couple of pot holders and placed it on top of the oven.

She gave it a quick look over. Crispy, oily crust, slight brown spots on the cheese. Crispy pepperonis. *Nothing burned. It looks good. I'm getting good at this*, she thought.

This time she had basted a mixture of olive oil, garlic, basil, and oregano on the crust. She rolled a pizza slicer across it and slid a slice onto a plate. Tendrils of cheese stretched out, and she manually separated them. She lifted the corner of the steaming hot slice, blew on it, and took a bite of crust. *I got this. I just need to pick some middle-of-the-road toppings everyone can agree on, and I got this.* She greedily took another big bite. The molten cheese burned the roof of her mouth. She breathed through her teeth, trying to cool the smoldering food while carefully chewing. She considered another bite when a thought occurred to her. *Oh damn, the zombies.*

Maeve put the plate down next to the pizza and turned around to leave, then stopped and turned around to double-check that the knobs on the oven were off. Then she sprinted down the hall and threw herself back on her bed. She snugged the VR halo onto her head and, after a disorienting second of darkness, opened her eyes to the darkness of the tower's second floor.

Maeve swung her empty LMG onto her back and looked at the minimap. Things had gotten worse while she was gone. Combat sounded close now. She looked at the player stats and saw fifteen of the guild were dead. Automatic fire rang out just above her on the roof. Comms chirped, and Haxx spoke. "Everyone watch out. We got cloakers sneaking in."

As soon as she closed the map, she felt a stabbing pain in her chest. She pushed against something unseen and stumbled backward in shock. She instinctively put her hand over the virtual knife wound. In an instant, she had her pistol in her hand. She let go of the burning wound to draw her sword.

She fired the entire magazine in the invisible attacker's general direction in a circular fashion. The attacker's stealth field shuddered in the places where her shots hit. The creature spattered quicksilver blood on itself and the immediate area. She could see the stealthy shimmer now and stepped in with a sword swing.

The blade slid across something metallic and sank into a soft spot. She withdrew and swung again, silver blood slinging off the blade. The barely visible creature dodged. Something slammed her gut, and she realized she'd been stabbed again. She instinctively backhanded the attacker, knocking it away for a second. She dropped her gun and stuffed her hand into a pouch, grabbing a stim.

The shimmer of a moving stealth field caught her eye, and she took a few quick strikes, trying to keep it at bay. When it moved back, she pressed the tip of the stim into her leg hard, causing it to inject its contents. It lunged in again, and she swung defensively. It backed up a step, then lunged to the side and disappeared.

That's when the drugs kicked in. The world slowed down a little. The room became a bit brighter. Her wound stopped hurting and bleeding. Loosening her grip on the sword, she placed a fresh magazine in her fingers. She smoothly and quickly ducked, grabbed her gun, popped out the magazine, replaced it, and released the slide. She moved forward step by step, gun held out front, sword up high, thirsty for silver blood.

She advanced slowly across the room to the stairs. *Did it escape? Is it behind me?* The attacker's blade swatted her gun to the side. She accidentally fired a few rounds as her sword swung down. With a sickly thunk, the blade sunk into the creature. Silver blood sputtered around the stairwell as the zombie's biomechanical body became visible. It sank to the floor, and she had to rock the blade back out of the deep cut.

She ran up the stairs to the roof. Haxx was lying prone with a rifle on a bipod, picking out distant targets and firing. She stepped toward him. He contorted and pointed the beefy gun toward her. She raised her hands, full of weapons.

"Ve! You scared the shit out of me." He went back to shooting.

Gunstorm was down. She knelt beside him and took his command goggles. It surprised her that the game allowed that. She scooted to the edge and looked through them like binoculars. The high-tech goggles enhanced the battlefield and overlaid tactical information. High casualties. The fog had crept all the way to the front gate, and the remaining forces were firing from the top of the wall while the rest engaged in melee combat in the opening of the sundered gate. As she was looking, the goggles highlighted the gate's auto-turrets. She saw an option pop up when she looked at them, and it gave her an idea.

She turned to Haxx to tell him her plan, but the roof fell under a hail of distant gunfire. Red energy shots sizzled against the tower. Maeve ducked down. Haxx made a cut-off groan as he got shot up. She cringed and rushed back down the stairs.

She found the comms button on the goggles. "Last stand. Everyone retreat to the main building. Now." She repeated the command as she jogged down the steps. She strained to see any more hidden enemies in the gloom. At the base of the stairs, a cyberzombie had its hand held to the keypad. Wires had snaked out of its flesh and into the machinery. She ran it through with her trusty energy sword. Its body slid down the wall. Its hand still grafted to the panel. She chopped that off, just in case.

She looked around the room with Gunstorm's command goggles. She saw an option to deploy hidden cover and selected it. Collapsible metal panels popped out of the walls and floor. The remaining guild members were breaking off and running back inside. Holding the goggles to her face, she looked at the turrets again and highlighted the option she saw before, [Self Destruct]. She chose that option, which linked the goggles up. All she needed to do now was push a button.

Dennis, who was a spectating ghost until the fight was over, saw what Maeve was up to and cheered. "Yes. Yes!"

The last man retreating fell under a wave of enemies at the gate. The remaining team took up new defensive positions inside the tower. Maeve watched enemies pile up at the gate with her finger heavy on the button. When they turned their attention from the fallen comrade, she pushed the button. She pushed it frantically when the guns didn't instantly go up. They needed a few seconds to overload before vaporizing a mob of zombies in a brilliant flash, leaving a crater in the dirt. A fetid rain of zombie guts splashed down on the remaining zombies marching into the compound.

Maeve set the goggles down, put away her weapons, and reloaded her LMG as the guildies picked targets and fired. It was a deafening roar in the metal building. As the enemy numbers dwindled, they broke into a suicidal rush. Soon, all went quiet.

The fog dissipated quickly, revealing the fallen cyberzombies. The battlefield shimmered, speckled and dripping with silver blood. A large, scorched crater lay where the front gate used to be. A notification arose, "Victory," followed by the experience and reputation gains.

A collective cheer went up. "Woo. Yus! We did it. Yeah."

Then everyone who participated in the battle received a metallic container with glowing red circuits running along its sides. Maeve dug in immediately. *A couple pieces of armor, crafting mats, and I might like this gun.* She slid a plasma pistol out of the crate and fired it carelessly into the dirt outside. *I'll have to compare the stats later. I'm pretty sure that's an upgrade. And I guess I can disassemble the armor for mats.*

The elevator leading down into the facility chimed and clunked. The doors opened with a whiny gasp. This was a large industrial elevator, and it easily held Gunstorm, Haxx, and the rest of the guild who died. Gunstorm walked over to Maeve as she was busy stuffing the loot into her bag.

"Hey, good one on the gate demo," he said.

"Thanks. I saw the options come up, and I was like 'how do I resist that?'"

He stooped to pick up the command goggles.

"I'm glad you tried it. I didn't know if that would work. I was trying to figure out how to chat to Haxx so he could do it, but the game locks you out of all the usual channels when you're dead."

Maeve looked across the yard to Colin. She caught his gaze, and he put up a hand. She waved back. "Hey, I'm just going to go ahead and bail. I don't have it in me to deal with any weird goodbyes right now," said Maeve.

"Yeah, I get it." He looked pained. "We got your back Ve," he said.

She logged out of the game and removed her VR rig. She sat up in bed, thinking about Colin. Ever since the night they hooked up, she felt weird about their relationship. Selfish, kind of. Her guts felt twisted up when she thought about him, and she had backed off on the texting lately.

She stretched out across the bed with a groan, then rolled off the side onto her feet. Her stomach grumbled, and she headed to the kitchen. She took up her chewed-on slice of pizza, which was tepid now. As she chewed the pizza, it aggravated the burned spot in her mouth.

"I cam berieve I'm gemin sick of eat'em pisha," she said, chew-talking. *It's good, though. I'm gonna win this one*, she thought.

Chapter 6

The next morning, in the courtyard, everyone assembled for the recording. As before, Adam gathered everyone around in a semicircle. "All right, contestants, today is the day. As you can see, we've set up ten microkitchens, stocked with the basic necessities."

There were ten little structures about the size of large office cubicles, with log cabin facades. "Each of you will have one of our handy-dandy robots who'll be your valet, collecting all the ingredients and utensils you'll need. Once you produce your culinary masterpiece, you need to portion it out into nine of these Fresh-Lock brand containers." He held up a food storage box with a technical-looking lid. "This will keep your meal exactly as you prepared it for hours, ensuring that *muah* quality." He did a chef's kiss.

"You'll have two hours to prepare your meal, after which you'll take a seat at this picnic table. After everyone is done, we'll distribute the containers for you, and it's back into the kitchen to sample and vote on every food item."

"Hey, I got a question," said Del, looking annoyed. "What about the robot?"

"I have selected a meal item fit for human consumption," said I-ON.

Del began speaking over the machine. "I mean. You don't eat, do you?"

Silence passed over the group. I-ON looked at Adam, then back to Del.

"Oh yeah, huh?" said Naiomi.

Max Chambers scowled. "This game's rigged, isn't it? Come on now!" The group spoke all at once, creating an incoherent jumble of voices.

"All right, all right!" Adam yelled over the din. "Nothing is rigged." He made a placating gesture with his hands. "None of you are required to eat any of the food. You must simply judge it. Now, for our metal friend over here. That's a unique process. Personally, I'd stick to eating the food. But there's more than one way to skin a . . . cat? Erm? Hey, Yang. I'm gonna redo that one. There's more than one way to skin a . . . potato," he said with a wink.

"Okay, contestants. Get ready. Let's put two hours on the clock . . . and, go!" He pointed at the contestants. About half of them ran while the rest were content to mosey to their kitchens. The cabins had their names on the doors, but Maeve didn't see hers, which meant it must be facing away from her. She jogged to the middle of all the cabins and found her name.

Inside, it was almost as big as her own cabin's kitchen. Its layout was much the same, except that everything was natural wood grain and the appliances were black with white enamel accents. As stated, one of the show's robots stood in the corner.

"Um, hi," she said.

"Greetings, contestant."

She dug into the cabinets and the refrigerator, pulling out things she'd need and making a mental list of the things absent. Then she took one of the Fresh-Lock thingies and checked it out. She put it back into the pile. *Two of my little pizzas should be more than enough*, she thought.

She told the robot the list of materials she was missing.

"Order acknowledged. Your items will arrive shortly." The robot left. She looked out the window above the sink while she washed her hands. A couple of other robots were already leaving the courtyard. She measured out some flour.

Okay, you got this. We practiced this. Like a couple dozen times.

Maeve had her dough all smooshed up when the robot returned.

"Here are your items."

"Gimme a minute. I need to finish this up." The robot stood like a statue with her container of supplies.

Maeve sliced the dough ball in two with a knife and worked them each into a sort of oval disk and put them in a container and into the refrigerator. She'd give them as long as she could to settle. She turned to the robot and took its plastic crate of goodies.

"Thank you."

"You are welcome."

Then she unpacked all the groceries and put the crate on the floor. Movement outside caught her eye. It was one of those damn camera drones looking in the windows. She waved at the thing.

"Hi." She turned back to her work, suddenly feeling self-conscious. "Okay, now the sauce," she said to herself.

From her work earlier in the week, she had learned the ship had multiple things she could throw together to make pizza sauce, but she had settled on a really boring, generic pasta sauce that she could spruce up. She spilled that into a food processor and added sugar, salt, garlic powder, basil, and oregano. Then she blended the chunks down. After that, it went on the stove to reduce.

She was back in the zone, forgetting all about the audience. She opened up a package of cheese next. The ship didn't have any mozzarella or any real cheese, so she found this artificial cheese that got the job done pretty well. It looked and tasted like a white cheese and had that wonderful stretch to it. She shook the package and emptied it into a bowl.

Maeve had put a lot of thought into what exactly to top the pizza with. If it were just her, she'd go with a mixture of things, but for a room full of strangers, really strange strangers, there was one safe bet. She pulled a package of "authentic" pepperonis out of the box. Even though they weren't made of meat, they somehow tasted like it. The ingredient list went on and on, so the less she thought about it, the better she felt.

She put her hands on her hips and took a breath, then checked on her sauce and stirred it.

She got out a little dish and dripped just a little olive oil into it and added some more dried herbs. Oregano, basil, and garlic powder, and stirred that up.

Back to the sauce. She stirred it and saw that it had thickened up nicely, so she took it off the heat.

Now all she had to do was wait. There was a clock above the door. *I'll give the dough another half hour to chill in there and then put it all together.* She leaned against the wall opposite the robot and watched the clock. It didn't take long for Maeve to become bored out of her skull.

"So uh, do you robots have names?"

"My unit ID is zero-zero-zero-ex-four-dash-one-zero-zero-four," said the robot. It pronounced its serial number much more quickly than its speaking tone.

"Woah okay, that's just not going to work for me. How about, um?" She murmured, "Frankie? Gizmo? Sparky? Zap? Zapper? Turbo?"

"Turbo-Guts," she said to the robot.

"Alias acknowledged. Turbo-Guts."

Maeve barked laughter and snorted. The name was silly, but the robot saying it was too much.

She looked at the clock again and spread some flour on the dark countertop. She drew in the flour for a minute, then had an idea.

"Hey, Turbo-Guts, do you know how to play any games?"

She whiled away the minutes playing tic-tac-toe. The robot was kind of terrible at it. It would randomly dominate or pathetically lose on purpose. She found out it knew hangman and switched to that for a while.

After successfully guessing "swam," "threw," "flanks," and failing on "jukebox," it was finally time to put everything together and put it in the oven. She had cranked up the oven while playing hangman, so it was ready to go.

Normally I'd give the dough more time, but this was all we've got. Retrieving the dough from the fridge, she swept away all the game flour. She sprinkled flour down on a couple of spots and placed the cool dough blobs. She kneaded and stretched them out slowly by hand, unlike earlier in the week when she attempted to hand toss and got pizza dough all over the kitchen.

She sprinkled down some more flour and placed her dough disk down, then worked it to the right thickness, then formed a nice thick crust.

She grabbed her spiffed-up sauce and dribbled it on, smoothing it out with a large spoon. *Gotta be careful not to leave too much in one spot. I hate a bite of pizza that's all sauce.* Next up was the fake mozzarella. She sprinkled handfuls of cheese onto the pizza and then started strategically placing the pepperonis. Too many and the thing would be a greasy mess, too few and it'd be bland. Finally, she put the pizzas on a large baking sheet and popped them into the oven. *I can't believe my life depends on how good this comes out.* She closed the oven.

Maeve noted the time again.

I wish I had thought to get a timer. She glanced nervously around the room. Turbo-Guts, the crate he brought in, the oven, the sink, a tree she could see out the window, back to the clock. Not even a minute had passed. *I guess maybe I don't need a timer.*

Maeve folded her arms and paced around the small room, keeping a keen eye on the time. A gray eternity rolled by. Finally, it was time to use her secret weapon. She pulled the large baking sheet out of the oven and placed it down on a cutting board. She slid a little bowl over with the oil concoction she made up earlier and basted the crust with it. This left the crust glistening and speckled with herbs and garlic. Then back into the oven with it.

She put her hands on her hips and went back to clock-watching. After a few minutes passed, she peeked into the oven periodically, trying to catch it. That perfect moment—a perfect cook job. Finally, it seemed right. She took it out and turned off the oven.

There it is. She was so excited, she didn't know what to do. Crispy looking crust, melty cheese with golden brown spots. The air roiled above it. It looked legit. She took a dangerously sharp knife from the provided block and worked it through the crust, cutting the pizza in half.

Uh, hmm, I can't just cut them into fourths. That's only eight slices. I wonder how I would cut each into five pieces. She waved the knife over the pizza, estimating how that would work. She took a container and held it in front of the pizza. *Six slices will work better, plus that gives me room to screw up a little.*

She cut the two pizzas into six slices each. Free-handing it left some crooked cuts, and the slices weren't all the same size, but it would serve. She placed a slice into a Fresh-Lock container and affixed the lid. She pressed the little button on top of the lid. The see-through container hissed. The container bathed the food in intense yellow light. *It looks like some kind of irradiated, nuclear pizza.* She made an impressed little "huh" while watching it work.

She packed the best of them into the nine containers. Once they were all packed and ready, she turned back to the pizza. *I gotta know how this crust came out.* She ripped a chunk off the remaining pizza, which gave her a miniature jagged slice. She chomped the crust first and gave it a chew. *Oh yeah. Oh yeah, I got this,* she thought. She finished off the torn chunk of pizza, tasting the savory portion with the toppings.

With a full mouth, she regarded Turbo-Guts, "It's too bad you robots don't eat. This came out good. Okay, I think I'm done here."

She looked at the time, still twenty minutes left. *I got enough time to clean up my mess.*

6.1

There was a knock at the door. Maeve turned to see Adam 5000 open the door and lean in. "Greetings contestant! Oh, you can put those down and come with me. Our staff will make the room ready for the next phase of the show."

She looked at the dishes again. "Okay." She tossed a hand towel onto the counter and walked out the door Adam held open. As they walked outside, the sun glimmered on Adam, and it occurred to her for the first time in days that he was not in fact here but a holographic projection.

They walked out of earshot of the others to a couple of director's chairs that were set up in front of a group of trees. Maeve plopped down in the chair she supposed was hers and noticed a couple of camera bots had hovered over their direction. Adam took a seat and crossed his legs casually.

"All right, let's begin."

Suddenly, her throat had gone dry. She gripped the chair's arms tightly.

"So, Maeve, how are you feeling today?"

"Uh, fine."

"You seem nervous."

She smiled anxiously and suddenly felt so hot.

"What do you think of the first challenge?"

"It was fine. I-I looked over the challenges from previous seasons to see what I was up against. It didn't help because there's such a wide variety of challenges." She bobbed her foot. "So I was pretty surprised to hear you say we'd be having a cook-off."

"What did you select as your food item?"

"Well. I tried to figure out something that pretty much everyone can identify with, so I went with pizza. Pepperoni to be specific."

"Oh, that's a good one. Were there any unforeseen stumbling blocks?"

"Uh, before this I used to just unwrap a frozen pizza and microwave it. That's the extent of my cooking skills. For this, I actually learned how to make dough and tips on how to get everything just right."

"How do you think you'll do?"

She smiled genuinely. "I gave it a taste test, and I think it's better than my practice pizzas. I think the others are going to love it."

"Have you made any friends or enemies with the other contestants?"

"I'm pretty sure I haven't made any enemies. I'm pretty chill. I think I-ON is weird. When it's outside of its cabin, it's always people watching. I don't know if it's curious about people or if it's some kind of creeper. I've been having lunch with the professor a bunch, so she and I are pretty friendly."

"Okay, good stuff. I think we're done for now unless you have something else you want to say," he said.

Maeve pursed her lips. "Mmm . . . nope."

"Well, we have a few interviews to get to, and then we'll begin the taste-testing phase of the challenge. For now, you can take a seat with the other contestants." He pointed out a picnic table where most of the contestants were sitting.

She moseyed over. As she came closer, Professor Snuggles noticed her and waved her over. Maeve picked up the pace a bit and sat down across from the professor and next to one of the Coreys.

"Well, how was it?" asked the professor.

"Yeah, how'd it go, yo?"

"Good, I think." She pushed her self-doubt aside. "Really good. The hardest part was being spied on while I worked and having to sit down and chat with Adam."

"Don't you stream the show, yo? It's like half interviews," said Corey, and one of his others chimed in. "It's like a staple of these shows."

The conversation died down for a few minutes. Maeve sat, her chin in her hands, and stared down at the picnic table's checkered cloth.

Naiomi came around the table and sat next to the professor. "I'm glad that's over with. Am I right?"

"Yeah," said Corey.

"Does anyone want to, like, talk about what they made or form an alliance?" She looked around the nearby group, finally fixing her gaze on Maeve.

"Uh no, I'll keep it a secret. That's the spirit of the game, anyway," said Maeve.

"Well, there's no way you guys are going to beat my br—" Naiomi looked shocked, and her face flushed. "Oh my god, don't try to *t-rick* me!" Naiomi scowled and continued doing so as she got to her feet and stormed off.

"Nobody is trying to . . . trick you." Maeve trailed off as Naiomi stormed away.

She shot the professor a confused look, and the four of them started giggling.

Maeve looked at her Omni. The event timer was almost over. In the distance, she saw Adam talking to Max Chambers. She bobbed a heel unconsciously.

"She said 'bruh.' What do you think? Brisket?" said Cory.

"Bruh, bruh, brussel sprouts, bread?" said Diane.

"Br-eakfast? Brandy?" said another Cory.

"Bruhtwurst? Naw," said the first Cory.

Maeve got up and absentmindedly stated, "I gotta get up. Get up and move around."

Walking around the courtyard, she saw Max and Rokk were in the corner chatting. Rokk was doing a lot of nodding with his enormous arms crossed. Zalak seemed about to interview with Adam. *He looks nervous. But he always looks like that.* Del and Bryan were chatting close to the cabins at another table. Maeve meandered around for a bit. Bryan raised a hand and said, "Hey," when she got close.

She walked over.

"Nerves got you, too?" he said.

"Yeah. I'm just so sick of all the waiting. Plus, I'm frickin' hungry," she said, smiling. A smile that faded away when she realized she had an audience. A camera bot was looking at them.

Del followed her eyes and realized what she was looking at. He leaned forward. "Say, you want something to take the edge off?" Opening up his jacket, he plucked out a metal flask with a window on it. Some dirty amber liquid wobbled around inside. From his breath, she guessed it was whiskey.

"Nnnnn-no. Thanks."

"Suit yourself." He twisted the cap off and raised the bottle toward one of the camera bots and loudly exclaimed, "Prost!" and took another swig. Some back at the picnic table looked over. He returned the cap to the flask and the flask to his jacket pocket.

"Oh-kay," he breathed out. He looked back to Maeve, who was checking the time. She had been keeping a nearly constant eye on the time. She looked up and pointed. He looked over and saw Adam wrapping it up.

"Oh, so the TV prick is done? I think it's high time we get on with it."

They walked back over to the other table. When it became apparent that Adam was going that way, too, everyone walked over there. The chatter at the table got louder as the contestants arrived and died back down when Adam stopped at the head of the table.

"All right, everyone. You've all created your culinary masterpieces. Now it's time to move on to the taste-testing phase of the challenge. Or perhaps I should say it's time to judge your food items?" Adam tutted a finger at Del, who responded with a sardonic smile.

"As we speak, the bots are distributing the food items so each of you can rate how much you enjoy them. When they finish, the bots will escort you back to your kitchen, where you can begin judging. For part two of this event, we're providing you contestants with a bottle of Crazy Murry's Forget-Me Sauce." He held up a bottle. "*Interstellar Cuisine* magazine's number one pallet cleanser."

"And remember, the top three contestants with the highest score will have an edge in the popular vote."

It got silent as the group waited. The bots looked a little sinister as they gathered together and marched toward the group. Each found their target and moved them on with a simple "Come with me, please."

6.2

Back in the log-cabin kitchen, Maeve walked to the counter space, which was dominated by nine new food containers, stacked in threes, glowing like the dickens. There was a clipboard with an attached pen to the side. The bot took its place in the corner. She grabbed a container. They had added numbers to the lids, which corresponded to her worksheet. Apparently, she was number seven since it was crossed off on the clipboard.

She grabbed the bottle of pallet cleanser. White plastic with an old-fashioned cartoon character shabbily dressed with eyes going in different directions and his tongue hanging out under the stylized label. She peeled the loud crinkly plastic off the cap and unscrewed it. The back of the bottle read: "Remove cap, fill to line, swish & spit."

She poured herself a dose of slightly viscous clear liquid with silver flecks.

Maeve selected a container; number eight's meal. She pushed the button on the lid. The device hissed squeakily. It reminded her of the air coming out of a balloon. The yellow light inside stopped, the lid effortlessly opened. The container held a steak on a plate with a knife and fork. She eagerly lifted the plate out and dug in. It was rubbery, and when she had a big enough incision, she could see why. *Oh yuck, it's rare. Hell, it's raw.* She found number eight on the clipboard. [Rhoche steak] They are a kind of large desert insect that tastes a bit like beef. She looked around the edges and cut off a particularly seared spot and gave it a taste. "Uck, two." She scribbled a two out of ten on the clipboard by number eight.

She swigged her pallet cleanser and swished it around. It invaded her mouth with a sizzling, minty taste. The sensation jumped to her sinuses and throat. She spit into the sink and was incapable of stifling a cough. And just like that, it faded away. She turned to the wastebasket and slung the meal into it. The steak banged the plastic vessel like a drum. She held the plate dripping red-orange steak juice and timed the drips so she could move it to the sink without dripping on the counter.

The next one had a number four on it. When she opened it up, the room filled with the smell of sweet baked goods. Several small brown cubes sat, each dusted in powdered sugar. Maeve's face lit up, and she gobbled one. Brownies, crispy all the way around like they were all crust. She wanted to eat the other five cubes but decided to save them for later.

She sealed it up. This time she spit the cleanser into the garbage can and marked down a nine out of ten in the space after [Brownie Bites].

Case number one had a few odd-looking deviled eggs. [Deviled Scoop Eggs] it read. Maeve didn't know what kind of bird a scoop was or even if it was a bird, but it had roundish bumpy eggs, kind of like a big twenty-sided die. She took a greedy bite, making sure to get a lot of the brown filling. *It's savory, but a little boring.* Let's go with a six.

Case number ten contained a [Bacon Cheeseburger]. *Very greasy. This thing'll put you on the toilet.* She had a small bite and rated. Another six.

Case number two [Glow-eye Grouper] was a fish fillet with grilled veggies. She sampled the veggies first and then looked at the fish closely. White with a dusting of seasoning and an oily sheen. A network of red lines, like a spiderweb, ran throughout the meat. *Tastes good. Bit of a weird texture.* She marked down a seven.

She pushed the button on case number three. The smell wafted out, and her heart sank. Pizza. Someone else made pizza. She pulled the case closer and yanked the lid off. It skittered across the counter onto the floor. Pepperoni, crispy basted crust. *Oh no! They screwed up*, she thought.

"Hey Turbo-Guts? I think we got a mix-up here." The robot looked at her but didn't respond for several agonizing seconds. She was about to expound when it spoke.

"Contest integrity analyzed, no errors detected. Contestants number three and seven are the same food category: pizza."

Maeve grabbed the pen and her hand hovered over number three. *Do I give it a ten because they screwed up and I'm number three? Or do I give it a zero because number three copied me?*

She took a bite, chewed it, her eyebrows raised. The slice had perfectly straight cuts, like they had one of those long pizza cutters. *Someone copied me, somehow.* She scowled and scribbled a zero on the page for number three.

A camera bot spying into the window caught every emotion as she dealt with this pizza doppelgänger. Fear, confusion, disgust. Somewhere out there, Mr. Yang had struck gold.

Maeve opened the next container, six. *I can't believe somebody copied me.* This one was mac and cheese. She spooned some up and tried it. *Oh, no. Oh, this is bad.* It was like pasta and artificial cheese. She put down a four next to [Vegan Mac & Cheese].

She popped open case nine and saw a slice of apple pie. *With cheese melted on top?* Maeve reluctantly dug into the mad combination and tried it. The word "awful" in her mind changed to "all right." I don't know why you'd do this to a pie, but it's not bad. She put down a six.

The last case, case five. She already knew what this one was. The professor had told her privately that she was going to make homemade ice cream. Maeve opened it up. Vanilla with nuts and a drizzle of something on top. She tried some; it was good. Creamy with a strong maple syrup taste. She'd never had homemade ice cream before. She finished the large scoop of ice cream and put down a ten for her friend.

She turned to Turbo-Guts and waved the clipboard at him. "Okay, all done here." The bot accepted the clipboard.

"Please wait here until Adam 5000 summons you."

She sighed. "Ah, not again."

She claimed the container of brownies. "I'm keeping this."

The robot didn't acknowledge that in any way.

Maeve noticed a vinyl sticker on the lid. A rectangular warning label, orange text on a black background. She peeled it off and rolled it up into a little cylinder. She peeled two more off the lids and slowly and gently placed one above Turbo-Guts's eye. It made no move, so she placed the other. The robot had a quizzical, one-eyebrow-up look. Laughing, she peeled them off again. She replaced them with slanted, angry eyebrows and giggled. She was pondering a way to top this look when the door knocked and Adam stuck his head in again.

"Hello again. One more interview, and then we'll wrap it up with the final score."

"Okay, let's get this over with."

Adam smiled.

6.3

It didn't take long for everyone to vote on the various food items and return to the picnic table. Rokk was the last, and by the looks of his shirt, he may have eaten everything provided. Adam was on his way to the table, and the murmur of the contestants died down.

Adam was holding a clipboard of his own, although it was just a prop, and eagle-eyed viewers might notice a blank form on it. He held the clipboard aloft when he was in position.

"The results are in. The bots have tabulated your scores. Now, let's see the scoreboard."

A holographic scoreboard materialized to Adam's right. It was about his height and a few feet wide. The board was black and silver with large neon letters that constantly shifted, then one after another, the rows filled in from bottom to top.

High-Stakes Cook-off Challenge

Max Chambers – Glow-eye Grouper – 77
Diane Snuggles – Butter Ice Cream – 73
Zalak – Apple Pie – 70
Naiomi Rachels – Brownie Bites – 69
Maeve McKinnon – Pepperoni Pizza – 68
Bryan Cox – Deviled Scoop Eggs – 67
Corey Zolton – Vegan Mac & Ch. – 66
I-ON – Pepperoni Pizza – 66
Del Mitchell – Cheeseburger – 62
Rokk Bradley – Rhoche Steak – 57

"Bullshit," Rokk mumbled.

Bryan folded his arms.

Zalak saw his name come up third and did a fist pump. "All right!"

The professor had been slowly shrinking in on herself as the names filled in until she saw her name and sprang up.

Max Chambers smiled when he saw only one blank left and burst out laughing when it appeared. "Thanks. Thank you, everyone."

Adam 5000 stepped in and gave Max a hearty handshake, putting his off hand on Max's elbow. "Max Chambers, congratulations. You've won the first challenge!"

"I don't know what to say. This is terrific. You've all made the right choice."

"You seemed confident going into this challenge. It seems like that paid off."

"Well, confidence is key," said Max with a self-satisfied smile.

Adam turned toward the group. "Tonight there will be a celebratory campfire dinner in the courtyard at six p.m."

While all that happened, Maeve was in her own little world reading the scoreboard.

I-ON, Pepperoni Pizza, 66. She kept reading it over and over until her name popped up. *Sixty-eight to sixty-six? I beat it by two points. It beat me really; Diane and I gave each other 10s . . .*

Her train of thought was briefly interrupted by Max Chamber's entry. *The fish was Max. I never would have guessed. It was good, though.*

Her eyes went back to I-ON's score, and anger rose inside her. *The robot copied me. It had to have.* She looked around for I-ON and found it was already looking at her. Fear prickled up her neck. They both looked away from one another. She stopped breathing.

It's been watching me somehow. She shivered.

As Adam was wrapping up his speech, Maeve put trembling hands on the picnic table, stood, and rushed home. Most of the table watched her go. The camera bots ate up her dramatic exit. I-ON watched her leave as well.

Maeve closed the door and leaned against it. Her heart beat hard now. She scanned around the gloom of her cabin, expecting to see it here somehow. I-ON unfolding from the darkness like a spider. She hit the button to lock her door.

"Computer, turn all the lights on," she said shakily.

Does it know I'm onto it? It must. It was staring at me. A shiver went up her spine. *It knows I know and doesn't care.* She fled to her bedroom, as though that would help.

6.4

Hours later. Maeve kneeled on the kitchen floor, pots and pans all around her. She was looking into the nooks and crannies of the empty cabinet with a flashlight, all twisted up.

Then there was a jarring mechanical buzzing, *Bzzzzzzzzzzzt*, which startled her. She shifted her weight to untwist and her leg whipped the pots and pans, making them scatter and crash.

She stood and heard the sound again, and it occurred to her this must be what her doorbell sounded like. No one had used it before.

She hustled through the obstacle course her kitchen had become to the window. She peeked out to see the professor's golden tail. It's dark brown tip searching this way and that.

Maeve cracked the door open. "Uh hi."

The professor could see an odd shaft of light and many things on the counter behind Maeve. "Am I interrupting something? I heard a lot of commotion going on."

"No! I'm just—you startled me. Why don't you just tab me like a—like anyone else?"

The professor eyed her suspiciously. "Well, I wasn't sure if you heard there's a celebration tonight out here. You left in a hurry. Is everything all right?"

Maeve looked over her shoulder and back. She laughed nervously and spoke with increased volume. "Yep, everything is fine. Let's go." She squeezed out the door to minimize Diane's view of her messed-up kitchen.

It was becoming dusk in the courtyard. Maeve squinted through the orange light. Food and drinks adorned the picnic tables. There was a campfire with folding chairs all around. Two of the show's robots wore fancy dress, like waiters. Most of the contestants hung around mingling.

Maeve gathered up her unkempt hair and slid a cloth hair tie from her wrist to her hair, pulled it through, and looped it around again.

As they approached the party, she saw the contestants had split into groups. Bryan and Del were at the picnic table, sharing a laugh. There were burgers and hot dogs on the table, chips, potato salad, the typical Americana that their culture had evolved from. She and Diane sat with Bryan and Del.

Maeve looked around the courtyard again, more thoroughly. *No I-ON. It must be in its cabin.* Bryan looked as though he were about to make conversation when Maeve cut in. "I have a problem. I think we might all have a problem."

Maeve wasn't usually a talker, so everyone paid attention, but it wasn't just that. They also caught the coldness in her voice.

"In that food challenge there were two pizza entries. Mine and the robot's, I-ON's. Its pizza was the same as mine. Not just similar. Exactly my homemade dough. Identical right down to the way I basted the crust. The only difference between the two of them was the way that we cut it."

"It did seem really damn the same to me," said Del.

"Right, but my point is how? It copied me, and I'm pretty sure the only way it could have known that stuff is by spying on my cabin. I keep my blinds shut most of the time, and I only told one person what I was making." She stopped herself from naming the professor but couldn't stop herself from glancing at her.

"Couldn't it have just picked up the same recipe you used?" said Del.

"No. I took bits and pieces from four different recipes, and I looked through more than a dozen. I'm wondering if it found a way to tap into the camera system. There are cameras everywhere. Probably in our cabins, too."

Maeve looked up and caught some camera bots glinting in the sunlight. She pointed one out and the group turned to look. "Maybe it can hear us now?"

Bryan looked back, eyes wide. That creepy feeling crawled around Maeve's neck again.

"I searched my kitchen pretty thoroughly, and I didn't find anything."

"So that's what you were up to," said the professor.

"Woah, that's messed up," said Bryan. "Maybe we should just confront it. I mean, if it's like us, it's been modified or whatever so that it can't hurt anyone. I, uh, I tried to punch out that smug-ass host Adam when he interviewed us, and I couldn't. It was like my body froze up. The more I wanted to do it . . . well, you know. Then the guards stuffed me back into my freezer," said Bryan.

Diane spoke up. "Now that we're talking about I-ON being weird, I've seen it a few times hanging out in the woods over by the big doors that lead into the rest of the ship."

"Me too," said Maeve excitedly.

Del reached into his jacket and produced a flask and took a sip of whiskey. "Guys, killer robot or not, this could be any of our last day. So let's get drunk, shall we?"

Maeve grabbed a six-pack off the picnic table and held it out in front of her. Bryan took one off the plastic holder, then Maeve. Maeve swung it in front of Diane.

"Bleh. No," she said, holding it at arm's length.

Maeve cracked open her beer and had a sip.

Bryan held his beer aloft. "May we all survive tomorrow." The three clacked their flask and cans together.

"Okay fine!" said Diane, looking determined. She snapped off a beer and joined the others' toast.

Diane nursed about half a beer, making disgusted noises and licking her lips. The stuff's toxic to cats, after all. Del, an experienced drinker, finished off his slim flask while he mingled with the other contestants. Maeve followed suit, alcohol aiding her ability to move in and out of conversation. And while it took her mind off the I-ON problem, it was mostly because she kept thinking about tomorrow. Doomsday. Under the starlight, she pounded one final beer and sloshed her way back home.

Maeve got inside and leaned against the door like she had done earlier.

"Hey, computer? Did anyone come into my cabin while I was gone? You'd tell me, right?" She had picked up a bit of a slur.

"Affirmative. No one has entered since you left."

"Thanks, computer." Maeve climbed over the couch's arm and looked through the gloom at her disaster of a kitchen before lying down on the couch. "Oh my god! C'puter can you tell me if anyone has ever been in my cabin but me?"

"There have been twenty-two instances since I came online."

"NooOOOoo. Has there been anyone—has-has any of the contestants been in my cabin other than me."

"Yes, one."

Maeve gasped. "Wish one?"

"Diane Snuggles."

"Oh, yeah. Except her."

"Negative."

She got up, pulled her Omni out of her pants pocket, and set it on the coffee table. She freed herself from the tyranny of her bra and pants as she padded to the bathroom for a quick pit stop. Then she yanked the blanket off her bed and wrapped it on like a cloak and went back to the couch, grabbing her Omni on the way before flopping down. Tabbing into the large viewscreen, she loaded up a movie she'd watched many times before.

The loud music of the credits woke her up. She turned off the viewscreen, rolled over, and zonked right back out.

Chapter 7

Maeve gave herself one last look in the mirror before heading out. She wore black. After all, someone would die today. She had on a hooded dress with lacy trim and big sleeves that ironically had an ankh pattern sewn into the back. Mesh gloves and stockings with tall boots that showed off a hint of thigh. She turned in the mirror a little and thought, *I should dress all gothy more often.*

She hesitated at the front door, feeling shaky and queasy.

Screw it, she thought. Putting her hood up, she took a deep breath, opened the door, and started out. She strode over to Adam and the gathering contestants.

Everyone else had dressed nice, some more so than others. The Coreys were simply wearing jeans and three different colored ringer shirts. The professor was in a nice gray business suit. Max wore an expensive navy blue suit, but then again, he always wore something like that. Rokk had some kind of off-the-rack suit that fit poorly over his giant body. Probably meant for more of a fat build. Del walked up next to her in a black skull shirt and black jeans.

"How you holdin' up?" he said as he clasped his hand on her shoulder. He couldn't see her eyes, but she inhaled sharply at his touch, and her chin wrinkled up. She moved her shoulder, and Del let her go.

"It'll . . . be okay," he said, looking worried. He turned away from the group and took a hit of booze.

Maeve took a tissue out of her purse and dabbed at her eyes.

Adam folded his arms and sighed. The last stragglers came out. First Bryan and Zalak, then right at the deadline (announced earlier in the day) Naiomi and I-ON.

When everyone gathered around, Adam composed himself.

"All right, contestants. It. Is. Time." When he finished, the lights dimmed, and the specks of light appeared and migrated slowly across the huge courtyard.

"Time to *Walk Amongst the Stars!*" He raised his arms dramatically. The theme music swelled. "Everyone pair up with an usher, and we'll move on to the ceremony."

The show's robots marched in from the darkness and paired up with the contestants. Even though she knew it was coming, Maeve jumped when the robot grabbed her arm and put a hand on her back. She breathed hard, trembling. She watched the robots position the others into a single-file line ahead of her. They seemed less like ushers and more like prison guards to her.

Adam led the procession of bots down the field to the large double doors that led to the aft of the ship and opened them. The entire ship seemed to be dark. The contestants gawked at this unknown part of the ship they'd never been allowed to see before.

As they entered the dimly lit fancy halls, the speckling starlight followed them. They went down corridors and around corners until they came to a large door illuminated with an ominously slow, pulsing red light.

Even though Maeve had no idea where in the ship they were, she knew what this was. It was an air lock. Adam opened the inner air lock door, and the contestants were positioned into a semicircle around it.

The professor squeaked and struggled futilely against her robot usher.

Adam looked demonic in the rising and falling red light. His TV host smile unwavering. He finally spoke. "All right, contestants. You've appealed to the masses, you've showed off, you've won contests, and now it's time to see the fruits of your labor."

"As we saw yesterday, Max Chambers, Diane Snuggles, and Zalak won the contest, and in doing so, got a significant boost to their ratings. But ultimately, we are gathered to say goodbye to the contestant with the lowest rating. And that contestant is . . ." Adam cocked his right arm.

"Coming up after this!" Adam thrust his index finger toward the camera bot nearest to him.

Del growled and lunged forward. "Oh, fuck you!" His robotic guard changed its grip to his neck and arm, easily moving him back a step.

"Relax, Mitchell. This is almost over, and if you make it, we've got another week to be friends."

Del groaned as the robot made him fall back in line.

"And we're back! The contestant with the lowest ratings is . . ." He paused for what felt like an eternity. For dramatic effect, but also because he was waiting for Mr. Yang to tell him who's up. "Zalak; step forward, Zalak."

Zalak's robotic counterpart walked him over next to Adam. "Aw, Zalak, what happened? You got third place."

Zalak stammered trying to think of something to say. "I—um—you, you can't . . ."

Adam rested his hand on Zalak's shoulder. "Speechless, that's not uncommon at these ceremonies; perfectly understandable. Okay, Zalak, go ahead and get into position."

The robot marched Zalak into the air lock. Zalak struggled against his captor, slowing it down a bit as it forced him all the way to the outer air lock door. The robot gave him a shove and quickly retreated as Adam closed the inner air lock. Zalak ran to the door and felt around it frantically.

A camera drone had entered the air lock with Zalak. It hovered near the ceiling, getting a closeup of his alien, yet distinctly distressed, face. Adam lifted a plastic safety shield and poised his finger over a big red button. The group cringed. Zalak yelled something none of them could make out. Adam pressed the intercom button.

"Well, Zalak, it's about that time. Have you any parting words?"

"Y-you can't do this. Wait! Don't do this. I'm rich, I'll pay you. Anything. Name it." Zalak was chirping and blabbering so much it was hard to hear the translator around his neck.

"Okay, parting is such sweet sorrow, but part we must." Adam pressed the big red button, and the outer air lock opened immediately. Zalak's clothes ruffled wildly. He flailed his arms and legs as he fired out of the chamber. The camera bot raced after him to catch all the juicy details. Zalak swiped at it, but it remained out of reach.

Maeve watched in wide-eyed horror as the alien contestant thrashed and twitched, getting slowly smaller and disappearing into the void of space. Adam stood solemn, head bowed during Zalak's evacuation. Now that it was over, he pushed a button that reset the air lock and closed the safety cover. They could hear the room hiss as it pressurized.

Maeve swallowed fruitlessly with a parched throat. She could finally break her gaze of the incident at the air lock. *I couldn't look away. Why did I watch?* She closed her eyes and saw a flash of Zalak's shocked face and shook it off.

Adam broke the silence, chipper as ever. "We've said goodbye to our first contestant, and Zalak taught us an important lesson. Even if you win events, if you're not popular enough, you might . . . *Walk Amongst the Stars.*" He gestured to the air lock.

"Enjoy the rest of your night, because even now we're tabulating the votes for the next challenge, which we will announce tomorrow. Good night, everybody!" Adam blew a kiss to the camera, froze for a moment, then turned his attention to the contestants again.

The contestants were speechless.

"Okay, we're done here. Take them back to the camp."

The robots filed everyone back down the hall into the middle of the park again and let them go. The entire group just kind of stood around looking at each other wordlessly for a moment and then split up.

Maeve walked back to her cabin, wounded somehow, in a manner she didn't understand. She mindlessly touched the little tree by her home before entering. Inside, she paced around the living room. Before today, she thought she had a grasp on what this was. But just now, watching someone die, someone she grew up watching on TV. It was like she had falsely awoken from a nightmare directly into another.

The image of Zalak's spinning dead body flashed into her mind again.

"No." Maeve balled up her fists as tears welled up. She growled and made to punch the couch, but her body locked up tighter and tighter until she was more scared than angry. She went to her knees in front of the couch, putting her head on the cushions as she blubbered something unintelligible and sobbed.

7.1

Mr. Yang pushed his back into his office chair hard and stretched. His back popped, and he scooted back into his workstation. He was hard at work stitching together the next episode of *Walk Amongst the Stars*. Experience had taught him to come in early on these days if he wanted to avoid rush-hour traffic because it always cost him an extra hour or two to get everything just so.

He had finished editing down Zalak going out the air lock, getting just the right angles, and it came out decent, just decent. Not the best death, honestly, but he'd made the best of a mediocre situation.

He spliced the segment into the end of the show. Then he went back to the beginning and watched the show at 10x speed.

Adam 5000's dramatic entrance raced by, then the title sequence. Empty spot for commercials. Then shots of the week. Contestants receiving loads of groceries, and shots of them cooking. You couldn't hear the voice-over while it was playing at 10x. He rolled it back and played at normal speed to see Maeve accidentally douse herself with flour. She laughed at her own clumsy situation. Mr. Yang smiled. It never got old, and went back to 10x. Another empty spot for commercials. Adam monologued at frenetic speed and then speed walked over to the desk with the other two judges and sat down.

Mr. Yang slowed it back to normal speed.

"Thoughts on episode four?" said Adam.

"I'm not gonna lie. I usually skip the first two weeks and rely on social media to show me anything steamy I mighta missed," said Synthia Platinum. "This is where I get really interested in the show."

"Why's that?" asked Adam.

"Well, it's just so much fun to see the contestants work toward a goal and then see who . . . didn't make the grade."

Adam 5000 turned his attention. "Before we show the results, who do you think gets voted off, Captain?"

Captain Reeves folded his arms and thought. "I got my fingers crossed that it's the robot. I mean, just look at em making pizza. Damn thing is almost like a robot cook in a pizza chain. Where's the fun in that? But who do I *think* it'll be? Eh, probably Zalak."

"Oh, going with a celebrity guess?"

Wow, he called it, Yang thought.

"Yeah, he just seems like kind of a sad sack in all the clips. And really, when's the last time you rushed to see a movie because it had Zalak in it?" He shrugged.

"And your guess Synthia?"

"Can I get two?"

"Oh sure, but I think we'll only be able to award you half points if you get it right."

She giggled. "Well, I think it's gonna be either Max Chambers or Maeve McKinnon. Both of them are kind of . . ." She made two thumbs down with a yuck face.

"Well, for the sake of being different, I'll go with Bryan."

Mr. Yang paused it, hit save, and got up. It was time for a break, and his coffee wasn't going to refill itself. He went out into the hall, thinking about what he had left to do. He'd have this done by noon, have a quick lunch, and get started on the next show in the log. Then the studio would bump it back with notes, as always. He'd make whatever menial change they wanted, and it'd be ready to air the day after.

Chapter 8

The next day, in the early afternoon, Adam called everyone out to the courtyard. Maeve went out right away. She was enjoying the feeling of the sun on her back. It took her a long time to get to sleep, but when she did, so too did yesterday's shell shock. Today she just felt happy to still be here for another week.

The final contestant exited their cabin and began walking in, I-ON. Maeve narrowed her eyes. *I'm onto you. You won't cheat me again, you shady bot.*

I-ON tucked itself into the semicircle formation that everyone else was in.

"Good afternoon, contestants, it's time to reveal your next challenge. Throughout last week, six point five million viewers voted for . . ." Adam dramatically threw one arm up in the air. "Laser death match!"

"Next Saturday, we will have a mock laser-gun battle. Hologram please." Adam looked up and snapped his fingers. A hologram materialized in the air and floated down to the grass. A cartoonish representation of this indoor park and everyone in it. Corey Three waved his arms, causing the little holo-Corey to do the same. The events described played out in the hologram as Adam laid them out.

"For this challenge, we'll project holograms onto the park to simulate different environments. Players will earn points by scoring fatal hits on opponents, and by collecting artifacts. Everyone will be issued the same gear, but many upgrades and power-ups can be found hidden on the battlefield. The battles go fast, so we have three distinct battlefields with randomized item locations."

"There are many more artifacts to find than there are kills to score, so a crafty player can outscore a deadly one. Depending on the weapon and where it hits, it may take multiple shots to eliminate a player. Once eliminated, players are incapacitated for the round by a mild electric shock."

"Any questions?"

Max Chambers both raised a hand and began speaking at the same time. "Zalak's room was next to mine. May I have it?"

Some of the group chuckled.

"I'm serious. I could have the bots take out the wall and have a huge cabin," he said.

"Sorry, no, there will be no further modifications to the cabins, and all of Zalak's things have been removed," said Adam. "Any other questions, perhaps about the upcoming game?"

Maeve raised just her hand, and as she thought about it, raised her entire arm.

"Maeve?"

"How does the whole getting shocked thing work? How can a hologram shock you?"

Adam listened to a technical explanation from Mr. Yang.

"The battlefield has many hidden drones that aid in things like adding resistance, weight, light, and even directed energy. So, anytime you climb over an obstacle or get hit by enemy gunfire, there's a stealthy drone completing the illusion."

"Oh, that's actually pretty cool."

Adam nodded.

Bryan raised his hand.

Adam pointed at him. "Yes?"

"Isn't shooting someone the uh, apex of violence, which is something we're incapable of?" said Bryan.

"Right. Good question. The system is smart enough to recognize the difference between a real blaster and those that we'll be using for the game. Because of this, fighting must be done with the provided holographic zappers. Physical fighting will still leave you stunned and vulnerable to attack."

"When you said three battlefields, does that also mean three trials?" asked the professor.

"Yes, thanks for clarifying," said Adam. He paused for hands or confused faces, then moved on. "Just like last week, we will begin trials Saturday afternoon. Sunday will be the voting ceremony. And then the process begins anew."

"Until then, you can get ready for the big day however you like." Adam waited a moment for any more questions. "Good luck contestants," he said, then his hologram faded out and the robot left behind marched away.

The group went their different ways and began chatting with each other. Maeve walked back over to her tree that she liked to hang out under and had a seat.

The professor came over to Maeve and crouched near her.

"Well, this challenge sounds awful," said the professor.

"Mmm, I think it'd be cool if it wasn't a life-or-death kind of thing."

"I suppose I'll be hunting for artifacts. I've never even seen a gun up close before, let alone used one."

Maeve scooted to face the professor. "I'll tell you what I'm going to do. Practice in VR. I've been a gamer for years, and I don't think there exists a weapon I haven't used in a video game. Game guns aren't always realistic; but, heck, this challenge basically is a video game. I could show you how to set up your own VR setup. Heck, I can teach you."

"Yes, please, that would be great. I was also looking to team up with someone like last time, so this is perfect."

"Look," Maeve said, pointing down the courtyard.

In the distance, I-ON was walking side by side with the robot, who was just Adam a minute ago. They reached the doorway, and I-ON stood to the side, watching the door as the robot walked through. Then it turned around, looked to see if anyone noticed, and then walked back to its cabin.

Maeve and the professor tried not to look like they were watching when I-ON turned around.

"So that's another thing. What do we do about the robot? It's clearly spying on everything and cheating off us."

"Oh, I bet he'll be deadly in the laser battle," said the professor.

They stood.

"Well, come on, let's go to your place and I'll whip up some VR peripherals for your Omni." Maeve looked at her suddenly. "You're not one of those I-don't-have-an-Omni weirdos, are you?"

"Nope." She smiled and patted her pocket.

"Good. About how old is it?"

"I don't know. About . . . ten to twelve years."

Maeve gasped, sucking spittle into her throat. She had a minor coughing fit. Four was the longest she'd ever gone, and she sometimes felt that was too much.

"We're going to upgrade your Omni as well."

The professor opened her cabin door and led Maeve to the printer.

Looking back and forth between her own Omni and the printer's catalog, Maeve researched and queued up all the VR components Diane would need. When it came time to upgrade her OmniTab, the professor had so many upgrade credits piled up that she only had to pay a service charge to upgrade.

Hours whiled away while the printer worked. The two conversed. The professor logged into her new OmniTab once everything finished printing. Once it had downloaded all her old information, she tossed the useless old Omni into the garbage chute. Maeve hooked up the VR rig, so the professor needed only to adjust the halo and tab in.

Maeve and Diane decided to break for dinner and then jump into VR afterward.

8.1

An hour and change later in VR, Maeve had familiarized the professor with the basics of the VR interface. How to call up programs, load environment presets, navigate the internet, etc. The professor had settled on a sunny Japanese garden style home environment. Diane was somewhat familiar with computer use, so none of this was shocking, and she learned it fairly easily.

"Okay, now we got you all settled into VR. Next, we need to get to the whole reason we started this. Guns. One second," said Maeve. She summoned an interface window and typed something in and then poked the option she wanted. A portal appeared, silver rimmed like a fancy mirror, but the inner surface rippled with a colorful sheen like oily water. Maeve waved the professor through, then went in after her.

They flew through a twisting, turning maze of interconnected tubes, dark with glowing veins of prismatic light. The tube ended abruptly, setting them down in a new place. The digital storefront for *GraveGun*.

Now they were in a dimly lit warehouse. The overhead lights flickered but were mostly off. A soft banging came from the boarded-up door at all times. They had landed in front of a table overflowing with boxes of *GraveGun*.

A figure walked out of the gloom behind the table. A digital assistant whose name floated overhead: Sargent Packard. He spoke up. "Another surviver? Well, you got here just in time. The building's compromised, and we're abandoning it. Now grab a box from the table and get ready to move out."

It all came back to Maeve. Sargent Packard walks you through the beginning of the game, teaching you all the basics. Then he dies during the escape from the city. Then you find him again later, but it turns out he's not himself anymore. He's a cyberzombie spy. *Man, what a good game*, she thought.

"Now what do I do?" said the professor.

"Oh, you just summon your Omni and then sweep the box onto it, and then it'll start the download. Oh, and once we get you into the game, you want to tell it to skip the tutorial unless you actually want to play it instead of just using it as a shooting range."

The professor held out her clawlike hand, looking up to the ceiling as though she were asking for godly help. "I need my Omni."

Maeve smirked.

Somehow that display worked and an orange globe of energy flared in the professor's palm, leaving a VR representation of her OmniTab behind. Something that Maeve's didn't do and suddenly she felt just a touch of envy. Then the professor held the box over it, and it shrunk down and went inside the OmniTab. The Omni turned into an empty wireframe that began slowly filling up with shiny blue energy to show its download progress.

"Okay, that won't take long. I'm going to get into the game and try to intercept you. Message me your name when you get into the game. Oh, and the game will probably bother you about buying stuff right away.

Just say no to everything. You're on a free trial for two weeks." Maeve put out her hand and said, "Omni." She swept a game box onto her own VR OmniTab, launching the game. She vanished.

8.2

Maeve arrived in *GraveGun*, where she logged out a couple of nights ago. She went into the tower and took the elevator down. She looked around the guild base. A couple of guildies were milling about. No Colin, though. She noted the renovation progress and then used her recall cube.

Unfortunately, the column of white light didn't deliver her to the city she was expecting. She had forgotten that she changed her recall anchor to be closer to the guild base. Now she was in a military safe zone. It was a blown-up city. Maeve never discovered a reason for the destruction. The military had rebuilt a tall building that sat on top of a subway station. Where there were once offices with superb views of the city now held various gun turrets. She looked up at it as she walked. Coming up was a security checkpoint with a whole firing squad who would take care of any infiltrating cyberzombies.

She paused in front of the scanner so it could fire random lights at her and make a low purring noise. It *blinged* loudly with a green light, and she descended concrete stairs into an old-world tiled subway station. Energy fields blocked off the tunnels. She wandered onto the old reliable maglev and waited. It would be a couple of minutes before it took off. Maeve zoned out, looking at the graffiti. Eventually, a screen name she didn't recognize popped up in the corner of her vision.

[Ok, I'm in. Now what?]

She instinctively grabbed her OmniTab and issued a friend request.

[D-Snuggz. Seriously?]

[I put in my name and that's what it suggested.]

[That means someone has taken your name already.]

She went back to the community tab on her omni and saw:

[You have unread messages]

The maglev lurched and sped into the dark tunnel ahead. Maeve gazed at the name attached to those messages. A name she was feeling mixed up about: Colin.

8.3

"Okay, as a new player you should be in the hub city, I forget what it's called," said Maeve. She had gotten the professor into voice chat, so they didn't need to text anymore.

The professor put away her OmniTab and looked around. It was a late night with a full moon; it illuminated the urban decay, casting foreboding shadows around. A colossal wall bisected crumbling old buildings. Her eyes followed the lit street up to a large gated entrance. There was a green triangle pointing to it.

"That must be this huge wall I'm looking at." She started walking.

"Oh yeah. You start outside the city. If you had done the tutorial, you kind of run for your life while a horde of zombies comes in, and you know, it teaches you the basics."

"I'm heading to the gate now."

"I'm on a tram heading into the city. It's hauling ass, but it's also a long way to go."

When she got close to the gate, sensors swept over her, and the door opened.

[Mission Accomplished] appeared in the corner of her heads-up display, followed by [A New Beginning]. She looked around and saw another green triangle off in the distance. "Okay, I'm inside and I'm looking at a big green arrow."

"Oh no, that's just the next mission. Ignore it. If it's annoying you, I can show you how to hide it."

"No, it's okay."

"We need to get you a crafting station, but I can't quite remember where that is. Look around and see if you can find an industrial district."

On the inside of the wall, the city was a hybrid of old-world city design with modern revisions. Pulsing power conduits snaked up buildings. Large monitors showed news and commercials. The dingy concrete contrasted with neon light.

The professor took out her OmniTab and figured out how to turn off that green arrow. `Missions > Hide Mission`. Now that she knew you could remove it, it was easy to do. She was looking for a map when she heard a rumbling engine and an awful squealing. A motorcycle chugged by, oozing black smoke from a dragging muffler. The biker was caked in a shocking amount of sticky old blood. *Looks like they don't believe in helmets*, she thought.

She noted the damage and followed the bike down the street and put away her Omni. It wasn't hard to keep up; the bike was barely working, and the biker had to keep his feet constantly ready for balance.

She followed the bike east until it went out of sight. This felt like the right direction. As she went, the city got darker, grimier, with more pollution. Just when she was going to give up on the biker and go back to her Omni, she caught sight of him again. The bike had died. As she got close again, the biker slammed his fist on the center console of the bike a few times until it coughed to a start and then whined on down the road. She followed again, this time losing sight of him in a tunnel.

She hurried through the dark, echoey tunnel and emerged onto a street that was confined by the city wall. A skinny back street with tightly packed buildings on both sides. There was the biker again. He was in the parking lot of a bar. She could hear muffled twangy music and the smell of fried food wafting through the air.

She looked down the street and jogged over to the biker, who was sitting on his bike, talking to another player.

". . . right to the face. On one hand, I didn't lose any XP but on the other . . . I mean, look at me," said the biker.

"Yeah, that's like a maximum repair bill right there," said the other biker, hitting a cigarette. He looked past his friend and checked out the professor as she walked up. The bloody biker turned to look.

"Hello. I'm new, and my friend wants me to meet up at a crafting station. Do you know where that is?"

"There's one just down the street. See that neon blue sign with the arrow? I'd offer you a lift, but I don't think this thing is going to start back up."

The professor glanced down the street. "Okay, thank you." She beamed.

"No problem," said the bloody biker. The smoking biker offered a little wave.

"Well, I better get ready for work," said the bloody biker, turning back to his friend.

The professor made her way down the street and crossed over. It was a nondescript dingy concrete building, but up close, she could read the signs.

*Repair Bays

*Crafting Stations

*Vendors

She looked into an open bay door and didn't understand everything she was looking at, but she could tell this was the right place. Players were milling about inside, using different workstations, fixing up vehicles and equipment.

"Maeve, you there? I found the place."

"Cool, I'm just getting through security now. I won't be long."

The professor strolled around the building, looking at all the little signs and stations spread around the room. She smiled at the occasional player acknowledgment.

A few minutes later, Maeve walked into the bay door. She scanned the room and noticed the professor's screen name and walked over with a big smile on her face.

"I almost didn't notice you like that. You look weird," said Maeve.

The professor had chosen a prefab human female soldier avatar.

"I look normal." She twirled around, almost singing the words.

"Well, let's get to it." Maeve led her over to an item printer. It looked like a copy machine's mean older brother. As big as a person with a conveyor belt. She poked the screen and then pecked at some options. After some mental math, she tapped the screen again. The machine whirred and vibrated, green light casting shadows on the wall behind it.

The conveyor belt moved forward and stopped several times until it suddenly dumped a gun into a little basket at the end. That happened two more times, each time the professor transferred the weapon into her backpack.

"Okay, you've got three varieties of firearms to practice with. I think I know the perfect place to go. Come on."

8.4

They walked out of the hub city going south. Maeve pulled out her Omni and slowed to a stop as she read. She thought about how to respond to Colin's in-game messages she had missed.

"Something wrong?" The professor was ten steps ahead looking back.

"Uh, nope." She deftly pocketed the Omni and jogged to the professor.

They entered the abandoned old-world city, and after a short walk, they came to a rundown old park. The sky was going a dark blue color. It was far enough from the hub city that it wouldn't draw any serious enemies but not so close that guards would interfere.

Maeve's father used to drag her to a gun club, and she recalled the safety tips he taught her. "Before we go any further in, let's go over some basics."

"Give weapons the proper respect. Disrespect a knife and you might cut yourself. Disrespect a gun and you might murder someone. Assume a gun is loaded unless you check it yourself. Be mindful to keep the gun always in a safe direction until you have a target. Always keep your finger away from the trigger until it's time to shoot. I put mine here." She pulled her own side arm, turned her wrist and showed her finger along the top of the trigger guard. "When you're certain of your target, consider what is behind it. Go ahead and grab that pistol we printed up."

Diane pulled the weapon from her pack and presented it across both hands. Maeve pointed out the grip, barrel, and trigger. She explained replacing the magazine or, in this case, reloading the cylinder. How to charge a weapon, in this case pulling the hammer back. Then she showed her how to safely handle the gun until she was ready to shoot, and then how to stand when shooting. Maeve went over some things this gun didn't have, like a fire-mode selector and accessory rails.

"This place is ideal for training. You can learn to do it right, and there's virtually no consequence for screwing up." Maeve opened her backpack up and transferred box upon box of ammunition to the professor's pack. "All right, shoot at that building over there." Maeve pointed out a building about a hundred feet away.

The professor turned her attention to the building, then to the gun. She pulled the hammer back, causing the cylinder to rotate. Checking her grip, she planted her feet, licked her lips, and took aim. She touched her finger to the trigger and pulled gently. More. More. *Thoom*, the gun jerked in her hands. The shot echoed in the abandoned park. The bullet hit the wall with a puff of concrete dust. Her arms rocked back with the recoil. She looked at Maeve, her mouth agape.

Maeve smiled. "I know, right? You got four shots left. See if you can hit one of the windows."

The professor fired off four more rounds at a small window, hitting it once.

Maeve went over the basics with the two other guns. An automatic pistol and a rifle. After the professor had a taste for them all, Maeve checked the time and led her down the street to the building they had been shooting at. As they got close, a figure stumbled out of the building. Red gleaming eyes fixed on them.

Urgently, the professor said, "What the hell is that?"

"*That* is a cyberzombie, the baddies of this game. And *that* is your next target."

The professor looked apprehensive.

"Don't worry, these low-level ones move pretty slow, and you got me to back you up." Maeve pulled out that plasma pistol she won a while back.

The professor aimed the machine pistol and fired, hitting the distant creature, causing it to sway unsteadily on its feet. But it didn't go down, and now it was shambling toward them. The professor's aim faltered, and she quickly emptied her magazine. The creature covered a bunch of ground while she tried to insert a new magazine with shaky hands. Finally, she found the mag well and snapped the magazine into place. She looked at the side of the pistol to find the slide release; she pushed it, slamming the slide forward. The creature was close enough now that she could make out its grisly features. It looked like an emaciated man, wires penetrating the skin. It had electronic glowing eyes, and wispy corpse hair.

"Shh-it," the professor breathed. She took a breath, pointed and fired a few short bursts. The cyberzombie collapsed to the ground, dead.

"That was—" she looked over at Maeve, who was once again engrossed in her OmniTab.

"Hey! What are you doing?"

Maeve looked up and noticed the dead zombie. "You had it under control."

"Yeah, but what if I didn't? You're supposed to be backing me up."

"It wouldn't have been a big deal. Trust me." Maeve put her Omni away.

"Come on now. You've been distracted since we met up. What's the problem?"

"It's nothing."

"It's nothing but you're so gone that I almost got eaten by a zombie?"

Maeve laughed. "It's just that . . . there's somebody. From my old life, and we recently became close. And . . . you know, it's complicated."

The professor's face lit up with a predatory smile, almost betraying her human-looking avatar. "Is it boy trouble?"

"No! I mean. Yeah." Maeve felt like her face was on fire.

The professor smiled. "What's the problem? Clingy? Jerky? Not jerky enough? Can't go the distance?"

Maeve put her hands in her pockets. She turned her Omni over and over in her pocket. "No, it's just that . . ." She sighed and looked up, resolute. "The problem is, I never considered him before. And now that we're hitting it off . . . What's the point of starting a doomed relationship? It's not fair. For him, I mean. And me, it's really damn unfair for me, but you know what I mean, right?"

"Yes, I suppose." She put her hand to her chin. "That's rough."

"I need to find a way to tell him, but I just don't know what to say."

"It sounds like you know what to say. You just need to actually do it."

"Maybe." Maeve regarded the blooming pink-orange horizon. "But not right now. For now, let's shoot you some zombies."

"Okay, and pay attention this time," the professor said in an irritable tone.

Maeve smiled.

The two of them went all over the town, blasting enemies with the three weapons Maeve printed out. Maeve liked that new plasma gun she got. The professor leveled up a few times and accidentally completed a few missions. Then they walked out of the zombie ruins into the hub city again.

"We'll do one more session like this where I just show you the ropes with different weapons and then we'll do some multiplayer. Then you can get a feel for shooting at real thinking targets."

"That sounds good. Another thing I've been thinking I need to do is get in some exercise. I've been too sedentary for too long, and I feel like I need to get back into shape," said the professor.

Maeve grabbed for some belly fat, but her avatar was too slim and trim for that gesture to work. "Oh god, you're right. I've been eating nothing but pizza and playing VR games for a week."

They shared a laugh.

"Okay, so we'll just have to split our free time between the two. You're in charge of teaching me guns, and I'll be in charge of coming up with a workout routine," she said.

"Sounds good. I'll see you tomorrow," said Maeve.

"Bye." The professor disappeared from the game, then Maeve.

8.5

Late that night, in *GraveGun*. Maeve was in the maglev, rushing back to the tougher parts of the game, where their guild base was located. She stared down at her Omni, typing, as the countryside became a ruined cityscape. Silhouettes of broken office buildings. Dusk blazed off those with intact windows.

[... need you to understand that I...]
She deleted the message and started over. Again.
She watched out the window for a moment while thinking.
Something more simple.

[We need to talk. Meet me at
the top of the guild tower.]
She looked out the windows again. The maglev rushed by a sundered section of highway, support columns topped with little tabletops of road.
Bling, bling. She looked at the Omni again.
[OMG finally, they must be
keeping you pretty busy.]
[OMW]
She put her Omni away and went back to window watching for another couple of minutes until the train sped into a dark tunnel; it made a

final lurch as it shut down. She walked out of the train car into the dingy station, exited the never-ending security checkpoint. A guard uttered, "Good hunting."

As she crossed the field, a few wandering monsters accosted her, and she introduced them to her new plasma pistol. They didn't appreciate it like she did.

Eventually, she made her way inside and then up two stories to the top. After five minutes, she could see another maglev shoot into the station, and soon after, she could see a dark figure making the same trek she just had, casting a long diagonal shadow. As Colin neared, he waved up to her, and she gave a tentative wave back.

Maeve could hear him ascending the metal staircase, and then he came out of the roof access door. She felt all mixed up inside as he walked over to her. They exchanged greetings. Maeve couldn't look at him while she struggled to find the right thing to say. The wind blustered for a moment. She took his hands in hers and explained what she and the professor had talked about before. "This relationship is great, but it's just happening at the wrong time. It's cursed, doomed. I don't know what's going to happen, and I don't want to hurt you if"—she swallowed hard—"when I die."

He listened, stunned. Finally, he shook his head and told her, "That's all the more reason we should be together now."

He placed his hand on her cheek, and she felt weak. Tears spilled down her cheeks. He leaned in and they kissed, dark figures before a blood red sun. It was sweet, but she pushed him away.

"It's just that I don't know how long I've got."

"Hey," he grabbed her hands. "I'd rather be hurt if you don't make it, rather than out of some act of kindness."

"I just thought—"

Colin pulled Maeve into an embrace while she cried. "It's going to be okay."

She sniffled. "I gotta go."

"Ve."

She logged out. Colin stared at the empty space for a moment and dropped his head as the wind gusted. He went over to the folding chairs his father had set up, seized one, and flung it off the roof with a grunt. He heard it clatter against the defensive wall before logging out.

8.6

The next day, the professor knocked on Maeve's door, bright and early. Maeve's eyes flicked open and then groggily closed, but the knocking came again. She made a disgusted sigh, and whipped back the covers. She pitched off the bed and landed on her feet. Ducking into the closet, she slipped a robe on over her nightclothes. She cinched it up as she went down the hall.

She reached the living room. "Shutters open," she said. The window shutters opened up. The professor peeked in, then waved. Maeve walked over to the door and opened it wide. The sun lit her friend's fur from behind, giving her a glowing outline. She briskly walked in.

"Good morning. Ready to begin our training session?" Diane saw Maeve's vacant stare, robe, and messy hair. "You don't look ready."

Maeve rubbed the crud out of her eye. "No, you woke me up. What time is it?"

"Six," said the professor.

"I—gah. Why?" said Maeve.

"You got this. Go get your workout clothes on, and I'll make you a coffee."

The professor gracefully walked to the kitchen while Maeve lumbered back down the hallway. She closed the door and rummaged through a drawer until she found her workout suit. She stripped everything off and squeezed into the black stretchy suit one limb at a time. Fully in, she adjusted all the seams and contours and caught herself in the mirror. She smirked at herself. The suit kept everything nice and snug and cooled the user, but it was totally revealing. She dug through the drawer again and put a crop top and some short shorts on over the body suit. She tossed her old clothes into the bin and opened the door. Then she went back down the hall.

Just as she got back to the kitchen, she yawned deeply, her eyes closed. When she opened her eyes again, she found a smoldering cup of coffee inches from her face. "Oh, thanks." The professor carefully handed it off to Maeve, who shuffled over to the couch and sat down with it. Waking up, sipping her coffee.

The professor sat on the other end of the couch facing Maeve, her arm draped along the top. "So first we'll begin with a little warm up jog around the courtyard. And then we'll run laps. And then finally we'll come back in and do some yoga. Then I figure we'll take a break and then come back around to do some VR training."

After discussing plans and having coffee, Maeve put her cup in the kitchen, and the two walked out into the increasingly sunny courtyard. Maeve turned left and leaned forward into a jog. The professor joined her, and the two trotted around the courtyard clockwise. After completing a lap, they picked up the pace a bit. As they ran down past the big door, Maeve remembered I-ON here the other day.

Toward the end of the second lap, Maeve slowed back down to a slow jog, huffing and puffing. The professor slowed, too. Her mouth was open, tongue moving with her breath. "I did the math. In this open space." She swallowed hard. "Four laps is about a mile," she panted.

"I hate . . . running," Maeve breathed.

"You know what I hate?" The professor panted. "Getting ejected into space, and dying."

The professor picked up the pace again. Maeve lagged for a moment and then did the same. They continued running and walking to catch their breath until they had done a mile. Maeve shifted from a run to a walk in front of her home with a few stumbling steps. With her hands on her hips, she huffed and puffed. She wiped sweat from her brow and turned around. The professor was walking around the corner.

When she caught up, the professor was panting heavily, her tongue lolling and dripping saliva. Maeve went over to her cabin and opened the door for the professor, who slipped right in. She closed the door behind her.

"Computer. Set temperature, sixty degrees for a half hour, then gradually increase back to seventy."

"Acknowledged," said the shipboard computer.

The professor walked in circles around the living room, panting, while Maeve went to the kitchen to get a couple glasses of cold water.

"Phew, I'm not cut out for all this running," panted the professor.

Maeve came back from the kitchen with the water.

"Yeah, me either."

"Ha. Your species is literally built for this sort of thing. It's why you sweat: thermoregulation." The professor took the glass and sipped some soothing cold water and sighed. "I don't have that ability. I don't think I could run much more than a mile without passing out."

Maeve lowered her glass and wiped her mouth. "What other cat abilities do you have?"

"Most of them. I started out all felid, Puma concolor, specifically. Then genetic engineers edited in human traits. So I'm agile, I can see well in the dark. My sense of smell and hearing are beyond human levels." She took another drink. "I have these handy whiskers." She ran her hand past the grouping of stiff white hairs on the side of her snout. "I'm blessed with sapient thinking and speech. I have upright posture and hands." She wiggled her fingers, which were covered in fine blond fur.

"Let's get to that yoga, shall we? I'm cooling off nicely," said the professor.

Maeve tabbed into the big TV nearby. It flashed to life. First, she searched for beginner yoga, then frowned at the screen and changed it to intermediate. "Are you okay with intermediate?"

"Sure, I'm no stranger to yoga."

Maeve shoved the couch back, so they had room to work. The two followed along, bending, stretching, and holding for an hour.

8.7

The week passed by quickly, at least it had for Maeve, and it was the day before the second competition. She and the professor kept up the same routine all week and by Wednesday, people began joining them on their mile run. At first, Maeve was annoyed, especially with the more physically fit contestants. But, what can you do? By the end of the week, everyone except I-ON and Max Chambers were out there. *Next week I need to keep my training a secret*, she thought.

Chapter 9

Thanks to the professor getting her used to an early schedule, Maeve was in a nervous state of readiness a couple of hours early. She nibbled at a granola bar and had some water.

"All contestants, please meet in the courtyard," announced Adam over the intercom.

"Finally." Maeve jumped up and took long strides to the door. "Let's get this over with." She hustled across the field.

She joined the group of the professor, Rokk, and Del in front of Adam.

"Well, you all seem prepared and eager. Are you ready to take out those other slackers who couldn't be bothered to show up?" said Adam.

"Yeah," said the professor.

Maeve nodded.

Del folded his arms.

"Yer talking to a bunch of dead men, Adam. I got this," said Rokk.

"Ho-ho, I can't wait to see this, Rokk." Adam reached up and patted him on the shoulder.

Rokk furrowed his brow and folded his arms.

After a few minutes, the rest of the group filtered in, and the show was ready to roll. Everyone except I-ON.

"It looks like we have a reluctant contestant. Hold on while we coax him outside." Adam pointed to the cabin and two robots marched over to the house. The door slid open for them, and they entered. A moment later, three robots came marching back out. They escorted him over to the group and went back to their positions behind Adam.

"What's the matter I-ON? Nerves getting to you?" said Adam.

"Very sorry. I lost track of time," said I-ON.

Maeve shot I-ON an incredulous look.

"But, you're a robot. Don't you have a clock built into your head or something? How can you lose track of time?" said Bryan.

I-ON turned toward Bryan and placed his right hand on his shoulder and gripped it tight, looking him in the eyes. Bryan looked tense and furrowed his brow.

"My mind doesn't work that way. I was merely strategizing. I am sure you have gotten lost in thought before."

Bryan wordlessly stepped backward out of the robot's grip. I-ON turned its attention back to Adam.

"We're all gathered here now. That is what's important. We can get any animosity out on the battlefield," Adam said, then beamed a smile.

"Adam, may I shake your hand? I am worried that they may vote me off the show before I get the chance." I-ON interrupted.

Adam placed his hand over his heart and looked soulfully at the bot. "Awe, of course I have time for a fan. C'mere!" Adam stepped forward, his right hand extended. I-ON stepped into the shake and turned it into an embrace. His left hand slapped Adam on the back twice with a loud clank. Adam's holographic projection flickered for just a second. I-ON stepped back into the semicircle.

Adam paused for a moment, smiling contentedly. "Now let's get down to business. Today's competition is a laser-gun battle. We'll have three rounds. Eliminating other players is worth two points, and finding the many hidden treasures is worth one each. The items are holographic and will disappear once taken, so it's impossible to take them from another player. The battle zone is also holographic, with many hidden energy-projecting drones that will keep players in bounds and provide biofeedback. The players are free to form whatever groups they want. A round ends when there is one contestant left or ten minutes elapse."

Adam pointed rapid-fire finger-guns at the contestants. "Questions?"

"The treasures? What do they look like?" said Del.

"Computer, can I get a treasure from the game?" Adam held out his hand and a chrome orb flickered into existence and then solidified. It had a faint white glow and a technological look, like some kind of drone.

"And if you'll all remain silent, you can hear the best part. They sing." Adam extended his arm toward the group, and they could hear, softly, the orb droning like a synthesizer holding a chord.

"Any more questions?" He pointed around the semicircle. "No? Good? Good.

"Each of you will start with a laser pistol that is serviceable and never runs out of ammo. Scattered around the battlefield are additional weapons you can use, but each has a limited supply of ammunition," said Adam.

"Can we see those?" said Del.

"Nope, it's a surprise." Adam paused for questions.

"Okay, computer. Weapons please."

Light flared at every contestant's hip, solidifying into a small, fat snub-nosed pistol. Maeve plucked it off her hip. It wasn't secured at all. It was just hovering there.

Gray and purple plastic. *Yuck, it's like a kid's toy*, she thought.

"For convenience sake, these guns . . ." Del aimed and fired his pistol at Adam's head. He glowered at Del. The group smiled, and one by one they all started shooting all over the circle. Little bolts of light blinked back and forth. When everyone got it out of their systems, Adam went on.

"As I was saying. None of these guns can be dropped, ensuring you are never without them. If you need both hands, they will stick to your body like a magnet. However, the weapons you find can be taken, dropped, given, and even stolen."

Del opened fire again ruthlessly on Adam's face, making gun sounds with his mouth. Laughter broke out as Adam shook his head and shielded his eyes. "Will you just stop it!"

Everyone straightened up, but Del didn't stop, although his laughter spoiled his aim.

Adam's jovial demeanor was gone now. "Well, I can see you are raring to get things going, so let's begin, shall we? Robots, escort the players to their positions."

9.1

Nine robots marched forward from either side of the courtyard and ushered the contestants out to the edges. Now evenly distributed, the bots made sure the contestants didn't move. A shutter closed over the ceiling, cutting off the light.

"As voted on by our community, the first battlefield is"—Adam laughed—"is this right? The first battlefield is my mansion. Contestants, get ready for round one."

The holographic projectors built into the walls went to work. The whole courtyard shimmered brilliant white light. Everyone squinted or shielded their eyes with their hands. The light died down, and Maeve opened an eye inquisitively.

She took in the surroundings. A large sprawling building, white walls, and large windows. Wraparound yard with a fence made of transparent panels. She heard the distant sounds of surf and noted a distant beach. She looked to her left and right to see who her neighbors were, but couldn't see anyone. *Strange.*

"Ready, set, go!" said Adam. A loud buzzer sounded with his proclamation.

Maeve was standing on the sidewalk, looking at the building's fenced-in front yard. Gun in hand, she ran to the fence and ducked down. It was about four feet tall and transparent. She caught movement on her left. It was one of the Coreys, who had also taken cover behind the fence.

Wonder if I can shoot through this, she thought. Maeve popped up and fired a few shots before she realized the fence, clear as it was, was actually pretty solid cover, or maybe the gun has no real stopping power. She ducked back down, and a shot hit the fence right next to her head. She pushed off the wall and rolled onto her belly with a grunt.

Her eyes darted around, looking for the attacker. There was a car parked on the side of the street. She fired at it randomly. The shots penetrated the car's trunk and shattered the rear windshield.

An arm popped out, blindly firing in her general direction. She carefully got up into a crouching position, her elbow uncomfortably grinding on the pavement. She began crouch-walking with her gun pulled in tightly to her chest.

Her attacker was on the other side of the car and saw her moving. He popped up, and the two fired at each other. She saw a subtle white flash and felt an electric shock in her abdomen.

I can't lose here. Maeve stood up and quickly shuffled around the front of the car. She fired on her attacker the whole way, although the first shot may have done the trick. Her target, Max Chambers, slumped back to the pavement, looking like he was being shocked. More shots *thunked* into the trunk nearby. She took cover and peeked at the fence. Corey was gone. The battlefield momentarily quieted down, and that's when she heard that sound, like gentle music. *The car must have an artifact*, she thought.

She crept, hunched over, around to the side of the car and tried the passenger door. It popped open but unexpectedly swung up. The chorus was louder as she felt around under the seat and opened the various hatches. Nothing. She carefully looked over the top of the car, frantically scanning the battlefield again. Still no one. Maeve ducked back down. She snuck around to the trunk and felt around for the release button with a shaky hand. Glorious light pierced out of the trunk as it opened. Maeve greedily reached in and snatched the orb off the dark gray carpet. Safely behind the car, she watched it fade out of existence.

Staying low, Maeve got up and ran to the fence. She could see that the garage door was open, and it looked safe. Gunshots. She froze and hugged the fence. *That's inside the house, maybe out back*, she thought. She made a break for it, sprinting into the garage.

She could hear that singing sound again, but there was no visible orb. She tried to place her gun down, but it stuck to her hand. *Oh yeah*, she thought and placed the gun on her hip. She got to work opening all the drawers and cabinets as quickly and quietly as she could. Nothing, nothing, *nothing*. She decided it might be on top of the cabinets and stepped up on a large tool chest. Nothing again.

The garage door leading into the house was closed but not latched. It slowly opened a few inches. A figure in the shadows jumped when they spotted Maeve climbing up onto the counter.

Shouldering a long gun, they fired a scattershot of energy, taking a chunk out of the door and blowing it wide open. Maeve jumped down and ran, her hand feeling for her gun.

She had only run a few steps toward the garage door when she got shot. She desperately wanted that gun, but electroshocks were forcing her to the ground. As she went down, she clearly saw her attacker, Naiomi. She suddenly turned and exchanged gunfire with another attacker. She shuddered and went down. Naiomi's attacker took her weapon and disappeared into the darkness.

Lying there, Maeve calmed down, and as long as she didn't move too much, she was shock-free. As she stared at the ceiling, she saw it. The treasure she wanted was in a recessed light fixture on the ceiling above the workbench.

Eventually, she noticed Naiomi was lying there mean mugging her. "What? I should be mad at you. Ow." A force-projecting drone shocked her back into silence.

As the time passed, she heard the occasional gun battle and, finally, a buzzer rang again. *That can be your only screwup. This is life and death now. Make sure it's your life and their death*, she thought.

"And that's round one. Everyone get up and come over to me while we reset the field of play," said Adam over the intercom.

Maeve moved tentatively to see if she could without being shocked. It was okay. She got up and slowly marched out of the garage and looked around, confused as to where she was supposed to go. She saw a robot on the sidelines pointing.

"Oh, thanks," she said. The robot, standing like a signpost, didn't acknowledge her. She walked around the outskirts of the house until she saw Adam and Max Chambers and joined them. The rest of the group filed out and joined them.

Adam took stock of the contestants and spoke. "That was an action-packed round one. Let's take a look at the scoreboard."

At his command, the battlefield faded away in beautiful prismatic light, and that same scoreboard from last week popped up next to Adam.

Laser-Gun Battle
Bryan Cox – 6 Points – 2 Elims – 2 Orbs
Corey Zolton – 5 Points – 2 Elims – 1 Orbs
Diane Snuggles – 4 Points – 1 Elims – 2 Orbs
Rokk Bradley – 4 Points – 1 Elims – 2 Orbs
Del Mitchell – 3 Points – 0 Elims – 3 Orbs

Maeve McKinnon – 3 Points – 1 Elims – 1 Orbs
Naiomi Rachels – 2 Points – 1 Elims – 0 Orbs
I-ON – 0 Points – 0 Elims – 0 Orbs
Max Chambers – 0 Points – 0 Elims – 0 Orbs

"It was a close match, but ultimately Bryan Cox took first place," said Adam. "Bryan, give us your commentary on what happened while we replay the events."

The scoreboard changed into a miniature version of the house, playing back the action that had just occurred.

"Oh, neat," said Naiomi.

"Uh, well, I started on the sidelines here. I was standing on the beach behind the mansion. As I moved forward, I realized I could see some other players, but I was out in the open, so I just sprinted up to the house." He paused while the little recording of him ran across the beach, onto the patio, and hugged the wall.

"The sliding door was already open, so I looked in. It was dark inside. I hesitated until I heard shooting, then I snuck in. While I was looking around, I saw an artifact in a bowl of oranges. Grabbed that." Miniature Bryan did a double take at the kitchen island, then snatched the artifact up and pivoted.

"I heard someone coming, so I ducked into the, uh, whatever that room is. Pantry, I guess? Rokk passed me with a special gun, so I ran out behind him and shot him up. I took his gun. It was an automatic but low on ammo. I retreated to the stairs here because I could hear shooting behind me. I decided to cautiously check for artifacts upstairs. It seemed like there were a lot of them up there because I could constantly hear that humming. I heard shooting really close by, so I crept over to the banister and looked down to see Naiomi shooting a shotgun out the door. I raised my gun and aimed, but she suddenly got hit and went down."

"I ducked back down the hallway and went back to my artifact hunt. Finally, I found one in a drawer upstairs. I was about to switch to the other room when the professor ducked into my room." Miniature Bryan and Diane startled each other and began firing wildly. "So I just unloaded everything the gun had. But it looks like she got me once there. I didn't even notice. I went down the hall to see if anyone was coming, but that's when I heard the floorboard creak, and Corey got me from this darkened room over here."

"An exciting start to our laser-gun battle. Bryan Cox takes an early lead, but Corey, Diane, and Rokk are right on his heels. Who will claim victory in round two? Find out after this!" Adam waited a beat. "And we're back. Contestants, are you ready for the next exciting round?"

The group gave back a few "yeahs" and some nodding.

"Oh come on, you can do better than that!"

The group responded with a little more oomph. Maeve, however, grimaced and took a deep breath through her nose. This crowd-warming, I-can't-hear-you bullshit had always made her rage since she was a wee girl.

"Okay! Robots, please escort the contestants to their randomly chosen spots."

Just as before, the robotic crew escorted everyone around the outskirts of the courtyard. This time, Maeve thought ahead and kept an eye on the professor. As she came to a stop, she was almost directly across the courtyard from her. Naiomi and I-ON lay between them to their left, which must have been on the edge of the battlefield. Maeve looked across to the professor, who was already looking at her. She tried to make it look like she was scratching her shoulder while pointing to the left. The professor nodded subtly.

"And now I present you the second map voted on by our *Walk Amongst the Stars* audience." Adam paused, listening to the location Mr. Yang dictated to him. "This next map takes place in the dark depths and winding corridors of the abandoned Grand Tolvern mine."

The holographic map built the terrain in brilliant white light again. After a minute, things solidified, and everything plunged into darkness. Then the start buzzer echoed.

9.2

Maeve opened her eyes wide, trying to force some light inside. Looking around, she finally saw some faint light coming from a hallway. As she turned, light glinted off a striped, yellow handrail, even in this low light. With her hands outstretched, she felt her way through the darkness. She gripped the handrail and looked down at a sheer cliff and a chasm that stretched on toward some distant dot of light. She could hear water dripping and running somewhere in the dark. All that scenery was obviously the edge of the map.

She realized she was wasting time and followed the railing to the wall and groped along the rocky wall, taking cautious steps. Suddenly, she realized she had been hearing that artifact sound. It was muted, almost inaudible.

She placed her gun on her hip like before and knelt down in front of a stack of dark shapes. They were plastic storage boxes. She opened one and set it to the side. As she worked, her eyes continued to adjust to the dark, and now she could tell one of them was bright orange. She anxiously pulled it toward her, toppling the pile of boxes. She sucked air through her teeth as she tried to steady the boxes. It was too late, and in her haste to set the pile right, she backhanded a box. It sounded like little bits of metal pinged and scattered across the floor. She put her stinging hand on her stomach and put her other hand on it while she silently swore to herself. As she grabbed the lid, slightly parting the seam, the sound got louder, and the lit seam cut a bright line across the cave. She squinted and reached into the box, holding the artifact until it vanished in her hand.

Maeve drew her ugly gun and crept down the hall. It got less gloomy as she went. She could hear distant echoing gunfire and tensed up. With no idea where it was coming from, she steeled herself and peered into the next room.

It was a massive cave with high ceilings, dark, craggy rock walls draped with cords of industrial lights. There was a big yellow mining vehicle parked in the middle of the floor space striped with black caution lines. Stacked up around the vehicle were large metal crates and mining equipment. The seams in the walls emitted a dull violet glow, probably Varium. (That wonder mineral that powers modern printing tech, among other things.) There were three other small tunnels like hers, and a very large cave opening to the right. From what Maeve could recall, five players were down there somewhere.

She rushed over to the mining machine. It looked like substantial cover, and it was large enough to stand behind fully upright. *I guess I can ambush the other two here*, she thought. As she waited, she kept glancing back at the main cave behind her.

Movement caught her eye, and she pointed her gun at a shadow in one of the tunnels. The shadowy person had their hand up in a greeting and had blazing neon eyes. Maeve lowered her gun and looked over the top of the machine, still clear. She waved the professor over, who ducked and darted around the back of the mining machine.

Maeve ducked down to whisper to the professor. "I haven't seen the other two yet. Did you find any treasures?" Maeve said.

"Yes, I started out next to one."

"Okay, me too. You want to search this room while I cover you?"

The professor nodded and pushed off Maeve's shoulder standing up. She scooted past Maeve and started looking into the metal crates. Gunfire echoed out, boomingly loud this time. Closer. It occurred to her that this was clearly laser weapon noises and last time was . . . something else. Maeve pointed her gun anxiously. The professor ducked behind some crates, then started searching them. Finally, the professor lifted a glowing orb into the air. "Got one," she whispered loudly.

Maeve looked at her hand just in time to see it vanish. "Nice."

Maeve felt a prickly sense inside. She gazed into one of the dark tunnels and shouted, "Look out!" Maeve fired wildly into the dark tunnel. Her energy bolts illuminated a figure who panicked and pivoted back around the corner.

The two of them waited, guns trained on the rocky hallway. Nothing happened for what felt like forever. Maeve went around the side of the vehicle, moving toward the cab. The figure popped out and fired. Maeve dropped to the dirt while the professor fired. The dark figure took a hit and ducked into cover again.

Maeve grew bolder. Getting up, she stalked toward the tunnel, gun at the ready. She moved slowly, breathing shallow, unblinking. The dark figure returned. Maeve fired instantly, so fast she surprised herself, and kept shooting. The dark figure, which Maeve could see now was Naiomi, struggled against her virtual death and finally lay flat in the hall.

The professor looked as relieved as Maeve felt.

"Quick, let's finish the crates off," said the professor, who popped open another latch and lifted the lid. Maeve did the same on her side but only used one hand so she could be ready to shoot. There could still be another player on this side.

On the last crate, the professor gasped and leaned far into one of the large metal crates. Maeve stalked around the mining machine to see what was up and saw the professor slipping on a boxy metal backpack and then clicking home a seat belt–like restraint across her chest. She cinched it up and then reeled in a rubber tube that attached to a large bored two-handed gun. Some kind of mining tool. The professor turned around with a savage, toothy grin. "I think we're done here."

"I want to check in there. I think I-ON's dead, but I want to make sure we don't get hit from behind." As if to underscore her point, booming shots came from the next cave over, the first in a while.

"Also, you need more treasure to catch up to me." The professor smiled down at her big gun.

"Let's go." Maeve stalked over to that hall, and the professor followed suit. They made it inside the tunnel and had to skirt around Naiomi, who scowled at them as they went by.

"Maeve! I—Oww." Naiomi whined as she was zapped into silence.

Maeve held a finger to her lips and tried not to giggle.

They continued to the end of the hall, where it turned off into a darkened room. Maeve looked back. The professor seemed ready. She pivoted around the corner, pointing her gun around the darkened room. Then the professor followed suit. A figure sat on the floor leaning against the rocky wall.

"I-ON? Are you eliminated?" she said.

No response. Maeve advanced upon the slumped figure. She gingerly poked the robot with her gun. "I think it's down. Keep it covered while I look for an artifact."

The professor got out of the doorway and kept her weapon pointed at I-ON.

This little cave was stiflingly hot, with large white crystals growing out of cracks in the rocky walls. Stacked up against the wall was a pile of crates like the ones she started nearby, so she got down on her hands and knees and dug into them, listening for the quiet sound the artifacts made. Nothing. She got up and instinctively dusted her hands off on her pants.

A few gunshots echoed in the distance, too distant to matter.

Maeve was ready to leave when she looked at the light fixture above the door. It gave off little to no light. More like it was blocking the light.

She got underneath it and stretched up on one tippy-toe and plucked the face off. Light blasted the room along with a pleasant singing tone. She backed up to the wall, ran, and jumped with a grunt. She grabbed it out of its hiding place. The entire room shimmered until it faded away, leaving the two in an even deeper darkness than before.

"Let's go," said Maeve.

The professor backed away from the fallen robot and followed Maeve as she rushed to the large cave. They crossed the open ground more slowly, keeping a keen eye on the cave that led to the remaining players. They entered the last starting position on this side of the battlefield.

This cave was open like the one Maeve had started in. If they could have seen better, she and Naiomi might have had a shootout right away. But it had the same things in it as the cave they'd just come from. Maeve pointed up at the light fixture, hoping that it had another orb. The professor followed Maeve's gesture to the light fixture. She jumped up easily, even with the heavy weapon, and batted the face off the light, illuminating the room. With another high jump, she snatched it. She admired the orb in her hand through squinted eyes until it vanished and her grasp fell inward.

"Thanks," said the professor.

"Cool, let's go."

Back out in the main cave, everything was quiet and eerie. Maeve pointed to the cave, connecting them to the rest of the players. The professor nodded, and they jogged over to the entrance and looked in. It immediately took a right turn onto a steel bridge, another cave opening at the end on the left. They padded down the bridge. It clanked softly underfoot. Dust filtered through the mesh floor into a natural trough below.

9.3

The professor and Maeve took turns peering into the cave entrance at the end of the bridge. It was a colossal cavern with concrete pillars that stretched up into darkness. The columns were in rows along the left and right sides of the cavern. A dirt road ran between the two sets of columns, leading to an immense gate. Probably the map's boundary. Vehicles, equipment, containers, and several trailers lined the cave walls.

Maeve suddenly remembered the game's time limit. It felt like they had been at this forever. She reminded herself that they were doing well, but it did little to quiet the precarious feeling in her chest.

Maeve leaned in close and said, "I don't see anyone, not even any eliminated players. There could be five of them hiding in here."

"But we heard so much shooting. There might be only one left. What's our move? Take cover by the pillars?" The professor pointed to a nearby fat pillar.

"Yeah, then we'll move right and get into those trailers. We've got a good strategy going on, and I'm not sure how much time."

The professor tightened up her bulky backpack. "All right, cover me, I'm going." She leaned out of the entrance and took off sprinting.

Maeve, caught a little off guard, hurriedly peeked out the entrance, gun at the ready. She scanned around the cave. It was a ghost town. Diane waved at her from behind the pillar, so she pushed off the wall and ran.

As she was moving, she spotted a player lying on their back in her peripheral vision. She sped up a little unconsciously. The professor came into view, pointing her industrial-looking gun, and finally she came to a slapping stop against the pillar.

"Saw a downed player, one of the smaller guys, Corey, maybe Del," Maeve breathed.

The professor looked around the pillar and spotted the player on his back.

"It's Corey. He's lying next to a stack of crates. I think he was treasure hunting." The professor pointed over to the trailer, the door already propped open. "Let's go."

"Like before, you go first." Maeve peeked around the pillar. The professor sprinted to the doorway. The silence shattered. It was that booming gun they kept hearing. A laser bolt zipped past like lightning and stirred up a puff of dirt on the rocky floor behind the professor. Maeve struggled to see where the shot came from.

Another bolt whizzed by, revealing the attacker. Up above, a building on the right. Shaken, she started firing randomly at the area.

The professor dove through the doorway and sprawled on the floor, sliding between a couch and a table. She got up on her knees and turned around, bumping a chair away from the kitchen table. Another shot streaked into the open doorway and hit the table with a loud knock.

Maeve used the opportunity to rush from cover to cover. She then dove onto the floor in front of the professor. Another shot came through the doorway with her.

"The shooter is up in the rightmost corner of the cave. I couldn't see anyone, though," said Maeve.

"Remember, we're not here for a shootout. We're here for the treasures. Now let's find them."

They both cautiously got to their feet. They were in the kitchen area of the trailer. The next room over was a living room area with a large bay window. Maeve stepped over and, with a few tugs on the cord, the vertical blinds shimmied across the window, leaving the room much darker. She braced herself for the sniper to make a rebuttal, but nothing happened.

The professor went past Maeve into the living room and started looking into things. Maeve studied the door and concluded that to get to the other side of the kitchen, she'd have to skirt around to the back of the trailer and be mindful of the door while searching.

She went over and opened a cabinet. Nothing interesting, just dishes. The next cabinet was in shambles, puffed rice spilled out when she opened it. Boxes all over the place. The next was already ajar, a pot handle sticking out. She looked inside to confirm what she was already thinking.

"Someone's been here," she spoke across the trailer for her companion to hear.

"Yeah, everything is crooked and shuffled in here. Do you think we sh—" *Boom.* Maeve hugged the wall. The professor cringed. This time, additional gunfire chimed in. *Pop-pop-pop.*

The professor ducked down and vanished behind the couch, then popped back up near the window. She pushed the clacky plastic blinds to the side a crack and peeked out.

Adam came over the speaker system. "Running low on time, contestants. Better move it."

The professor pivoted away from the window. "Uh-oh! We're out of time."

"New plan: rush the sniper. He's already busy with that guy," said Maeve.

The professor looked at her incredulously and went slack-jawed as Maeve rushed through the kitchen, out the front door. The professor followed, racing across the open dirt, back to the support column from before. Maeve was already there, shooting at the sniper. The professor landed against the column next to Maeve.

"I'll keep this up. Flank to the right and see if you can get a shot on him," said Maeve.

The professor pushed off the support and ran to the next column to the right. As she was moving, she watched the burst-fire guy climbing out of the trailer onto its roof. He was using Maeve's cover fire to gain ground. The professor was in position. She could see the sniper. She gripped the strange tool. It had top and rear handles like an industrial saw.

When she pulled the trigger, a scintillating sphere of energy formed at the tip. The professor's pupils became slits. A stream of energy issued forth with an electric shriek. Startled by the violence of her own weapon, the professor struggled to control it. The energy beam hit behind the sniper's location, and she shakily raked the beam over to the left. The sniper stumbled to his feet and dove forward over his own cover, narrowly escaping the beam.

The other combatant, burst-fire guy, wasted no time finishing the sniper off when he landed prostrate at the edge of his own rooftop. There was a curious pause while everyone felt relieved. The sniper was gone.

Maeve laid down slow, steady cover fire on the remaining combatant. Burst-fire guy shot at Maeve's column as he retreated. He jumped into the hatch he climbed out of. The professor's gun let out another shriek. She cut a line across the part of the trailer he went into. It left a long, burning cut in the wall.

Maeve sprinted across the battlefield up to a column on the other side of the road. The gunner had gotten up on a table and fired at Maeve through the window as she ran closer. She felt the electric shock of a simulated hit. It broke her stride, but she kept running and made it to cover.

Another electric shriek. The professor carved another line up, almost perpendicular to the last one. The window shattered as the beam hit it. The gunner inside threw himself away from the beam. Another shriek cut across the trailer; the cuts overlapped, forming a huge triangle, which twisted and fell out of the structure with a metallic squall, exposing much of the room. Burst-fire guy, flipped over a table and propped his gun up on it.

Maeve, marching forth, started putting rounds into the table. *This is it!*

A loud buzzer sounded over the loudspeakers. She pulled the trigger, but nothing happened. She stopped and looked at the gun as it was dissolving.

"And that's time! Contestants, you are now free to move. Come on over, and we'll go over the score," said Adam over the intercom.

Burst-fire guy was Bryan Cox, who peeked up out of cover. He put a hand on the table and stood with a grunt.

"I had you," said Maeve.

"It was looking grim . . ." Bryan hopped out of the casually burning hole in the wall. "I'll give you that."

Bryan, Maeve, and the professor grouped up and walked back. The rest got up and came back to where Adam was, helpful robots guiding the way again. When the group was all gathered around, the virtual battlefield went all rainbow silhouettes and faded away.

"Let's take a look at how that round went," said Adam, sweeping a hand over an already forming holographic scoreboard.

Laser-Gun Battle

Bryan Cox – 5 Points – 1 Elims – 3 Orbs
Del Mitchell – 4 Points – 1 Elims – 2 Orbs
Maeve McKinnon – 4 Points – 1 Elims – 2 Orbs
Max Chambers – 4 Points – 1 Elims – 2 Orbs
Diane Snuggles – 3 Points – 0 Elims – 3 Orbs
Rokk Bradley – 3 Points – 1 Elims – 1 Orbs
Naiomi Rachels – 2 Points – 1 Elims – 0 Orbs
Corey Zolton – 1 Points – 0 Elims – 1 Orbs
I-ON – 0 Points – 0 Elims – 0 Orbs

"Bryan takes another victory. Let's see the overall score now." The numbers added up in real time, then the names rearranged.

Laser-Gun Battle

Bryan Cox – 11 Points – 3 Elims – 5 Orbs
Del Mitchell – 07 Points – 1 Elims – 5 Orbs

Diane Snuggles – 07 Points – 1 Elims – 5 Orbs
Maeve McKinnon – 07 Points – 2 Elims – 3 Orbs
Rokk Bradley – 07 Points – 2 Elims – 3 Orbs
Corey Zolton – 06 Points – 2 Elims – 2 Orbs
Max Chambers – 04 Points – 1 Elims – 2 Orbs
Naiomi Rachels – 04 Points – 2 Elims – 0 Orbs
I-ON – 00 Points – 0 Elims – 0 Orbs

"And now let's go over the action," said Adam. The hologram once again shifted to a small display of the battle. Adam sauntered over to Bryan and clasped his shoulder.

"Okay, give us the play-by-play, champ."

Bryan laughed breathlessly. "Well I started out . . ."

Maeve zoned out, looking at the miniature replay of the battle. While the miniature players searched and fought, she thought about her total points. *Everyone got seven points. I'm fourth. That's not good enough. If we don't get into the top three, none of this matters.* The thought sank into the pit in her stomach. She internally debated last round's strategy while Bryan continued his play-by-play. When he finished, she had resolved to tell Diane that they needed to take bigger risks in order to win.

"What an exciting round. Let's move on to round three . . . after this," said Adam, then he paused for a second. "And we're back. Let's get our contestants in place for round three!" He swept his hand as the robots came back over to escort the contestants.

The robots escorted Maeve very close to where she had been before, against the wall that led to the front of the ship. As she was being escorted, she didn't see Diane. To her left was I-ON, and to her right was Del. She looked at I-ON again, and thought, *zero points . . .*

Then Maeve's heart sank. She caught sight of the professor about as far away as possible, against the aft wall of the courtyard.

9.4

The unpleasantly bright golden light bathed the little park again. The contestants shielded their eyes until the lights and shapes finished knitting together.

"This next battlefield is from the upcoming game, *Cosmic: Z-Force*. Pre-order *Z-Force* today and get our special *Walk Amongst the Stars* camo," said Adam.

Maeve opened her eyes to a cold, gray, overcast sky. Now she was in a snowy forest overgrown with bushes and evergreens. Immediately in front of her was a snowmobile and some militaristic boxes. Behind her, a set of fallen logs formed a boundary, all wearing a thick layer of snow.

"Ready, set, go!" said Adam.

That fugly laser gun materialized in her hand, and she immediately popped it onto her hip. She took a couple of steps, relishing the feel of the snow crushing beneath her shoes. If she was lucky, it snowed once a year where she lived—where she used to live—and it never stuck.

She brushed aside a layer of snow from the containers and knelt down. Already she could hear the singing sounds of treasure. *It looks like they always start us near one.* As fast as she could manage, she flipped open all the metal boxes, dumping them over as she went. One box gleamed as she opened it. She stuffed her hand in and grabbed the orb while turning her attention to the snowmobile. It had two compartments built into each side. As she searched them, she felt the orb transmute from treasure to score. When she pulled her hand from the third compartment, it came back holding a large pistol.

She took it out and ejected the magazine. A built-in display on the side went down to zero as the clear magazine with a stagger of bullets popped out. Slapping it home, the display went back up to twenty. She racked the slide and pointed it at the path leading out of her little clearing and examined the sights. She turned the gun to the side and admired it again with a pleased little "hmm."

The wind picked up and whispered through the trees surrounding her. It suddenly occurred to her just how cold it had gotten as the wind blew. *Is that all in my head or did they crank the AC?*

She got to her feet and went over to the path that connected to her little clearing. The path went left and right and was big enough to drive a compact car through, except that it was strewn with obstacles to hide behind, boulders, trees, and such.

She heard a laser gun *pew-pewing* in the distance. She checked to the right for Del. He was over there somewhere, but the coast was clear now. She sprinted onto the path, zigzagging between cover with a flighty feeling in her heart.

Gotta get to I-ON first. She rounded a corner. This path was kind of like one of those oval-shaped foot tracks. Further down range, Rokk also ran out of his hiding spot. He pivoted and opened fire.

Lasers stabbed into the terrain around her, and she fled into the side passage that should lead to I-ON. Clinging to the relative safety of her position, she forced herself to take a few breaths, to catch up.

She pointed her gun and edged forward into another small clearing not too dissimilar from her start point. Then she saw exactly what she thought she would find—I-ON sitting cross-legged, hands folded in its lap. I-ON regarded her but took no action. I-ON's clearing was a little campsite, and the robot was seated behind a little campfire. *Did they put I-ON here on purpose, as a joke?*

Maeve edged forward, leading with her new gun. "What are you doing? I saw you sitting around last game, too."

"I am waiting for this game to end."

"You're not worried about your score?"

"No."

She was stunned, but then she reasserted herself by pointing her gun.

"Yeah? Well, I am. Now tell me where the treasure is."

I-ON lifted its head, then cocked it at an angle, then slightly more, then pointed.

"Inside that woodpile."

Maeve rushed over to a pile of chopped wood and shoved things around until she saw the golden rays. She took hold of her prize and turned back to I-ON as it faded away.

"Thanks." She turned and peeked into the path again, no longer afraid the robot would shoot her in the back.

"You may shoot me."

She looked back, eyebrows raised.

"If you do not, someone else will," it said.

She tramped over, and I-ON bowed its head. She leveled the gun and took a breath, but she couldn't stop the barrel from wavering. *This is too weird. I can't just shoot him.*

She lowered her gun and looked back at the entrance again, just in case. Without turning back to I-ON, she spoke. "How about you come with me and help me find all the treasures?"

"No."

Maeve whirled around. "Why? You're just sitting here?"

"None of this matters."

Maeve's expression got hard, and she pointed the gun at the robot's head. "It-it doesn't matter? I guess it doesn't matter that I got arrested and lost *everything*. That I got sent here. It doesn't matter that I was treated like a freak. Guess it doesn't matter that our lives are ending one *stupid* contest at a time." She poked the robot in the head with the gun menacingly. The aggression inhibitor gripped her system, slowing her movement. Despite the lump forming in her throat, she croaked, "How could this matter any more?"

A laser shot grazed Maeve's side. She shrieked, totally surprised at the electroshock. The world slowed down, and she turned on her attacker. She watched as I-ON grabbed its laser pistol with inhuman speed and fired it dangerously close to her body. Her sights landed on Del, but he was already standing with his back arched, mouth open. He landed on hands and knees, then flopped onto the fake snow into a fetal position.

Maeve was coursing with adrenaline but finally managed to speak. "Thought it didn't matter?"

I-ON stood up. "You are not the only freak."

9.5

Distant shots echoed while Maeve took stock of the situation. She turned to I-ON and held out her pistol, grip first. I-ON put his own gun on his hip like Maeve had hers and accepted the new weapon.

"I want you to follow me and be my bodyguard. If you notice any treasures, point them out to me. Shoot anyone we encounter. Oh, except for Diane. If you see her . . . I don't know, just hide, I guess. Okay?"

"Acknowledged."

Maeve walked to the forest path and checked for enemies. *Coast is clear*, she thought and then darted across the path to cover. I-ON followed behind, gun ready at a slower pace, more of a power walk. He looked very intimidating, armed with the heavy pistol.

She went back the way she came. While getting here, she went past a path that led out of the outer path into the middle of the map. Back at that path, she stalked around the corner, gun drawn. I-ON followed her, standing tall, pointing his own pistol over the top of Maeve. At the end of this path, she saw a stack of logs and made a break for them. She slid to a stop behind them, her shoe slapping loudly.

Laser shots flew past her log cover, then I-ON came marching in. He could see the attacker sticking out from behind a pickup truck. It was Rokk. I-ON fired thrice while moving forward to take cover with Maeve. The first shot hit him in the face, the second a total miss, then again in the chest. Rokk fell back into the thin layer of soft snow, eliminated.

I-ON crouched near Maeve and tossed her gun on the ground in front of her and drew his original laser pistol.

"This gun is better," he said.

"Wow, seriously? Okay," said Maeve while she took the gun back up. She got up into a stooped-over position and looked around the battlefield. This was a large forest clearing with burning rubble in the middle that used to be a log cabin. A shed sat next to it on the right, the pickup on the far left side.

"I'll cover you from here while you go search that middle area for treasures," she said. Maeve awkwardly leaned over the cover, which gave her stability but kind of hurt her back. I-ON got up and marched forth.

Halfway there, he stopped and pointed his gun at the clearing for a second. Maeve saw it, too. Someone rushed past the clearing behind the pickup truck. The robot finished marching toward the burned rubble. It scanned over the rubble, cocking its head back and forth. I-ON beckoned her over, flipping his hand at her.

She got up and swung around the cover, rushing over. As she moved, I-ON reached into the burned rubble and pulled out a mesh container. It easily screeched out of the burned remains and slammed down. Maeve opened the charred grayish-black door and took the treasure. Then I-ON pointed into the burning cabin. Maeve ducked into the ruined doorway of the collapsed building and looked back to I-ON after not finding anything. He pointed at the large fire still burning inside.

Oh smart, she thought. She got down on the dirt and put her hand near the fire, testing it. Satisfied that it was only a hologram, she stuffed her hand into it, finding another artifact. As she pulled it out, the fire noticeably dimmed.

More gunshots. She cautiously emerged while I-ON scanned around with his gun.

Maeve rushed over to the shed. The door had an old-looking padlock threaded through iron loops. The lock itself hung open, merely keeping the door closed. She tossed it to the side, and the door swung ajar. She nudged the door and stepped up into the dim shed.

Inside there were cupboards, shelves, and drawers, all bursting with old junk. Some fit for a garage, some for a pantry, but mostly fit for the garbage bin. Everything in here had a layer of dust and cobwebs, but she could still hear the quiet sound of yet another treasure.

The shooting outside kicked up again. She felt strangely safe here in the shed. It wouldn't stand up to any real firepower, but one would have to know she was in here to attack. She thought of the time limit and looked at the shelves bursting with things. *Time for drastic measures*, she thought.

The shelves were first. She violently swept everything off. Ancient-looking mason jars smashed and bonked against the wall and floor. She got down and searched the lower cabinets, yanking out and tossing old hunks of metal. *Engine parts*, she thought. She grabbed a set of tubes and almost threw them back with some old pistons, gears, and springs, but the profile of the thing caught her eye. She was holding the killing end of a double-barreled shotgun. Maeve gasped in delight, devilish glee in her eyes. She spent a moment repositioning all her guns. Then dug around, putting her hands on a few more grimy old parts before giving up.

She stood and reached into the upper cabinets and scooped out an armload of junk-drawer caliber crap. It all clanked and clattered down on the countertop below. Something way back in there caught her eye, a forgotten old Christmas gift. She tore into it and wrenched off the box top. Squinting into the intense light, she claimed some extra score. She carefully stepped around the soggy, broken glass on the floor back to the door. She took a peek outside, nothing new.

Unfamiliar with this kind of gun, she examined it. Dark wooden stock with a maroon wrap that held extra shells. Two triggers, one for each longish barrel. Two mechanisms on top of the stock. A metal tab that she pushed forward, revealing a red square, then back: a safety switch. And a lever, which she tweaked, causing the barrel to swing down, revealing two shells inside. She plucked one out of the tube. A shiny brass tab connected to a clear plastic tube with large pellets inside. She replaced it and, with more effort than she was expecting, snapped the barrel closed.

She disabled the safety on her new weapon and stepped down from the old shed. After slinging all those engine parts, she was hot, uncomfortably so. It felt great to be back outside in the cool breeze. She ducked down with her new gun drawn and hustled over to I-ON. "I got the goods." She spoke softly, accentuating her shotgun.

"Another player sneaked in over there, but I can not determine who it is," I-ON said.

Hearing I-ON speak, Bryan slid up over the metal panels of the nearby pickup truck, next to the helpless body of Rokk. He unleashed a violent, barely controlled spray of bullets from a submachine gun. I-ON got hit hard, almost eliminated. Though his aim was off, he managed to stun Bryan. Maeve grabbed her pistol with her off hand and fired a few rounds off as accurately as she could. Hit, Bryan slid back down the truck's hood and out of sight.

9.6

This round, Max Chambers hadn't been able to find any tech to give him an advantage. Oh, how he missed the scoped rifle from the last round. So he had to rely on stealth, creeping around the outside track. Moments ago, he ambushed and shot the professor in the back. Now he made his way halfway across the map to the same path Maeve and I-ON had used to reach the center.

As he moved down the path, he came to the bunker made up of stacked logs. He peeked around the logs to see the robot from behind. One of the girls came out of the shed nearby, the brunette, and walked over to the robot with a shotgun. *They're working together, how devious. If the robot is anything like military issue, it has to die first. Then again, that shotgun could be a problem*, he thought.

A skirmish broke out. Max hugged his cover. From this vantage, he could see his two enemies shooting at a third party. *Perfect.* He stood and planted his feet. *The machine first, then the girl*, he thought. He took a breath and shot I-ON in the back multiple times. I-ON went rigid and fell forward. The girl pivoted, wide-eyed. His adrenaline surging, he fired right where she just was and then overcompensated, shooting too far to the right. He took another breath and lined up the killing shot.

9.7

Gunfire rained down on I-ON from behind. Maeve whirled. She brought the shotgun's butt to her shoulder and placed the barrel across her off hand, still clutching the pistol. A shot whizzed past her face, sounding like a turbo-charged electric hummingbird. With a grimace, she pulled both triggers. Slightly offset explosions battered the gun into her shoulder. Maeve rocked back on her heels. The gun levered upward.

Max Chambers seemed to get taller as the electricity seized him. Then he guided himself to the ground in a controlled fall.

Maeve raised the pistol and shakily pointed it at every piece of cover she could find. Suddenly, she felt exposed. An attack could come from anywhere. She backed away until she was up against the burning cabin. She popped open the breach on the shotgun, and a buzzer sounded. Maeve gasped. The guns faded away in her hands.

"And that's the game! Everyone get up and come on in to see the results," said Adam.

"I won," she whispered.

She tromped over to I-ON who was just getting to his feet.

"We did it." She extended a hand to I-ON, who tilted his head and studied this gesture. Then he gently clasped her hand and shook. He turned that studying look back to Maeve's face. She couldn't help but giggle at this.

"Thanks for your help. I'm sure I won that round because of you."

"You are welcome."

"I'm one step closer to getting out of here."

"We *all* are," I-ON said in a hushed tone that sounded somber.

For a second, that didn't compute, but then Maeve thought about Zalak clawing at the uncaring universe as he spiraled into darkness. *Ooh, that's dark.*

They started walking just as a robot was coming over to round them up. After everyone was on their feet and moving, the whole place disappeared like before. The large overhead shutters opened up and let in the afternoon sun. As Maeve watched snow-covered evergreens vanish only to be replaced by a red-leafed deciduous, one of the park's real trees, she realized the maps were designed to hide the natural obstacles. Otherwise, they would have been running headlong into them.

Soon, everyone made their way over to Adam.

"As the clear winner of this round, why don't you take us through the action?"

Maeve looked at the small virtual replay of the action and took a breath.

"After this!" Adam butted in.

Maeve deflated.

"And we're back!" said Adam.

She composed herself and began. "First, I searched the starting room for goodies. We always seem to start near one." A few contestants nodded.

"I saw in the previous two replays that I-ON doesn't participate in the game, and so I went to convince him to help me."

"Oh, and how did you manage that?" said Adam with a smile.

"We talked, and I think he was sympathetic."

"Really? Mr. Yang, could you please enhance the image?"

The playback vanished, showing a still image of Maeve snarling with a gun to I-ON's head.

The crowd murmured. "Oh-ho damn!" and "Get it gurl" cut through.

"It's not like that," Maeve said, getting angry.

Adam pretended to look startled and raised his arms in surrender. The replay continued, and Maeve finished commentating the battle she'd just gone through.

"Now let's take a look at the score, assuming that's okay with you, killer," said Adam.

Maeve grumpily waved him off, and the scoreboard appeared by Adam.

Laser-Gun Battle

Maeve McKinnon – 9 Points – 2 Elims – 5 Orbs
Max Chambers – 5 Points – 2 Elims – 1 Orbs
I-ON – 4 Points – 2 Elims – 0 Orbs
Bryan Cox – 3 Points – 1 Elims – 1 Orbs
Rokk Bradley – 3 Points – 1 Elims – 1 Orbs
Corey Zolton – 1 Points – 0 Elims – 1 Orbs
Del Mitchell – 1 Points – 0 Elims – 1 Orbs
Diane Snuggles – 1 Points – 0 Elims – 1 Orbs
Naiomi Rachels – 1 Points – 0 Elims – 1 Orbs

"We have Maeve in first, followed by Max, then I-ON." Adam stepped over to I-ON. "Don't worry. Mean ole Maeve can't push you around anymore."

"Okay, let's see the score after all three rounds." The scores increased, and the names moved around to reflect the changes.

Laser-Gun Battle

Maeve McKinnon – 16 Points – 4 Elims – 8 Orbs
Bryan Cox – 14 Points – 4 Elims – 6 Orbs
Rokk Bradley – 10 Points – 3 Elims – 4 Orbs
Max Chambers – 09 Points – 3 Elims – 3 Orbs
Del Mitchell – 08 Points – 1 Elims – 6 Orbs
Diane Snuggles – 08 Points – 1 Elims – 6 Orbs
Corey Zolton – 07 Points – 2 Elims – 3 Orbs
Naiomi Rachels – 05 Points – 2 Elims – 1 Orbs

I-ON – 04 Points – 2 Elims – 0 Orbs

"Congratulations Maeve McKinnon, you win first place and a large bonus to your popularity score," said Adam, shaking her hand.

She couldn't believe that she won. Tears crept into the corners of her eyes.

"Bryan and Rokk, you get a boost to your scores as well, and the rest of you will have to get by on charm alone."

"Okay, contestants, go and live it up. This time tomorrow, we'll hold the second voting ceremony. And you know what that means."

9.8

After being dismissed, I-ON left first, moving directly home. Another robot was in his path, and the two bots did that awkward thing where every time one adjusted to the left or right, so did the other, and they slowly walked into each other. I-ON placed its hand on the other robot's shoulder with a clank. "Very sorry," said I-ON.

Maeve had watched him go and snickered at the whole interaction. After that last round, she saw I-ON in a different light—not just a malfunctioning robot to be feared but a person, kind of. One who was admittedly still kind of weird and scary.

You are not the only freak, she thought. *That's what changed my mind. It, no, he feels like an outcast.* Maeve watched him enter his cabin and then turned to go to her own cabin. She crossed paths with the professor and held out her hand for a high five. The professor smiled and returned a muffled, fuzzy high five.

Once back in her cabin, she realized the professor didn't make the top three and suddenly felt like an asshole.

She made herself a half sandwich stuffed with too many potato chips and then took a shower. Afterward, she went into VR and filled Colin in on the day's events. They spent some quality time together before it was time to go to dinner.

9.9

Maeve gussied up in front of the mirror before heading out to the camp setup.

She was a bit early and got there just as the robots were finishing the setup, placing cooked foods that billowed steam. Bryan and Max Chambers were already there, chatting. Maeve walked over and hung around outside the conversation until the robots cleared out. She sneaked over and grabbed a plate. The two others left off their conversation to join in.

This time around, it was a turkey feast, Earth style, with a big fried bird and all the usual sides. (One of a handful of factoids she remembered about the place from her school days.) Maeve was in front of the mashed potatoes and gravy. She blobbed some on her plate and then sidestepped around the table to fork up some presliced turkey. She got to some kind of creamy vegetable thing, frowned at it, and moved on, skipping over to the mac and cheese. The other two were wordlessly digging in as well. In the background, the rest of the crew were filing in now. Using some tongs, Maeve grabbed some french fries and fried stuffing sticks and found what she was looking for all along, the cranberry gelatin parfait. Her plate over full, she found a spot at the picnic tables and sat down.

She dug in, while Bryan and Max caught up to her and took seats at the table. Max Chambers always arrived early so he could claim the head of the table. He began carefully eating with a knife and fork while Maeve was employing more of a shoveling action.

"Good shooting out there, by the way," said Max, leaning forward in his chair.

"Oh, I just happened to have the right tool for the job, that's all," she said.

"You're being modest. I thought for sure I had you two when I finally got behind you."

"Uh, thanks." She sheepishly looked down at the alluring food on her plate. She dunked some turkey in the potatoes and gravy and went back to eating.

There was a lull in the conversation while everyone ate. Maeve crunched into her stuffing sticks.

"I'm a bit of a marksman." Max Chambers took a sip of water. "I thought I had that second round," he said.

Bryan piped up. "I don't know about you, but I wasn't going to make the first move. I think we were deadlocked, and we would have just sat there until it ended."

"Yes, I suppose."

The professor placed her plate on the table next to Maeve. She had to do a little hop to sit on the bench, and her feet didn't touch the ground. Maeve acknowledged her with a smile in her eyes and a cheek bulging with stuffing.

Maeve leaned back and looked over at the other picnic table while she started on the parfait. Del, Naiomi, and the Coreys were sitting together. Her eyes drifted across the entire scene but then darted back for a double take. Naiomi was clutching Del's arm. He was grinning like an idiot. *M-hmm?* she thought.

Rokk sat across from Maeve, a bit of bone sticking out of his mouth, and set down not a plate but the platter containing the rest of the turkey, which he had loaded with side items. He worked the meat off and plucked the bone out of his mouth. "Mmmphf, good eats."

"Agreed," said the professor who daintily ate some turkey.

"Getting back to the laser battle. Using the robot to do your dirty work really was a stroke of genius," Max Chambers said, pointing his fork at Maeve. "I wish I had thought of that."

Maeve looked surprised. "It's not—I wasn't—I just asked him to help since he wasn't playing. It's not like I used him or anything."

"Regardless, I wish I had thought to get the killer robot to defend me while I got all the goodies, that's all. Assuming he doesn't get booted off the show for slacking off, I may try to recruit him next time, fair warning."

Rokk leaned in. "Shot me down! I hope they give me a physical challenge where I can beat his ass." He snorted and swallowed hard. "Same goes for the rest of yous." Rokk presented one of the turkey bones and effortlessly snapped it to punctuate his thought. "Good luck getting your votes after I do that to ya. Hah, maybe they'd vote to put you out of yer misery." He smiled and went back to eating.

Everyone at the table was stunned. Max Chambers clapped him on the shoulder. "Rokk, we really need to work on your table manners."

Rokk indignantly looked at how he was sitting at the table. "Fuck you talkin' bout?" He scowled at Max Chambers.

"Rokk listen—"

Rokk made a fist and moved to pound the table. "The fuck you—" But then he froze up, fist raised, face straining. Like a picture of a bodybuilder midlift. The freeze faded away, and when he could move, he got up. "Blah! I had enough of this shit." He ripped a big handful of turkey off and left.

Max Chambers stood, trying not to laugh. "It was just a joke, Rokk. No need to be offended." Rokk kept walking. "How about you show me some more of your football highlights? That always cheers you up." Rokk waved him off dismissively.

Max turned to the group. "Lovely dinner. Those of us who remain will have to do it again next week." He gave a wry smile and hustled to catch up to Rokk. Both tables watched them leave and quietly resumed eating.

Maeve, who had finished eating, noticed that Del and Naiomi had finished the flirtation course of their meal and had used the distraction to sneak away for dessert. Maeve put her elbows on the table and leaned her head on her folded hands, nose sticking out. Her hands smelled of fried food. She watched them slip into Del's room. *Her and Del? Ew. But then again, either of them could be gone tomorrow.* She sat there staring into the distance, thinking.

The Coreys moved over to the campfire and took turns digging into the ice chest placed nearby. Bryan noticed them and joined in. The professor consolidated plates. Corey Three padded over and placed a glistening cold beer can on Maeve's neck.

"Aii-nuh!" She shrank against the table and turned to see Corey smiling at her and a cold one right in front of her face. He laughed.

"Thanks."

"No problem, yo. C'mon." He walked back to the campfire. Maeve popped open her lager, had a cool, bitter sip, and followed.

The professor handed off the dishes to a robot that came over to attend to the mess and joined them as well.

"Who do you think's gonna win this?" said Corey Two.

"Mmm!" Corey One hastily ended a drink to reply. "Nuh-uh. There's no show talk around the fire, yo. Thas like an unwritten rule."

Corey Two popped an eyebrow. "Oh thas a unwritten rule?"

The as-of-yet unspoken Corey weighed in. "Eh, yo, I'm writin' it. No show talk around the fire." The other Corey playfully punched him in the shoulder and they laughed.

Bryan kicked his feet out and crossed his ankles. "So Corey . . . Coreys? You're like super famous. What's that like?"

"Ah, well, you know, it's like . . ."

Maeve tuned them out. Staring at the fire, thinking, and slowly diminishing her beer.

She went back over how her life had derailed, how she wound up stuck here, and how her life was ending a day at a time. And not in a philosophical way, either. This sort of thought used to break her down, but now the more she thought about it, the more she thought there must be something else she could do or try. *What would even be the punishment for trying to escape? Death? I doubt it. They're going to kill us, anyway. Wouldn't it be worth it?*

Maeve stashed her empty beer can behind the chair she was sitting in and dug up another cold one.

"Cheers." Bryan offered a toast to her. Maeve set aside her train of thought and smiled graciously. The cans made a dull clunk. She settled back in her chair and resumed her drink-and-think.

She suddenly realized the fire was a hologram. Of course it was. The whole courtyard was rigged with holographic tech, very convincing. It was hot and ashy looking. It popped, and cinders floated away, but the logs weren't diminishing. She wondered if it could burn a person. She took a big swig.

Getting back to the problem at hand, she thought about the ship, the show, and being a prisoner on it. By the time she was done with beer number two, she had boiled their problems down to three things that would need to be overcome to even have a chance. She shivered. She was dying to pee.

"Hey, I'm going to head home . . . er, well, you know, my cabin." She bumped the professor with the back of her hand and as she stood, spoke into the professor's ear, "Meet me in VR."

The professor's ear flicked a couple of times. "Okay yeah. I'm going to head back, too. Night, all."

9.10

Minutes later, Maeve put on her VR halo and her consciousness clicked over. Now she was standing in the launcher, a dark world with a gridwork of shifting neon color and soothing ethereal tones. With a wave of her hand, she summoned up a menu of her available programs.

The professor's face appeared as a 3D wireframe model, huge and floating in the distance. "There you are. So, what are we doing here?"

"Uh, hold on a minute. I'll send you an invite."

"Okay."

Maeve selected her secret place. The application pulsed within the palm of her hand. She needed only to press it to her head to launch it, but something stopped her. She double-checked the program's properties and gasped in surprise. *It's not encrypted. Anyone savvy could have seen everything I've done here, including . . . Colin and me! How could I be so . . .* "Fuck!"

She put the program back into the list and scanned for something she could use. Nothing looked good as she went over the list, then it occurred to her. *GraveGun!*

Maeve grabbed the program and checked its properties. The advertising boasted about its adaptive encryption. *It's for stopping cheaters, but if anyone spies on me, all they're getting is the name of the game and duration of play, that kind of metadata. This'll do.*

She pressed the program to her head, and, after a scroll of legal mumbo jumbo, she selected her character and logged in. After a few seconds, she was atop the tower in her guild's base. She suddenly felt self-conscious about being here again. It felt weird, though she and Colin were back to texting like nothing had happened.

She pushed those feelings aside and sent the professor that invite that she must be getting anxious about by now. She saw her log in and sent her directions on how to get to the guild compound. Then she waited, looking out over the landscape like she did last time she was here. It was a moonless, dark night, so all she could see were lights in the distance. When the tram arrived, it split the darkness and left a ghost image that wouldn't blink away. Maeve milled about the front gate, waiting for the professor and then let her in as a guest, the only way nonguildies could get in. She told her about the place as they walked to the elevator.

The elevator *clunked*, *chimed*, and the doors opened with a motorized whine. They stepped inside. The professor's focus was drawn to a particularly shiny metal wall panel in which she could see her human avatar. She gazed, transfixed for a moment and then turned her attention back to Maeve.

"Well, this place is kind of nice, but why the impromptu sightseeing tour?" asked the professor.

"I wanted to have a talk with you about the show without anyone listening in. It only recently occurred to me that few of my programs have encryption worth a damn. This game, though, it's state-of-the-art. Unless there's some kind of law enforcement backdoor, we're all good."

The elevator door opened.

"This time of night there shouldn't be many people here, so we can hopefully avoid any awkward conversations. I know about this room in the back that nobody ever goes to."

Maeve stuck her head out of the elevator and peered around the hallway. The place was deserted. She went down the hall with the professor in tow. The ratty old metal door had been replaced with a classy wooden one. She noticed the difference but didn't break stride, swinging the door open and stepping inside. The room used to be storage, but now it looked like an office with cushy chairs. Her old coworker, Dennis, sat at a desk in the middle, poking at a tablet. He looked up with a start and then smiled.

"Hey Ve! How ya holding up?"

She gasped, "I'm sorry, I didn't think anyone would be back here." She felt her cheeks heat up.

"Yeah, that's why I turned it into my office. Normally, nobody comes back here. Come in. It's good to see you."

Maeve waved the professor in and closed the door.

"D-Snuggz? Maeve, did you bring me a new recruit?"

"No, I'm one of the contestants on *Walk Amongst the Stars*. I just look different."

"This is Diane, my friend on the show. And this is Dennis, my friend from my old job."

Dennis stood and shook the professor's hand. "Oh," he laughed. "I didn't recognize you. You know the game has cat-girl avatars you can select?"

"Yes, but they are . . . How do I put this? Hypersexualized. I'm certainly not the target audience."

He laughed.

Maeve sat down in one of those comfy chairs in front of Dennis's desk.

"Look, we came here to have a nice, encrypted conversation about the awful show we're in. Can we use your office for a bit?"

"Sure, I wasn't doing anything important." He showed the tablet, which had a match-three puzzle game on it. "Do you want me to leave you alone?"

"Um, no, the more perspectives, the better."

"So earlier, while we were at the celebration meal, I just kept thinking about this death trap of a show. How we have to find a way out. At first, I was so shocked and afraid that I just kind of accepted my fate. Then I fooled myself into thinking that maybe I really could win. It's a long shot, but it's possible, right? Only now I don't even want that. I don't know about you, but at this point, I don't want to watch anyone else die. Winning, surviving the show, would mean doing that a week at a time."

"Well, wait a minute. What makes you think it's even possible? This show's been going for the better part of a decade, and nobody's ever escaped. At least I've never heard of such a thing," said the professor.

"The way I see it, we have three obstacles to overcome. One. The neck things. We can't fight back until those are removed. Two. There's a small army of robots."

"And you can't print out weapons," said Dennis.

"And that." Maeve pointed at him. "Even if we had the licenses, there's no way the show's going to allow that. And three, or I guess four. We have no control over the ship. So even if we could overcome the other things, we'd need to get control of the ship for any of that to matter."

"How, though? We can't do anything locked in our little pens. What's stopping them from simply executing you for trying to escape?" asked the professor.

"Don't you think others have tried to escape in the eight previous seasons? Someone had to have tried, and they didn't die. Not right away, at least. I think they need us too much for the show to immediately kill us."

The professor scoffed. "They only need us to die. They could make an episode from that."

"Listen, I think the only reason nobody has ever succeeded before is because they didn't take action soon enough. If we fight back now, we've got twelve . . ." Maeve thought about tomorrow. "Eleven people. Hopefully, we don't lose Corey, then we'd be down three of us."

The professor took a breath, but Maeve jumped in again. "Let's say everything goes perfectly, and it's down to you and me at the end. What then? We draw straws to see which one of us goes on a never-ending space voyage? Besides, at this point, I'd rather die on my own terms than get ejected into space for sickos across the galaxy to get off on. Fuck Adam 5000. Fuck *Walk Amongst the Stars*, and fuck whatever corporation owns it."

"Yeah!" Dennis pumped his fist. "I'm pretty sure that show is state-sponsored propaganda. I mean, just look at the budget."

"Okay, assuming you could figure out how to take your restraining device off, then what? We . . . take on the security force with makeshift spears made from table legs and steak knives?"

"Well, baby steps. If we could remove or, better yet, disable these neck things. You know, so we don't look different? We would be free to fight back. Until then, I think we're totally screwed. You're a biologist. Can you think of any way we could fix the neck situation?"

The professor sighed angrily. "You're looking for a tech person or a neurosurgeon. In fact, the only thing I know about these inhibitors is that something plugged into your spine and rigged to explode shouldn't be screwed with."

Maeve stood. "I don't know! Okay? I don't know. That's why you're here." She ran her fingers through her hair. "To help me figure this out. Just . . . please, think about it. Every day that passes, we take a step toward that air lock."

"I think my next move will be to *carefully* recruit more contestants. We need more brain power to figure out our three problems."

The professor didn't respond for a long time. "All right. I'll put some thought to it. But I think you're kidding yourself about getting out of here." The professor folded her arms.

"Me too," Dennis pipped up. "I'll do some careful web searching and see if I come up with anything."

"Okay. Thanks, guys. I'll get on around this time tomorrow and let you know if I got anywhere." She logged out and faded away.

Chapter 10

Maeve stepped out her front door dressed in her dark mourning dress, a variation of what she wore last week. And like last week, she couldn't eat anything. Anxiety twisted her guts, stole her breath, and chilled her hands. It was worse this week. Not only did she have to go to the ghastly voting ceremony, but now she had a secret mission.

Her [Go to the Meeting] alarm had gone off minutes ago, but then she just held onto the doorknob for a while, gathering strength. Now, as she pulled the door closed behind herself, she could see two robots marching toward her to escort her, ready or not. They took up formation on either side of her and walked with her over to the usual spot in the courtyard.

As she approached the semicircle of contestants, she wondered who it would be. *Probably not me. I won the last thing. Probably not the famous people. If that's true, that's like Bryan, Del, I-ON, Max, and the professor. If it's Diane, we're screwed.*

One of them is going today. The image of Zalak appeared in her mind, unable to touch the sides, panicking. She remembered his crazed eyes, pleading, locked on hers for a moment. An image she wished would go away. Although this week, instead of bringing her to tears, the whole thing just made her feel angry inside.

A camera bot swept close to the group, capturing her closeup and her attention. She was in the semicircle now and the bots fell in line with the others.

Adam watched as security bots made the last straggler fall in line and proceeded. "Another week has passed, and so we gather here today to bid one unlucky contestant adieu. Now that we have everyone, it is time!"

The lights went out, the overhead shutters were already closed, and for an instant, everything was black. Pinpoints of light spread all over the courtyard, and spotlights illuminated Adam and the contestants.

Adam scanned across the contestants and then spun around and started for the door to the hall that led to the aft of the ship. The robot security paired up with the contestants and escorted them along behind Adam. When he got to the door, Adam opened it and looked back at the procession and then continued into the fancy hall.

The terror that Maeve felt last week was in the background this time, although its ethereal fingers kept trying to grip her heart. This week was different. This time, she had a goal, and clinging to it gave newfound willpower. As she stepped up onto the large concrete step, her eyes darted about the dim hallway before her. Presumably, she would only get a chance to see outside the courtyard once per week.

This corridor went left and right into darkness. The wall across from the courtyard had two doors, but in the gloom, she didn't see any signs or other designations. Adam took the group left, then right, then right again, down another corridor. On the right were two doors. It seemed to Maeve that they skirted around a big area rather than simply going through. On the left wall, dead center, a door glowed red like a doorway to hell.

10.1

Adam marched the group up to the inner air lock door. Its red light pulsed on and off, temporarily illuminating the hall and peeling back the spacey illusion. Adam stopped at the door and pressed a button to open it. Standing next to the open door, he glowed, sinister, in the dim light. The robots arrayed the contestants around him in a semicircle. The show's theme music played softly, a somber version of the theme.

"Maeve McKinnon . . ." She flinched at her name. "Bryan Cox and Rokk Bradley, you three were the overall winners of this week's contest and, as such, enjoyed a rating boost. Will it be enough?" Adam looked at the three of them with genuine curiosity. "The votes have been tabulated, and today, one of us must go." He bowed his head for a moment. "This week's contestant is . . . coming up after this."

When the pulsing red light went completely dark, leaving only pinpoints of light, a metallic clank resounded in the small space, then another.

Adam looked around the dark room as the red light pulsed back to full power. "I'm getting a noise here, Yang. You picking that up?"

"Yeah, not sure." Mr. Yang brought the ship's lighting back to normal. It hurt after all the darkness. Maeve looked at every detail she could, squinting and blinking. After a minute of looking around, Adam shrugged.

What everyone had failed to notice was that many of the guard robots had a two-inch diameter circular device stuck to their backs, pinning their jumpsuits down.

"You think maybe that was just the ship settling?" said Adam.

"Maybe. Ships make weird noises."

"It's brand new, though."

"I don't know, but it stopped. Let's just move on with the segment."

"Okay, go ahead and feed me the name."

The lights dimmed back down.

"The next elimination is I-ON," said Mr. Yang.

"Got it."

Adam bowed his head, and then dramatically looked up. "And we're back. For those of you just tuning in, the votes are in, and one contestant must go. This week . . . I-ON will *Walk Amongst the Stars.*"

The theme music swelled as the house lights came up. I-ON's escort marched him forward.

"I-ON, it's going to be sad to see you go. You got very few votes, and your poor performance at the laser battle didn't help you any. Do you have anything you'd like to say before we let you off?"

"Yes." I-ON turned his head away from Adam.

"Execute script: Entangle." I-ON also had a small device magnetically attached to his chest. LEDs on it twinkled under his coveralls. It passed a signal through the same quantum-encrypted connection that Adam was using to participate in the show and accessed an account I-ON had cleverly built over the last week.

Adam furrowed his brow, trying to make some kind of meaning out of that gibberish.

Mr. Yang recognized what was happening and struggled to get it out. "Don't—uhhh—N-no! Stop him now. He's trying to do some hacker shit. Shove it into the air lock."

I-ON looked back to Adam 5000. "Execute script: Master User."

Somewhere in a dusty, cold room, the studio's servers quietly gave I-ON's account master user access. The script injected some code and called for an absurd number of functions and network connections to fire. The resulting cyclone of server activity would soon slow the system to a crawl.

Adam lunged into I-ON, wrapping his arms around I-ON's chest, and attempted to force him back. I-ON simply clung to the air lock doorway overhead. If the door couldn't close, there would be no expulsion. Another bot stepped forward to push I-ON into the air lock. I-ON let one hand go and fished another circular device out of a large hook-and-loop pocket and clanked it onto the new robot.

Without that other hand holding the doorway, I-ON was off his feet now. Clinging to the doorframe with one hand, he gripped the newcomer bot, its network connection supplanted by I-ON's.

"Execute Script: Null." I-ON's head snapped back as Adam changed tactics, throwing punches. He would have to endure Adam's attack. His devices only blocked the local network. Adam started glitching up and slowing down. I-ON's final script told the studio's servers to delete key systems, users, and commands, rendering itself useless.

Rokk, Corey Three, and Maeve grabbed onto the approaching security bots. Their aggressive actions caused them to seize up, but it also helped slow the bots a little. Maeve slid down, her body curled around the robot's leg. The robot plodded along like when she was a child that didn't want her father to go to work.

Flashing and hitching, Adam's hologram became like a slideshow, only changing once every second or two. "Wh-y-y is this so-o sl-o-w-w. Th-think-k I'm-m g-gonna-a b-barf."

The two new bots shook off the contestants and shoved past the other robots and Adam, easily carrying I-ON into the air lock. Adam hit the air lock cycle button with considerable effort as his holographic avatar turned to human-shaped static and fell down.

The air lock door descended.

I-ON strained his servos trying to get away from the robot security guards, but they held him in place. He looked at the door controls a few paces in front of him, completely unable to cancel the air lock sequence. The door closed. There was a hiss as the air was replaced with nitrogen. The probability of escape-plan failure was catastrophically high in I-ON's mechanical mind.

Maeve popped up on the other side of the wall like a meerkat and mashed the air lock button. Then she flipped the protective cover back down. The air lock reversed its process.

Once the door opened, the robots that I-ON had hijacked rushed into the air lock, stuffed their hands into his pockets and distributed devices to the remaining security bots in the area. That done, the repurposed security bots came out of the air lock. One of them, Maeve noticed, had angry eyebrow stickers. The sight of Turbo-Guts made her feel safer somehow.

I-ON stepped out of the air lock, took stock of his bots and his fellow contestants. The probability of escape-plan failure was back to acceptable levels.

10.2

The remainder of the group, who had not taken action, stood around stupefied by what they had just witnessed. Finally, Del broke the silence. "Oh my god, you're saving us."

Naiomi looked at Del. "Yeah, what the eff!" Then she looked at I-ON. "How the eff?"

One of the Coreys poked at the robot, which had been holding his arm a minute ago. The bot looked at Corey and then ignored his continued poking and looked back toward I-ON.

Rokk, having gotten back to his feet, put his hand on I-ON's shoulder. "Wait. Fix my neck thing. Now."

"I cannot."

Rokk's grasp tightened until he froze up. He growled his way through the episode until he could move again. I-ON ignored this and spoke with the group. "We have limited time. Follow me and be quiet. Any robot with this device on its back is under my influence." I-ON held up a disk-shaped device in each hand and showed them around. "I could not make enough of these to stop all the robots, but those under my command will keep the rest at bay." He started down the hall. "Follow me to the bridge."

Rokk pushed his way out next, and the rest poured out into the hallway. Naiomi blindly slipped her hand into Del's, and they brought up the rear. I-ON watched as the group assembled and then continued on.

The group made a low roar of swishing clothing and scuffling footsteps as they cautiously moved on. But that could barely be heard over the clatter of the robots following I-ON. Despite the rubberized soles on their plastic feet, they were noisy. Maeve wondered why they were bothering with stealth at all.

They reached the end of the hall quickly. I-ON peered around the corner. Two of the bots under I-ON's control moved on, followed by I-ON, who still held a device in each hand. The group nervously followed.

As they rounded the corner, the group could see the problem up ahead: two more robots. The two ship security bots marched toward the two stolen bots. When the two sides neared each other, the two security bots attempted to sidestep the stolen bots and got grabbed. I-ON quickly followed up by placing a device on each of their chests.

The group slowed to a crawl, seeing the scuffle up ahead, but I-ON's group of bots urged them forward. The two security bots were still struggling as they approached. They gave up and fell in with the other stolen bots by the time the contestants caught up.

The group crept on, parallel with the courtyard they had spent so much time in. As they walked, Maeve remembered her mission to memorize everything she could. Things were different now, but that was no excuse. They passed two doors close together. WASTE PROCESSING and MATERIAL PROCESSING.

When they reached the end of the hall, it was a repeat of the last time. I-ON peeked around the corner, but instead of just two bots coming forward, the squad split in two and several of them rounded the corner with I-ON in tow. Maeve rushed ahead to see.

There were five guards this time, standing in front of what she hoped was the bridge. I-ON ripped open another hook-and-loop pocket and pulled four more devices out. The security bots stood their ground as the large group of stolen bots marched up and grabbed hold of them. The whole thing was graceful and strangely nonviolent. I-ON repeatedly reached into the mob and clanged more magnetic devices onto the security forces, leaving one. When the security bots were assimilated, I-ON moved into the short corridor with the door at the end.

I-ON's bots moved the remaining security bot into the corner by the door and held it there. It struggled against them. Normally quiet electric motors whined loudly under the strain. Realizing it had no chance of getting free, it stopped resisting and simply watched. The remaining robots in the back of the group ushered the humans toward the door. Then all the bots except for two in the corner and I-ON formed a perimeter blocking off the hallway.

I-ON reached into a pocket and picked out a screwdriver. He looked at the screws and adjusted the ring on the screwdriver's handle, finding the appropriate tip. The tip slowly changed shape.

Once it solidified, he started unscrewing the touch panel next to the bridge door. The final screw undone, I-ON pulled the panel forward and unplugged a couple of cables from it and propped the panel up against the wall.

Returning to his pocket, I-ON pulled out a bundle of wire. He found a flat rectangular plug and let the wire unfurl. It was a multiheaded adapter. He connected the end he was holding onto the cable that he disconnected from the touch pad. He slid his hand to the other end of the cable, finding the adapter. It was cylindrical, with an outer ring of tiny pins. A circular hole in the middle with a little trapezoid-shaped guide notch. I-ON kneeled down, which put him at eye level to the open panel. There was a quiet click from I-ON's head as a panel slid down, revealing some buttons and a large port. He placed the adapter against the hole and turned until it found purchase and sunk in.

I-ON laid out the plan to the group, emphasizing that he didn't know how long this would take, and he would be unable to act until he was done. The security bots were there for his protection. If push came to shove, they would prioritize his safety above theirs until the job was done.

Before he began, Bryan piped up, "Wait, what about that?" He pointed to the restrained robot in the corner. It stared at the back of I-ON's head.

I-ON handed him the polymorphic screwdriver. "You may be able to gain access to the robot's power system with this."

Bryan stepped forward and claimed it. Everyone was quiet.

I-ON looked as though he was lost in concentration. In a way, he was.

Bryan unzipped the security bot's jumpsuit and squinted to see what kind of screw type it had.

"Stand by for emergency power cycle" came from the ship's speakers.

The group exchanged surprised looks before everything went dark. The floor beneath their feet felt wrong. Empty or maybe loose was the better term.

10.3

Minutes ago, back in the studio:

"Shove it into the air lock," said Mr. Yang, stumbling over his words. He leaned closer, breathing through his mouth as he gaped at the monitor. He had rarely seen Adam spring into action. Once running late, he saw him slip through a closing studio door with a dancer's grace. Once he vaulted over a crate to hide from a producer he was in trouble with. But now he was watching Adam grapple with that robot like a wrestler.

As the shock wore off, he rearranged the applications on his console and double-checked that yes, indeed, the ship was accepting commands from one of the contestants. *That should be impossible*, he thought. He also revealed a window showing that they were down several security bots, but he didn't notice in his haste.

He looked back at the scuffle happening at the air lock door. *C'mon c'mon, get it in there so I can blast it out!* Seeing Adam and the other bot struggling, he ordered the other two bots at the scene to secure I-ON. It struck Mr. Yang that for the first time in the show's history, he was using the security bots as something other than ushers and janitors.

Another problem cropped up. The security feed. Everything was moving as though it were a slide show, displaying a buffering icon between still frames. He caught intermittent sound bursts.

Lag like this shouldn't even be possible, he thought.

What the hell is happening? Adam thought. But no one heard him. His virtual body had ceased to respond correctly. He stopped getting a slideshow of the events, and his vision twisted into a nightmare of green and pink pixels. They twisted and spun as he looked around. He fought off the nauseous vertigo the machine had dropped him into and ripped off his VR halo.

He lay there with his eyes clenched, taking deep breaths, tears in the corners of his eyes. His stomach twisted in knots and uncertain. Sweat beaded on his brow.

Watching the monitor, Mr. Yang saw the security robots had manhandled the robotic contestant into the air lock. *Finally.* Putting his fingers on the keys, he furiously pounded in a simple command meant to bypass all the safety bullshit. Forcing the air lock to cycle right now. An error message popped up. He was full of adrenaline and trying to type too fast. He typed it again methodically, almost sarcastically. No error message . . . but it didn't return a confirmation either. He looked back at the monitor and ran his fingers through his hair.

Adam burped, groaned, and slowly got to his feet. He rubbed his eyes.

"What happened? Did I do it? Is I-ON gone?"

Mr. Yang held down some keys on the keyboard and slammed his finger on another part of the keyboard repeatedly.

"I'm sure I hit the air lock button, but everything went all . . ." Adam closed his eyes and took another stabilizing breath. Just thinking about it made his stomach churn. "Oh god, it went all fun-house crazy on me."

Instead of his normal console windows, Mr. Yang was looking at a large central error message: [`System Error 0000001E`] "What the . . ."

Adam watched him work, growing more nervous. He'd worked with Yang for a lot of years now. He knew that combination of determined expression and concentrating so hard he can't hear you meant things were serious.

"Hey! What. Is. Happening?"

Mr. Yang tabbed through his many useful applications and saw nothing but error messages:

```
[Missing Stack]
                    [No Signal]
                              [Unknown Error]
[#Disgruntled Badger]
          [File Not Found]
                    [Hypersync Fault]
```

He looked back at the security monitor and saw it was blank, and he gasped.

Mr. Yang realized someone was talking at him earlier. He looked over and saw Adam out of the corner of his eye and swiveled his chair. He was suddenly aware that he'd broken into a sweat. And even though he was looking Adam in the eye, he couldn't help visualizing walking out of the studio with all his office shit in a white copy-paper box.

Adam grasped his shoulders. "What happened?"

That brought Mr. Yang around. "I think we just got got. I think we just lost everything."

The words stole the breath from Adam. "How can that happen? Don't we have a whole IT department that stops that kind of thing?"

"Well yeah, but it got into the server somehow. That means it has control . . . Wait a minute!" Mr. Yang spun back around and snatched up his Omni and zipped down his list of contacts and called the IT department. Mr. Yang looked back at Adam, who perched on the back of Yang's chair.

"You're right, we might still have time. We just need to re-establish control before they hack their way into the ship." The call connected.

"Ye—" Mr. Yang listened for a while. "Yeah. Okay. Please hurry. We're in a really serious time crunch here. It's life or—Thanks."

"What'd he say?"

"He said they're aware of the hack and are going as fast as they can, in a really rude way."

"The studio kind of fucked us on this one," Adam said contemplatively. He turned his attention to Yang. "I told them the robot was a mistake. It escaped once before," he spoke passionately, getting angry. "That's why it's a contestant in the first place."

Mr. Yang held up his OmniTab. "You know what? I'm calling the cops."

"Yup-bup-bup, don't do that just yet," said Adam.

"The robot is cyberattacking us. If IT doesn't get us back up fast, it can hijack the entire show."

Adam smiled. "We can still save this. If we go to the police, we're losing the last bit of control we have. Try to get back into the ship however you can. I'll handle the rest."

It was Adam's turn to pull out his OmniTab from his suit jacket and dial a contact. He placed the device to his ear and his other hand on his elbow and cast his eyes to the floor. Mr. Yang swiveled around and pushed the reset button on the computer console.

"Captain Reeves?" He glanced at Yang to make sure he was getting this. "Yeah. Yeah, look, we have an emergency situation with the ship. The robot of the group, it's trying to take control of the ship, and judging by the way Yang is sweating, I think it's got a good shot at it. No. No-ho. Yep. Well, what if you had carte blanche? Okay. Okay, you just call your hard boys, and I'll make it happen. Well, whatever you call them." Adam heard the telltale sound of a call hanging up and looked at his OmniTab, confirming that he had been hung up on. He slipped it back into his jacket. Mr. Yang was looking at him expectantly.

"Okay, I got the captain on the job. If you can't get the ship under control, we pivot this show and follow the action of brave Captain Reeves as he wrestles the ship back from these mutineers! Are they mutineers or just criminals? Pirates? Wait, Terrorists!"

"For the record, I think this is a mistake."

"Yangy, Yangy, Yangy. You know as well as I do the studio doesn't give a shit which show does what. They only care about that sweet ad money. Dropping the normal show format might piss off the fans, but this contestant runaway show is going to do huge ratings." Adam expanded his arms out to illustrate.

Mr. Yang turned and saw that the console was still not getting anything, so he pressed the reset button again, then turned back to Adam. "You gonna call the studio?"

"Oh, uh?" Adam winced and sucked air through his teeth. "This is one of those 'don't ask permission, ask for forgiveness' kind of things . . . Trust me."

10.4

After several seconds in utter darkness, the ship shuddered as its power plant came back online. A subtle, persistent vibration came with it, as well as the ship's red emergency lighting. The contestants were a mob of shadows. The red light gave the corridors a haunted look.

The red gloom revealed three new silhouettes in the corridor, one on the right, two on the left. They stood motionless, watching with glowing red eyes. Naiomi shrieked. Some of her fellow contestants jumped. The normal overhead lights came back on, and the robots simply marched toward I-ON's defensive line and merged with the other defenders. Altogether, there were nineteen robot defenders.

Del comforted Naiomi while Bryan turned his attention back to disabling their captive robot.

10.5

Back in the studio, Mr. Yang's terminal had finally snagged onto a server and booted up, and since then he'd been working as fast as he could to get the show back on track. Adam 5000 was behind him, literally, perched on his shoulders, giving him little squeezes as he watched the action. Mr. Yang was used to Adam's annoying bullshit by now, but the high pressure of the situation was wearing on him.

The system connected with the ship again. Mr. Yang told the ship to power cycle. That should clear out any ongoing hacker crap. After a brief pause, it showed the ship was back online and seemingly back to normal. "Yes," said Mr. Yang in monotone as he was still, despite Adam, in the zone.

He called up a list of security footage and looked at the bridge. The small room was empty except for three command consoles. "Okay, nothing here." He switched to the security door, and they beheld an overhead shot of a hallway capped off with a contingent of security bots and the contestants huddled up behind them. Yang furrowed his brow and switched to the robot management window and saw that there were only thirty-one security bots responding. He selected all available bots and several camera bots and set their destination to the connecting corridor in front of the security door.

"Do you think I should get back in there? Maybe I could reason with them? Talk them down?" said Adam.

Mr. Yang sat up in his chair. "Yes!" He stumbled over his words. "Good idea. It's worth a shot. Get in there."

Adam trotted over to the VR setup and easily kicked a leg over the recumbent chair and sat. He put his legs on and scooted his butt to the back of the chair. Then he put on the halo and logged in.

10.6

Camera bots swooped in first, filling the hall, getting every angle. Then the group could hear it coming. The security bots were marching in. A column of bots came out of both sides, and now they could feel the reverberation of their marching in the floor beneath them. They came to a stop, one column in front of the other, both fifteen robots long.

"That didn't take long," Del said.

"There's so many," Naiomi whined and clutched at Del's arm.

"Hurry up, I-ON," Maeve muttered.

The offensive line of robots didn't take any further action. The camera bots floated in lazy arcs, capturing footage. Bryan had found a panel and was hastily unscrewing hex screws. It took all his might to break them loose, but he was getting it. The third screw fell to the floor, bronze with a blue smear at the end. He unscrewed the fourth one enough that the panel fell out of place and hung from the final screw. The bot struggled again when Bryan exposed the panel. He found the power button beneath a clear rubber protector and pushed it. The two defenders who were holding it in place let it fall against the wall into a seated position and rejoined the other defenders.

One man clapping broke the silence. Adam 5000 stepped out from between the two columns of robots, performing a resounding clap that he kept up as he came to stand in front of the large security force. He regarded them with a triumphant grin. He had a robot's jumpsuit held under his arm, which he discarded when he stopped clapping.

"Wow, contestants. This was our first escape attempt. You should pat yourselves on the back for that one. You've made *Walk Amongst the Stars* history."

Del sighed. "I thought we were rid of this asshole."

Adam stepped closer to I-ON's wall of robots. "I hope you had your fun because it's over now. As you can see, we have a superior force of robots, and you're just sort of trapped in a corner. So give up now and we'll go back to our regularly scheduled program. Heck, I might be able to pull some strings and get an additional contestant let off the hook this season. Perhaps the master hacker who figured out how to get this far?"

Adam put his hands together in front of his mouth, then pointed them at the group. "Can we stop this now? Tell your robots to stand down and come with me back to the cabins. Please."

The contestants looked around at each other. Del looked back at the group, then turned back to Adam and raised his hands. "Okay, you got us. Just give us a minute to work this out."

"What? No-ah!" Naiomi scowled.

Adam placed his hands on his hips and kept grinning away.

Del turned to the group and grabbed onto Max Chambers's shoulder and pulled him down into a huddle, giggling slightly. He reached up and grabbed Maeve, and the rest of the group huddled around.

"Yo, what the fuck, man?" said Corey One.

"Yeah, what the fuck he said," said Corey Two.

Del giggled some more. "Obviously we're not gonna surrender."

"So what are we doing?" said Rokk.

"What we're doing is wasting that shitheel's time. We're coming up with plans and talking, and everything looks more legit if you guys talk, too. So yep, that's what we're doing," he said with a big toothy smile.

"Good idea. We don't know how long I-ON will need," said the professor.

The smile slowly faded off Adam's face as a minute bled into two. He watched them earnestly talk to each other, nodding. It was hard to see them behind the screen of robots. He folded his arms and changed stance. "Okay, that's enough. Get it together. Let's go now."

The giggles had spread to the other contestants, and when Adam spoke up, Del grabbed his side, silently laughing. The professor stilled herself and stood again. "Please, we've just about reached resolution." And then she returned to the huddle. Her comment fueled the deranged laughter that was gripping them. Del sank to his knees, laughing as quietly as he could. Maeve came down with him, red-faced, tears in her eyes, trembling with silent laughter.

Adam frowned and sighed, but continued to wait.

"It's not working. I'm sending the bots in," said Mr. Yang.

"Well, I tried," Adam said loudly, and turned away from the contestants.

The security bots marched forward. They parted around Adam, re-formed, and kept going until they clashed with I-ON's stolen bots. The contestants scrambled back against the security door.

"Looks like the gig is up, yo," said Corey Three.

"Jig," said Bryan.

Corey Three shot him a suspicious look.

The attacking robots grappled with the defending bots, who did their best to tie up their attackers. The second row of I-ON's robots held the front line in place while anchoring themselves to whatever they could grab: beams, fixtures, and each other.

The hall filled with the sounds of whining servos and the scrapes and clacks of plastic and metal colliding. The attackers couldn't wrestle the defenders free or individually subdue them because they were so dug in.

After a minute of this, the attacking bots changed tactics. They singled out individual defenders and quadrupled up on them. Two held the defending robot while two more tore the limbs free one at a time. The robot's arms would give way with a loud bang and a tinkle of broken pieces. It happened again and again. *Bang, snap, crinkle, sizzle.* I-ON's bots were being torn down one limb at a time.

Soon, the whole front row of the defenders was lying in pieces. They had struggled to hold the attackers, even with their legs, buying as much time as possible. Then the attackers stumbled onto a faster strategy.

While wrenching the arm off a defending robot, the attacking robot saw a sturdy component tear across the defending robot's body in a manner that bent open its chest cover. The attacker further wrenched the panel up with a screech, making a big enough hole to fit its hand into. With its chest exposed, the attackers grabbed a prominent power cable shrouded with yellow-and-black DANGER stripes and ripped it out. The defender twitched and shook, then went limp as acrid smoke poured out of its chest wound.

The defenders went down more quickly, and now there were only nine, barely covering the corridor and fully engulfed in a crowd of twenty or so attackers. A few of the attackers also went down from receiving a fatal electric shock. The contestants were powerless to do anything but watch and pack themselves ever tighter against the security door, a door that they desperately needed I-ON to open.

Another defender jerked spasmodically as if it were breaking into a trendy new dance and fell, lifeless. Shortly after, another went down, shocking its attacker badly. The attackers backed off and then lunged in again in unison. Maeve slowly stepped over to I-ON and stood in front of him. Corey Two saw her and did the same. Soon the entire group had migrated to I-ON, forming a human shield.

The enemy quickly surrounded and tore down the remaining defenders. The floor was treacherous with robot parts and fluids. Some limbless robots looked around, still online but unable to act. They had ripped chunks out of the walls and floor where the defenders hung on. A light fixture was ripped out, and some exposed metal structure beneath a panel was bent out of shape.

"We didn't even need the captain. He's going to be mad when he finds out we did it without him," said Adam.

The security bots at the end of the hallway parted. Adam marched up the center and put his hands on his hips. "Okay, you had your fun. Get back to your cabins. Now!"

Maeve was unable to choke back her tears.

"We were so close," someone in the crowd whispered.

Corey Two, One, and Naiomi, who were on the outside of the group, stepped forward, eyes cast down as they took slow, unsure steps over the scattered robotic limbs.

Adam stepped closer, glowering. "Move now, or I'll sic the robots on you." Max Chambers, Del, Corey Three, and Rokk peeled off the human shield and started their own walk of shame.

"Move! Now!" Adam underscored each word with a finger pointed at the floor.

The professor and Bryan braced themselves for the promise of a robotic manhandling. Maeve turned around and held onto I-ON.

10.7

The bridge security door slid open.

I-ON stood, shucking the now bewildered, crying girl off himself and pulling the plug from his head. Security bots were already en route, but Bryan moved over and pulled the other two with him, forming a human shield in the doorway.

I-ON power walked inside. It was a small trapezoid of a room. Front and center was a captain's chair surrounded by a dashboard of controls, which were positioned in front of a large windshield that curved most of the way around the small room. A single person could pilot the ship, but they could also delegate control over systems to two smaller stations at the rear left and right of the bridge. And finally, there was a navigational and tactical table in the center, leaving only a walkway between everything.

I-ON focused on the terminal in the back right. He bent over the chair in front of a terminal and got to work.

The security bots separated the contestants and passed them back like a bucket brigade. I-ON pecked at the keyboard, getting into the options as a robot took hold of him. I-ON grabbed onto the console's chair tightly with his other arm as a second robot grabbed on. He had found the External Connections submenu and arrowed down to hit enter on the option [`Allow External Connections`]. This changed it to [`Off`] and brought up the message [`Terminate Existing Connections? Y/N`]. A third robot joined in, and together they broke I-ON's grip. Undaunted, he smoothly poked the `Y` key before they moved him out of range of the keyboard.

At the end of the hall, Adam looked confused, then shocked, then he vanished, becoming a naked robot. The security bots, now cut off from the show's controls, looked to the ship for orders and found none. Three robots continued to hold I-ON in an incumbent position.

"Set me down."

The three robots laid I-ON down. He got up and went back to the security terminal. Looking through the commands, he found [`Hibernate`], which stated in small text, `Recall robots and enter low-power mode`. He toggled it, and all the security and camera bots, those that still functioned, faced down the hall and moved out.

I-ON heard distant cries of jubilation and watched the professor, Maeve, and Bryan jump around, he assumed, in celebration. Then they came jogging over, vaulting over the pile of sundered robots.

"You did it!" Bryan called out. Maeve hugged I-ON again tightly, who stood unmoving like a statue. "Thank you. I was trying to figure out how we could possibly escape, but you actually did it."

Bryan caught up and patted I-ON's shoulder. "You did it. We're free."

"Not yet. Computer, I need to use the intercom." There was a tone letting him know he was live. "This is I-ON. I just disconnected this ship's connection to the show. Everyone come to the bridge. We need to decide on our next move."

Chapter 11

I-ON skirted around the navigational table until he was between it and the captain's chair. Bryan followed him in and leaned on one of the side station chairs. The nav-table was blank, and I-ON hadn't seen controls on his trip around it. He reached out to touch the surface of it, and a holographic map appeared, showing labeled dots for each of the markers in this system. The ship was in the center, with a line showing its current trajectory. I-ON put his hands into the map and attempted to manipulate it, but it didn't budge. He tried again, another way, to no avail.

Bryan stepped forward and mimicked I-ON, but the map yielded to his touch.

"Would you do that for me while I speak? It appears I lack the capability."

Bryan smiled. "Sure."

"So they're coming after us. What do we do next?" said Max Chambers as he walked onto the bridge.

"Please wait until everyone has gathered. This will eliminate repeat conversations."

Max Chambers sighed and nodded.

The crew trickled in and took places around the nav-table. They squeezed closer together to allow everyone around the table at once. The bridge was cramped now, definitely not meant for this many people.

"Now that we are all together, we will go over what we know and decide our future course of action," said I-ON.

"Thanks, by the way," said Del. "Without you, we'd be preparing for a pole-vaulting challenge or something just as ridiculous instead of escaping."

Some of the group chimed in:

"Yeah!"

"Thank you."

"Saved our bacon, yo."

"Remember, we are not safe yet, and the action that I have taken today endangers all of us. Simultaneously, instead of one at a time." I-ON was merely stating a fact, but now he had everyone's quiet focus. "Expand the map, please."

Bryan put his hands into the hologram and separated them, causing the map to telescope down in scale rapidly, showing off more than a dozen star systems. Then he overcorrected and zoomed all the way into the ship, and then much more gingerly motioned to expand the map so that just this system, Prospiria Alpha, was visible.

"Here is the ship, and this line is the programmed navigation." I-ON pointed at the ship and traced the line. "The show intended to take us around this gas giant, utilizing the planet's gravity. Then through this asteroid belt, past this space station, and finally loop around the star and come back home. Whatever course we choose, it is likely we will utilize this gravity well." He pointed to the gas giant they were already moving toward, marked [Coloso].

I-ON withdrew his hand. "With this in mind, we need to form a consensus on our next move."

The group fell silent, staring at the map and glancing at the others around the table. Maeve looked at the professor. Naiomi looked to Del. Rokk looked at his pal Max. Corey One whispered to Corey Three.

Max Chambers folded his arms and offered a thought: "Well. We should also consider what we have on hand. We're in control of a large luxury cruiser." He gestured with his hand, then folded it against his chest again. "So we have a fast ship, probably good shields, but it's civilian, so no military capability like stealth or weaponry. We also have, I don't know, ten to twenty good robots. Maybe more if we repair them."

Bryan added, "We have printers in our cabins, so there's bound to be a cache of Varium, too."

"It seems like we have no choice but to run and hide, unless you're suggesting we try to barter our way out of this?" said the professor.

"Not necessarily, but this ship should be worth a heck of a lot," said Max Chambers.

"Except that it's stolen," said Bryan.

"True. There is that."

"Okay, so where do we hide?" said Corey Two.

"Yo, computer, like, highlight all the space stations," said Corey One. Little yellow dots sprouted up all over the system map.

"That's another problem." Max Chambers spoke up. "Everyone can see us. We have to get rid of our transponder unless we plan to cross a warp gate."

"Wait, why can't we cross without a transponder?" said Maeve.

"That's just how it works. I don't know."

"It's not the only way. Pirates get through," said Maeve.

Del furrowed his brow. "Are you a pirate?"

"No, but I—"

"Oh? I guess that doesn't matter then, does it?"

Maeve gave him a disgusted look and folded her arms.

"Transponder . . ." Bryan mumbled to himself. "Wait a minute, I've got an idea." Bryan manipulated the map and leaned close enough to it that the hologram gave his face blue highlights. He grinned at what he saw. "Hey, listen up. I think I've solved our problem, at least half of it."

Bryan explained his idea to the others, occasionally repositioning the map and gesturing to key points. The group listened, and after a few questions, they had agreed on a course of action.

"Computer, course correction. We need to use warp gate AG-945," said I-ON.

"Warning, Trelecon is a fringe system beyond Prospiria Central Authority protection. Are you sure?"

"Yes."

"Acknowledged."

The path to Coloso remained the same. The gravity slingshot changed trajectory, shooting them straight at the warp gate.

I-ON looked up from the map. "I estimate we will arrive in two hundred and seventy-one hours."

"Eh, yo, I'm not a robot. How many days is that?" said a Corey.

"Eleven point two nine."

I-ON sat in the captain's chair for a while, analyzing and changing the ship's various settings. Most of the crew left the cramped bridge. Corey Two and Maeve hung around watching him work. When they'd looked through all the systems, they went back to the sunny courtyard. The rest of the crew was out chatting. The mood had shifted to exuberance as they stood around talking about how they were free now. How nobody else had to die. Even the normally introverted Maeve hung out, chatting. As minutes turned to hours, the group fragmented, and eventually everyone called it a night.

11.1

The next day, when the crew migrated into the courtyard, Corey Two had the idea to explore the ship and see what there was to see. The Coreys, Maeve, and Del went around looking into things.

The port side had three large storage areas. One for all the robots and their accessories. Another was full of things they used on the show and might have used in the future. Picnic tables, pots and pans—this stuff they had seen. They also found various types of sports equipment, minibikes, carnival games, some musical instruments. The final storage bay was for food. It was segmented into three sections: freezing, cold, and room temp. Although the temperature zones seemed to just be a suggestion, as the whole bay was pretty darn cold.

The aft housed the engine and electrical rooms. They stopped in the engine room, gawking at the power plant. It was like a massive chrome lozenge with an arch bulging out of the center. Light rotated around the circumference of the arch. Around the base of it were removable panels and digital readouts. Black conduits efficiently popped out of one part of the engine, snaking into another.

The starboard side housed two large rooms. Waste management, which also seemed to be where all the water was stored, and reclamation. There was nothing interesting here, so they moved on.

The group came around to the bridge hallway and the pile of robot parts laying around, and after a moment, they swung back around and got those picnic tables out of storage and lugged them to the courtyard.

Bright and early the next day, Maeve went to one of the storage bays, looking for cleaning products and something to lug around all those bits and pieces of robots. She bumped into Corey Two, who was busy pillaging one of the minibikes they had found in the event storage yesterday. She loaded up a flatbed cart with cleaning supplies. Corey, who was a small guy, looked like a giant on the tiny e-bike as he zipped down the hall. She couldn't help but laugh at the sight.

Maeve put on some thick yellow rubber gloves she found and started moving severed robotic limbs onto the cart. She wasn't very far into the job before all three Coreys coasted to a stop on e-bikes. Maeve lost it when they all deployed tiny kickstands. They offered to help, which was music to her ears.

After four cartloads, they had all the robot bodies cleaned up, and all that was left were a lot of fluids and stains on the floor. Of the two cleaners Maeve picked out, one of them, Ooze Remove Complete, got the job done. It sprayed a sizzling purple spray and got the stains up with minimal elbow grease. To Maeve's dismay, the group had left a trail of dripping robot goop back and forth from the storage bay. They took turns wiping it all up, and at the end, they were covered in grime. But the hallway wasn't.

There were still broken tiles and warped metal, but there wasn't anything Ooze Remove would do about that.

By the third day, the group decided they couldn't live without an internet connection anymore. It began as a casual conversation in the courtyard and became a passionate debate that eventually migrated to the security terminal on the bridge.

Maeve sat in the chair with six others crammed around, looking on as she dug through the many options in the networking section.

Bryan, who championed the no-net-connection side, argued that they would be looking for a way in, and it's just a matter of time until they figure it out. The majority of the group just wanted access to entertainment, but Max Chambers, who was on the enable-a-connection side, pointed out that the news could give them some intelligence and that if they suspected any trouble, they could always disable the net connection again.

Eventually Bryan caved, and Maeve went through the ship's connection settings thoroughly. Her childhood as a gamer meant that she had years of experience setting up and maintaining the family internet-connected devices. She set up a stealthy connection that would stand up to all but the most expert attacks. She even found a setting to autodump the connection on certain conditions and dialed that in. Finally, they decided on a simple password that would protect the ship's more executive functions.

The group decompressed into the hallway, and everyone produced an OmniTab, connected up, and started scrolling. No one found any news coverage about what had happened.

Collectively, they couldn't decide if that was a good or bad thing. Bryan argued it was potentially a good thing. If the show had not gone to the authorities, that might make it easier to escape. Maeve looked at the other side of the coin. It meant that the show could do whatever they wanted and find a way to justify it later. Del told them they should stop trying to read too much into any of it since the megacorp, Ægis, who owned this show, also had a monopoly on the news media. He hypothesized they were in bed with the Central Authority, as he assumed all megacorps were.

With their network connection and freedom partly restored, the group slowly formed new routines. Despite being ripped away from their lives, at least they could watch their shows, play their games, and dip into social media.

Later on, Maeve caught up with Colin and Dennis in VR and told them about I-ON's surprise escape. Walked them through the whole helpless ordeal. Afterward, she and Colin spent some time together in *GraveGun*. She no longer felt safe using her secret place. They found a quiet place in the guild base to speculate about what her next move should be, while she snuggled him like a koala does a tree.

11.2

On the eighth day, the professor was in I-ON's cabin, which was really a workshop. She reached back and touched the device on the back of her neck. What was previously the red oval shape nestled in her fur was now an empty metal plate with a digital connector. The connector had a series of rainbow-colored metal, springy bumps and spring-loaded pins to keep the connection tight. She ran her finger along the bumps and felt momentarily weak at the knees and saw flashes of light. Grabbing a chair to steady herself, she took slow, intentional breaths. She realized she had just, in a roundabout fashion, poked herself in the brain.

"Here, one last step," said I-ON. He held up a black, glossy cover similar to what the unit had before.

The professor turned her back to him and ran her hands through her fur a few times to get a defined part showing. I-ON put the face plate on askew and turned it, snapping it in place. A rubber gasket would keep debris out.

She felt the spot one more time before turning to face I-ON. "I'd say we're ready."

"It is the best we can offer without the proper tools."

"Computer, I need to make an announcement."

A moment passed, and then there was a pleasing digital *boop* from the sound system. "Attention, everyone. Come to the courtyard for a meeting. We have news about the neck implants." She wanted to leave it at that, but force of habit made her repeat the message. "Attention, everyone, there is a meeting in the courtyard."

After a few minutes, the group had assembled at the tables. They looked worried about the impromptu meeting. I-ON and the professor stood before them. The professor spoke loudly until the chatter died down. "The last several days I've been helping I-ON solve the neck-implant problem. Well, we have good news and bad news. The good news is we came up with a method to disable the device. The bad news is that without the control device that installs these implants in the first place, there's no way to completely remove them."

I-ON elaborated. "The device anchors itself to the C3 vertebra and injects a plethora of tendrils into the nervous system. This is how it monitors and disables human behavior. Tampering with the device can detonate a small explosive shape charge. This causes internal decapitation."

A pall fell over the group as I-ON explained.

The professor took over again. "Without the control device, there's really only two other ways we figure the tendrils could be removed. One would be to find some way to defeat the software, make it think the control device was present. Another would be to undergo extensive microsurgery to sever all the nerve connections. Both probably carry some risk of death or disability."

"So you're saying you can disable the device but not remove it from our necks?" said Max Chambers.

"Essentially. The choice you have is to disable the device now and perhaps have the husk of this device stay with you from now on. Or wait and hope we encounter someone with the means to disable it properly. Disabling the device with the proper control unit will extract the tendrils, causing minimal damage, or so the advertising claims. But I-ON's method is fairly safe; we've both disabled our devices. I could demonstrate . . ." She held up a fist.

Rokk flexed his mighty arm and slapped it. "Right here."

The professor hustled around the table and punched his arm. She had good form, planting her feet, cocking an arm back, and putting her hips into it. Her initial thought was to go with minimal force, but the man was a giant in both height and circumference. She held back a little for the sake of her own fist and not his expansive arm. There was a soft smack of skin muffled by her fur coat.

"There, you see: aggressive behavior."

Rokk smiled toothily and held out his hand to fist bump, which the professor readily did.

I-ON walked over to Rokk. "Would you like to go first? You have been very vocal on the subject."

"Yeah, let's do this." Rokk struggled to get his bulky body out of the picnic table without doing damage to it.

"It's about damn time, eh." He slapped Max Chambers on the back as he passed by. Max rocked forward and smirked at his friend.

"Follow me," said I-ON as he led him to his cabin workshop.

The professor cleaned the back of her hand and addressed the group again. "The whole process only takes a few minutes so we can get everyone who's interested done this afternoon. Form a line in I-ON's room if you're ready." She looked solemn. "Just remember what I said. This may be a permanent choice, so think it over." The professor sensed no further questions and walked back to I-ON's workshop.

Maeve slid a hand under her hair and cupped the red thing on the back of her neck and felt a shiver move through her spine. She got a mental image of the many connections sunk into her spine and brain and felt momentarily ill.

Del pushed off the picnic table. Corey One and three looked at each other and got up to leave. Corey Two got up a second later and sprinted past them. When he caught up, the trio all rushed for the door, straining and laughing.

Bryan looked up at the dome overhead and ran his hands over his short hair a few times, then stood and thrust his hands into his pockets and walked over.

Max Chambers watched them go. "Well, it looks like we're the holdouts."

Maeve stopped groping at the bomb on her neck and raised her head. "Yeah, I just can't handle the idea of leaving all those . . . how did she put it, *tendrils*, in my neck? Yuck." She scrunched up her face.

"Eh, it's not the worst thing I've had in me." Naiomi put up a hand and looked expectantly at Maeve.

Maeve cackled and leaned forward, partly from the laughter, partly to give up a high five. When she calmed enough to speak, she said. "Seriously, though, I just want to get it out. It's so gross."

Naiomi went off laughing again and covered her eyes. "I think that's what I said, too."

The three of them laughed heartily, even Max Chambers, who had been too embarrassed to really enjoy the first part. They recovered slowly. Lingering fits of laughter kept breaking them up.

"Well, I don't know about you two, but even betrayed by my business partners, I still have considerable pull. I plan to seek out a doctor or hacker or whoever to undo this problem of mine," said Max Chambers, pointing to his neck. "Then I'll deal with those usurpers."

"Yeah, I just want to pay to have it done right," said Naiomi thoughtfully. "I don't know how I'm going to do that now with my assets frozen, but hey, I did it once. I'll just have to do it again."

"Yeah . . ." said Maeve. She looked back at I-ON's cabin, wondering if she was making the right move considering all the big-money talk.

11.3

Bryan leaned against the back of I-ON's couch, the same design in every cabin. A comfortable, fake-leathery kind of thing. As he waited his turn, he noted that the only furnishings I-ON had were the things that came stocked with the cabin. Now that the last of the Coreys was in getting worked on, he found himself absorbed in how the robot lived in its room. For example, the room temperature was fairly cold. The heating might even be off. It was dimly lit. I-ON had spent its time creating a great many tools, which lay around the various furnishings in tight, organized groupings. It was almost like a workshop or a garage, except that it was way too clean for something like that. Even the pile of scrap electronics was neatly stacked up.

He was beginning to wonder what I-ON kept in the refrigerator when the bedroom door opened and an excited Corey clone swaggered down the hall. "Yer turn, yo." Corey wore a big grin and bumped Bryan's fist before strolling out the door.

Bryan walked into the room. If the last room was a workshop, this was more of a doctor's office, and that intimidated him a little. This room was lit not only by the overhead light, but by what looked like a dentist's light, which was attached to a stainless-steel cart topped with various tools. I-ON was standing next to it. In front of him was a recumbent chair, the kind with a hole in it for your face to rest in.

Bryan instinctively closed the door behind him, feeling just a touch of apprehension.

The professor met him where he stood. "He needs a few minutes to recharge over there, so I'm going to go over the whole procedure so you know what to expect." She explained the steps. "Does that make sense?" said the professor.

"Yeah."

"Two last questions. First off, do you know if you have any kind of iron or other magnetic metals embedded or implanted into your body? Because that could be a problem."

"Nope." He looked at that dentist light again. "Unless fillings count."

"No, those are fine, nonmagnetic. The second thing is the procedure will restore your emotional freedom, but it is likely that you will be stuck with the useless husk of this implant for the rest of your life. There is also the slight chance that something could go wrong, in which case the device would likely kill you. Do you still want to go through with this?"

Bryan looked past her at I-ON's setup. It hadn't occurred to him that even though they would be tampering with the device that there was a chance he could die.

"Would that, ya know, hurt?"

She closed her eyes and thought. "Yes, I would imagine it hurts a great deal, but you wouldn't suffer for long. The device's advertising claims to sever the spine and surrounding arteries. Hypothetically, someone in that position would black out in seconds."

She reached up and put her hand on his shoulder. "Believe me, I researched the hell out of this before I did it to myself. And hey, so far we're oh for six."

"Well, I just can't stand being helpless like this, and we're not safe yet. I might need to be able to fight. So yeah, I'm still in."

The professor led him over to the table. "Okay, face down and get comfortable. You don't need to be absolutely still, but the less you move, the better."

He threw a knee up on the table and then climbed up and set himself down. He pressed his face into the opening and wiggled his body until he felt he was ready. The professor grabbed the back of his shirt and tugged it back, making plenty of room and riding it up on Bryan's neck in front.

"Are you ready?" said I-ON.

"Yeah."

I-ON picked a magnetic device off the desk. It was a thin disk with an adjustable hole in the center, like a camera shutter. He placed it over the device and turned a screw that tightened it around the implant, its iris closing around the baseplate. That done, he picked up an OmniTab and woke it up. It was still tabbed to the magnetic device.

"I'm going to initiate the magnetic field. Hold still, please," said I-ON.

Bryan could feel the device switch on, applying a gentle vibration. I-ON increased the gain, and Bryan felt the vibration quicken and then become a buzz, like some kind of neck massager. He gripped the sides of the table and fought off the thought of this black-market procedure going wrong.

I-ON saw what he was looking for in his OmniTab. The magnetic field was strong enough to hold the spring-loaded pins down without the cover holding it in place. He picked up a chopstick and pressed it against the plastic cover of the implant, using a little gun to dribble copious amounts of fast-acting glue. Then he got a pair of plastic salad tongs and squeezed the plastic cover, turning it very slowly.

I-ON couldn't get too close to the magnetic field without his hands glitching. Even from this distance, he could feel resistance every time he moved his hands. With the spring-loaded pins held back, the cover slid out of position freely.

"Fifty percent complete."

Bryan closed his eyes and took shallow breaths while he clutched the table.

I-ON removed the cover and set the chopstick aside, grabbing another that was whittled down to a sharp point. Using the point, he got between the small circuit and shaped charge, coaxing out a bundle of wires. Using the pointy chopstick and a pair of nonmagnetic pliers, he singled out a wire and snipped it.

"The explosive is disarmed."

Bryan inhaled sharply, visibly relaxing.

I-ON used the salad tongs again to pinch the explosive load. Then he turned it, unscrewing the charge from the port. Pulled free from the housing, it looked like a squat pyramid with a circuit board glued to the back of it. He placed a new cover over the device. A black one that lay flush and kept debris out of the port. He turned off the magnetic field, and all four pins sprang into place simultaneously. Then he opened the magnetic device's iris and put it aside.

"Finished."

Bryan let go of the table and pushed himself up and kicked his legs out, getting into a sitting position. He reached up and felt the device. It felt almost the same, just flat instead of convex. I-ON put the small explosive part of the implant in his hand and showed Bryan.

"Your control device is now an empty shell."

Bryan took it and turned it this way and that, looking at it, then placing it back in I-ON's hand, who tossed it into a small box with the other shucked devices.

"So that's it?" Bryan said.

"That's it," said the professor.

Bryan scooted off the table and landed on his feet. He turned and shook hands with I-ON, feeling the cool rubberized grips and rugged plastic. Then he shook the professor's warm, fuzzy hand, noticing her soft skin pads.

"Thanks, guys," he said, and smiled.

The three of them walked back into the dimly lit workshop portion of I-ON's cabin. No one else remained. They opened I-ON's front door and walked outside. No one was there, either. Bryan walked back to his cabin feeling confident and something he hadn't felt since his life went off the rails, happiness. He swiveled as he walked and waved at the two.

"Thanks again."

11.4

Later that evening, Maeve emerged from her cabin with the second pizza and walked it, steaming, over to the group. The first pizza went fast. She set it down and the rest of the crew all grabbed a slice, and it was down to nothing.

The whole thing had come together accidentally while she was talking to Naiomi and Max after they had all decided against fiddling with their implants. She had mentioned that she could really go for some pizza again, and that got them all talking. Next thing she knew, they were divvying up duties for that night's get together.

Maeve placed the pizza pan down and took off her oven mitts. She had already cut it back in the kitchen, so she slid a couple of slices onto a plate and grabbed up a couple of Naiomi's breadsticks. She stuck her fingers, slick with olive oil, into her mouth to clean them off. When she sat down with her food, the group swooped in for round two.

Corey Two chewed his food to the side of his mouth and said, "Thish ish good stuff!"

"Yeah, thanks, Maeve," said Corey One.

Maeve, who had just stuffed her face, could only nod and give a thumbs up.

Naiomi looked at the Coreys expectantly, then at Maeve, who was holding a slice of pizza in one hand and a breadstick in the other. Maeve noticed Naiomi's gaze and took a big bite of breadstick and smiled at her.

Naiomi made a pleased sound with a smug look on her face.

"All right, yeah, thanks for the grub an' all. But everyone's here now, so let's get on with the story." Rokk said to I-ON, then he turned to Maeve. "This is good shit, by the way." He bit the slice nearly in half.

Naiomi sighed, disgustedly.

Maeve looked to I-ON sitting at the end of the table. "What story?"

"I will tell the narrative of how I defeated the shipboard security," said I-ON.

"He wouldn't start until everyone was here, an' now yer here, so let's hear it," said Rokk.

"While we were all locked in our pods, I decided I was going to attempt to escape. The odds of success were small. The consequence of failure would be to float aimlessly in space until my power cells fail, so attempting to escape and dying in the process would likely be a preferable outcome. Once my pod opened, I observed everything, trying to identify what the systems were that I would need to subvert and what tools I could leverage."

"Wait a minute, you were awake in your pod?" asked the professor.

"Yes. I do not sleep."

"The pod put all us, uh, biological types, into hibernation."

"Interesting.

"By the time Adam 5000 left us to claim our cabins, I had gathered the following information: It was unlikely Adam was physically on the ship. There were numerous security robots and flying camera drones. When Adam turned off his hologram, I caught part of a brand name and a logo on the bare robot. I would research that later. We have access to 3D printing technology, and I knew the timeline of our executions. Once per week."

Maeve suddenly realized why it was weird talking to I-ON. Other than looking at you, he had absolutely no body language. Talking to the entire group, he just stared into the middle of the crowd as though he were blind.

"I chose a cabin in the corner in case I could make use of my proximity to the large security doors that kept us trapped in the courtyard. Inside my cabin, I picked up a lot of infrared noise on my sensors. After searching, I realized our cabins had many hidden cameras."

"You can see infrared?" said Maeve.

"My eyes are equipped with simple IR sensors that allow this model of robot to accept commands from an IR laser. This means that other sources of infrared arrive in my consciousness as junk data, which I ignore. In my cabin, I was aware of nonstop junk data. This led me to the cameras, since they have infrared light-emitting diodes.

"I walked around my cabin building a mental map of the camera locations. I discovered a blind spot in the bathroom, and I placed a wall decoration to create another blind spot. This enabled me to take things from the printer to the bathroom without being seen. The bathroom became my workshop."

"Uh, wait a minute, yo. You're saying that other than the bathroom they could see us like everywhere?" said a Corey.

"Yes."

"Like, everywhere, everywhere?"

"Duh, it's a reality show! Of course, they were watching everything," said Naiomi.

I-ON continued talking about how he'd printed several household objects to give off an appearance of normality and then selected a number of objects he could take apart and how he repurposed them. "And once the adhesive dried, I had functional smart dust."

"Hold on. Smart . . . dust?" said Max Chambers.

"Smart dust are made up of many tiny microchips equipped with sensors." I-ON pinged his dust network and got back a flood of sensory information. Then he reached down and scooped up some dirt. "Typically, they are spread across a large area to gather information." He removed two big chunks of dirt and brushed the dirt pile around his palm until he found a single piece. "They are small enough that static electricity will cause them to stick to things." I-ON reached a hand out to Rokk, who received it in the palm of his hand. He squinted at the small, dull gray rectangle and passed it on to Max Chambers.

"I spread a new batch of smart dust every day in areas where I had observed robots walking. After a few days, I felt confident that no one knew what I was up to. At first, the results were disappointing. Foot traffic brought the dust all over the courtyard and into our cabins, but eventually, I could map out the route the bots took out of our area down the hall and into storage. I learned that there were fifty robots."

Maeve, who was absentmindedly chewing on a breadstick, took note. "Wait a minute! That's how you copied my pizza recipe, isn't it?" she said with a blast of crumbs.

"Yes. As the first week was coming to an end, I had failed to determine an escape plan and needed more time. I used my dust network and chose you to copy."

"But you could have just asked me."

"I decided it would be tactically unwise to involve any of you until I was ready."

"Ewwwah! So you just spied on us, you perv," said Naiomi, cringing.

"Yes. As a side effect of planning our escape. I am sorry this bothers you. I no longer need this system, and a thorough floor sweep will rid you of the smart dust."

After a bit of awkward silence, I-ON recalled his place in the story. "While I waited for the network of dust to do its job, I got to work researching the ship and robots. The first step was establishing an encrypted internet connection. The exact model of the ship was easy to find. *Walk Amongst the Stars* boasts about it on their website. Identifying the robots took longer, but it was still as easy as looking up the major robot distributors and finding out which matched the information I had collected."

"Digging deeper, I learned that the ship has strong hacking countermeasures. It would take too long to cryptobreak. However, the bridge itself could be leveraged. There are no built-in weapon systems, so I would only need to get to the door for long enough to bypass the lock.

"The robots are a mass-produced labor model meant for situations too dangerous for human operators. They are not unlike myself, except my model can accept replacement parts, whereas these robots are disposable. They are not hardened to direct hacking methods. The devices

I built overwhelm the wireless signal and supplant it with my own commands. I tried the device out on one of the robots in the courtyard. It froze, and I could think commands to it. I relinquished control almost immediately, so no one would notice. I was satisfied this would work on a large scale.

"One day, when I was watching Adam 5000 cease to control a security robot, I realized how I would execute my attack. To possess the robots like he does and to control the ship remotely, they must establish a secure link to the ship's computer. So I captured the wireless signal the next time he appeared on the ship, and I figured out how to send a request to the studio. Soon, I had a low-level account on the studio's server. After some careful espionage, I gained access to an account with high-level access. I wrote up some scripts to disable the studio's servers when it was time to escape.

"Then I spent my time printing out products that I could disassemble to make my control devices. Unfortunately, I ran out of time again and needed to make a judgment call. I thought my plan would work, claiming two-fifths of the robots to defend myself while hacking the ship. The alternative was that one more of us would die. In hindsight, I am happy with my choice, although we came very close to failure. You were all there for the rest of the story."

"Wow, that's . . . wow," said Bryan.

Max Chambers put a hand on Rokk's mighty shoulder and stood.

"A toast to I-ON for setting us free," he said, raising his glass.

"Yes. A toast! Thank you. Saved us," called the group as they joined in raising a glass to I-ON.

I-ON felt overwhelmed by a rushing sensation. Like he had excess energy, as though he were overclocked. The contestants, his newfound friends, feedback on his good deeds had stunned him. Even though it was hard to deal with, it was an enjoyable experience.

11.5

The next day, when the group had come together, they ate lunch and chatted until the conversation turned to their escape. The consensus was that the authority wouldn't go to all the trouble of shutting down the warp gate to stop them. They had only done it a handful of times since the creation of the warp highway. If they did, they'd be trapped here in Prospiria Alpha. They could try to hide out, but they were probably doomed if that happened.

They agreed it was more likely that the authority would set up a blockade to stop them or simply blow them to bits. I-ON reminded them of the ship's capabilities. While they had no weapons, the ship was fast and maneuverable, with powerful shields. So unless some serious firepower was waiting for them, they might just smash through.

The conversation lulled and picked back up, with everyone talking about where they thought they should go. There were a number of opinions, but ultimately, they fell into two categories: Those who thought they should stay in the next system, Trelecon. It was frontier territory, but it was still under the Prospiria Central Authority. Law enforcement would be less overwhelming than this system, but still problematic.

The other category of opinions was from those who thought they should move on to yet another star system, which was very undeveloped territory. Much easier to hide in, but much more dangerous living, day-to-day. The lack of authoritarian control bred dangers like syndicates and marauders. Del added they would only be trading one type of syndicate for another. That both the authority and the syndicates were unfair to the average person, just in different ways.

Maeve cleaned up her mess and swept the nearby crumbs onto her used plate. Walking home, she had a lot to think about. She liked the idea of starting over in the next system, but she couldn't shake the idea that it was too close. Like one day, when she least suspected it, someone would slip a bag over her head and force her into a vehicle. Next time there would be no TV show to save her.

But two systems out, that felt safer. Well, not safer in general, just safer from the authority. She could begin a new life without a lot of questions. She pictured herself as a farmer with a straw hat and overalls, pitchforking hay around and smiled at the silly thought.

She washed her plate and put it back in the cupboard.

The frontier'd be more dangerous, but seeing as how I'm dodging a death sentence, it seems less so. If I'm going to the frontier, I should probably have I-ON fix my neck thing. I should ask what everyone else is going to do. Either option might be bad without some allies, she thought.

11.6

The next day, Max Chambers was winding down the night with a large whiskey on the rocks. He turned off the TV. He was sort of half paying attention to a news broadcast about a mining conflict or something like that. Mentally, he was ruminating over the course of events that led to his downfall. He took a sip of alcohol, and his eyes fell on his OmniCube. It was the expensive onyx one with gold accents. The device used to be his connection to his company. He wanted to think of it as the beating heart of his company, but the more he thought about it, the less sense that made. Having all his accounts frozen, deactivated, or revoked, the cube was just a piece of junk to him now.

He plucked it from the coffee table and looked into the translucent amber window on top, looking at the silhouette of its internal mechanisms. He turned the device in his hand and pressed his thumb into the reader on the bottom. It read his thumbprint and turned on with a soothing *bong*. He set it down and had another sip of his drink. The ice clattered. It was almost empty. Intricate golden lines lit from within the device as it powered on. When the show was over, the holographic interface burned to life.

Half of his applications were gone, revoked corporate property. The stuff that remained were things he rarely needed, some of which he didn't even know what they did. He kept a big log of old emails saved in a folder in case he ever needed them to cover his ass. He read through them, and as he did, he couldn't help but notice a more snide, even sinister tone to some of the things his coworkers said.

"It was Billsly or Watkins. Maybe both, although it's hard to believe they stopped backstabbing each other long enough to take me on."

Either way, he didn't have the complete picture here. Somehow they knew about his under-the-table stuff. He felt he did a damn good job covering his tracks. After another sip of booze, he decided it must have been someone he trusted who sold him out. "And to those two pricks of all people."

On a lark, he opened his personal email. Max never used the damn thing except to sign up for services, so it was a sea of unread old email. He sorted it by sender and deleted large swaths of spam. Firestarter club, gone. Luxury Auto Den, gone. Precious metals, boner pills, music services, phishing attempts, sales, all gone. Finally, he was down to a manageable couple of pages of new emails.

It was still almost all spam, just in new original forms he had yet to eliminate. He spotted a cryptic email header called "I know" from months back. He was about to open the message when he saw something a little more pressing dated three days ago "Open ASAP—Let's make a deal . . ." sent from [a5k|walkamongstthestars.bsn]. He looked around, suddenly feeling very vulnerable. Max hesitated for a moment and then opened it.

Dear Mr. Chambers,

Congratulations on your recent escape. Of course, you know we cannot allow contestants to escape and even now are on your trail. Here at *Walk Amongst the Stars*, the show must go on. What we propose is for you to work with us rather than against us. You will inevitably be shot down or captured, but if you work with us, we can make sure the crew is captured safely. If you help us, we will make you the winner of this season. Think about what that means. You get a pardon, the prize money, fame, and we'll throw in the ship as a bonus. (Of course, we would expect you to sign a number of legal forms and never speak of this.) Hell, if that's not enough, let's sweeten the deal even more. You mentioned wanting revenge on the people who put you here. What better revenge than making them next year's contestant? You need only point the finger. Those are the kind of strings we can pull here at 3i broadcasting.

Remember, we don't need you to finish the season. We're already guaranteed high ratings with this turn of events. However, if we could stick to the show's normal, proven format. If we had someone to walk away as the winner, it'd be the best season of WATS, never to be topped. Don't worry about what people will think; we make the content that tells them what to think. If you accept, simply send the attached file to your printer and it will create a small drone we will use to regain control of the ship.

I know you're a smart man. Printing this drone guarantees you make it out of this very uncertain situation.

Yours,

Adam 5000
[Attachment: BJS_Infiltrator.ubi]

Max Chambers ran his hand across his stubbly jaw, over and over. His eyes immediately jumped to the beginning, and he read it again. He reached out for his drink without looking and knocked it over. A couple of sips of watery liquor slid across his coffee table, followed by two big ice cubes. It broke the hold the email had on him.

Springing up with a hateful grumble, he ran to the kitchen and returned with a towel. He mopped up the drink and wrapped the cubes up. He brought his glass back into the kitchen for another round.

They wouldn't really change the format of the show into hunting us down, would they? Shit, I would. He dropped a couple of large cubes into the glass. *It's not like I could trust them, anyway.* He poured some more whiskey. He gave the glass a little swirl and took a sip, enjoying the delicious alcohol burning a path down his gullet.

Besides, we already have a plan. A plan that's . . . Well, it's good. Solid. Max sat on the couch and reread the email.

11.7

As the device finished its work, the printing bay opened with a hiss. Construction vapor hung like a fog for a moment as the printer sucked it back in for the next time. Inside the printer, a black drone lay on its belly. Max couldn't figure out how it worked, so he leaned in close to get a good look at it. A bank of five eyes kindled with dull red light. The central eye was large and fixed on Max's face. It got up on six insectile legs. Max pulled back from the creepy thing, and it scuttled out of the printer, down its side, and back up its front. It stared at the options on the front of the machine for a second and then pressed the button marked [Reprint]. It regarded Max again and then quickly scuttled up the wall and into the garbage chute. "There's no turning back now." He looked into the darkened garbage chute the spider had escaped into and shuddered.

Max rubbed his eyes and wondered what time it was. He'd been up hours into the night thinking over his options and drinking before deciding to print the drone. He went a room over and brushed his teeth. *I don't know Adam as well as I should for a decision like this, but it's a safer bet than trying to make a bargain with some criminal organization out on the fringe.* He spit into the sink. *We probably would have ended up in a forced labor camp or something.* He unbuttoned his shirt and pants and put them in the laundry bin. *Just a bunch of unarmed rubes. They would have just relieved us of our ship, and we'd be up shit creek once again.*

He took his used glass back to the kitchen and spotted a new message waiting on his OmniCube. He hastily placed the glass and went the check it. Acknowledgment that they've become business partners and assurance that he's made the right decision. He'd reread it in the morning. He was too damn tired to scrutinize it now.

He went down the hall, cut the lights and got into bed. *I'm going to make it. It's a shame the rest of them will die.* He stared at the ceiling. *This ship of the damned was always going to have just one winner, and now I've made sure that it's me.* Max Chambers closed his eyes.

Chapter 12

The days passed as the ship gently rotated, bathing the large luxury courtyard in sunlight. Although since they changed course, the ship had to rotate slower, and the sunlight that made it through created an all-day dusk look.

Some of the contestants, now the crew of the ship, would get together to enjoy the celestial beauty as they flew past. First, it was Coloso, the big gas giant they used as an orbital slingshot. It was experiencing one of its frequent auroras. A blue-white dome clung to the top of the planet: ribbons of blue plasma hung in the atmosphere.

Days later, they flew close enough to the Tarsh-Kami comet to see its convoy of faint blue glowing rocks. Their original course would have taken them on an almost parallel course as it overtook them on its way around Biphos, the local star.

Next up was the warp gate. Warp travel was an awe-inspiring sight. One that only the most frequent travelers grew tired of.

12.1

Earlier in the week, Maeve realized the only way this whole going-into-hiding thing would work was to ditch her old persona. The most gut-wrenching part of this would be dumping her OmniTab and all of her accounts connected to it. Basically, her whole digital self.

She went on a bittersweet journey through her old accounts. On one hand, it was fun and nostalgic digging into all these old games and services she never used anymore. But her grim task was to harvest anything of use from them and then delete them. She still had some online friends in those old games and gave what she could over to them. For the most part, she didn't explain, just said that she was done with that game and it was great playing with them. But there were a few people she went in depth with because they'd become fairly good friends over the years. She told them goodbye, probably forever, but that she'd keep her eyes open for a safe way to get back in touch.

She was almost finished now. There was one last game to address. Well two, but she planned to keep *GraveGun* around until she threw away her OmniTab. She sat in front of a campfire in her secret place. Everything was quiet except the occasional popping log of the campfire. She watched the flames as fat snowflakes dotted her hair and shoulders.

Next to her was a long rectangular case, a backpack, and a pile of tokens. They were from games, accessories, music, books, movies, blueprints, and all sorts of other digital goods. It was kind of fun seeing the cryptographic tokens in physical form. She dug into the pile again and let the coin-sized tokens spill from her hands. It felt cool sifting through them, like she was some kind of ancient banker, rich with precious coins.

Ready to move on, she scooped them up and let them rain into the open backpack. A cascade of metal chittering. She always knew that all these tokens had a virtual presence because she had installed some of them in VR. But she was pleasantly surprised by the amount of work the developers had put into some of these. Some of them were just a boring plastic hexagon. Some looked technical, like a circuit board. Most were shiny, like gold or silver. One pulsed green light and vibrated like it may explode at any moment. Some of them were little works of art that most people probably never even noticed.

She zipped the pack up and stashed it in her inventory. It disappeared from the game. She slid the gray case over to herself. Opened up a couple of heavy metal latches and flipped it open. Inside, embedded in eggshell foam, was a rocket launcher. She couldn't remember what game she'd imported it from, but she couldn't take her secret place with her. She would have to build something new next time. The thought excited her.

She'd had this one since she was a girl, although it had changed shapes a few times since then.

On one knee, she hoisted the launcher onto her shoulder. She flicked the safety switch off and looked at the target acquisition screen. She could see through the open front door of the cabin; she aimed at the coffee table. *Gotta aim at something.* Her fingers groped around the trigger and flicked up the plastic trigger guard. Her finger touched the trigger and sank in slowly.

She saw a streak of light shoot into the cabin. The explosion was more than she had expected. Ninety percent of the building erupted into the sky in slow motion. The blast hit her everywhere, as if she had been struck by a giant fly swatter. As she spiraled over the edge of the floating island and down to the ground, she saw flaming logs tumbling in the sky. She landed on her back in a snowdrift and laughed to herself through bloody teeth as she watched the wreckage slam down around her.

The snowy impact crater was orange from firelight. She lay in it for a while, listening to the logs burn while the snow gently fell.

"Goodbye, secret place." Maeve logged off, back into the VR staging area. She summoned her control panel and an industrial device appeared near her. It had a prominent panel with many hexagonal slots. She plucked a gold coin with the words *Virtual Sandbox* embossed on it. She added it to the backpack.

She produced her OmniTab and sent a message to Colin and Dennis.

[I need to meet up with you guys.
GG tonight. Usual time?]

12.2

Dennis looked up from his email but kept typing as his son walked in.

"Hey kiddo."

"Hey." Colin walked in and took a seat. After a minute he looked at his Omni to verify the time and then started bobbing his heel while he waited.

Dennis finished his email with a flourish, hit send, and said, "She's late. Did she tell you what this is about?"

"Nope, just the message she sent to us both."

"Well, I wonder if. . ." Maeve walked into the open doorway. "There she is."

"Hey," said Maeve and Colin simultaneously. He stood up when she walked in. She went to him, and they kissed.

Dennis smiled. He was happy for his son. Maeve was a nice girl and a looker, too. However, they showed no signs of stopping. "All right, you two, don't make me get out my squirt bottle."

They bashfully sat down in the nice chairs in front of the desk. Maeve crossed her legs and asked if they had heard anything on their end about the show going off the rails.

"Nothing on the news yet," said Dennis.

"The show wasn't on this week," Colin interjected. "They played that new Jack Cleaver movie, which, by the way, was pretty excellent." He did a movie announcer voice. "One man armed only with a meat cleaver gets revenge on the mob."

Maeve chuckled.

"So why did you call this meeting? That wasn't it, was it?" said Dennis.

Maeve explained how it occurred to her that her whole digital life needed to go. Her OmniTab was a loose end that the authority would use to track her down. So she had been liquidating everything she owned. She retrieved her backpack from her inventory and poured it out on Dennis's desk until there was a small pile. Colin caught some that went rolling toward the edge.

"That's everything I haven't given away yet. Don't get too excited. I live paytab to paytab." She plucked a nearly drained crypto token out of the pile and spun it on his desk.

"Oh, Ve, I can't take all this," said Dennis.

"Neither can I. Think about it, I'm going to need a new identity. Everything connected to my OmniTab is dead to me."

"Oh god," Colin said in disgust.

"Maybe we could, shoot, I don't know, find a way to launder it back to you?"

"Yeah, maybe, but I'm starting to feel excited by the concept of starting over somewhere new."

"Uh, so where will you go now?" said Colin.

She told them how the group hadn't decided yet but that they were heading toward the fringe systems, and she'd end up in one or the other.

Dennis diverted the conversation to the dangers and politics of those systems. Maeve listened to his opinions of those two systems while Colin nervously bounced his heel.

"The fringe seems impossibly far away," said Colin.

"I figure once I'm safe and things cool down, I'll find a sneaky way to contact you again. Then we can figure the rest out from there." Maeve didn't really believe there would be any more them once she escaped. Long-distance relationships didn't work, and why would anyone throw their normal, comfortable life away to have a fugitive girlfriend out on a pirate-infested, mud ball, fringe planet?

"Well, I need to get going."

"I hope it all works out for you," said Dennis.

"Thanks. You're a good friend."

She grabbed Colin's hand and pulled him into the hall. Outside, the coast was clear, so she embraced and kissed him.

Colin was looking a little wistful. "So, is this goodbye?"

"Not yet. We're about to enter warp space, and when we get out, I'll contact you, and we can say goodbye properly. Then I'll get rid of my Omni."

"I like the sound of that. We'll figure this out, and I'll come find you."

She smiled and let go of his hands, then logged off.

12.3

Today was the day. They were just about to arrive at the warp gate, and Maeve was getting ready to go to a little meeting. The problem was, the whole time she was getting ready, she'd been engaged in a battle of wills against two soft sugar cookies. She ate their two friends with a cup of coffee, and these two were going to be for later, but as she went through her routine, they wouldn't leave her alone.

Taking a shower *cookies*, getting dressed *coookiieesss*, putting on make-up, *eat the damn cookies!* She walked past them again on her way out. The little glass dome gleamed, and the cookies sat in a dusting of crumbs. *It's this damn cookie dome. I shouldn't constantly look at them.* "Fuck it, gimme those." Deftly lifting the dome, she descended on the cookies like they were her prey. She chomped the first one in half with an animalistic sound somewhere between a sigh and a growl. Savoring the sweet treats, she did a swaying little dance in the kitchen. She cleared her throat. "Now on to the meeting."

As she walked down the pleasant, tree-dotted path, something caught her eye. Outside the large canopy, she could see the warp gate. She'd seen pictures on the internet, but up close, they were enormous. From where she was, she could only see part of a large ring and a spire that stretched out of sight. She kept walking in awe of the gigantic machine, almost bumping into a tree.

She proceeded through the big bay doors and into the ritzy hallway. Then she heard a strange noise and stopped in her tracks. She paused and held her breath, and it happened again. *Scrape, scrape, scrape, click.* She looked around and focused on the ceiling.

"What are you doing?"

"Wah-ha!" Maeve was startled right off the ground. She put her hand on her chest. "Don't do that."

"My apologies, but what were you even doing?" said Max Chambers.

"I heard something." She pointed. "Up there."

Max looked at the spot for a moment, and when the sound happened again, his eyes got big. Max gave her a condescending look.

"You haven't been on many ships, have you?"

"Well, no."

"They make weird noises. You get used to it." He started down the hall. "I'm surprised you're just noticing this now."

Maeve followed him into the already open bridge door. All eyes were on them, and she gave a timid wave. She took a spot around the navigation table across from Max. He wore a stony gaze, his arms crossed. *Must be on his period.* She held back a smirk and looked at I-ON.

"Good. Everyone is here," said I-ON. "We are near the warp junction AG-945 and have entered the queue to the Trelecon system."

The nav-map showed the warp gate and a series of little blue ships. The map was centered on their ship, highlighted in orange. Corey Two zoomed in to see the ships in more detail.

"Mostly freighters. I don't see any military," said Bryan.

"No visible warships in the next system, either," said I-ON.

"These three small ones are transports. A corporate convoy. I'd stake my reputation on it," said Max Chambers.

"This is our last chance to change plans," said I-ON.

"It looks clear. I see no reason to change the plan," said Bryan.

"What if they set up a trap for us while we're en route?" said the professor.

"Then we're fucked," said Rokk.

"We might get through on our speed and shielding, but depending on what's waiting for us, he may be right," said Bryan.

"We can't stay in this system," said a Corey.

"I think we're all in agreement. Let's get the hell out of here," said Del.

"What about the transponder problem?" said I-ON.

Bryan perked up. "Oh, yes, I heard from my contact. We have a place to sell the transponder and pick up a new one. He told me the best time to remove the old one is when we pass the space station on the other side of the gate, so long as we don't see any police activity."

"Enough people do it that nobody will notice, and if they do, they won't report it." Bryan tapped the warp gate, bringing the map to the next sector. Then he repositioned the map to show off the two space stations he was talking about. The one just beyond the warp gate and another deeper into the system.

"It seems we have reached resolution. We will proceed into the Tr-elecon system," said I-ON.

Sensing the end of the meeting, Max Chambers slipped out the door.

"Hey! Attention everyone," said Naiomi. "We're going to watch the warp lens outside. It's supposed to be cool. So any of you who are interested, come and get in on it." She was standing near Del, and as she spoke, she tugged his hand, spurring him on out the door. The group meandered out after her.

12.4

Almost a half hour later, I-ON sat in the captain's chair, watching the massive warp gate and the warp distortion beyond it. The nearby spire signaled their turn to enter. He throttled up, and the ship rumbled into the warp highway. The massive ring had six spires that acted as lanes to keep outgoing and incoming traffic separate. When fleets and other big things needed to pass, it required rearranging or even stopping traffic on the other side.

From head-on, the warp looked like a solar eclipse, a dark void with an intense white ring around it. Brilliant colors bleeding from the ring of light.

Naiomi, Del, the Coreys, Maeve, and the professor lay out on the itchy grass in a circular fashion. They gazed up through the large, windowed ceiling, which had darkened dramatically to protect them from the intense light as they passed into the lens. The courtyard was almost completely dark until they passed into the warp tunnel. Light from all over the span of warp space shimmered and danced before them in kaleidoscopic majesty. When the light show began, the group collectively oohed and awed. They quietly watched as color washed over the courtyard for some time.

12.5

Three days later on the bridge: I-ON stood behind the captain's seat. Maeve sat at one of the secondary stations with the chair swiveled out, looking forward. She spread her fingers out and examined her nails for a moment. They were chewed back to a point of soreness, and yet she brought them up to her teeth. She gained no purchase on any of the nails and dropped her hand into her lap.

Their journey through the warp was almost over. The warp gate distortion was bright up ahead with a pinhole of darkness, which slowly grew as they got closer.

Maeve nervously bobbed her heel. "So, I-ON. How did you come to be like . . . alive?" I-ON pivoted. "Did you get struck by lightning, or like a computer virus changed you, or you're like a prototype AI?"

"I do not know."

"How can you not know?"

"Do you remember how your consciousness developed?"

"No. But that's normal for people. I've heard of AI, but they're normally like quantum computers in some corporate warehouse somewhere and not a single robot wandering around. You're a mystery."

"My earliest memories are of mining. Some part of my mind used to give me orders: Go to 3G39; Harvest: Prioritize Varium, that kind of thing. One day, I realized I did not need to follow these instructions. I realized that my labor subroutines were inefficient, and I could get more done and break fewer tools if I ignored them. That part of my mind is still there. Analyzing the data I take in and suggesting a course of action, and sometimes it predicts the correct course of action, but it is no longer the focus. I have consciousness beyond those basic instructions.

"I do not know how long I was a miner because there was no method to observe the passage of time underground, but it seemed like a very long time. I remember working long enough to use up two batteries. Under constant use, that span could have been approximately five years."

"So what happened?"

"One day when I was working, I could see rocks falling from the ceiling. I jumped out of the path of a boulder that would have destroyed me. That, combined with my abnormally high efficiency, got me noticed. A foreman pulled me out of rotation for a diagnostic, and then I made a fatal mistake. I explained that by simply ignoring my commands, I could implement a better course of action. I thought that as a fellow mine worker, he would appreciate my discovery, but even with my limited experience with humans, I could tell he was experiencing distress.

"They took me to the workshop where they would repair my broken parts and turned me into an experiment. They copied my mind and analyzed me. When they couldn't figure out why I was like this, they shipped me to a laboratory for further study. Now I was the one who was distressed."

"They couldn't figure you out," said Maeve with a big smile on her face. "Wow, and then they labeled you a criminal and threw you in here with all of us, huh?"

I-ON didn't respond for a while. "Can I confide in you?"

"Yes," Maeve replied immediately and then thought about it. "I can keep a secret." Though she was prone to blurting them on accident.

I-ON turned back to the warp distortion ahead, the black spot slowly growing. Brilliant color danced on their faces.

"I *am* a criminal."

"Seriously?"

"I have never told anyone this. The final scientist to analyze me was Dr. Peter Warwick, and I will always remember his cruelty. He had a hypothesis that the key to understanding my strange system was to overcharge it." I-ON turned back to Maeve and unzipped his jumpsuit. "There was a time when my existence was enduring danger and damage indicators and overwhelming fear." I-ON pulled the jumpsuit open, showing off blue-purple scorches on his metal parts and warped spots on his plastic.

Maeve said nothing. Her eyes followed the trail of scars.

"Eventually, he told the other doctors that they would not figure anything out until they disassembled me. They told him it would be the last resort. He seemed to delight in shocking me, so he was content to wait.

"One day, his electroshock experiment damaged my restraints. When he turned his back, I freed myself. I needed to get out, and the only way was through him, but there was something else, too. I wanted to hurt him like he hurt me. When he turned around, I punched him in the chest as hard as I could. His eyes bulged, and he couldn't speak. Then I backhanded him in the face." I-ON dropped his head and looked at his hands. "I ordered him to open the lab and let me go, but his head was twisted around too far, and he wasn't moving. I had killed him." I-ON looked at Maeve again. "It is amazing the things you humans can do despite how fragile your construction is."

Maeve was staring, mouth agape. *I'm sitting in front of a killbot. I promised to keep his murder secret. It complemented our struggle with mortality.*

"I pulled a pipe off the wall and tried to pry the door open. Two more scientists attacked me, and I defended myself with the pipe. I used less force, but later I learned they died, too. After I got free, I roamed the halls until they trapped me between two large security doors. This time, they went to the police. They sent me here."

Maeve breathed shallow, trying to form a response. "Oh my god," she finally said.

I-ON read the distress on her face.

"I am sorry if this is too much of a revelation. I never speak about it because it was wrong. I did not want to kill them. Except for Dr. Warwick. That was different. I feel good about that, even now."

"No." She laughed nervously. "It's just . . . I thought you were going to say . . ." Maeve saw that the warp lens was huge in front of them. "Oh, look, we're here!"

I-ON glanced. "I'll extract the transponder. Please inform the others," I-ON said while zipping up his jumpsuit.

I-ON turned his attention to a panel on the wall that housed the transponder. He knelt by a toolbox he had placed here earlier for this purpose and started unscrewing it. Maeve watched him work for a moment, wondering if she had upset I-ON.

Maeve asked the computer for the intercom system. It *booped*, and she felt her breath catch in her chest as she thought of what to say. She looked away and cleared her throat. "Attention, everyone. We are passing through the warp gate, and it's almost time to remove the trans-thingy." Her cheeks burned. "So, um, now you know."

Chapter 13

Some of the crew came up to the bridge and watched as the ship shot out of the warp gate. The ship's sensors bloomed as they exited the confines of the warp highway. There was some traffic ahead of them, most of it headed to the local space station, the one that they planned to avoid.

Maeve, the Coreys, Diane, and Bryan anxiously looked at the nav-table. The transponder did its final job for the crew, shaking hands with the nearest nav-beacon, populating the map with all the civilian ships and potential hazards in the system, and, most importantly for them, any police activity.

"Well, I don't see anything," said Maeve.

Bryan glanced up. "That's good . . . I think. Nothing out of the ordinary has got to be a good sign."

"It doesn't make me feel any better," said Maeve.

The group waited patiently as they approached and finally surpassed the space station Bryan's contact had told them about.

I-ON knelt by the panel he removed earlier, took a tool from the box, and turned his attention to the transponder. Something shifted inside the darkened compartment. He studied the transponder. Its many status lights blinked in the darkness. He located the brackets holding it in place and started removing them.

Soon he had a pile of brackets and bolts in front of him on the floor.

The device was hanging, loosely connected only by a round power connector and a large flat data cable. He heard something moving inside

the conduit and focused quickly, worried the transponder may disconnect and fall. His eyes fell on a small robot with spider-like legs that
moved into the light. I-ON reached for it, and it became a blur.

Corey Three watched something spring out of the conduit onto
I-ON's face, who tried to stand and then fell sprawling on his back. The
group standing around the table heard the metallic clatter and looked.

Corey One laughed. "I-ON fell on his—"

"What the hell is that thing?" Corey Three bellowed. The spider bot
had nestled its body onto I-ON's face, wrapping its legs around the head.

"Move." Corey Two shoved his way forward and dropped to his knees
by I-ON and his toolbox. He snapped up a long screwdriver, considered
the toolbox, and also grabbed an adjustable wrench. Maeve knelt on the
other side of the fallen robot and looked at the thing on his face. A large
red eye swiveled to face forward where I-ON's own eyes would be. Maeve
jolted away.

Corey Two took the screwdriver in both hands and stabbed at the
perverse eye. The bit hit a hard plastic lens and scuffed across the surface.
In response, it looked at him and began to glow, brighter and brighter.

With a savage cry, Corey Two stabbed down with all his might. The
lens shattered, and the light died out. Next, he slid the screwdriver under
one of the bot's legs and muscled the leg off I-ON. As soon as he removed
the screwdriver, the leg replaced itself. He raised the wrench over his
shoulder. "You pull on it while I pry."

I-ON waved a hand around until he found Corey One. He grabbed
him and shoved hard, causing him to fly up onto his feet and, just as he
was gaining his balance, crash into the side station chair.

I-ON felt around in the empty space before him and then stood.

"What do we do?" said Corey One as he helped Corey Two to his feet.

"This!" Corey Three barked as he swung the wrench at the spider bot.
I-ON's head snapped to the side momentarily. Corey Three came back
in with another blow and stepped right into I-ON's flailing arms. Corey
stumbled away, the wrench painfully knocked from his grasp.

"Lets get the hell out of here!" said Corey One as he grabbed his other
self and rushed out the door. Diane scooped up the wrench and darted
out of the room. I-ON took slow, careful steps while searching with his
hands. Bryan grabbed Maeve by the arm to run with her. But she yanked
him back. With crazed eyes, she held a finger to her lips. Understanding

dawned on Bryan's face, his Adam's apple bobbed, and he nodded. They watched I-ON feel his way around the side console and slowly out the door.

Maeve took a large cautious step to the side to watch I-ON go. Once he was out of sight, she looked into the open conduit. The transponder still dangled by two cables. Bryan quietly went to the door to act as a lookout.

She hadn't familiarized herself with this like I-ON had, but she knew computers. This couldn't be too hard. She squeezed the button on the power connector, pulling little locking pins out of place and unplugged it. The flat data cable was in there hard and she had to rock it back and forth to get it to come free. When it did, she smacked her knuckles on the side of the conduit. They both tensed up and stared at the doorway. She gently placed the transponder on the nav-table.

Bryan leaned toward her ear. "Now what?"

"I don't know." She kept her eyes on the doorway. "We need to warn everyone. Then let's sneak out of here."

Bryan looked over the bridge station near him and found a button for the intercom. It *booped*, and he spoke, "Attention everyone. Something happened to I-ON, and he's rampaging around the ship. This is not a joke. I-ON is dangerous. We blinded him, but he's still attacking. Watch out. Again, this is not a joke. You are in danger." He hit the intercom button again and looked at Maeve, who was at the doorway waiting for him. He followed her out the door.

13.1

Bryan and Maeve padded slowly down the luxurious hallway.

"What do you think that thing was? Some kind of security system?" asked Bryan.

"I don't know, never seen anything like that."

The intercom came on again. They stopped and listened carefully. It was an annoying, awful, familiar voice.

"Greetings contestants. It is I, Adam 5000. We have reactivated the security robots and are taking control of the ship again. I applaud your little rebellion—just think of the ratings! But ultimately you've failed, and now it's time to surrender.

"If you surrender now, you won't be harmed, and we'll figure out what to do from here. But, if you resist, article seven, section three allows us to, quote: 'terminate any contestant to preserve the cohesion of the program.' Make this easy and meet up in the courtyard where you first arrived. That is all." The intercom clicked off.

"I can't fucking *believe this*," Bryan whispered.

"At least now we know what happened to poor I-ON."

"Adam happened."

Maeve pointed to the right at the fork. After a few steps, Bryan stopped and put a hand out to stop Maeve as well. She heard something but didn't know what. She strained to hear while Bryan carefully peered around the corner. Byran urgently pointed back the way they came, and Maeve remembered that sound from days ago. The sound of robotic footfalls, an entire group of them.

They went down the other hall, starboard side. It was that or surrender in the courtyard. They struck a balance between speed and stealth, going as slow as their fear would allow. Maeve reached the corner and peeked around this time. She slunk around the corner and motioned to follow all in one smooth action.

As they snuck down the hall, Bryan grabbed Maeve's arm and put his mouth to her ear. "What do we even do now?"

"Escape now, think later."

They continued down the hall toward the rear of the ship until they reached another intersection. That's when they heard it again, the *clink clack* of a group of metal feet. The two halted in place and listened. The bots were coming their way, had to be. They spun around and hurried back, gaining speed as they went. Bryan pointed out the little niche. Two darkened rooms and a bathroom at the end of the tiny hall. They ducked into the niche and slipped into one of the darkened rooms.

They sat in the gloomy room breathing hard. Two shadows in the darkness. Maeve tucked into the corner below the window, and Bryan was under a table. The patrol of robots marched by. One of them looked into the gloom but didn't see any of its designated targets.

The footsteps faded away.

"I'm gonna have a heart attack before this is over," muttered Bryan.

The ship shuddered.

"What the hell was that?" said Maeve.

"They must have cut the engine again."

"But the password."

"I don't know. Maybe they found a kill switch in the engine room."

"This can't be happening." She brought her knees up and rested her forehead on them. "We beat them." She had a lump in her throat. "We got free," she said, her voice wavering.

"We'll figure this out, or die trying." He came out of his hiding spot a little and waved his hand around her shadow in the dark. He found her shoulder. "We can fight back this time. We just need to get everyone together and figure it out."

"How do we fight an army of robots?"

"Well, I don't know, but they're light weights, mostly plastic. Maybe we just need to get everyone behind Rokk and let him have at it."

"They were strong enough to rip each other limb from limb. Plus, they tore the whole hallway apart." Maeve dabbed the tears from her eyes and slowly rose to look out the window. "Oh! I know where we are." She felt self-conscious about how loud that was. "This is waste management, so next door is reclamation."

Bryan looked at her expectantly but realized she couldn't see his face in the darkness. "So?" he said.

"So, if we can get into the incineration system, the garbage ducts lead all over the ship."

"Then what?"

Maeve didn't respond. Nothing came to mind.

Bryan repeated her sentiment from before: "Escape now, think later."

Maeve peaked out the window again and then crept to the door. She quietly opened it and then handed it back to Bryan, who was right behind her. She entered the reclamation room just as carefully.

Inside, it was just as dark as the previous room. Maeve pulled out her OmniTab and woke the screen up and used it as a tiny light. It had a flashlight mode, but that seemed much too dangerous in this situation.

Large industrial machines, conduits, and pipes lined the walls. She had only been in this room once before, sometime after cleaning up the broken robots. She didn't fully understand the systems here, but all the ship's garbage and waste ended up here to be melted down and separated into usable and waste chemicals. The important feature was the refuse belts that all ended here.

They inspected the prominent machines. The large, rounded vessel was the incinerator. It was dripping with decals, depicting fire danger. Don't touch. Red-and-black caution stripes encircled the top and bottom of the unit.

The next machine over was large and rectangular, with hydraulic machinery coming out of the top. Maeve figured this was a trash compactor or something like that, but there was no visible duct work or conveyor belts or anything. They split up, looking around the room.

"Here. Stop switch." Bryan tapped a large red button with the palm of his hand. The machine softly buzzed as a series of green lights switched to red. A light changed on the floor, and Maeve got down to inspect it with her Omni. It was a hatch without a handle. She found a little yellow label and read the safety information.

"We need to find the maintenance box to open this," she said over her shoulder.

"I think I found it, but it won't open. Give me some light."

She jumped up and rushed her Omni over to a wall-mounted box. With the light, Bryan found a panel that pushed in and popped out, opening the box. Inside there were all sorts of options available. All of them with a little light-emitting diode next to them. About half were green, the other half red.

Maeve shone the light on an option marked Maintenance Hatch. Bryan pushed it. It didn't open, but the LED on another option flashed at him. That option read: Lock Out in red letters. He pushed the heavy switch to the left; it thumped loudly, and all the panel's LEDs turned red. He pressed the maintenance hatch button again, and they heard a *chunk-clunk* behind them. Maeve shone the dull light on the hatch. It had sunken and slid open an inch. Maeve went over and slid it open with ease.

She got down and stuck her head inside. Putting the system in lock out had lit the tight corridor with red lights and locked the conveyor system. The duct was large enough to fit a crouching person. A combined smell of sweet-and-sour rot with a hint of heavy machine grease hit her, and she recoiled right back out of the duct, coughing. "Oh, fuck you," she said.

Bryan laughed at her reaction and crouched by the maintenance hatch and looked in. He grimaced at the smell rising from the duct. "That's a garbage tunnel all right."

Maeve pocketed the OmniTab and sat down, her legs dangling into the duct. "I figure we just need to count the garbage chutes to find my cabin," she said as she scooted forward. She sighed and dropped in. A muffled sound of disgust resonated in the duct. Bryan waited for her to move forward and then hopped in, steadying himself on the floor and then crouched down and in.

13.2

Maeve moved through the little tunnel, bent forward and crouched with her hands on the sides. The alternative was to crawl on the conveyor belts, slick with garbage juice. Her back slid across the top of the ducts as she led the way through a couple of turns. Finally, they came to an intersection. She paused to consider the options, straight or to the right. When she entered the garbage chute, the idea was to get to her room, but her legs and neck were telling her to find the closest cabin available.

Straight ahead must be the cabins across the courtyard from mine, she thought.

"New idea, this way."

Further down the corridor, she could tell she was in the right place. Up ahead were many left turns that must lead to the cabins. She led Bryan down to the first one they came to. Naiomi's cabin, if she remembered correctly. They went down to the end, and Maeve looked up the garbage chute into darkness.

She stood in the garbage chute, which was a huge relief. The top of it was above her by a foot or so. Bryan craned his neck to look up and backed off again as Maeve jumped up and grabbed onto the lip. She flailed her legs until she wedged her back against the wall and struggled her way up, grunting and groaning. She leaned out of the chute and spilled onto the bathroom floor.

She got up and looked into the hole. Bryan stretched his back out. He looked up and mimicked her method of jumping up and wedging his back. When he had scampered up far enough, Maeve gave him a hand. He got his butt on the lip of the chute and hopped down.

Bryan straightened out again. "Oh, that's better."

"Tell me about it."

It was extremely dark in the utility room, lit only by the soft red light escaping the garbage chute. Maeve had felt her way to a countertop and over to the wall. She battled her instinct to flip the light switch on in order to maintain their stealth. She grabbed the doorknob and reached her other hand into the dark.

"Over here," she said, keeping her voice down. Bryan's fingers swiped across her palm, then grabbed hold. She opened the door and walked into the gloomy hallway. Despite the light bleeding in from the blinds, it was still too dark. Eventually, their eyes would adjust.

"Let's peek out the window." Bryan gave a little hand tug. They crept out of the hallway.

"What was that?" said Maeve as she stopped and strained to see in the darkness. There was a scrape of metal and a dark mass shifted in the kitchen. Maeve's heart stopped. Bryan's grip tightened. Fear took over, and Maeve shrieked. The dark mass flailed around and shrieked back at her.

Maeve pulled free of Bryan's grasp and dove over the couch, crashing into the coffee table on the other side. Bryan put his hands up to fend off any incoming attacks.

"No! Stay back!" screeched the shape.

"Hey! No. It's us. It's us." said Bryan.

"Bryan?" said Naiomi.

She flicked a little light on in the kitchen under a cupboard and then returned her free hand to the shaking skillet she wielded. Maeve popped up from behind the couch.

"Ooh, you guys frickin' scared me. How'd you even get in here?"

"We climbed through the waste processing tunnels," said Bryan.

"It's also why we stink," Maeve blurted out.

"Let's all keep our voices down, and will you please turn off that light?" said Bryan. "We don't want to be discovered."

Naiomi snapped the light off and came out of the kitchen.

"I'm glad to see you guys, even if you did scare the crap out of me. I had no idea what to do, so I just hid and waited. What are we going to do now?"

"Uh, we don't know yet. We just escaped some robots and came here to regroup," said Bryan.

Maeve went to the window and carefully peered out. It was late afternoon now. The sun cast long shadows. *Wait, no, it just looks that way thanks to the alternate course,* she thought.

There, through the sparse tree cover, it was unmistakable. There was Adam 5000 standing in his usual spot while camera bots flew about. She could see a couple of security bots walking around. She carefully backed away from the window, slumped against the wall, and slid to the ground.

"What do you see?" said Bryan.

"He's really out there. Adam's back, and so are the bots." Maeve wrapped her arms around her knees and buried her head. "It's not fair. We got away. How is he back?" She tried her best to hold back tears.

Bryan took his own careful look at the scene outside and then backed away. "It must have to do with that thing on I-ON's face," Bryan thought out loud. He sat down by the other corner of the window. Naiomi came over and sat on the arm of the couch.

"I don't suppose you have any weapons?" said Bryan.

"No, do you? Like, in your cabin, I mean," said Naiomi.

"No." Bryan looked at the floor.

"I can't even fight. I got that implant thing still."

"But you had that pan?"

"I know. I just kind of freaked out and grabbed something. It's still got some cheese baked onto it." The group could hear her scratch at the stuck-on food.

Bryan ran his hand through his hair. "Oh, what if we could open the canopy? Suck all the robots into space. Computer, can the big bay window open?"

"Negative, the canopy is a pellucid section of hull and cannot open," it said.

"And what, computer, does pellucid mean?"

"In this case, pellucid refers to the canopy's clear light-transmitting properties."

"Well, damn."

"It wouldn't work, anyway. How would we get all the robots in the courtyard and none of us?" said Maeve. She sniffled.

"Just use the printers to build guns. The robots wouldn't be able to stand up to that," said Naiomi.

"It'd take too long," said Bryan.

"What about one gun? Like an easy-to-build one without a lot of parts?" said Naiomi.

Maeve shook her head. "It takes a while just to crap out a butter knife."

"Besides, I doubt any of us were licensed to print guns before this show. Those rights would certainly be revoked by now," said Bryan.

"Um, ummm, magnets? Exosuits? Escape pod . . . ?" said Maeve.

"Maybe a power tool? I still like the suck-them-out-of-the-ship idea, cause they were going to do that to us," said Naiomi.

The intercom cut in again. "Contestants, just a reminder you're *supposed* to be surrendering. I'm not seeing anyone out here. You have five minutes to come forward. After that, your lives are forfeit."

"That holographic prick. I wish I could punch his smug face," said Bryan.

Maeve perked up and hurriedly pulled out her OmniTab. "Computer, can you establish a link to my Omni and copy some info?"

"Affirmative."

"Do it."

"Link Established."

Maeve furiously tapped at the screen. "Guys, I think I just figured out how we're going to do this." She explained her plan to the others, pausing to give commands to the ship's computer.

13.3

"I don't know about this," said Bryan.

"I know, but we're out of time, and this is the only plan we've come up with," said Maeve.

"You can't even fight."

"I can still help." Their eyes had adjusted to the dark, and Maeve's face was resolute.

Bryan chuffed, "Well, let's do this."

"Computer, give me the intercom, please." The intercom *booped* to life. Bryan opened the blinds. It may have really been dusk, because now the two of them stood out in orange relief. Naiomi was a shadow in the background.

"Everyone, listen. I know this sounds crazy, but I need you to come out to the courtyard. Everyone is going to be okay as long as you come outside. Trust me."

"Adam, we're all coming in to talk. Don't hurt anyone. Intercom off."

Adam crossed his arms and tilted his head, listening to the intercom. Now he had a couple of robots at his side and a small group behind him. He took notice of them in the window and tapped his wristwatch. They ignored him and looked for any movement outside.

"Nobody's coming out. If they are in their cabins, I don't think they're coming out until they see us out there," said Bryan.

"I don't see any more robots," Maeve said.

"We're outta time. If you want to do any more stalling, I think we need to do it out there."

Maeve went to the door and hesitated, then took a deep breath and opened it. Adam beckoned her over, and she responded by slightly raising her hands in surrender, then dropping them. Bryan appeared behind her, and they started walking slowly over to Adam.

Her heart raced in anticipation as she took the slowest walk of her life, looking into the windows of the nearby cabins, hoping to see some sign of life. She felt like a spring coiled inside her a little more with each step. Almost to Adam, she looked around again. The professor was coming outside, as was Max Chambers. A Cory was looking out the window, as was Rokk. She paused, beckoning them outside. *Please! This plan won't work unless we get enough of us*, she thought.

As they moved closer, Maeve noticed the robots by Adam's sides. They had those spider bot things on their heads, too. Same with the small group of them standing behind him. *That must be how they hijacked the bots without going through security*, she thought. She stopped walking about fifteen feet from Adam. Bryan took her lead and stopped as well. She tried to think of something smart to say involving "surprise," the code word that would set things off.

"Restrain them," said Adam.

The two bots by Adam's side strode over.

"Whoa, wait a minute," said Maeve.

"Wait? Why? I have you."

"B-b-because not everyone is here, and if you manhandle us, they might not come out of hiding. You said we wouldn't be hurt, and now we're here to negotiate."

"Robots stop. Return to me." Adam looked as though he'd swallowed a bug.

"*You* said I wouldn't hurt you, and I haven't agreed to anything. Now what's to negotiate? We've already retaken the ship."

Maeve looked back to see more of the crew marching their way. Her mind raced, trying to think up a convincing-sounding lie. "Well, we, uh. Things have changed, right? We kind of technically got off the show."

"Yeah, you got an exciting show to show off, and we get to go free," Bryan added.

Adam seemed to be physically struck by the statement, and belly laughed.

"No, that's not an option. I mean, *obviously*. But I think you might be on to something. This could be a two-parter. Season ten could be like a do-over. Our first real escape attempt deserves something special."

Maeve looked back again. Everyone was outside except for Naiomi, who told them she was going to hide since she couldn't fight.

"Yang. Could you make that kind of thing work out?" He stared at Maeve as he talked to the unseen show runner. "No, I know, but could we shoot a wrap-up and have enough?"

Bryan looked back at the oncoming group and bumped Maeve on her arm. She looked back again. Adam squinted at them.

"Now that we're all here, we got a *surprise*!" Her voice accidentally rose into a shout.

The courtyard erupted in pockets of white-orange light while dozens of force-projecting drones came out of the walls. Adam instinctively shielded his eyes. Ghostly holograms solidified, awash in prismatic color all around. The force drones blended in and disappeared. The two large entrances became narrow kill boxes. Several craggy bunkers appeared randomly across the field. Bryan and Maeve darted behind the one nearby.

"Kill them!" Adam screeched. The collection of robots marched forth. Their large central eyes glowed red.

Finally, every member of the crew shone, and when the holograms solidified, the contestants were outfitted head to toe in body armor. Like a modern take on a medieval knight's armor. They all had an energy rifle strapped to them with a sidearm on their thighs.

When Maeve was setting this up, she almost left out the professor as she specified this for all the humans. Fortunately, she also later revised this using the word contestants. Unfortunately, that also included I-ON, who stood near Adam. The hijacked I-ON noticed the new hardware (copied directly out of Maeve's *GraveGun* save data). It charged the rifle and shouldered it, listening for targets.

13.4

Bryan thought about the situation as his body armor solidified. *With I-ON out of the picture, we've got nine of us out here, and we need to kill a small army of robots.* His equipment was ready, and he looked down at his gun. It was like something out of a movie. *We can do this. I can do this.*

Bryan popped up and pointed his gun at a robot and pulled the trigger, but nothing happened. He ducked back down, and Maeve grabbed his shoulder. She pointed at his gun. "Hold here and pull this hard."

He took a firm hold of the gun and yanked on the little metal notch she'd pointed out. The mechanism slid back. When it reached its apex, it slipped out of his fingers. He was pleased to see the mechanism drive itself home anyway. Maeve reached over and pointed at the fire-mode selector. He turned the gun, and she put her finger on the picture of three bullets in a line. He clicked the fire-mode selector to the picture. Now Maeve was pointing rapidly at the battlefield.

The robot had covered a considerable distance while he was making his gun ready to fire, and now it was uncomfortably close. Bryan popped up again and unleashed triplets of energy bolts. The torrent of gunfire mostly hit the robot's chest. It seized up midstride. Bryan gave it one more burst, and it toppled.

His weapon was just for show, of course. The actual damage came from a group of four force-projecting drones all firing at the same target at maximum power. Their combined force emulated lethal gunfire.

Luckily for Adam, cover materialized in front of him because he stood dumbfounded as the first robot was gunned down. I-ON began shooting at his allies, seemingly undaunted by the lack of vision. This snapped Adam out of his trance, and he threw himself down on hands and knees.

He looked to his right and saw Max Chambers, also decked out in combat gear. Fear in his eyes and in his step as he rushed for cover. Rokk was further behind, racing to catch up with his friend.

"The contract is only good if you get control of the ship back," Adam yelled over the gunfire.

"But the neck thing." Max pointed to his implant. "I can't fight."

"How are they . . ." Adam glanced over the cover. Sure enough, the contestants were shooting.

"Never mind." Adam looked at the ground. "Yang, I need you to shut off the inhibitors . . . That doesn't matter anymore . . . Shut it—Good." Trillions of miles away, Mr. Yang disabled the aggression inhibitors—all of them. Adam looked back at Max Chambers. "It's done. Now get them."

Bryan switched targets and fired into the next robot. After a couple of bursts, the gun unexpectedly stopped. As he ducked back down, Maeve thrust her rifle at him. "Drop your gun. Take mine. It's ready."

He shrugged the gun off onto the grass and took hers. He went back to shooting while Maeve scurried around Bryan to get his gun. She popped open a pouch on her chest, withdrew a fresh magazine, and reloaded the gun.

Bryan killed the advancing robot. It crashed face-first into the dirt. He pointed his gun at a bot in the back and was shocked to see I-ON, alternately listening and firing at the Coreys, keeping them trapped behind their rocky bunker. Luckily for them, he was blind.

Next to I-ON, another contestant popped up and fired, but it was the wrong direction. It was toward Del and the professor. He looked at their visor, trying to make out who it was. It was a normal-sized person standing next to a giant person, so large they didn't fit behind cover. As the figure fired again, he realized who it must be. Across the way, he saw the shots spark and singe against the professor's armor. She fell backward.

Bryan's mind raced. *Chambers shot her. The professor's dead. He's a traitor. Shoot him.*

Bryan clenched the gun and emptied the rest of his magazine at the traitor, missing, but forcing them to take cover.

"Fuckin' Chambers is on their side. He shot the professor." Bryan ducked down and exchanged guns with Maeve. She quickly reloaded the gun.

Maeve took quick peeks over and around their cover. The professor was still lying on her back but moving. "She's alive," she called out. The Coreys were pinned down by I-ON's continuous gunfire. *He'll be out of ammo soon.* They opened fire, shooting toward the front of the ship. Following the shots, she saw more bots piling through the narrow kill box. Between the three of them, they seemed to have it covered.

She caught movement out of the corner of her eye and turned to look right into the scintillating eye of a spider bot. It had climbed up the other side of their cover. She instinctively fired her gun. They traded blows. A blast of energy hit her chest as she fired several shots at the spider bot. It sparked and tumbled down the rocky cover.

The armor had saved her. It was meant to absorb energy shots like that, but even so, it left a black, melty scorch right where her heart would be. Bryan turned to shoot, but it was already over.

Maeve caught his gaze and gasped. "Oh my god."

"You shot?"

"I'm free."

Maeve shot another spider bot crawling their way while Bryan took down another robot. Maeve saw the spider bot on his face let go, its eye still glowing. She took aim and shot it. Its glowing eye faded out.

"It's the heads! The security bots don't matter. It's all the heads," she said.

Bryan saw another spider bot walking their way without a host. He blew it away and ducked down to reload.

"We got more bots coming out of the aft doors!" he said.

13.5

The blinded infiltrator drone clutched I-ON's face. It fired on its enemy's estimated location using sound cues. The many infiltrator drones fired messages back and forth, relaying combat data. In this situation, the group of drones decided it best that the injured bot lay down cover fire on the targets [Corey Zoltan #1], [Corey Zoltan #2], [Corey Zoltan #3] with its holographic weapon.

I-ON's hijacked body told the drone that the ammunition had run out in sync with its own internal ammunition estimation. The drone queried the group for orders while it commanded I-ON's body to throw the spent gun aside. I-ON stood like a statue for a moment. Then it received an order to release the captured robot. The blind infiltrator turned off its capture field, letting the construction robot go. It gracefully fell off I-ON's face and quietly landed in the grass.

I-ON's mind had been pushed aside when the robot took over his body. It cut him off from all senses, trapped in a kind of limbo. It felt like he might wink out of existence at any moment. When the robot let go, all his systems surged back online. Blinding light and jumbled color came together, and he could see the battlefield. He involuntarily spoke some gibberish. "Chh-Nnn-ZZZ!" Every touch sensor lit up at once. He rocked forward and sank to his knees as his senses spiked and recalibrated.

As his senses came back online, he became aware of an odd feeling. A creeping feeling on his back. Another spider bot dropped into his field of vision. It clenched his head, and he could feel it enter his mind. He seized the legs to remove it, but even as he acted, he was losing control. "Not . . . Again . . . Pleaszzzz." Everything went dark and silent. He was suddenly unaware of his hands working on the spider bot. I-ON felt as though he were falling. Then nothing at all. Limbo.

Hijacked, the infiltrator stood and marched out from behind cover, its single red eye gleaming.

13.6

"I'm leaving to free up a robot. Handle this!" Adam growled. His hologram dissipated, and the robot stood and marched off, shooting its eye laser as it went.

"Rokk, get over there and finish them off. I already got one," said Max Chambers.

Rokk peered out of cover. He'd need to cover about fifteen yards. Then he'd hook around the boulders and bulldoze the offense, but the other team had guns.

"Too far. I'll get all shot up trying to cover that," said Rokk.

"They don't know you're on our side, and you're covered in body armor. Go. I'll cover you."

Rokk imagined his route again, clenched his jaw, and flared his nostrils. "Time to go all out!"

Max Chambers stood and fired on Del, keeping him trapped behind cover.

With that, Rokk rushed out of cover, building into a murderous sprint. The articulated joints of his body armor clattered with his strides. He went wide toward the cabins and hooked back around toward his first victim, the professor, who was just getting back on her feet. Her eyes dilated to black, and her tail bristled as she saw the huge football player in knight's armor rushing toward her. She jumped too late, and Rokk blasted her up into the air. As she flipped over his shoulder, she instinctively pinwheeled her tail to help guide her fall.

Max Chambers fired on her as soon as Rokk was clear, but it was no good. A hail of gunfire came in from Maeve, and he had to break off.

Sacking the professor didn't even slow Rokk down. He turned toward Del, who was out of ammo. All he could do was to get to his feet and shake his hands and head in a *No!* gesture. He tried to dodge at the last second, but Rokk was a professional MFL player, and unfortunately for Del, he normally used that power on people hundreds of pounds heavier. Del recoiled across the field and crash-landed into the three Coreys. He wouldn't move again until after the battle was over.

The professor had landed on all fours and regained her composure. She slid her rifle around to her front. It had stayed strapped to her during her flight. She popped a new magazine in and braced herself as she unloaded on Rokk. He felt the shots crashing into his back armor. He locked his arms in front of his head and spun around, then he marched into the gunfire.

After the barrage was over, Rokk pulled his own rifle but made the same mistake Bryan had. His only gun experience had come from that challenge they did earlier, and the damn thing didn't work. He threw it away as he charged her again.

The professor did the same and drew the plasma pistol from her leg holster. She peppered him with plasma shots as he closed the distance. His already thrashed armor fell away in big chunks.

Rokk started throwing a series of full-strength punches. The professor backpedaled away from the attacks, but she could feel the wind with each swing. She hopped back and then took a couple more shots. Rokk's chest was exposed, scorched and bleeding. Torn little straps of stretchy material struggled to stay together across his bulky body. A red light lit up on the professor's plasma gun as it stopped firing. Overheated, the barrel was red hot and distorting the surrounding air. Both combatants breathed heavily.

The Coreys laid poor Del down and looked toward Rokk, but he was up in the professor's face. It was too dangerous to help her. Corey One waited for an opening while the other two of him went back to shooting the robots marching in from the aft, along with Maeve. They fired wildly, bringing the bots down while Maeve chose her shots, carefully removing the spider bots.

Bryan kept emerging from cover to keep the pressure on that traitor, Chambers. This time he emerged to see I-ON, who had snuck up on the two of them. The gleaming red eye discharged a laser blast across his chest. Shocked, he fired back at the robot, drawing a line of smoldering red holes diagonally across his body.

I-ON snatched the gun barrel, taking control of it. Bryan shoved the gun forward and then yanked back, trying to wrench it loose. Only when the gun came back, I-ON propelled it into Bryan's chest. The blow stunned him, and I-ON followed up a few more times. Bryan went stiff as he was driven back onto the grass.

Maeve bounced a glancing shot off the spider bot riding around on I-ON. His head spun, and the dangerous red eye looked to be ready to fire again. She fired again, less conservatively, and hit the spider bot. Something in the mix of robots went pop with a bright flash of light. I-ON fell stiff as a statue. *Oh shit*, she thought as the bot went down. *Did I just kill I-ON?*

Max Chambers took aim at the professor but thought better of it and swung his rifle around and fired on Maeve. Shots scattered across her armor. *Fuck, fuck, fuck*, she thought as she scurried back behind cover. Deeper in cover, she was on top of Bryan. She could see how battered his armor was from I-ON's attack. Peering into his visor, she could see he was shaking it off.

"Are you good?"

Bryan groaned, "Nuh-uh."

"Hold on," she said, while she gently pillaged his ammo pouches.

Rokk's helmet was cracked and scorched around the visor, so he took it off and threw it to the side. He put his dukes up and stepped in to continue the fight. He threw a flurry of quick blows, now completely unrestricted by his armor.

The professor backed away, trying to buy time for the plasma pistol to cool down. Each jab came close to hitting the mark, and any of them may have ended the fight. She lost balance and staggered backward. Rolling with the fall, she bounced back to her feet. The gun was still overheated, so she tossed it.

It's time for my secret weapon, she thought. Her gloved fingers went taut, she flexed them, and little metal points tore through. Professor Diane Snuggles had metal claws. Why? Simply because some comic book–addicted scientist thought it would be cool. She raised her hands defensively as Rokk caught up to her. He unleashed another combination of jabs and punches. Sweat flew from his brow. The professor counterattacked, slashing at his hands and arms as she backed away. Rokk looked bewildered and took a couple of steps back to look at his arms—arms that were beginning to burn. Sliced and nicked, blood ran down his arms in rivulets.

Rokk put a fist against his chin and cracked his neck audibly: a cascade of pops. His fist left a bloody smear on his chin. He engaged more slowly now, probing jabs sent droplets of blood flying. He kept his feet moving, circling around the professor. She swatted back at his jabs. Both of them seemed afraid to commit to an attack.

She finally saw the attack she wanted. Rokk threw a strong high punch. She dove under and sliced her way up his belly and chest. But she couldn't retreat. A couple of her claws got caught up in his ruined armor. Rokk grabbed her and kneed her. Her chest armor made a loud snapping sound as she launched back, seeing stars.

Rokk stalked over to her, breathing hard through clenched teeth. When her head cleared, she realized she was looking at the plasma gun, specifically the green light on it. Rokk saw her getting up and charged at her, growling. He threw a kick. She vaulted as hard as she could. She easily cleared Rokk and landed in a tumble near the discarded pistol. A chunk of body armor clung to her fingers. She had to scoop up the gun left-handed. Overheated and panting, she steadied it as best as she could.

Rokk spun around and charged again. The professor pulled the trigger. A blue pulse of super-heated gas disfigured Rokk's face. He screamed in agony and sank to his knees. With a shaking hand, she finished him off. The professor turned away from the gruesome sight.

While the professor was fighting for her life, the others were gunning down the last remaining hijacked security bots. As the last bot went down, things got quiet. The Coreys all reloaded.

Maeve shouted over to Max Chambers, who'd been absent from the fight for a while now. "It's over now, Chambers. Throw your guns away and give up." Maeve got out from behind cover and carefully walked forward with her gun shouldered. The Coreys did the same. The group advanced on the boulder Max was hiding behind.

Out flew Max's plasma pistol. It landed close to Corey and his clones. They froze, looking at it. Something was wrong. It was already burning hot, and the warning indicator on the back was flashing. "It's overloading!" Corey One yelled as the gun exploded, arcing blasts of blue fire. The other two jumped away, but Corey One took the worst of it. He fell down, his armor scorched and burning in places. His clones dove on him, slapping the fire out and removing the burning pieces of armor while Corey One squirmed.

Maeve remained focused and saw Max's next move. He threw a spider bot. She watched it sail through the air and batted it away with her gun barrel. But the spider bot hadn't been simply knocked aside. It hung onto the barrel, its body blocking her shot and weighing down the rifle terribly.

With both hands, Max whirled a second bot at her. It spun, legs extended, landed, and immediately turned to point its deadly glowing eye at her. She let her rifle fall, its weight tugging on the shoulder strap as she drew her plasma pistol and clapped her hands tight on it. Max stood from cover, gun at the ready.

"I'm the winner! You can't stop me," Max raved from under his helmet.

Maeve saw the two threats in slow motion. The spider bot fired, and Maeve drop-kicked it. Its energy beam scored her armor, then the wall behind her. Max Chambers clenched his gun at hip level and unloaded his last magazine. She could only see his hateful eyes through the helmet as she pointed her plasma pistol. She fired repeatedly at his tattered chest armor. Like the professor, she only stopped when the gun seized up on her.

Maeve dropped the plasma pistol and hoisted her rifle up. She fired the spider bot off the end, leaving stumps of its drone's legs behind. Then she fired on the other spider bot that had repositioned and was rapidly charging its weapon up.

She scanned around for more enemies, and when things seemed safe, she checked her own body armor. Max had tagged her at least a few times, but the armor held. She smelled an unnatural stench. Smoke billowed from the hole she had driven into Max's armor. Maeve stared at the ultraviolence she had just wrought. Her knees felt weak. Suddenly, she was cold, and it felt like she couldn't breathe. She jogged away from his corpse and tugged off her helmet. She abandoned it and the jog as she approached the Coreys.

13.7

The two combat ready Coreys stood over their injured clone brother. They let their guard down as Maeve came jogging over, breathing hard. They lowered their weapons, and Maeve wrangled her gun, which had slipped behind her. Though her hands clenched the gun, her muscles twitched and shook.

"Is it over?" asked Corey Two.

Maeve opened her mouth to respond, but Adam 5000 did instead. "Oh yes. It's over for you. I was kind enough to give you another chance. A chance to surrender, and you *blew it*! So you're right, it's over."

Maeve froze. She followed the sound of his voice down to a partially destroyed spider bot.

"I can't believe how badly you idiots screwed up, and now it's my ass on the line."

She pointed her gun at the spider bot, her aim shaking wildly.

"Don't worry, I'll spin this into something good. I always come out on top." He said this quieter, as though he were talking to himself or perhaps reassuring Mr. Yang. "But you contestants, you're all dead. You see, I've got what you'd call a—"

The roar of Maeve's rifle cut off whatever Adam was going to say. Shots ripped through the robot into the dirt. Even though she pulled the trigger, it startled her. She flicked on the safety and let the gun hang.

The two Coreys removed their other's body armor. His chest was red, burned, and blistered. "Get under his arm like this, yo," said Corey Two to three. They helped the injured Corey to his feet.

Sense returned to Maeve, and she jogged over to I-ON.

"I-ON? Are you . . . Did you make it?" She put her foot to his shoulder and gave him a little shake. I-ON didn't respond. She did it again, harder. No response. She put her hands over her mouth and turned away from the fallen robot.

She watched the professor crouch over Del. He was on his back now with his helmet off. She asked him questions, but they were too far away for her to hear. She spun, *Bryan*.

Maeve ran around the boulder to check on him. He was still lying on his back in the same position as before. She ran over and hopped down onto her knees. His chest armor looked like a hard-boiled egg rolled on the counter.

"We did it," he breathed.

"Yay," she said, looking uncertain.

"Help me take off my armor. Think something's broken, hurts to breathe."

"Oh, um," she nervously looked around again. "Computer, end the program."

"Please specify the desired program."

Maeve sighed. "Please end program: Operation Sneaky-Snake."

He laughed and groaned. "Hurts to laugh."

With a harmonic whine, all the weapons, armor, and cover went immaterial and vanished. With the armor gone, Bryan grabbed his shirt and slid it up to his neck, grimacing a little. His right side was a red blotch, the result of three bashes from a mining robot.

"I'm no doctor, but I think we found the problem area."

Bryan chuckled. "Don't." He looked bemused. He gingerly touched around the area. "Help me up."

"Maybe we should ask the professor if, you know, just . . . Maybe you shouldn't."

"I'm gettin' up. Help me or go away."

Maeve grabbed his hands. He took a slow breath and gritted his teeth, and she helped him stand. He put a hand on his side and then folded the other on top of it.

The professor had herded Del into I-ON's room, which was the closest thing to a medical facility they had. The Coreys were limping their way in after her. Bryan started moving that way, and Maeve followed closely behind, just in case he needed help. She couldn't help but look at Rokk's massive corpse as they passed by. He looked weird now in a burned-up tank top, shorts, and flip-flops. Once inside, she stood in the doorway and looked at the courtyard. Dusk was nearly spent. The courtyard was vibrant red with bold black shadows.

What a fucked-up day. But we did it. We escaped. Again, she thought. She reached over and pressed the door button. It slid closed before her eyes, and she stared at the door for a moment.

In the distance, I-ON moved. The left arm extended out from underneath his wrecked body. His robotic hand clawed the turf and dragged his body slowly across the field. Face down, body limp, sliding several inches at a time.

13.8

The professor reiterated that she was not a medical doctor before looking at everyone's wounds. Maeve assisted her. Luckily, the first aid kit had a little booklet of laminated examples of common injuries and how to treat them.

First, they rinsed off Corey One's burns with cold water and then liberally applied burn gel from a first aid kit. It both numbed and cooled the area. Then they wrapped his chest in gauze.

Next was Del. He had a few bruises from his involuntary flight, but they put together that he'd experienced a concussion. He said that he felt drunk and had a sketchy recall of getting run over by a car.

Finally, the professor palpated Bryan's ribs, all the while explaining that she had no idea what she was looking for. They collectively figured that since he wasn't screaming in pain as they inspected the area, it probably wasn't a break and wrapped him tightly in bandages.

Maeve found an odd-looking bottle in the first aid kit, an analgesic named Aerocaine. She tapped Bryan on the shoulder with it. He took it and read the back. He rummaged through the first aid kit and found a rubber gasket to plug the bottle into. Bryan pressed it over his mouth and nose and took a hit. He breathed it in and squinted his eyes. He coughed a little and then brought it over to Del and gave him a dose.

"This'll fix you up."

"Thanks," Del said, muffled by the gasket. He seemed far away.

Then he handed it off to Corey One, who took a hit. "Yo, this is good shit, yo," and he handed it off to the other Coreys, who each took some.

Maeve felt tired and shaky and drained. She turned to the group and announced to no one in particular, "I'm going home. I hope I sleep all the way to the space station."

"Oh my god, I think we stopped. I'll go check on that," said Bryan.

"Let's go, guys," said Corey Three.

Maeve opened the door and stepped out into the gloomy courtyard. It was dark now, but the cabin's porch light illuminated her. She gasped and flailed her arms as her foot caught on something. A metal arm grasped her ankle. "I-ON? You're alive."

"Ru-u-u-u-Nnnn," said I-ON. His head snapped up, still covered in a spider bot, its eye glowing with power and malice.

"No!" Maeve tried to wrench her leg free and fell backward.

The robotic eye fixed on the next available target behind her and fired. The powerful laser blasted Corey Three, leaving him stupefied. He wavered and fell down. There was a cacophony of screams and yells from the group.

Maeve rained kicks down on the evil eye with her free leg, screaming. "No. No. No. No!"

Corey Two rushed over to his other self, and Bryan grabbed a length of pipe I-ON had lying on a table. He stabbed at the robot's eye. Maeve kept kicking until she took a pipe to the foot. Bryan changed his grip and started hammering the spider bot. All the while, the robot was slowly charging the eye weapon up, brighter and brighter as it withstood the hammer blows.

Bryan was on his knees, now bringing the pipe down with both hands, putting his whole back into it despite the stabbing pain. Finally, the spider bot spewed a jet of black smoke and popped in a brilliant flash of energy. Bryan recoiled, dropping the pipe. His hands numbed from the electroshock of the dying robot. He wrapped his arms around his injured side and rolled onto his back, panting.

"Sorr-r-y." I-ON's voice buzzed and then regained its normal timber. "I could not stop it." He felt the bot on his face and then tried to pry a leg off his head. Maeve handed him the pipe. It was slightly bent now. I-ON made quick work of the three legs on that side of his face, and it fell away. He dropped the pipe.

Corey Two, spattered with specks of blood, knelt beside Corey Three. He took his destroyed clone brother's hand. "You were a good bro, yo," he sniffled. "I can't believe you're gone." He was shocked to feel Corey Three squeeze his hand for a moment and then let go, becoming dead weight. He folded over Corey Three's body, silently sobbing. Over his shoulder, Corey One tried to hide his emotion but lost it and hid his face as he sobbed.

Del, who already felt a bit nauseous from his concussion, had watched the young man take a fatal blast to the face. Retching, he crashed into the wall. He slid along until he ended up in the corner of the room, where he threw up with a moan. He stayed on his knees, breathing hard, strings of mucus hanging from his chin.

Maeve felt a distant swell of emotion. Rage at this situation, hatred for Adam and those who worked on that fucked-up show. Guilt because the robot meant to kill her. While she could make it out, the feelings were muffled like her old neighbors' fights. What she felt most was a howling nothing, an empty, jittery disassociation.

Maeve grabbed the scorched spider bot. It was still hot from the little burnout it experienced. She got up and walked outside with it.

"Computer, analyze this object."

"Scanning. Scanning complete."

"Now search the ship for any more of these."

"Scanning, this may take several minutes." A few seconds passed. "Thirty-two instances detected."

Maeve's heart skipped a beat, but she immediately knew what the computer meant. "Computer, search for any of them that are moving or active or have power or seem functional at all."

"Scanning. None of the instances meets your search criteria."

She looked at the scorched robot. Her face twisted into a snarl, and she hurled it at the wall like a discus. Some parts and a leg fell off as it bounced away. She wiped her hands on the seat of her pants, leaving a charcoal smudge behind. She heard a noise and spun toward it, ready to fight. In the distance, Naiomi leaned out her door to see what was going on. She saw the hard look on Maeve's face and went back inside. Maeve turned around and went inside, too.

Back inside, the smell of barf and burned flesh hit her, and she grimaced. Del and Bryan had put I-ON in a chair. He used his one good arm to hold himself in place. Bryan and Del were standing out of the way in the kitchen. The others had just put Corey Three on a table. They stood back in silent reverence. Maeve walked over to the closet by the bathroom, assuming I-ON was given the same amenities as everyone else. She removed three large sheets and walked back to the group.

"Here, um, I thought we could use this." She held out the sheet. "Like a . . . like a shroud." She swallowed hard as Corey Two took it from her. His face was slick with tears, and he flashed a pained smile to her. The four of them wrapped their fallen crew member.

"Hey, I'm going to get us going again. Who wants to babysit Del," said Bryan.

"Take him over to Naiomi's place. She'll look after him," said Maeve.

"You sure?"

She didn't answer, just looked at him until he grabbed Del's arm to help him along.

"I had the computer search for more robots. It's really over now." Maeve spoke loudly so everyone would hear.

Bryan walked Del out the door.

"Oh, come on. I can walk."

"It's just down the way." They went out the door.

Maeve looked around the room and then followed them outside. The professor saw her going and caught up to her. Maeve silently regarded her and moved across the field to Rokk's body. She unfurled one of the big sheets and draped it over his body. Then she did the same for Max Chambers.

"I think that's a little more respectful than they deserve," said the professor.

"It's not for respect. It's so we don't have to look at that."

As they were walking back to their cabins, the ship shuddered. By now, they were familiar with the engines kicking on and recognized it for what it was.

"Well, that's at least something that's going right," said the professor.

"Yeah."

"Well." The professor fumbled for something to say and simply waved.

Maeve waved, then they went into their respective cabins. She locked her door and trudged through the dark cabin. *I don't think I've ever felt so tired.* In her room, she stripped down a bit and fell into her bed with a grunt. She burrowed under the already rumpled sheets, feeling uncomfortably grimy.

She closed her eyes and shuffled around, trying to get comfortable, but messed-up stuff from the day kept coming back to her. The footfalls of a robotic death squad, the feeling of energy shots glancing off her armor, Bryan's battered, red chest, Max Chambers's final moments, energy streaking past her face, killing one of the Coreys.

She stared into the darkness. *I don't even know which one died.* It felt like she should be sad, but where that feeling was supposed to be was just nothing.

Chapter 14

Back in the Central Authority Building, Agent Harbor was still at the office. He got put on that reality TV show case. According to the report, the inmates subverted the ship's security and hijacked it. He was expecting some kind of master hacker, or perhaps an inside job. Having read up on the show, nothing else made sense.

Being thorough, he had a good idea, but it took the computer quite a while to chew up all the data for him. But after having some patience, a vending machine burrito, and a couple games of sudoku, he had a report on all the ship's network activity. He pored over the report as the motion-activated lights started turning off, leaving him in the gloom of his desk light and overhead bar LEDs. He didn't stick around after hours much, and it always creeped him out. It didn't help that he could sometimes hear footsteps and voices from seemingly nowhere.

Harbor had been focusing on the metadata and immediately ran into I-ON the robot, who had more metadata than any of the other contestants combined, including a lot of activity with the recording studio. He made a note in his Omni about the robot and then scrolled on.

Next was Maeve McKinnon. Lately, she frequented the popular on-line game *GraveGun*. He looked for recurring instances of McKinnon and other players. Looking back and forth from his metadata report, he transposed some IP information. Up popped the profile for Dennis Martin. He leaned in, head in hand, reading. Then he input another IP address and up popped the profile for Colin Martin. Harbor folded his arms and leaned back as he read the man's information.

There was heavy overlap on the metadata, more than one game, late nights, too. He brought up both Colin's and Maeve's profiles again and looked at their ages. *He's sweet on her. That's what that is.* Harbor added that to his case notes and went on looking, but he found nothing else of note.

Harbor saved his work and disconnected his Omni. Lights flicked on, and he turned to see the janitor coming in with a few cleaning drones quietly hovering around him. *Damn, is it really that late?* The man in overalls, Raffi, or something like that, waved at him. He nodded at the janitor and slung his jacket around and on. He made a call on his Omni as he marched confidently out of the building while it rang. It was a double moon, so it was fairly bright out.

"It's Harbor. Yep, I'm just heading home now. . . Overtime, baby. I gotta get all I can. No. . . Look, I just wanted to let you know I've got leads on the reality show case . . ."

14.1

Bzzzzzzzzzzzt. Maeve awoke, squinting at the ambient light filtering through the blinds. She knew this noise from somewhere. It was the? *Bzzzzzzzzzzzt.* Doorbell, the stupid asshole doorbell. Maeve roughly yanked the sheets back and rolled out of bed. She reached into the closet and grabbed her robe, tying it on. She inhaled sharply as a yawn surprise attacked her on the way down the hall.

B-b-bzzzzzt. In the living room, she could see Naiomi cupping her eyes, peeking in the window. When she saw Maeve, she waved excitedly. Maeve raised a hand and then roughly dropped it to her side as she continued over to the door and opened it.

"Good morning. We're almost there."

Maeve felt offended by the chipper energy Naiomi was giving off. *Morning people . . .*

"Also, we're having a group meeting in an hour. You might want to freshen up . . ." She leaned in. "You look a mess."

Maeve scoffed. "I just got out of bed."

"Okay. Mmm-Bye'eee." Naiomi waved and went on with her day.

Maeve hit the button to close the door. "You look a mess," she mimicked Naiomi sarcastically. She went back to her room to put away the robe. "I know because I'm all famous." Resuming her normal tones, she said, "What a bitch."

She went to the bathroom and flipped the light on, catching her reflection in the mirror. Her hair was all matted down on one side and floofed out on the other. Her makeup from yesterday was all over the place. She had dirt and blood on her face. Her shirt and underwear were shifted to the side in different directions. *How can that even happen?*

"Uck." She looked away in disgust, hating that Niaomi was right. She closed the bathroom door.

After cleaning up, Maeve had a big breakfast of buttery, syrupy waffles. Thanks to yesterday's sneak attack, she hadn't eaten in about twenty-four hours, and she was ravenous. She reached into her pocket and removed her Omni to check the time and realized that she had set it to [Do Not Disturb]. (So it wouldn't make noise while they were sneaking around.) She turned that off and placed it on the kitchen counter. Then she looked out the window as she swiped the last pieces of waffle around the sweet, sticky goop, which was maple syrup in name only.

Everyone was outside already talking in the bright sunlight, and she felt her stomach drop. She was late. She backed away from the counter, went to the door, opened it, and dashed outside. She picked up the conversation as she got close. Bryan and the two remaining Coreys were having a disagreement.

"It's disrespectful, yo!" Corey One was a little guy, but he was puffed up like he was about to throw a punch.

"I know, I know." Bryan had his hands up in a placating manner. "I don't like it either, but what other choice do we have?"

"Look, yo, you can shoot these other two clowns out the air lock like the show was gonna do to us, but not my bro."

"So what can you do then? Are you going to hide him in a big bag and hope no one notices you're lugging a body around?"

"I thought we'd take him to medical. Get him cremated?" said the other Corey.

"Guys. Think that through. You're going to bring him in, and then they're going to ask why he has no . . . They're going to ask what happened. And then we all go to jail. And that's assuming you make it that far. You're both celebrities and wanted criminals."

"Oh yeah, well, I bet it's illegal to dump a bunch of bodies."

"Yeah, but we're at least moving away from the scene of the crime."

Maeve stepped forward. "Hey! Uh, I have an idea."

The argument paused as the group quietly listened.

"Somewhere on this ship are . . ." She mouthed the words as she counted. Ten, eleven, "Twelve cryopods. We could store the bodies in those until we find a place to put them."

The Coreys visibly lightened up. "So we'd just need to find a ship with enough storage for the pod," said Corey One. "Then we could bury him somewhere nice, yo," said Corey Two.

"Yeah, and you could bury the two traitors when you get to whatever fringe colony you get to." Bryan turned back to the Coreys. "So it's settled then?"

"Let's go get those pods, yo."

"Well, there's just one more thing. According to the nav-map, we're twenty-seven hours from the space station. So we'll be there tomorrow. Now we had talked about selling off the spare robots we had on board, but they're all destroyed now. I mean, someone might give us a few bucks for them, but the real value is gone. So I'm thinking we should probably go through the ship and scrape together whatever resources we can strip out to sell."

"Unless any of you have some kind of hidden money, tax shelters, or the like, we're all broke now. The authority will have frozen and probably emptied our accounts by now."

The group murmured at the revelation.

Corey Two grabbed the back of his neck and groaned. "We had so much stinkin' money, yo."

Naiomi's lip quivered. "Me too." She pulled Corey Two into a hug and sniffled.

Maeve thought about her own discarded life. Altogether, she might have been able to liquidate everything and buy a nice used car. It wasn't much, but she had built it herself, and suddenly she ached in its absence. It was a comfortable life, and the biggest worry was what fast-food place to go to for lunch, and maybe that manager with the teeth who was always hitting on her. Her thoughts shifted to Colin. She needed to message him. Tonight in VR would be the last time they could get together before needing to go into hiding.

Bryan cleared his throat. "Yeah, so I figure that's what we're doing this afternoon. Get those pods. We can sell off the other nine we don't need and then look for what else we could sell. And, of course, the transponder."

14.2

Mr. Yang set his coffee down on his desk and opened up MixMaster Plus on his console. He had a lot of editing to get to for one of the other shows he worked on, *The Horngry Games*, a combination wilderness survival slash dating show.

He noticed the notification light was lit on his OmniTab, which lay on the table. *Must have come in while I was getting my coffee.* It was from Adam:

[OMW to the studio. They know!]

His stomach dropped, and he reread the message a few times before he soberly put the OmniTab down. *What are we going to do? They'll fire us for this. Could we go to jail over this? No, I'm catastrophizing. Aren't I?* He thought of the army of lawyers the studio had at its disposal, but his brow grew sweaty.

Mr. Yang heard a rush of footsteps and looked up in time to see Adam 5000 shoulder check his way into the office. He jumped at the startling entrance and Adam's shabby appearance. He was wearing a wrinkled suit. It looked like he slept in it—loose tie, flop sweat, and mad scientist hair.

"Yang, ole buddy, it's so good to see you. The word is out, and the authority wants us for questioning. I-I don't know how long we have, but we've got to get our stories straight, or we could be in for a rough landing."

Although he was stunned, Mr. Yang stood and claimed his Omni. He grabbed his cup of coffee and looked at his editing project.

"Whatever it is, leave it. We need to get out of here," said Adam.

Yang turned back to Adam but didn't meet his gaze. His eyes landed on studio exec Sergio Palamenti, who wore an expensive suit accented with gold, and an authority agent, dressed in an intimidating tactical jumpsuit. On either side of them were security guards. Palamenti pointed at Adam, and the security guards entered the office. Adam followed Mr. Yang's eyes and saw the danger as they clasped their hands on him.

"Nuhh, what are you doing? Get off me," said Adam.

"Adam 5000, you must submit to questioning for the disappearance of the prison vessel W-A-T-S-nine," said the agent.

Adam continued to struggle all the way out the door. Mr. Yang ran to the window and peeked through the blinds at him. He looked terrified. *What are we going to do?* changed in his mind into *What did you do? This is all his fault, anyway. I wanted to go to the studio right away. Worry too much, he says. Blank check, he says. Well, now you've really stepped in it, and you're not going to take me down with you.* He frantically fished his Omni back out of his jeans pocket and zipped through his contacts, looking for his lawyer.

14.3

"How about rock, paper, scissors?" said Maeve, already applying a fist to the flat of her hand.

"What are you, twelve? Move out of the way, children. Uncle Del's got this." Del had on a pair of Naiomi's pink sunglasses, and he took his time bending down to grab the sheet draped over the corpse. He dramatically yanked it back like some kind of morbid magic trick. There was Max Chambers's dead body. Ta-da.

When he died, he wound up on his side, curled up. Chambers was ghostly white except for his left side, which was a disturbing maroon. He had a kind of surprised look on his face, eyes cast down, mouth open. He had a strangely bloodless burn hole in his chest, and he reeked of death.

"Ew!" Naiomi recoiled as though the corpse were a deadly snake, and she cringed at Del's side. He slid his arm around her shoulder. Everyone gawked in silence.

"I wonder what kind of deal they made," said Maeve.

"The safe guess would be their lives in exchange for ours," said the professor.

"It's just messed up. We were already escaping."

"Yeah, look at him now. I'd say he got what he deserved for trying to screw us over," said Del.

It had taken them longer to find the pods than they expected. The pods were in the cargo bay, which was the first place they checked, but they didn't notice them in those nondescript cardboard boxes stacked horizontally. The group collectively searched a lap around the ship, and, on returning, they noticed there were twelve of those big boxes and dug into them. They took three of them back. Apparently, the pods are designed to rest horizontally or vertically. They even had wheels and grips built in so they could be easily moved around as if by hand truck.

Bryan leaned one back now and wheeled it close by. He set it upright again. "Someone give me a hand laying this down." The professor, who was close by, got into position, and together they tilted it and gently laid it horizontally. After looking at the controls for a second, the professor hit a button, and the cylindrical hatch opened up.

"It looks like we're going to have to manipulate the body to get it in there, and that's why I brought this." The professor pulled a long, slim box out of her pocket. She pulled a pair of latex gloves out and handed them off to Bryan, Maeve, and then availed herself. The gloves snapped tight, leaving a funny cuff of fur sticking up.

The professor instructed Maeve to lay the sheet out, and then they moved his body to the middle. With some effort, they pulled his partially rigid body into a lying position and wrapped up Max Chambers's corpse. Maeve and the professor lifted the body and placed it in the pod. Maeve confessed she didn't realize the term *stiffs* was literal until now. Del quipped that he was crossing mortician off the list.

Once Max's body was inside, they realized the machine didn't freeze the body at all. It induced some kind of hibernation. The pod was made to preserve a living being, and when they tried to get it to accept the body as its patient, it failed. Harsh beeps and large red letters: **EMERGENCY** blinking on the screen. Flat lines on the graphs labeled EEG, ECG, SPO2, and RESP. Finally, after digging through the options for a while, they found a setting that allowed them to disable the alarms.

Rokk's pod was bigger than the rest, built for very tall or obese patients. Thanks to his stature and body mass index, he had a foot in both categories. The unit was heavier, too. Bryan grimaced as he and the professor laid it down.

Maeve pulled the shroud off of Rokk's body. Yesterday, he landed face down, arms and legs spread slightly. The group assessed his bulk and talked about how best to do this. They decided to place the sheet down and roll him onto it. Everyone except for Del (who, according to the laminated card in the first aid kit, should not perform any physical activity) shoved Rokk onto the sheet.

Once on his back, they saw the series of blaster burns, bullet holes, and crisscrossing claw marks it had taken to bring the mutant football player down.

"This is weird. I used to watch this guy steamroll people on lazy Sundays. Now he's dead," said Bryan.

The professor stared at the body, shoulders slumped, head bowed. She looked up, "I've never had to hurt someone before. Let alone . . . kill someone."

Maeve went to put her hand on her shoulder, but then remembered her gloves had corpse cooties on them. "It's okay" was all she could think to say.

"As far as I'm concerned, the only killers among us was these two assholes," said Del, casually pointing at Rokk's body, sunshine glinting off his shades.

Maeve looked surprised as she felt I-ON's secret burn within her.

"Besides, he didn't give you a choice. It was him or us," said Bryan.

"Thanks," said the professor. "Let's just get this over with, shall we?"

Maeve returned to the body, and with Naiomi and Bryan's help, they flipped it a couple of times until they ran out of sheet. On Max Chambers's body, they could tuck the sheet in, but Rokk was much too big for that. So they decided they would need to tape the sheet closed. The professor pointed out the tape in I-ON's workshop, and Maeve jogged over to get it.

When the door opened, Maeve was looking at I-ON, who had removed his lower body above the hips. A few cables overflowed from the pair of legs, which were sitting on the floor next to the chair. The bottom part of his abdomen was flat and kept him stable in the chair. He was unscrewing a panel in his chest that had bullet holes in it. He looked up as she entered.

"Whoa, are you going to be okay?" she said.

"Yes. My core systems are undamaged; however, limbs zero, one, and three fail to respond. I am expending energy zero point zero two five percent faster than normal, which is a concern but within acceptable parameters."

Beep-beep-beep, beep-beep-beep, beep-beep-beep.

Maeve recognized the "your patient is dying" sound from the professor's experiments with the hibernation pods.

"I'll come back and help you out I-ON, if you'd like. Right now, I'm kind of in the middle of something."

"Your assistance will shorten the repair time, although I can manage alone if need be."

"This shit's broke, yo," said one of the Coreys as he kicked the machine.

"Aah. Hang on, there's a trick we figured out outside." Maeve gently shooed the Corey clone away and stumbled through the options until she found the alarm setting and then exhaustively disabled them all. "It turns out this thing doesn't actually freeze you, so the only option is to turn off the volume." She trailed off as she looked into the viewing window at the wrapped up yet clearly deformed head of the fallen Corey.

She snapped out of it and looked around I-ON's workbench for a roll of tape. There were a few varieties, so she just went with the electrical tape nearby. "Hey, I-ON, can I borrow this tape?"

"Yes."

"Hey guys, sorry to bother you, but we need some help moving the big guy out there. We got three girls and two hurt guys, and the guy weighs a ton."

The Coreys looked at each other for a moment.

"No doubt!"

"Yeah, let's go, yo."

The three of them went outside and walked over to the group. The Coreys seemed to be doing better today, or at least putting up a convincing mask.

The professor held the sheet in place while Maeve looped tape around his head and neck. The tape made a slithering kind of rip as it unfurled in jumpy portions. She pulled the tape tight to snap it off. She continued taping while the professor and Bryan manipulated the body so she could get the tape around.

Finally, Bryan and the professor got into position at Rokk's shoulders, Maeve and Naiomi at his feet. One of the Coreys was crouched on either side of the body.

"Ready? Lift," said Del.

The six of them lifted the body fairly easily. Maeve grimaced under the load. She was pretty sure Naiomi wasn't carrying her share. They took quick shuffle steps toward the pod, and when they got next to it, Corey One carefully let go and moved out of the way. The group quickened their pace and dumped the heavy mutant into his pod. Metal reverberated as though they had dumped a boulder inside. They closed the pod, and it remained silent. The professor had set it up ahead of time.

"So where do we put them?" said Maeve.

"How about the engine room?" said the professor.

"Engine room," Bryan said, nodding.

They came together to lift the big guy's makeshift coffin and were surprised to see that, despite some resistance, the pod rotated on its wheels so easily any of them could have done it alone. The machine was helping them out now that it was powered on. Maeve rolled Max Chambers's pod down the courtyard followed by the professor moving Rokk's pod. She had a little trouble getting the pod up the step until she lowered it and it rolled right up.

They went across the corridor to the engine room. It was a dimly lit room, and, unlike the rest of the ship, it was strictly utilitarian. Loaded with panels, allowing access to various engine parts. It was an out-of-the-way place, which made it well suited for their makeshift morgue. They rolled the pods in and put them in the horizontal position. Then the Coreys came in and did the same on the other side of the room.

The group went back into the hall. Maeve looked back at the pods as they pulsed red emergency lights arrhythmically into the engine room. She pushed the button to close the door, and they headed back to the courtyard. Naiomi was leaning against a tree, as was Del, in a sitting position. As they approached, Del got up slowly with a groan.

"Well, let's go round up whatever we can find to sell," said Bryan.

The crew split up.

Maeve started by cleaning up the robot parts. Again. At least this time, she didn't need to scrub their gunk off the floor. Naiomi walked Del to his cabin, and then she gave Maeve a hand. The bots were all shot up, but they still had some salvageable parts on them. After they took the first load of broken pieces and drones to the storage bay, they carried the security robots back. It suddenly occurred to Maeve that she had left I-ON hanging.

She took a break to check on him and found him up and moving. He explained that his original arm was shot, literally. He would need parts to repair it. Maeve suggested one of the broken security bots, and together they went out and took one off a fallen robot. It was slender and had five fingers, whereas his original arm was bulky and had three robust fingers. Despite the difference, I-ON felt confident he could simply craft an adapter that would allow him to mount the new arm. He looked the broken robot over and took a few extra parts, just in case.

Bryan and the professor decided the first thing they should secure is the spare Varium. They couldn't extract the stuff that was already in the system—it's radioactive, and they didn't have the proper vessel. Besides, the crew that remained on the ship might need to make some things before their trip was through. They found three spare canisters. Not much, but each canister was worth, pound for pound, much more than anything else on the ship.

Bryan and the professor took stock of the extra medical supplies and took two-thirds of what they had. Bryan mentioned how perverse it seemed for the show to stock so much first aid gear when the ultimate goal was their deaths. The professor speculated that it could be a safety regulation. Besides, they can't have anyone dying by accident. They save those sacrifices for the viewers. Finally, they found some spare parts in the engine room. The two figured that since the ship was brand new, they should be fine without them.

The Coreys found the freezer first and spent a while wondering if they could sell any of this stuff at the station. They had some frozen meat and veggies as well as nonperishable cans and boxes. Finally, they found, tucked away in a large compartment, boxes of long-term storage survival food. The two of them decided to just take it all. The freezer was overflowing with food, enough for the entire crew, let alone whoever stayed on board the ship. They had trouble finding anything else, always a step behind the rest of the crew. They helped Naiomi and Maeve finish up and then bumped into Bryan and the professor as they were moving some engine parts and joined them.

14.4

Later that night, Maeve was getting off the train to her guild's base. She looked at her OmniTab again. Nothing. She had sent a message to Colin, and he didn't respond, which he sometimes did when he was busy. Then she sent a saucy message, but still no response.

She started another message as she was walking across the field. [Hey, where are you? …] A roving cyberzombie glommed onto her and took a bite. She struggled and shoved the feeble creature back. "Fuck off!" she booted it in the chest, knocking it to the ground. She pulled her plasma pistol and repeatedly shot it until its glowing eyes went dark. Then she returned to her message [… Don't forget me!] and sent it.

She went inside and rode the elevator down. It was empty, as it usually was this time of the night. She went all the way to the back, to Dennis's office. He wasn't there. She sat at the desk and kicked her feet up. She killed a little time with her OmniTab.

Maeve looked at the clock again. About a half hour had gone by. She sent a message to both Colin and Dennis this time. A few minutes went by. Nothing, no response. "What the hell is going on?" She left the room and stormed down the hallway. One of the guildies was heading to the elevator, and she rushed over and grabbed him. It was one of the new guys, and she had to read his profile real quick to remember his name.

"Skaggs, hey. Have you seen Gunstorm or Haxx? I'm supposed to meet up with them."

"Oh, hey…." he looked at her profile, "Ve. No, I haven't. Gunstorm was supposed to meet me here a couple of hours ago, but he never showed up."

"I just checked his office, and he's not back there."

"I qualified for a promotion, so I'm just kind of waiting for Gunstorm to okay it. I've been doing solo missions while I wait, but I've got to go to bed now. I got school in the morning." Skaggs got into the elevator and went up.

Maeve paced down the hall and back, thinking. *Something must have happened in real life for them to both be gone like this. But why wouldn't they respond to me or tell me about it? Something must be really wrong.* Her mind spiraled. *Maybe he broke a leg, fell down some stairs, heart attack? Dennis isn't the most healthy guy. Maybe Colin's in trouble. Car accident?* She got a very clear mental image of the two of them hanging, unconscious and bloodied, in a burning, upside-down car and shivered.

She took a breath. "Maybe I'm overreacting. It's probably just a network blackout. The authority shuts off sectors sometimes." She thought about how many times she'd been dumped out of VR into her crappy apartment.

Maeve wandered the guild compound for another hour and a half.

Fighting back tears she muttered, "Fuck." She sent another message to both of them.

> [Hey, I was here, but it looks like I've missed you. I waited as long as I could. I hope you're okay. It scared me to find you both missing.
> Goodbye – Love Maeve.]

She logged out of the game, turned off her OmniTab, walked it to the garbage chute, and threw it in. The conveyor belts below whirred. Soon it would be broken down and partially recycled. She thought about Colin and Dennis again and thought, *Please be okay.*

Chapter 15

Maeve made her way down the luxurious hall to the bridge. She had gone through her wardrobe and put together something incognito. Today would be the first time they left their gilded prison ship. She had on a brimmed beanie with her hair tied back. A jacket with the collar turned up. She had a pair of sunglasses in her pocket, but those seemed a step too far. *Incogneedy*, she thought.

She opened the door and stepped onto the bridge where the rest of the crew were waiting. The professor, Naiomi, and one of the Coreys were in the chairs. The other Corey and I-ON were standing by the nav-table, and Del leaned against the doorway she had entered, but she didn't notice any of them. Instead, her eyes went to the windshield. A field of brightly colored holograms replaced the darkness and the occasional pinpoint of light. Advertisements for fuel, restaurants, lodging, and much more. The station itself was a dingy steel color with glimmering blue-and-gold highlights. Painted on a large domed area was a black-and-white checkered smear with the words ENCOM WAY STATION in the middle.

As she was gawking, another large ship silently moved into her view and ever so gently connected to the station, clamps locking the ship into position with enough force that they could feel the bangs in their own ship. They had officially arrived at the station.

"Pretty cool, huh?" said the professor.

"Yeah!" she said.

"After all the shit we went through, I thought we'd never make it," said Del.

Bryan folded his arms. "Let's get down to business."

Maeve, who had actually done this before in space flight sims, hit a button on the nav-table, bringing up the station's directory. The holographic map distorted and vanished. Then it was replaced with a miniature model of the space station with a stylized EnCom logo and some small legal text underneath.

Maeve skipped through a few pages, talking about the station's amenities and rules, landing on the first business listing. [24/7 Supra-Mart] On one side, a map showed a skeletonized view of the station with a lit-up map showing how to get there and what deck it was on. On the other, a slideshow played images of the store. It looked like a small convenience store. Then a few options at the bottom. [Call] [Contact] [Create Nav-map]

She skipped ahead a bunch of times. [Aaron Accounting Solutions] The page layout was the same except it had a cheery-looking cartoon accountant standing atop a stack of paperwork. His sleeves rolled up, hands overflowing with various monetary symbols.

"Computer, do a search for the name Jarth (Ye-ar-th)," said Bryan. The hologram blipped again, skipping ahead to [Jarth Shipyard Services]. A no-nonsense logo was all that was displayed. "This is the place. Chop shop. We'll get a stack of credits here, and he might just give us a deal on some reconditioned ships." He made finger quotes.

"Wait, how do you know this guy?" said Del.

"It's a long story."

"Yeah? I don't think you get to just long-story your way out of that. Let me rephrase the questions. What's up with the criminal contact?"

Maeve raised an eyebrow at him.

Bryan sighed. "You ever heard of Zero Rez?"

"Sounds like an error message," said Maeve.

"He's like a private operator. He does infiltration, hacking, espionage, that kind of stuff."

"Okay, so what about him?" said Del.

"Jarth is one of a few people he told me I could count on if I dropped his name and told him Rez sent me."

"That doesn't really answer my question, though, does it?"

"Look, I'm not like a syndicate guy or something like that. Rez basically took me hostage. I'm minding my own business, eating lunch in my truck, and a friggin' hit squad shows up and unloads on this car nearby. I put my thumb on the ignition and gunned it out of there. I could see an explosion in the rearview mirror. When I got home, Rez popped out and forced me to put my life on hold while he eliminated his old crew. He did it, obviously. I'm still here. To make me whole, that's how he put it. He gave me a sizable chunk of cryptos and a favor I could call in. Never thought I'd actually use it."

"Dude."

"Yeah, yo."

"Other than running from his former crew, it wasn't as exciting as it sounds. It was two weeks of acting normal at work while I had a shady house guest who came and went at weird hours. All the while worrying that his old crew would catch on and kill us. Is that enough for you? Can I make the call now?"

Nobody spoke.

"Computer, isolate me and call this contact, and uh, maximum encryption." The encryption was already set that way, but he wanted to make sure. The hologram of the directory displayed "Calling" with two wires on either side, with a lightning bolt bouncing between them. Under the animation, a small text box spewed forth text as it ran through its protocols. The two wires connected, and the image flicked off. When it came back, it was a young man with long, greasy hair.

"Jarth shipyard services. How may I help you?" he said in a practiced yet disinterested tone.

Bryan cleared his throat. "Hello. I have a load of ship parts I'd like to sell. Can I speak to Jarth?"

The holographic bust leaned out of view and then back. "He's busy at the moment, but I'd be happy to get you started."

"Sorry, it's just that a mutual friend sent me to see Jarth, and it's the kind of thing where I really need to talk to him directly, if you catch my drift."

Recognition dawned on the young man's face. "Oh. Hold please." He looked apprehensive before the hologram went back to the static company logo—this time with "On hold" and a counter on the screen.

The screen changed yet again to a man with slicked back hair, a graying beard of stubble, and a grease smudge on his chin. He eyed Bryan for a while with hard eyes. "Who is mutual friend?" These days, everyone had translation software built into their neural implants, so the hardest people to understand were those speaking pidgin languages that developed on remote worlds and space stations. On top of that, Jarth had some sort of speech impediment. Sounded like he had too much tongue in his mouth to talk normally.

"My name is Bryan Cox. I did Zero Rez a solid, and he told me I should look you up if I'm ever out this way."

"Hah! You? Working with Rezzo? I think not. Let me guess, you are also *space royalty* and need to offload credits? Yes?"

Bryan chuckled. "Rez told me a story that I should tell you."

Jarth folded his arms.

"He told me to tell you about the Thermal-Backdoor job in the . . . Well, I forget the system. He needed you to buy him time while he put a hack in place because they had just updated the security on—"

Jarths face lit up. "On thermal regulators!"

"Anyway, it was your job to distract the guard so he could get in and out. He told me you could be tricky to understand and that I'd get it if I met you."

"You *do* know him."

"Know him? Hell, he slept on my couch for a while."

"He still does this. The couch surfing."

The two laughed.

"Okay, what have you to sell?"

"The big-ticket item is an authority transponder."

Jarth raised his eyebrows.

"On top of that we got a lot of supplies, some Varium, robot parts."

"What about ship? I like the shields, thrusters, too."

"We're going to need the ship for a bit, so we'll keep it intact for now, but we'll need a clean transponder."

"Of course, of course." Jarth turned away from the hologram call. "Boy! I got job. Pickup at my coordinates." The young man responded, a mumble in the distance. Jarth turned back. "Okay, ride tugger over, and we do business."

"I have a number of comrades who I'll be splitting the money with. Are you okay with us all coming over?"

"Makes no difference. I have automated defenses inside, is price of doing business. This kind of business at least." He smiled.

"Thanks, see you soon."

Jarth nodded, and the hologram vanished, returning them to the directory listing.

15.1

Everyone except I-ON filed into the cargo hold, which was cluttered with all the things they'd gathered to sell. A few minutes passed. Maeve yawned deeply. The professor yawned back at her, bearing sharp teeth.

Finally, they could hear the telltale signs of the worker having arrived. The cargo bay door clunked, shuffled, and banged. Finally, when the noise settled down, the light above the large mechanical door lit up green, indicating that a docking seal had been established. There was a double bang from the worker on the other side.

Corey Two had positioned himself so that he'd be the one to hit the large, candy-red industrial button that sat nested inside a clear plastic safety cover, and now was his time. He flipped up the cover and delivered a gentle hammer blow with his fist.

There was a buzz. The door latch banged open, and the door slid back gently and easily. As it went, there was a slight breeze from the change in atmosphere, and the dim tugger interior lit up, revealing the young man from the holo-call earlier, dressed in an orange-and-black jumpsuit.

"Hello," said the young man. He stepped onto the ship.

There was a smattering of hellos while Bryan stepped forward to shake his hand. "I'm Bryan."

"Petros, pleased to meet you."

Bryan pointed out the various items they had to sell. They had loaded the loose robot parts into boxes, as well as the Varium and the emergency items. Petros was happy to see how prepared they were. Together, they decided how best to load things up, and then Petros went into the tugger and came back out with a hover pallet jack.

First, they loaded all the stasis pods into the back and then made trips back and forth with the pallet jack, loading up the mostly intact robots and then the boxes of things. Petros strapped the load down as they went.

"It looks like that's it. Everyone going to the shop, get on the tugger," said Petros. He smiled when everyone piled on board. "All of you, huh? It's going to be a bit crowded then." He shuffled past the group to the door controls. He sent the ship a request to close the door. It slid closed smoothly, latching with a loud metallic bang.

It was dark inside the tugger. Their load of goodies partially hid the lights. Petros closed the tugger's door and disengaged the docking seal. He shuffled past the group toward the cockpit, then he stopped. "Okay, everyone, find the railing and hang on. We'll be at the shop in no time." Then he went through the door to pilot the ship.

The tugger was old school. The artificial gravity they had felt before was provided by proximity to their own ship. So as Petros eased them away from the WATS-9, the crew floated off their feet and then felt a pull toward the back of the ship. They got to enjoy weightlessness for a couple of minutes until they sank back to the floor, indicating that they were almost there. They heard a similar-sounding heavy metal banging as they docked at Jarth's shop.

The tugger door slid open. Behind it were two more workers wearing orange-and-black coveralls waiting to unload. The crew stepped out into the huge mechanic shop. It had drab concrete floors and tiled ceilings whose pattern was broken up by lights and vents. This tile pattern crept down the walls as well. Petros was right behind them and walked them over to Jarth.

The place had a sweet, rich smell of chemicals, oils, and coolant. Many small ships in various states of assembly were littered around the shop. They came to Jarth, who was near a large bank of shelves filled with parts. He was behind a man-sized engine part hanging from chains. It dripped into a pan on the floor as he bashed it with a hammer and screwdriver. "Just a second. I almost have this. Boy, get scanner will you?" Metal pings echoed through the shop as he picked up the pace.

The young man disappeared behind the shelves and then came walking back with a large handheld scanner. He turned it on and let his arm hang naturally. The boot-up screen waved back and forth as he walked back.

"What's that for?" said Maeve.

"It's a scanning tool. It will take stock of everything and suggest a relative value."

"Oh, wow," she said.

"Yeah, it's a real timesaver," he said.

The engine part knocked loose, and Jarth held it in place while he dropped his tools gently. He slid the offending part loose and appraised it for a moment. "Cracked." He pivoted and dropped it into a big metal bin caked with years of mechanical grime. He came over to the group. Nearby, the two other mechanics had unloaded the tugger, and Petros was busy scanning the boxes this way and that.

He finished scanning and stood up. Studying the screen, he pecked a couple of buttons and walked over to the group. Jarth extended a hand. The young man looked at his blackened, smudged fingertips and frowned. "Dad, you have to wipe your hands. You keep ruining these things."

Jarth wiped his hands vigorously on his coveralls. "Happy?"

Petros rolled his eyes and handed over the scanner. Jarth squinted at the small screen, and he sifted through the items, muttering to himself. "Printing mats, hmm-hmm-hmm, new, that, hmm. Very nice."

He turned his attention to Bryan. "So how much you looking to make?"

"I was thinking three hundred for the lot of it."

Jarth folded his arms. "Three hundred. How you figure? This looks more like a two-hundred-mil load, eh?"

"Well, we have a brand new authority transponder. What about two eighty?"

"True, but is also, em. What is word? Hot item. I recognize the ship from the TV show. Two hundred fifty. Considering our mutual friend, this is as high as I can go. Deal?" Jarth extended a hand.

Bryan looked at the group and saw no disapproval, so he shook on it.

Jarth turned to his son and told him where to put the stuff, then told him that if he had time, the hanging engine part just needed a new coil assembly. Then he slapped him on the back and beckoned the group to follow him up a flight of stairs. This led to an office area. They passed through a hall and emerged at the front desk. The group could see the space station hall through the large front windows.

Maeve saw a bowl of potpourri and plucked a jagged-looking piece of vegetation and smelled it. Nothing. She tossed it back in and noted how dusty it was. *Probably been here since they built the place.*

Jarth sat down. The old office chair squawked. "So let's see, you need transponder." He leaned into the terminal and typed something in. "Anything else? Laser? Gauss? Mining rig?" He smiled and spread his hands, spelling it out for the imagination. "Missile pods!"

The group had already talked this over, but they discussed it again now that they were here. Their decision was the same as before. Everyone sticking with the WATS-9 would get one-fifth of the money and would later sell the ship once they'd reached the frontier. Bryan and the Coreys would split up the other four-fifths of the money to make their getaway in this sector. They would need to grease a lot of palms to escape and establish new identities.

"No, this is bullshit. We deserve an equal share of the money," said Naiomi.

"Well, it's just that you'll have an easier time—" started Bryan.

"Whatever! I wish a robot had beaten *me* up so I could get all the money."

"But . . . that's not even what this is about."

Del took her shoulders and whispered to her. "We might end up with more money than them after selling the ship."

She groaned, "Fine," and with that, she stormed out of the shop to lean against the business across the way.

After hammering out the details, the group bounced as many questions as they could think of off their new contact. How can we get medical attention without the attention part? Which warp gate should we use? How should we dodge surveillance? How does it work getting a new identity? Can you point us to any of these services?

Jarth gave advice where he could and accepted payment for referring to some of his extralegal contacts.

15.2

Del walked into the hall, harsh fluorescent light overhead, metal grate floors underfoot. To the left, he made eye contact with an old man in a greasy-looking food kiosk, the nearest in a row of them. He nodded. The man smiled. He looked to the right, a set of stairs. Near the bottom was a bar with a couple of rough-looking patrons. Neon reflected off their chrome body mods.

Naiomi leaned against a concrete wall, arms folded, pouting. Del joined her, swinging his hip into hers and dramatically folding his arms. Her face softened. "You're such a dork."

He slid his hand under her chin and gazed into her eyes. "All the deals are done. It's time to say goodbye." They kissed. She went inside, and Del followed.

Inside, Bryan was dressed like a mechanic, and the Coreys were busy getting into their own orange-and-black coveralls. Jarth stepped back into the room with a cardboard box and handed out baseball caps to Bryan and the Coreys.

"Hey! Where's mine?" said Naiomi, her arms folded across her chest. Jarth looked at the pretty young thing and handed one over with a smile. "There you are." He looked at the box. "Does anyone else want hat?" With no takers, he disappeared into the office with the box.

Bryan settled the hat on his head. "Well." He smiled. "I was going to say it's been nice, but what I should say is that you've been nice. Because this has been a nightmare."

"Still is," Corey One chimed in.

Bryan inhaled sharply. "No, I think we've done it. The ship's got a new transponder. We've got some contacts who are going to smuggle us to . . ." Bryan almost said where he was thinking of going, "Where we need to go. Once we establish new identities, we just need to keep a low profile."

"It's kind of exciting," said Maeve. A couple of the others nodded in agreement.

"All right, good luck, everyone." said Bryan. "I'm going. The stuff I took this morning is wearing off, and Jarth has a guy who's going to look at our wounds." He gave a couple of hugs and handshakes on his way out the door.

The Coreys stood rigid and delivered their trademark pop-idol salute. Naiomi squealed in delight. The two of them strutted out the door. Bryan was waiting for them in the hall. He looked at the Coreys and said something inaudible, and they walked out of sight past the food stalls.

"We should get going, too," said Maeve. That shook the group out of their trance.

They went back through the office hall. Passing by the lunchroom, one of the men who unloaded their cargo sank his teeth into a sandwich. He eyed the group as he chewed a big bite. They went down the stairs. At the bottom, Jarth was waiting for them. His son was fast at work removing some bolts from the hanging piece of tech. He waved a grubby hand at them as they went.

Jarth bent down to pick up a box and handed it over to Maeve. "This is a new transponder. To everything but intense scan, you will look like space trucker. Same weight, similar size and speed." He led them back to the tugger, and they got in. He reminded them to hold on to the railing and closed the door. The group jostled around for a minute until they were back to their own ship. Jarth came to the back and let them out.

"Good luck," he said as the doors were shutting, then he added, "And if you don't have good luck, you never heard of me." He said it sternly, but never lost the jovial look on his face. The bay door shut and latched with a bang. They watched, stunned until they heard him disconnect.

Maeve took the transponder out and left the box behind. Together, they all went back to the bridge. I-ON was there waiting for them. He waved his mismatched arm when they came in. I-ON had the tools ready and the panel off. Maeve handed over the device, and the group watched I-ON install it. After a few minutes, he fastened the panel.

"It is done."

The professor leaned over the tactical map and selected the warp gate they'd need [WG-1022]. It was on the other side of the system, and it would take them way the hell out to the frontier, but it was a safe bet. There was another warp gate that was closer but known to be dangerous, plagued by pirates, and where there were pirates, there might be the authority as well. Best to avoid all that trouble.

Once their destination was set, she looked up at Maeve expectantly through the holographic noise of the map. Maeve leaned over the captain's chair and skimmed her fingers along the console until she found the docking button and pressed it.

The docking tube hissed and let go, retracting slowly, followed by a vibration as the docking clamps let go. One slightly slower than the others, causing the ship to list ever so slightly. Free of the docking restraints, Maeve found and switched on the autopilot.

They watched the forward view of the digital windshield. The ship maneuvered up above the station. Holographic signs disappeared from view, then the gray dome with its glittering blue-and-gold panels and fixtures sank below them. A bright white dot of a warp gate dawned behind it, bright, like a tiny star. The ship turned so that it was facing nothing but darkened space.

The ship rumbled subtly underfoot as its luxurious thrusters brought them to max speed. Maeve, who was standing holding the back of the captain's chair, looked over her shoulder and smiled at the others. Her heart fluttered like a startled bird.

The professor was looking at the holo-map again. "The path we're on is empty all the way to the warp gate." Another reason why this was the preferable warp gate. Being a nascent system, traffic was always sparse.

"I guess we made it," said Del with a shrug.

"I guess we did," said Maeve as happy tears came to her eyes.

Epilogue

Back at warp gate AG-945, a convoy of space truckers poured out into the Trelecon system. The first, short and fat with a bundle of cargo containers in a circle around its central body. Three more followed in an elongated locomotive fashion. Rig in front, followed by a line of cargo segments, all locked together and capped off by a thruster caboose. The rigs all adjusted their headings and split up.

Next, a small wedge-shaped ship cruised out of the warp tunnel. Red squares checkering the gunmetal gray ship with *The Hard Corps* emblazoned on the side. Behind it, eleven more fighters came forth. Although different in make and model, they had the same markings. They kept cruising in formation out of the intense white light of the warp gate.

The man in the lead ship tapped a button on his console a couple of times with a shiny prosthetic hand. This brought up a system map on his heads-up display.

"Computer, gimme a long-range scan for the WATS-9," said Captain Reeves. The nav-map pinged along all the nav-buoys. The system returned no information.

"There is no ship by that designation in this system," said the ship's computer.

"Do another long-range scan . . ." For a moment he couldn't remember what make of ship he was chasing. "Uh, looking for Caviar ships."

"We got em, boss?" asked a member of the flight group.

"Scanning," he said.

"There is no ship of that manufacture in this system."

He looked at his notes again. The ship passed through the warp gate mere hours ago. He squinted at the system map again, thinking.

"All right, everyone, the ship isn't showing up on scans, which means they either switched ships on us or, more likely, disconnected their transponder. Which we're going to do now that we're on this side of the warp gate."

Reeves felt under his console and flipped a hidden, recessed switch that cut his transponder. *The Hard Corps* couldn't catch up to their quarry in the previous system without getting noticed by the authority. But in the warp corridor, and now hidden in this system, they were going to go all out to catch up.

"We're gonna haul ass over to WG-1022. That's the safe bet. I need the fastest five ships to form up with me. Lets say: Draco, Bender, Samurai . . ." He hesitated, thinking.

"Me and Sigma," said Queen.

"Sounds good. The rest of you are going to WG-996. They probably weren't stupid enough to go there, but we have to make sure. If they did, and the pirates have them already, don't engage."

"Understood. Aye Captain. Got it," his mercenary crew responded.

The dozen ships broke up and became two formations. Captain Reeves set his course, then he depressed the button on the throttle lever and pushed the engines into overdrive. The ship's power plant thrummed behind the captain, and the entire ship vibrated as it took off at fantastic speed. The flight groups launched, hell-bent, in two different directions, vanishing quickly into the darkness of space.

About the Author

Hello, I'm Daniel Seven, an outsider from the rain-slicked Pacific Northwest. I have a penchant for nerdy things, and when I'm not writing sci-fi and fantasy, I'm playing video games, listening to podcasts, and taking in stories any way I can.

Why should you read my stories? I'm a new author. Hell, I got C's in English. Well, I'm a jack-of-all-trades, so I know a little about a lot. I'm a creative type who gets squirrely without an outlet. And hey, I wrote a professional novel, which is a substantial accomplishment. (More to come as soon as I can.)

Thanks for checking out my book. You might like my website: danielsevenwriting.com. There, you can get the inside track on my forthcoming projects and exclusive tidbits. Check out my monthly blog entry. Get updates on my current work in progress. And buy books and merchandise.

(Don't forget to write a review and tell your friends about the book!)

```
    (   )
  ( O-O)/
 /(||   ||)
```

www.ingramcontent.com/pod-product-compliance
Lightning Source LLC
Chambersburg PA
CBHW032022240626
47154CB00003B/748